David Peace was chosen as *GQ* Man of the Year in 2007 and one of Granta's Best of Young British Novelists in 2003. He is the author of the *Red Riding Quartet* and in 2004 he won the James Tait Black Memorial Prize for his novel *GB84*. *Tokyo Year Zero*, the first book of his *Tokyo Trilogy*, was published in 2007 and *Occupied City*, the sequel, was published in 2009. *The Damned Utd* was made into a film in 2009 starring Michael Sheen. David Peace lives in Tokyo.

Further praise for *GB84*:

'On one level *GB84* works as a historically precise, week-by-week account of the strike. But it is also a conspiracy thriller laced with apocalyptic poetry. Its power lies in it mixture of documentary realism and enigmatic fantasy, its exploration of the intimate betrayals that constitute an epic social tragedy.' *Independent*

'David Peace's *GB84* will serve as a record – it brings to life the reality of the miners' strike in all its grisly detail . . . It's as flecked with blood, spittle and bile as the conflict itself, and will serve as a fitting testament to the real cost of Thatcher's iron will.' *Arena*

'The novel's bite is matched by its swallow . . . The writing is clever, terse, incisive. The sentences short. This mammoth conspiracy tale is a thriller daubed with horror, a mirror signalling Britain's future . . . GB84 is a commentary, a how-dunnit without revisionism, sentiment or nostalgia . . . In the end his triumph signals tragedy. You read. You weep. You ponder. In the pondering lies the portent of the tale.' *Tribune*

'Like British James Ellroy, Peace has also moved from the crime genre to a broader, bloodier canvas, excavating the dank world of Eighties politics . . . When the reader comes up for air at the apocalyptic end, it is with a sense of the futility, the waste and above all the ugliness (on all sides) of the strike that changed British politics forever. Highly recommended.' *Jack*

'*GB84*, David Peace's insanely fatiguing, self-proclaimed "occult" account of 53 weeks of brutal political, social and ideological confrontation . . . taunts us with the idea that it could be absorbed into a conventional aesthetic framework. This, rather than the obvious weight of its subject matter, is what makes it an enormously significant novel. It also makes it a profoundly moral one . . . Peace is telling us that the people whom the events of 1984 were ostensibly about have been, and perhaps always were, relegated to the interstices of a much bigger and, almost unbelievably, much more frightening picture. It's hard to think of another writer who could capture that picture so suggestively and so thrillingly.' *Sunday Times*

'Two decades ago a mighty confrontation happened between the forces of a Stalinist class warrior and a monetarist state led by an equally fanatical fighter. What feels like a lifetime later, David Peace has written the best novel of the year, and what may well be the finest English novel written since the hellish days, weeks and months he so faithfully describes.' *Ink*

'What David Peace captures brilliantly are the colours, the postures, the language, and the intricate webs of emotion and sociology that lay at the heart of the conflict . . . If the recent flurry of ineffectual television programmes dedicated to the twentieth anniversary of the end of the Miners' Strike left you unfulfilled, *GB84* will not.' *Leeds Guide*

'Internalising J. G. Ballard's suggestion that because we live in a world ruled by fictions the writer's task is to invent the reality, [Peace] has brought that very old-fashioned strike kicking and screaming into modernity . . . A violently original novel.' *The Times*

'Peace's trademark clipped, poetic style tears through the strike year, piling on the battles, betrayals and blunders while counting the psychic cost . . . As TV wheels the strike out for cheap 80s nostalgia, Peace sees it as a time of national breakdown, haunted by Orwell's ghost, leaving villages of the damned.' *Uncut*

'Peace's style builds slowly, cloyingly, until you almost have to take a deep breath to shake yourself free of the overpowering sense of endemic corruption and political cynicism that domintated the era.' *Observer*

'[It] reeks of working-class England, of the eighties, of despair; of blood and spit, the risks people take and how they always seem to get it wrong. It is a tragedy. If you have a heart, it should break it. Broad in scope, truly ambitious, and unrepetenant about its agenda – the miners' strike – *GB84* is equal parts pacy crime thriller and tricky history assignment, putting the reader inside the soul of the events, close enough to smell the blood on the knuckles of the strikers and hear the crack of the policemen's truncheons . . . David Peace's bruising fictions are unlike anything else; based on fact and meant to make a significant historical contribution, his books are not merely written to entertain but to educate as well.' *Herald*

'He shows a clarity of purpose and a control of his material that very much justify his inclusion among *Granta's* twenty Best of Young British Novelists last year. *GB84* is a novel of ambitious political scope and sustained anger, defiantly out of step with these times.' *Literary Review*

David Peace

GB84

ff

faber and faber

First published in 2004
by Faber and Faber Limited
Bloomsbury House
74-77 Great Russell Street
London WC1B 3DA
First published in paperback in 2005
This paperback edition published in 2010

Typeset by Faber and Faber Ltd
Printed in England by CPI Bookmarque, Croydon

A CIP record for this book
is available from the British Library

ISBN 978-0-571-25820-8

2 4 6 8 10 9 7 5 3 1

For my father

Author's Note

With the exception of those persons appearing as well-known personalities under their own names, albeit often in occult circumstance, all other characters are a fiction in a novel based upon a fact.

Oh these deceits are strong almost as life.
Last night I dreamt I was in the labyrinth,
And woke far on. I did not know the place.

Edwin Muir, 'The Labyrinth'

The Argument

Electricity –
   Harsh service station light. Friday 13 January, 1984 –
   She puts a cigarette to her lips, a lighter to her cigarette.
   A dog starv'd at his Master's Gate –
   He waits.
   She inhales, her eyes closed. She exhales, her eyes open.
   He picks at the solid red sauce on the plastic ketchup bottle.
   'Early March,' she says. 'South Yorkshire.'
   He rolls the solid red sauce into a soft bloody ball.
   She stubs out the cigarette. She puts an envelope on the table.
   He squashes the ball between his fingers and thumb –
   Predicts the ruin of the State.
   She stands up.
   He shuts his eyes until she's almost gone. The stink still here –
   Power.

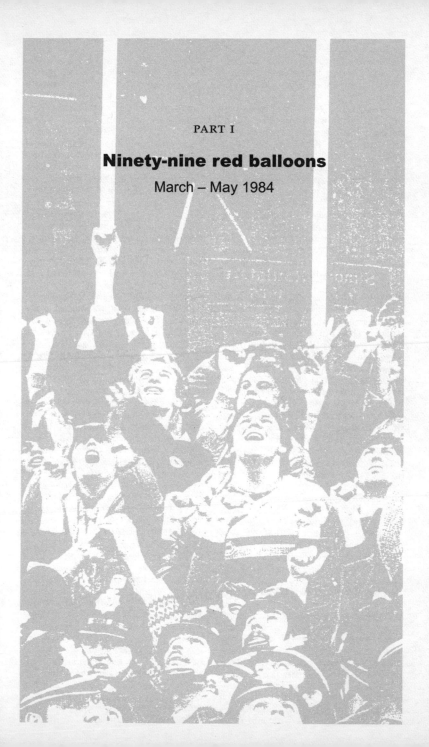

PART I

Ninety-nine red balloons

March – May 1984

The dead brood under Britain. We whisper. We echo. The emanation of Giant Albion – Wake up, says Cath again. Wake up, Martin. I turn over. I look at her. They're closing Cortonwood, she says. You'll be out now. I sit up. I reach for my cigarettes. She moves packet out of my reach. I say, Pass them here. She throws them on bed. Expensive habit that, she says. Bloody Manvers. I don't drive. Geoff Brine picks us up. I wouldn't be here if he'd not rung – *Click-click* – Asked us if I wanted a lift into Thurcroft. Not way Cath's been going on. But she's gone into Sheffield to meet her mate. On way we stop for one in Rising Deer. Neither of us fancy Hotel. There'll be enough talk later. They've begun by time we park up, get inside Welfare – We've fought sixty years to get these snap times, now they're going to change them so coal will be coming up whole time – It's packed. They put it to vote, show of hands. Three to one against. Let them sort it out themselves, says Geoff. But it's all bollocks. We all know it is. Just a matter of time now. On way home we never mention Manvers. Just Sheffield bleeding Wednesday. Geoff stops car when we get to top of our road. I open door. It's sleeting. I turn back to say ta. He's staring at us. I shake my head. He nods – Eighteen weeks with no overtime. Fights every day. Rag-ups across area – It's just a matter of time. Fucking Cortonwood. **Monday morning.** I'm on days. It's quiet when we go in but there's about forty blokes from Silverwood waiting for us when we come off. It's about more than Manvers fucking snap times now. They've been into Barnsley for Area Council meeting. They're stopping cars. I've got my window down. Don't come tomorrow, they're telling us. I say, I won't. Don't you worry – Stick your telly on when you get home, they shout. I say, Don't worry. I will. Pete Cox from our Branch comes over to car when he sees it's me. Few of us are going over to Manton tomorrow, he says. If you fancy it? I tell him, I'll be there. Nice one, he says and bangs twice on roof of car. I put window up, switch on radio and drive straight home. Cath's waiting for us, front door open – Television and radio

both on: Jack Taylor stood outside Area HQ on Huddersfield Road, telling everyone how Yorkshire have voted to implement 1981 ballot – To stop them butchering our industry and our jobs. Our pits and our communities – All out from Friday over closure of Cortonwood and Bullcliffe Wood. Cortonwood has best coal in South Yorkshire. Least five more years' worth, says Jack. No more running. That's it then? asks Cath. I nod – That's it, we're out. **Day 1.** It'll be National now. Fucking MacGregor. Twenty pits and twenty thousand jobs over next twelve months. Arthur's been right all along. There's no talking to Cath though. I drive into Thurcroft. Mini-van's already gone over to Manton, so I have a drive over with a couple of lads who were just hanging around like me. When we get there it's solid. There's talk of a run down to Creswell because that won't be. Pete and some of older blokes say we best wait for tonight. See what score is. They're going to set up some kind of Strike HQ at Silverwood. They'll be telling us where to go. Where we're needed and where we're not. Lot of lads have been here since first thing so we have a pint and head back to Thurcroft. I run into Geoff. Have a bag of chips with him in car while Hotel opens. We have one in there, then go across to Welfare. There are that many tonight they're having to stand out front in car park – Motion to back strike is proposed. Motion is seconded. Motion is backed 100 per cent – Folk head off to Hotel or Club. Lot of talk about '72 and '74. I'm having a piss in Club when this bloke says to me, It'll be right then? I say, How do you mean? We'll win? he says. Yeah, I tell him. What you worried about? Be summer soon, he says. I look at lad. I say, Do I know you? No, he says. You don't. **Day 3.** Thousand pounds for every year of service. We'd have fifteen grand, Cath says. I say, And what'd that buy us? Peace and quiet, she says – And for how long? I ask her. Fifteen thousand pounds, Martin – I can't be doing with it. I leave her to it. I drive into Thurcroft. I play darts and drink. Booze. Sup. There's nothing else to do. They're telling us to stay put. Let Nottingham

The First Week

Monday 5 – Sunday 11 March 1984

Terry Winters sat at the kitchen table of his three-bedroom home in the suburbs of Sheffield, South Yorkshire. His three children were squabbling over their scrambled eggs. His wife was worrying about the washing and the weather. Terry ignored them. He took an index card from the right-hand pocket of his jacket. He read it. He closed his eyes. He repeated out loud what he had just read. He opened his eyes. He read the card again. He checked what he had said. He had been correct. He put the card into the left-hand pocket of his jacket. He took a second card from the right pocket. He read it. He closed his eyes. He repeated out loud what he had read. He opened his eyes. His children were taunting each other over their toast. His wife was still worrying about the washing and the weather. They ignored him. He read the card again. He had been correct again. He put the card into the left pocket. He took another card from his right pocket. He read it. Terry closed his eyes. Terry Winters was learning his lines.

Neil Fontaine stands outside the door to the Jew's suite on the fourth floor of Claridge's. He listens to the telephones ring and the voices rise inside. He thinks about the coincidence of circumstances, the meeting of motives and the convergence of causes. Neil Fontaine stands outside the Jew's suite on the fourth floor of Claridge's and listens to the corks pop and the glasses chink. He thinks about the start of wars and the end of eras. The timing of a meeting and the opening of an envelope –

The closing of a pit and the calling of a strike –

The lighting of a corridor. The shadow on a wall –

Fear and Misery in this New Reich.

Neil Fontaine stands outside the Jew's suite. He listens to the toasts – Inside.

They had their breakfasts across the road from the County Hotel on Upper Woburn Place, Bloomsbury. Four tables of them. Full English.

Terry Winters just drinking sweet tea. Dick after more toast. No one else speaking. Everyone hungover –

Everyone but the President. He was on the early train down from Sheffield.

They mopped their plates with the last of the bread. They put out their cigarettes. Drained their teas. Terry Winters paid the bill. They got four cabs down to Hobart House. Terry paid the drivers. They pushed through the press and the sleet. They went inside.

The President was waiting with Joan, Len and the news from South Yorkshire –

Solid.

They had their last cigarettes. Looked at their watches. They went upstairs –

The Mausoleum –

Room 16, Hobart House, Victoria:

Bright lights, smoke and mirrors –

The orange anti-terrorist curtains always drawn, the matching carpet and the wall-length mirrors, the tables round the edge of the room. In the middle –

No man's land.

The Board at the top end; BACM and NACODS down the sides –

The National Union of Mineworkers at the foot of the table.

Fifty people here for the Coal Industry National Consultative Committee –

But there was no consultation today. Just provocation –

More provocation. Real provocation –

Fifty people watching the Chairman of the Board let his Deputy get to his feet.

The Mechanic hangs up. He closes up the garage. He picks up the dogs from his mother's house in Wetherby. He puts the dogs in the back of the car. He takes the A1 down to Leeds. He pulls into the car park. He leaves the dogs in the back. He walks across to the transport café –

Paul Dixon is already here. He is sitting at a table facing the door and the car park.

The Mechanic sits down opposite Dixon.

'Nice tan that, Dave,' says Dixon. 'Garage must be doing well.'

The Mechanic says, 'Look like you could do with a fortnight in the sun yourself.'

'Not all as fortunate as you, Dave,' says Dixon.

The Mechanic shakes his head. He says, 'I owe it all to you, Sergeant.'

'I'm glad you appreciate the advantages of our special relationship,' says Dixon.

The Mechanic smiles. He says, 'That why they call it Special Branch, is it?'

Paul Dixon laughs. He offers the Mechanic a cigarette.

The Mechanic shakes his head again. He says, 'Never know when you might have to quit, do you?'

'How about a nice cup of Yorkshire tea then, Dave?' asks Dixon.

The Mechanic smiles again. He says, 'Coffee. Black.'

Paul Dixon goes to the counter. He orders. He pays. He brings over the tray.

The Mechanic has changed seats. He is facing the door. The car park.

'Expecting company?' asks Dixon.

The Mechanic shakes his head. 'Just keeping an eye on the dogs, Sergeant.'

Paul Dixon sits down with his back to the door. The car park. He passes the Mechanic his coffee.

The Mechanic puts in four spoonfuls of sugar. He stirs. He stops. He looks up –

Dixon is watching him. The dogs barking in the car –

They want to go home. Out.

Terry Winters didn't sleep. None of them did –

It was never dark. It was always light –

The bright lights on the train back North. The TV crews outside St James's House. The fluorescent lighting in the foyer. In the lift. In the corridors. In the office –

Always light, never dark.

Terry phoned Theresa. *Click-click.* Told her he didn't know when he'd be home. Then he got out the files. Got out his address book. His calculator –

He did his sums –

All night, again and again, over and over.

First thing Wednesday morning, Terry Winters was across in the Royal Victoria Hotel with the finance officers from each of the Union's twenty separate areas and groupings. Terry made them all stand up before the meeting could begin. He made them search the room for hidden microphones and bugs. He made them frisk each other.

Then Terry Winters drew the curtains and locked the doors. Terry made them write down their questions in pencil and seal them in envelopes. He made them pass the envelopes forward.

Terry Winters sat at the head of the table and opened the envelopes one by one. Terry read their questions. He wrote the answers in pencil on the other side of their papers. He put the answers back in the envelopes. He resealed them with Sellotape. He passed them back down the table to the individual authors of each question –

The finance officers read the answers in silence, then returned them to be burnt.

Terry Winters stood up. Terry told them how it was –

The government would come after their money; hunt them through the courts.

He told them what had to be done to cover their tracks –

Nothing on paper; no phone calls; personal visits only, day or night –

He handed out sheets of codes and dates for them to memorize and destroy.

The finance officers thanked him, then returned to their areas.

Terry Winters went straight back to St James's House. Straight back to work.

He worked all day. They all did –

Each of them in their offices.

People coming and going. Meetings here, meetings there. Deals made, deals done.

Breaking for the *Nine o'Clock News, News at Ten, Newsnight* –

Notebooks out, videos and cassettes recording:

'I want to make it clear that we are not dealing with niceties here. We shall not be constitutionalized out of our jobs. Area by area we will decide and in my opinion it will have a domino effect.'

Cheers again. Applause –

Domino effect. Essential battles. Savage butchery.

Then it was back to work. All of them. All night –

Files, phones and calculators. Tea, coffee and aspirins –

The Communist Party and the Socialist Workers arguing in the corridors –

Tweeds and Denims at each other's throats. Their eyes. Their ears –

Shostakovich's Seventh Symphony on loud upstairs in the office of the President –

All night, through the night, until the brakes of dawn.

Terry put his forehead against the window, the city illuminated beneath him.

Never dark –

You couldn't sleep. You had to work –

Always light.

Head against the window, the sun coming up –

The troops were gathering on the street below him. The Red Guard in good voice:

SCAB, SCAB, SCAB –

The dawn chorus of the Socialist Republic of South Yorkshire.

Another cup of coffee. Another aspirin –

Terry Winters picked up his files. His calculator.

Terry locked the office. Terry walked down the corridor to the lift.

Terry went up to the tenth floor. To the Conference Room –

The National Executive Committee of the National Union of Mineworkers.

Terry took his seat at the right hand of the President. Terry listened –

Listened to Lancashire: 'There is a monster. It's now or never.'

Listened to Nottinghamshire: 'If we're scabs before we start, we'll become scabs.'

Listened to Yorkshire: 'We are on our way.'

For six hours Terry listened and so did the President.

Then the President stopped listening. The President stood up with two letters –

It was their turn to listen to him now.

The request from Yorkshire in one hand, the request from Scotland in the other –

The President talked about the secret December meetings between the Chairman and the Prime Minister. He talked about their secret plans to denationalize the coal industry. Their secret nuclear, electric dreams. Their secret hit lists –

Their open and savage schemes to butcher an industry. *Their* industry –

For then the President spoke of history and tradition. The *history* of the Miner. The *tradition* of the Miner. The legacies of their fathers and their fathers' fathers –

The birthrights of their children and their children's children –

The essential battles to come. The war that must be won.

The motion from South Wales was before them –

7

'It is now the crunch time,' said the President. 'We are agreed we have to fight. We have an overtime ban. It is only the tactics which are in question.'

They listened and then they voted –

They voted twenty-one to three to endorse the striking areas under Rule 41.

It was the only vote. The only vote that mattered –

The vote for war.

The President put a hand on Terry's shoulder. The President whispered in his ear –

Terry Winters nodded. Terry picked up his files. His calculator.

He went back down to his office. He closed the door.

Terry walked over to the window. He put his forehead against the glass –

He listened to the cheers from the street below. Terry Winters closed his eyes.

Neil Fontaine receives the call. He fetches the Mercedes from the underground car park. He drives up to the front of Claridge's. The doorman opens the back door –

The Jew gets into the car.

Neil Fontaine looks up into the rearview mirror. The Jew strokes his moustache. The Jew smiles. The Jew says, 'Chequers, if you would please, Neil.'

'Certainly, sir.'

'Zero notice,' laughs the Jew. 'So don't spare the horses.'

Neil Fontaine nods. He puts his foot down.

The Jew picks up the car phone. The Jew starts dialling and chattering –

The Jew wants the world to know where he's going.

Neil Fontaine watches the Jew in the mirror. The Jew plays with his moustache. The Jew sits forward. The Jew looks out of the windows. The Jew prattles into the phone. The Jew never shuts up until the Mercedes is in sight of the place –

Her place.

Neil Fontaine stops before the gates –

Before the guns.

Neil Fontaine winds down his window –

The car is surrounded.

Neil Fontaine says, 'Mr Stephen Sweet to see the Prime Minister.'

The officer speaks into his radio.

Neil Fontaine glances up into the mirror. The Jew isn't stroking his moustache. The Jew isn't smiling. The Jew isn't on the car phone –

The Jew is sweating in his pinstripe suit.

The officer steps back from the car. The officer gestures at the gates –

The gates open.

Neil Fontaine starts the car.

'I told you, Neil,' laughs the Jew from the backseat. 'I am expected.'

Neil Fontaine drives slowly up the gravel drive. He parks before the front door.

The Help is waiting. The Help opens the back door of the Mercedes for the Jew. The Help slams the door behind him.

The Prime Minister appears in blue. The Jew gushes. The Prime Minister swoons. They disappear inside, arm in arm.

'You want a fucking picture?' asks the Help. 'Round the back.'

Neil Fontaine starts the car again. He parks in an empty garage. He sits in the car. He can smell exhaust fumes. He can hear peacocks screaming.

Terry Winters opened the front door of his three-bedroom home in the suburbs of Sheffield, South Yorkshire. His family were asleep upstairs. The lights off downstairs. Terry quietly closed the door. He stood his briefcase in the hall. He caught his face in the dark mirror: Terry Winters, Executive Officer of the National Union of Mineworkers; Terry Winters, the highest non-elected official in the National Union. Terry applauded himself in the shadows of South Yorkshire, in the suburbs of Sheffield –

In his house with the lights off but everybody home.

make up their own minds. Chadburn and Richardson had a rough time of it yesterday. Chadburn saying Notts will have a secret ballot with a recommendation from him to strike. But we all know what that fucking means. **Day 4.** Cath wipes her face. Cath dries her eyes. Cath looks at television. Cath says, She hates us. **Day 5.** Fucking hell. She's getting on my nerves. She doesn't want to use Hoover so she's on her hands and knees with a dustpan and brush in front of television. She's singing bloody hymns so I can't hear *Weekend World*. There's no Sunday dinner either. Frozen Cornish pasties and baked beans. Same as last night. When adverts come on she makes me switch it off for two minutes. I go out into back garden. It's pissing down. I have a cigarette. We'd talked about having a patio this summer. A conservatory. I go back inside. Pasties are on table. Cath's crying again upstairs. Phone's ringing. I close my eyes – *We suffocate. We drown* – **Day 8.** Panel in Silverwood has twinned us with Bentinck, just south of Mansfield. Doesn't matter what any bleeding High Court judge says. It's a quid a shift and there's a coach and some cars. I put my name down for nights. I play darts with Geoff all afternoon. Pete comes in about four o'clock and tells us coach will be out front at six. Geoff says he's off home for his tea and his duffel coat. I don't fancy going all way back to Hardwick for another set-to with Cath, so I have a bag of chips and a walk up Pit Lane. It's quiet. Almost dark. Getting cold and all. I sit across from brickworks and eat my chips, staring up hill at colliery. Folk must think I'm crackers. Chips are wrapped in a photo of Scottish pickets and police at Bilston Glen. I smooth it out and read it. I think about phoning Cath, but what's use? I stick paper in my pocket and go back down hill. I have a quick pint and a piss in Hotel, then go over Welfare and get on coach for Bentinck. **Day 9.** Middle of night. Pissing it down. Absolutely fucking freezing. Police won't let us light brazier. Not local. Not tonight. Last couple of nights they've been from Lincoln and Skegness. Even shared a flask of soup with them. Not that they'd put

that on television or in papers. Even manager was decent at first – Canteen. Cups of tea. Toilets. Knew that wouldn't last – Wasn't for us, they'd all be working. He knows that. We know that. Make me laugh – Quick enough to tell you how they'll vote, how you can count on them. But you know half of them are heading straight round back to get in under fences on their bellies. How they are round here. Always have been. Even their Branch. Minute you left, they'd be backed up for five mile in their brand-new Fords. There are them that don't even bother to lie to you. Just drive straight in. Won't even talk to you. Then there's them that fancy themselves. They stop. Give you a mouthful. Their cars get a bit of hammer in return. Least you know where you are with them – They're cunts. But they're honest cunts – Wish I'd gone back on coach now. Just standing about, taking it in turns to go and sit in cars, waiting for day picket to show up. Freezing to death. Then these lads from Dinnington and Kiveton pull up. They've killed one of ours, they say. He's fucking dead. I say, You what? It's right, they say. Where? Ollerton. We're off there now. Hold up, says Geoff. We'll follow you there – We take A6075 through Sherwood fucking Forest. Get there about half-two. It's ugly – five hundred police, five hundred of us and counting – CB radios got cars coming in from all over as news spreads. Everyone with a different fucking story – He was hit by car; he was hit by a truncheon; he was hit by a brick – Women and kids from houses are all out in street hollering at us. Pit manager appealing for calm. Blokes from their Branch doing same – No one's listening like. Then word comes down that colliery is closing for night. That Arthur's coming. There's cheering then. Three o'clock and Arthur gets up on roof of a car. He asks for two minutes' silence – Mark of respect. Police are first off with their helmets – Say that for them. But there's no cheering now. *You took us from the mountains.* Only silence. **Day 14.** I get my head down about five. *You took us from the sea.* I wake up at one for news. Leon Brittan promising all police in world to make sure anybody who wants to

The Second Week

Monday 12 – Sunday 18 March 1984

The Jew has his orders. Neil Fontaine has his.

Neil Fontaine picks up the Jew outside *The Times* building at ten o'clock sharp. He is on the steps in his leather flying-jacket with his camera and his tape-recorder –

'I am her eyes and her ears,' he tells Neil Fontaine.

They do ninety up the M1 with the Jew on the car phone. He's in a good mood. South Wales have voted overwhelmingly to reject the Union's call to strike; Nottinghamshire have called for a pit-head ballot; the pickets are flying –

The Jew wants to be where the action is –

Two rooms reserved at the Royal Victoria Hotel, Sheffield –

In the Heartland –

A suite for the Jew upstairs, a single for Neil downstairs; fried kidneys and champagne for the Jew in his room, a burger and Coke for Neil at the bar –

Familiar faces, Union faces, in and out all night –

Other faces.

Neil Fontaine lies on his single bed in his single room with the single light on.

He can't sleep. He never can. He has his own orders –

Other eyes and other ears.

The telephone rings three times at three o'clock.

Neil Fontaine brings the car round. The Jew is waiting in his leather flying-jacket. The Mercedes drives out of the city centre up through Rotherham and onto the A631. They cross the A1 into Nottinghamshire.

There is snow on the roads. The hedgerows. The fields –

The police van parked at the bus stop.

The Jew can't sit still. He looks out of the left window, he looks out of the right –

'I am her eyes and her ears,' he tells Neil again.

They come to the Harworth Colliery on the Yorkshire–

Nottinghamshire border; this the place where the Spencer Union was finally defeated in a last bloody battle –

It's 1937 again.

Harworth's men have voted to cross the Yorkshire picket line in military columns; there are one hundred and fifty policemen here to help them; five hundred of Doncaster's hardest out to hinder them –

The men of Harworth turn back to their homes and their families –

First blood to Arthur's Fliers.

The Jew is in a bad mood now. They park in a lay-by with the radio on:

'The National Coal Board has applied to the High Court for an injunction to prevent Yorkshire miners picketing other areas.'

The Jew is in a worse mood. Livid. The Jew is on the car phone. Furious –

'There'll be a bloody general strike if the Chairman does this. Tell him from me, it's absolute insanity. You will hand that red prick the entire labour movement on a plate. He saw it on TV, did he? He saw it on TV? Well, I'm bloody here in fucking Harworth and you can tell your Chairman from me, the answer isn't the 1980 Employment Act. The answer is more fucking police. More fucking police with more fucking balls from their so-called senior officers. That's your answer. Bloody dogs, too. More fucking dogs. And you tell him that's what Stephen Sweet will tell the Prime Minister –

'Because I am her eyes and her ears. Her fucking eyes and her ears out here!'

The Jew hangs up. The Jew sits back. The Jew sighs. The Jew shakes his head.

Neil Fontaine watches a minibus of miners go past –

Bare arse-cheeks pressed against the back windows.

'The gloves are off now, Neil,' shouts the Jew. 'The gloves are bloody off!'

Jen looks fucking gorgeous under these lights. Her hair. Her tan. That blouse. That skirt. Frankie for the thousandth time. Fucking gorgeous. The Mechanic could sit here for the rest of his life. They put on Your Love Is King. *She waves him over. He finishes his drink. Onto the dance floor of an empty club on a Tuesday night in March. He puts his arms around her. Holds her. The rest of his life.*

*

It's been a long Wednesday –

Harworth, Bilsthorpe, Bevercotes, Thoresby.

The police vans in convoys now, checkpoints at every junction –

The Jew takes the credit.

The Yorkshire pickets abandoning their coaches, marching through the fields –

The Jew back on the phone.

It's been a long Wednesday and it isn't over –

This is Ollerton.

The police had to march in the afternoon shift in columns.

Ten p.m. and the Jew is where the action is; the Jew is in the Plough –

Packed. Pickets waiting for the Nightshift. Pissed.

The Jew is talking. Taking notes. Sending Neil to the bar to buy the drinks.

The barmaid says, 'Must have some brass, your mate Biggles.'

'Four pints of Mansfield's and a gin and tonic,' says Neil Fontaine.

'You not having one?'

'Given it up.'

'Well,' she laughs. 'I hope she's worth it.'

'Keep the change,' Neil tells her.

He's halfway back with the drinks when the roar goes up outside –

The Nightshift here.

Everyone heads for the door –

'Neil!' the Jew is shouting. 'Come on, Neil. This is it!'

Neil Fontaine sees the Jew disappear through the door. He goes out after him –

Everyone running. Pint glasses breaking. Car doors slamming.

Neil Fontaine can't see the Jew anywhere –

Fuck.

Neil Fontaine starts up the lane towards the pit, the pickets and the police –

Bricks and bottles, sticks and stones, flying through the air –

There's a hand on Neil's arm. There's a voice in his ear: 'Hello, hello, hello.'

Neil Fontaine turns round –

Paul Dixon is stood beside an old Allegro. He's in his best new sweater, his jeans with a fresh crease and his polished size tens.

'Paul?'

'The fuck you doing here, Neil?'

'Don't ask.'

'I knew you were going to say that,' laughs Paul Dixon. 'I just knew it.'

Neil Fontaine looks up the road. Everyone by the gates now. The Jew too.

Paul Dixon opens the door of the Allegro. He says, 'Got a minute, have you?'

Neil Fontaine looks back up the road. He shrugs. He gets into the Allegro –

The car smells bad. The car feels dirty.

They sit and watch four coppers dragging a picket down the road by his hair.

'So what are you doing here, Neil?' Paul Dixon asks again.

'Like I say –'

'Don't ask,' winks Paul Dixon. 'Well, I am asking.'

'In what capacity?'

Paul Dixon opens his wallet. He taps his warrant card. 'In this capacity.'

'Don't be silly, Sergeant.'

Paul Dixon closes his wallet. He looks out of the windscreen. Embarrassed –

Six coppers are handcuffing two pickets round a lamp-post.

'All right,' sighs Neil Fontaine. 'I'm driving this Captain of Industry up and down the country so he can write little pieces on industrial relations for his mate at *The Times*. Happy now?'

'I'd heard you were –'

Neil Fontaine turns to stare at Paul Dixon. He asks, 'Were what?'

'Nothing. I must have misheard.'

'Yeah,' says Neil Fontaine. 'You must have misheard.'

Paul Dixon looks out of his window again. Embarrassed again –

Local lads are setting about the pickets' cars parked up and down the street.

'So what brings *you* to a pretty place like this, Paul?' asks Neil Fontaine.

'National Reporting Centre. Liaison officer.'

'Nice work,' says Neil Fontaine.

'If you can get it.'

'And you got it,' smiles Neil Fontaine.

'Thanks to the Yorkshire Stalin, aye.'

'Old King Coal to his friends,' laughs Neil Fontaine.

Paul Dixon looks out of the windscreen again. He says, 'Few of them about tonight.'

'How about our old mate?' asks Neil Fontaine. 'The Mechanic still about, is he?'

Paul Dixon shakes his head. 'Man's in love. Married. Two dogs. Retired.'

'That's a shame,' says Neil Fontaine. 'Our Dave had his talents.'

Paul Dixon points through the windscreen. 'How about your new friend?'

Fuck –

There are six men carrying another man back down the lane towards the pub –

The Jew has an arm.

Neil Fontaine opens the car door. He gets out.

Paul Dixon leans over the passenger seat. He says, 'Stay free.'

Neil Fontaine slams the door.

Terry Winters had been home twenty minutes when the phone went. Theresa picked it up. She didn't speak. She just listened and rolled her eyes. She handed it to Terry –

Click-click.

Terry Winters drove back to St James's House.

Terry unlocked his office. Terry got out his calculator. Terry went upstairs.

The music was loud. Terry knocked once. The music stopped. Terry waited –

'Come.'

Terry opened the door. Terry went inside.

The Tweed Jackets were sitting around the table. The President at the window –

His back to the room.

Terry Winters coughed. Terry said, 'You wanted to see me.'

The President didn't turn. He said, 'They're not moving fast enough, Comrade.'

'I've told them,' said Terry. 'I –'

'They're in the pub talking about it when they should be on the phone doing it.'

Terry Winters nodded.

The President turned now. He said, 'Twenty-four hours from now they will have outlawed this Union and every union in the country which believes they still have the right to strike to save their jobs, the right to picket to save their jobs. Every working man and woman in this country will have to rise as one to defeat this government. This Union will be in the vanguard of that battle, as it has been in every struggle, as it has been in every victory.'

Terry nodded.

The President stared at Terry. The President turned back to the window.

One of the Tweeds emptied his pipe into the glass ashtray with three sharp taps. He looked up at Terry. He said, 'The President is counting on you, Comrade. We all are.'

Terry Winters nodded again.

'So get rid of the fucking money.'

Terry nodded again.

Someone switched the Shostakovich back on.

Terry Winters went back downstairs. Terry knocked on Mike Sullivan's door. Terry told him the President wanted them to go out to the Yorkshire Area Headquarters on Huddersfield Road in Barnsley. The President needed Terry and Mike to double-check. The President didn't trust Yorkshire any more. He never had. Not since he'd left the place. The President didn't trust anyone any more. The President was paranoid –

They all were.

The Tweeds made Terry and Mike change cars twice. The Denims had them take the long way round. They travelled the ten miles in an hour and in three different cars. They had two empty suitcases in the boot –

Theresa had taken them down from the loft.

Terry and Mike arrived in Barnsley unannounced. Terry and Mike went upstairs. Terry and Mike took over an office. Terry and Mike searched the room for microphones. Terry drew the curtains. Terry sent Mike out on a wild paper-chase. Terry called in the finance officer for the Yorkshire Area. Terry locked the door. Terry frisked Clive Cook. Terry made Clive put the radio on while they talked. Terry taught Clive his latest code. Terry told him to use it in all future contact. Then Terry put the two empty suitcases on the table and asked Clive about the eight million quid.

The Jew is in shock. He spent Thursday on the phone in his double bed at the Royal Victoria. He sent Neil out to buy an electric type-writer and every single newspaper he could find.

The Jew had met the dead man. They had both helped carry an injured miner back to the pub. The dead man was a picket, the injured man a scab. The dead man had tended to the cut above the scab's eye. The dead man had called an ambulance from the pub. Then the dead man had gone back to the front –

The Jew has spots of blood on the lamb's-wool collar of his leather flying-jacket.

'Her eyes and her ears, Neil,' says the Jew. 'I am her eyes and her ears.'

Neil Fontaine drives the Jew back over to Ollerton on Friday morning. The Jew wants to see the place in daylight. The Jew wants to take notes. Take some pictures –

Upturned cars, ripped-up pavements. Uprooted hedges, boarded up windows.

There are a lot of police vans and a lot of television crews and no pickets –

There is a forty-eight-hour truce while the Nottinghamshire men have their vote.

The Jew puts his arm around a woman in her ruined garden. He tells her how the pogroms drove his family out of Russia. He tells her how his family lost everything. He tells her how they started over again. He tells her how his father worked eighteen-hour days, seven days a week. He tells her how he himself was sent to Eton. He tells her how they bullied him –

He tells her bullies never win –

The Jew promises her that.

Neil Fontaine drives the Jew back to his hotel suite.

The Jew has some fresh orders for Neil Fontaine –

The Jew wants Neil to hire a van. Neil Fontaine hires a van.

The Jew gives Neil a shopping list. Neil Fontaine goes shopping.

The Jew gives Neil an address:

The Proteus Territorial Army Barracks, Ollerton.

Neil Fontaine makes his delivery:

500 bottles of whisky, 500 bottles of vodka, 1000 mixers and 4000 cans of lager.

The Jew should have laid on some ladies –

A thousand Met boys with nothing to do and nowhere to go on a Saturday night in the North of England; two thousand more at the Beckingham Camp in Newark; another thousand at the Prince William Barracks, Grantham –

Three hours from now they'll be wanking in circles –

'These men are the backbone of this nation,' the Jew tells Neil. 'The backbone.'

The Mechanic is screaming into the phone in a service station, southbound on the M6 –

'Schaub? Julius fucking Schaub?' he's screaming. 'You think I'd have gone anywhere fucking near this if I'd known that little cunt was going to be in on it?'

'Relax,' says the voice on the receiving end. 'Relax –'

'Relax?' the Mechanic shouts. 'You're telling me to fucking relax? I got the wife in the fucking car, you fucking wanker. You think I'd have brought her along if I'd known fucking Schaub was going to be there?'

'Someone dropped out,' says the voice. 'We needed –'

'Wise fucking man.'

'Let me finish,' says the voice. 'Someone dropped out. We needed a body at short notice. We called Vince. Vince called Julius. Julius was available.'

'Schaub's always fucking available,' the Mechanic says. 'Because no one wants to work with the fucking cunt.'

'Please,' sighs the voice. 'We need you on this one.'

'You should've fucking thought of that before you went and invited that fucking little pervert along then.'

'We will make it up to you,' says the voice.

'I'm listening.'

'An even four for your troubles.'

'I should fucking think so,' the Mechanic says. 'I should fucking think so.'

'Have you ever seen anything like this before, Neil?' shouts the Jew from the backseat.

Neil Fontaine shakes his head. He never has seen anything like this before –

An entire county completely sealed off –

All roads in and out of Mansfield and Nottinghamshire blocked with checkpoints; the motorway down to a single lane in each direction; tracker dogs in every field; helicopters and spotter planes over-head; three thousand police deployed –

Every taxi and coach firm in Yorkshire and Derbyshire told not to accept fares from miners or face immediate arrest; every taxi and coach stopped just to make sure; every private car and van –

The Dartford Tunnel closed. The borders with Scotland and Wales.

Neil Fontaine parks the Mercedes in sight of the Mansfield Headquarters of the Nottinghamshire NUM; the Jew waiting in the back by the car phone for the result –

The sound of helicopters in the sky and the Attorney-General on the radio:

'If it does involve a lot of extra police work, then so be it. It is not involving the government in the dispute.'

The car phone rings. The Jew picks it up. The Jew listens –

'Two hundred and seventy for a return?' he says. 'That's seventy-five per cent. That's fantastic news.'

The Jew hangs up. The Jew dials South –

'What did I tell you?' says the Jew. 'He's already lost.'

work can. Threatening anybody who obstructs them with jail. I mooch about house all afternoon. Telly and crossword for company. My name's down for nights again this week. Cath's got more hours at shop. Never see each other. I go down into Thurcroft for about half-five. One in Hotel. One in Welfare. Folk start to meet up about seven-thirty. Now they've had their little vote and one of ours has died, it's different. Up a notch. Don't need a coach now either. Can see how it's going to be from here on – Hardcore unless it's a rally or something. No firm will hire us a coach anyway – None would get through either. Private cars and vans, that's us. Fifteen to twenty per shift. Pete gives out pieces of paper with name of pit and best way there. Bloody Bentinck again. He gives us quid for shift and money for petrol. Me and three other lads are in with Geoff again tonight. Dayshift have told us police are all over shop. *Krk-krk*. Not messing about either. Numbers, names, and piss off back to where you come from. Told some lads to be down their local nick first thing with their driving licences. Lip and they'll have your keys. We've got maps out in car. Don't even bother with usual ways, ways Pete's written. Fields and farms for us. Helicopters with big bloody searchlights overhead. Everyone but Geoff with their heads down – Hour later we give up on Bentinck. Like a fucking police state. Geoff calls Silverwood. *Click-click*. Tell us to try Harworth. But then a carload of lads from Markham pull up. Got a CB radio. Heading to Bilsthorpe – Know a good way up there. We follow them – Anything's better than lying among crisp packets on floor of Geoff's car. It's gone half-nine by time we get there. Never seen so many fucking police. We park up on side of main road and join picket at entrance to pit lane. Some of scabs have already started showing up. They don't hang about either. Leg it straight in. Can't even see them for police half of time – Shove. Shout. Scab. Shove. Shout. Scab – There's a song every now and again from us. Sneers and jeers from police. This goes on for a couple of hours – Shove. Shout. Scab. Shove.

Shout. Scab – One point I'm right up against this copper. Won't tell us where he's from. Not from round here though. Tell from his accent. Things he says. They've had their vote, he tells me. They want to work. So why don't you lot fuck off back to Yorkshire. About midnight, we do that. **Day 17.** Cath's laid out my suit on bed. Ironed us a shirt. I watch end of breakfast telly. Have a couple of hours. *You took us from the wild-fields*. Get up. Put on my suit. Sit there till it's time. Just thinking. We meet at Welfare at one. There're about twenty cars and banners going. Everyone to be at South Kirkby cricket club for two. We have a pint then into cars. I go with Geoff again. Unbelievable scene at their cricket field: hundreds of buses and cars parked up; thousands and thousands of men in their Sunday best; banners from every lodge in Britain; other unions here and all. Hearse sets off from lad's house. Five cars follow with family and friends. There's a drummer up at head with Arthur, Jack Taylor and all big shots – our lads and all banners walking behind them. First banner is from lad's own lodge, Ackton Hall. Procession goes for a mile up to All Saints' Parish Church, village streets lined with women and kids. Three hundred of lad's family and friends inside church. Everyone else outside in silence. Blokes with tears down their faces. Big blokes: Pete; Geoff; me. It's hard – Two kids. No dad now – Follow them up to cemetery in Moorthorpe. Lad goes into ground for last time. We call in Robin Hood on way back. Long faces and short drinks. Lots of both. Big disputes develop a logic of their own, Pete is saying. It'll be right. Back in Thurcroft, King Arthur's on television in Hotel. Dead lad's dad had told him, Under no circumstances must we give up now. We must fight to save pits and jobs because that is what their son gave his life for. We all get right fucking smashed. Nothing to eat. I walk all way home. Pass out. *You took us from the whale-roads*. Wake up in my suit and I can't stop fucking crying. **Day 20.** Cath's on warpath again. Every time he comes on news, she switches it off. I tell her, You're blaming wrong bloke. Blind,

The Third Week

Monday 19 – Sunday 25 March 1984

They wake up in a four-poster bed in an olde hotel in the centre of Stratford-upon-Avon. They are hungover. It takes a minute to remember why they're here. The Mechanic switches the radio on. 99 Luftballons. *They have a shower. Eat breakfast in the room. They check out. Feel better. They take the* A46 *and the* A422 *into Worcester. Jen drives. They park outside the Pear Tree. They go inside. The Mechanic makes the phone call. Gets the address.*

They have a drink. A bite to eat.

An hour later they stop at Diamond Detectives to pick up the key and the money. Vince Taylor isn't about. Just his old secretary Joyce. Jen has never met Joyce before. Joyce gives them a cup of tea. Tries to get hold of Vince. She says Vince is a bit down in the dumps at the moment. Looks like she's had enough herself. The Mechanic asks her if there's anything him and Jen can do. She shakes her head. Locks herself in the toilet for ten minutes.

Vince isn't going to show.

They finish their tea. Make their excuses. Joyce gives them the key. The money. They take the A44 *out to Leominster then the* A49 *straight up to Shrewsbury. Jen counts the money. They find the house. Two-up, two-down terrace near Sutton Road. They let themselves in. The Mechanic makes another phone call.*

They sit down. Stick the telly on. Wait –

Bad weather. Bad dreams all night.

The Yorkshire Area Executive had defied the High Court injunction on picketing and the pickets continued to fly. The Yorkshire Area had been found in contempt of court and the bailiffs dispatched –

The Yorkshire Industrial Action Fund already exhausted.

The President sent Terry Winters and Mike Sullivan back to Huddersfield Road again.

This time they weren't alone –

Two thousand from the Yorkshire Coalfield had answered the President's call; two thousand miners here to defend the battlements of King Arthur's (former) Castle, ringing the black, stained bricks of the Yorkshire HQ –

Four thousand eyes watching and waiting for the bailiffs.

In an upstairs room Terry and Mike shredded papers.

There were scuffles outside. The men attacked photographers and camera crews. The police stepped in. Punches were thrown. Arrests made.

Clive Cook brought in more boxes. Terry and Mike shredded more papers.

There was a sudden, huge cheer from the men outside –

Terry and Mike went to the window.

Clive came back with the last box. He said, 'The Board's abandoned the action.'

The Tinkerbell doesn't knock. They never do. He has his own key. Doesn't introduce himself. Never do. Wise men. He has a good look at Jen, then takes his gear straight up to the little bedroom. The Mechanic sends Jen out to buy a pint of milk. He reads yesterday's paper again. Jen comes back. It's raining outside. She makes a pot. The Mechanic takes a cup up to the Tinkerbell. He's sitting on the bed with his headphones on and his notebook out. The Mechanic taps him on the shoulder. The Tinkerbell jumps. The Mechanic hands him the mug. The Tinkerbell nods. The Mechanic goes back downstairs.

Half-twelve, Jen goes out for fish and chips. The Mechanic sits and waits for The One o'Clock News. Jen comes back with the chips. The Mechanic sticks some on a plate for the Tinkerbell and takes them up. He's still sitting on the bed with his headphones on. He nods. The Mechanic goes back downstairs to Jen. They eat lunch. Jen makes a fresh pot. The Mechanic does the dishes.

Three o'clock, the Tinkerbell comes downstairs. He hands the Mechanic a piece of paper –

The Mechanic reads it. Picks up the phone.

Hour later, Julius Schaub arrives with Leslie in a red Ford Escort. Schaub's grown his hair out since the Mechanic saw him last. Leslie looks exactly the same. The Mechanic doesn't introduce them to Jen. Schaub keeps it shut. He's been warned. He's on his best behaviour. The Mechanic gives them their instructions. He takes Jen up to the little bedroom with him. The Tinkerbell is sitting on the bed with his headphones on. Notebook out. He turns to look at them. He shakes his head. They sit down on the bed next to him to wait –

Bad weather. Bad dreams all night.

Just after half-seven the Tinkerbell nudges the Mechanic. He taps his headphones. He puts his thumb up. The Mechanic and Jen go back downstairs. Wake up Tweedle-dee and Tweedle-dum.

They leave the house.

Schaub and Leslie take the Escort. The Mechanic and Jen take the Rover.

Both cars drive to Sutton Road. The Escort parks at one end of the street, the Rover at the other. Schaub gets out of his car. Leslie stays put behind the wheel. The Mechanic gets out the Rover. Jen stays where she is.

The Mechanic takes the bag out of the boot. He walks along the street. He comes to the house. He goes up the drive. Schaub already has the back door open. They go inside. The Mechanic opens the bag. He hands Schaub a camera –

Schaub takes the upstairs. The Mechanic the downstairs.

The Mechanic goes through the kitchen into the living room and then the study. He searches drawers and bookshelves for twenty minutes.

Schaub comes back downstairs into the study. He shakes his head.

They leave the house. They close the back door. They go down the drive.

The Mechanic walks back to the Escort with Schaub –

Schaub gets into the front. The Mechanic the back.

Leslie turns round –

The Mechanic shakes his head.

Schaub says, 'She must have it on her.'

'Like where?' Leslie asks him.

He pulls out a large white pair of women's knickers from the inside of his jacket. He holds them up. He laughs and says, 'Hide all sorts in these sexy things.'

The Mechanic leans forward. He grabs Schaub by his hair. Pulls his head over the back of the seat –

Whispers in Schaub's ear, 'I thought it was kids you liked. Your own.'

'Fuck off,' shouts Schaub. 'Fuck off!'

The Mechanic pushes him forward again. He leans over the seat with him –

Bangs Schaub's forehead once onto the top of the dashboard.

'Fuck!' screams Schaub. 'Fuck! Fuck! Fuck!'

'Take him back to the house,' the Mechanic tells Leslie. 'Wait for me there.'

Leslie nods. He starts the car.

The Mechanic gets out. He walks back down the street to the Rover. Gets in.

'What's wrong?' asks Jen.

'Nothing,' the Mechanic says. 'Have to go out to the cottage.'

Jen starts the car. They drive out to Four Crosses and turn off up to Llanymynech. They stop at a phone box. The Mechanic calls the number –

Lets it ring. Ring and ring. No one answers.

They find the cottage. They park.

The Mechanic takes the bag off the backseat. He gets out –

Jen waits in the car.

The Mechanic walks up the path. He does the door. He goes inside. He searches the place. He goes back outside. He locks the lock. He walks down the path –

Jen starts the car.

The Mechanic puts the bag in the boot. He gets in. Shakes his head.

They drive back to Shrewsbury. They park outside the terrace –

The Escort isn't here.

They go inside. No Schaub. No Leslie. The Mechanic goes upstairs –

The Tinkerbell is still sat on the bed. Headphones in his hand. He looks up –

'What the fuck happened in there?' he asks the Mechanic.

'What do you mean?'

'The phone's dead.'

'What?'

'I can't hear anything –'

The Mechanic goes straight back down the stairs.

Jen's just put the kettle on. She says, 'What is it?'

'Come on,' the Mechanic tells her. 'Quick!'

They go back outside to the car. They drive back to Sutton Road –

No Escort here either.

They park at the end of the road –

'Wait here,' the Mechanic tells Jen.

'You're never going back in there?' she says. 'She could come –'

The Mechanic gets out. Closes the door. He walks along the street. Comes to the house –

The curtains are drawn. Lights on inside –

Fuck.

He goes up the drive. Round the back of the house. The door wide open –

Fuck.

He leans inside. Shouts out, 'Hello? Anybody home?'

There's no answer.

He steps inside the house. Dirty washing scattered all over the kitchen

*floor. Two handbags emptied on to the table. The telephone ripped from the
wall.*

He goes into the living room then the study –

No one.

He goes upstairs. One of the railings in the banister is missing.

He goes into the front bedroom –

No one.

Into the bathroom –

No one.

The back bedroom –

Fuck –

Wet towels on the floor. The bed stripped –

Blood and semen on the mattress.

The Jew hasn't been to sleep for days. He's too excited. Too busy –

He's just had his tour of the thirteenth floor of New Scotland Yard –
The National Reporting Centre.

Neil Fontaine opens the back door for the Jew. The Jew gets in.

'Downing Street, if you would please, Neil.'

'Certainly, sir.'

The Jew tells Neil of the twenty-four-hour operations and the
banks of telephones, the walls of maps and the coloured pins –

'They keep them in biscuit tins,' he laughs. 'Would you believe it?
Biscuit tins.'

Neil Fontaine stops for a red light. He glances at his watch then the
rearview –

The Jew is wearing a dark blue pinstripe suit, a pale blue shirt and
a white silk tie. The Jew has another report to make; another speech
to give –

'There will be no ballot. That much is clear,' the Jew is saying aloud
in the back. 'The strategy of the committee must be based upon this
reality. The Employment Acts have to be kept in reserve. No resort to
ballot, no resort to court. In the very unlikely event of a national ballot and an even unlikelier vote for a strike then, and only then, should
the Employment Acts be used to protect those areas that will
inevitably defy the ballot and continue to work –'

The Jew is practising his speech again. The Jew is out to turn the
screw –

He talks to himself in the back of the Mercedes. He talks about

Social Security. Talks about the non-payment of benefits. About late payments. He talks about the Electricity and Gas boards. Talks about demanding weekly payments. About cutting the strikers off. He talks about the banks and the building societies. Talks about mortgages –

About repossession –

The Jew wants to turn the screw. To turn it again and again –

Week by week, little by little, day by day, piece by piece –

'To roll back the frontiers of Socialism for ever, Neil!'

Neil Fontaine stops at the checkpoint at the end of Downing Street.

The Jew puts on a pair of aviator sunglasses and his large-brimmed panama hat. He takes a deep breath. He says, 'Wish me luck, Neil.'

'Good luck, sir.'

Neil Fontaine watches the Jew disappear into Number 10, Downing Street.

Neil Fontaine looks at his watch again. He starts the Mercedes –

He has his own screws to turn. Different screws.

Midnight Wednesday into Thursday. Dark side of the moon. They pull up outside Vince's bungalow. No lights on –

'Wait here,' the Mechanic tells Jen.

He gets out. He goes up the drive. Rings his bell. Bangs on his door.

'Who is it?' shouts Vince from inside. 'What do you want?'

'It's me,' the Mechanic says. 'I want a word.'

Keys turn. Chains fall. Vince Taylor opens the door –

The Mechanic shines the torch full in his face. Vince's hand goes up –

Vince knows.

'Dave,' he says. 'Put that away.'

'Vince,' shouts his wife down the hall. 'What the bloody hell's going on?'

'Nothing, love,' he says. 'Go back to sleep.'

The Mechanic lowers the torch.

Vince tightens the belt on his dressing-gown. He looks down the drive. He says, 'Who you got in the car with you?'

'Jen.'

'Fucking hell,' says Vince.

The Mechanic nods. He says, 'Schaub? Leslie?'

'Just Leslie,' says Vince.

'Schaub?'

'Fuck knows.'

'So where's Leslie?'

26

'He's afraid, Dave.'

'We're all afraid, Vince,' the Mechanic tells him. 'Now where is he?'

'Dave –'

The Mechanic shakes his head. He asks him again, 'Where is he?'

'They call it Little America,' says Vince. 'But, Dave –'

'Where is it, Vince?'

'Atcham on the way to Telford. It's a disused airfield.'

'What's he doing there?'

'He's hiding. What you think he's doing there?'

The Mechanic looks at his watch. He says, 'Put some clothes on, Vince.'

Vince shakes his head. Vince says, 'Dave –'

The Mechanic grabs Vince Taylor by his dressing-gown. He says again, 'Put some fucking clothes on.'

Vince goes to get dressed. Vince comes back out. Vince sits in the front seat –

And off they set.

Thirty minutes later, Vince points to the left –

The Mechanic switches off the headlights. He turns off the main road –

Drives through an industrial estate.

Vince points straight ahead.

There is a fence with a gate and an old USAF sign. A red Escort parked up.

The Mechanic pulls in beside the Escort. He switches off the engine.

The Mechanic turns to Vince in the passenger seat. He says, 'So where's Leslie?'

'Fuck knows,' says Vince.

The Mechanic grabs Vince Taylor's fat face in his right hand. He squeezes those pasty cheeks tight together. Turns him towards the backseat –

'You know who that is?' the Mechanic asks Vince.

Vince nods.

'That's the woman I love,' the Mechanic tells him. 'So don't speak like that in front of her.'

Vince nods again.

The Mechanic pushes Vince's head back into the side-window. Lets him go.

Vince holds his face. He says, 'I'm sorry, Dave.'

'Right,' the Mechanic says. 'Then let's go and find Leslie.'

They all get out into the dark. The cold and the rain.

'Shall we split up?' asks Vince.

The Mechanic switches the torch on. He shines it in Vince's face –
Vince puts his hand up again.
'Vince,' the Mechanic says. 'Splitting up is always a mistake.'
Vince shrugs and opens the gates.
They start walking towards the airstrip and an old control tower.
Vince cups his mouth in his hands. He shouts, 'Leslie! It's me, Vince!'
Nothing.
'Leslie! It's me, Vince,' he shouts again. 'Dave and Jen are here with me.'
'There,' says Jen. She points at a light flashing on and off up ahead.
They wave their torches at the signal. They walk towards it.
Leslie is standing in front of a small shed. He is shaking. He drops to his knees. He looks up at them –
'It was fucking Julius,' he sobs. 'He only went to put back them fucking knickers. I told him not to. But he thought you were going to hurt him again. Then he was inside and she come home. I went to help him. But –'
They stand in a semicircle. They look down on Leslie.
He looks up again –
'He lost it.'
'Where are they now, Leslie?' the Mechanic asks him.
'I don't know. I swear. Really. I don't. I went upstairs. I didn't want any part of it. I went back to the car. I didn't know what to do. Then Julius come back out with her. Took her off in her car. That was last I saw of him. Them.'
The Mechanic squats down next to Leslie. He takes Leslie's face in his hands –
The Mechanic holds it up to his –
Little Leslie is crying.
The Mechanic wipes away Leslie's tears. He looks into his eyes.
'I swear that's all I know,' says Leslie.
The Mechanic lets go of Leslie's face. He stands up.
Vince is staring at the Mechanic.
The Mechanic nods.
Vince spits into the ground.
'What?' says Leslie. 'Vince? What is it?'
'You two wait here,' the Mechanic tells Vince and Leslie.
The Mechanic takes Jen's hand. They walk back to the Rover.
'Lock the doors,' the Mechanic tells her. 'Put the radio on.'
Jen nods. She gets in. She locks the doors. She puts the radio on. Loud.
The Mechanic goes to the back of the Rover. He opens the boot –
Takes out the spade.

Terry Winters walked the floors and corridors of St James's House. His ear to the doors, he listened to the voices. The telephones ringing. The typewriters –

Terry was the boss now. The big man –

The President had left him in charge. The President was touring the coalfields. The President was making certain that the lessons had been learnt. That through solid unity and with more trade union support, pits and jobs could be saved. The Tory anti-trade union legislation resisted. That now was no longer the time to ballot. Now no longer the time when the Haves could stop the Have-nots fighting to save their homes and their communities. Their jobs and their pits –

There were standing ovations. There were songs in his name –

Autographs for the wives and kids. Big boots to fill for Terry Winters –

Terry called meetings. Asked for briefings. Terry demanded updates. Analysis.

The President would call. The President would need to know –

Not tomorrow. Today. Now.

Terry Winters sat bolt upright at his desk under the large portrait of the President. Terry waited for the phone to ring. For the President's call –

At five o'clock, it rang.

Terry picked it up. *Click-click.* Terry said, 'Chief Executive speaking.'

'Hello, Chief Executive,' she said. 'Guess who?'

Terry swallowed. He said, 'Diane?'

'Who's a clever boy then?'

'How did you get this number?'

She paused. She said, 'Well, if you're going to be like that –'

Terry stood up behind his desk. He said into the phone, 'No, wait.'

'You gave it to me,' she said. 'Remember?'

Terry nodded. He said, 'Of course.'

'Guess what?' she said. 'I've got a present for the Chief Executive.'

'For me?'

'But you have to guess what it is,' she giggled.

'I –'

'I'm looking at it right now. I'm touching it.'

'I –'

'I'll give you another hint,' she whispered. 'It's wet and it's waiting for you.'

'Where are you?'

'Now that would be telling,' she laughed.

'Where?' he screamed.

'I'm sat at the bar of the Hallam Towers Hotel, holding your vodka and tonic.'

Terry Winters hung up. Terry dialled Theresa. *Click-click.* He told Theresa lies. Terry hung up again. He got his coat. He switched off the lights. Terry locked the door. He went down the corridor. He took the stairs –

Two at a time.

There was a Tweed at reception. The Tweed said, 'In a hurry are we, Comrade?'

'No,' said Terry. 'Just off to meet the wife.'

'Now, why don't I believe you, Comrade?' smiled the Tweed.

'What?' said Terry. 'What do you mean?'

'Just pulling your leg, Comrade,' laughed the Tweed. 'Just pulling your leg.'

Terry Winters left the building. He ran up the street to the underground car park. He drove out to Hallam Towers. He sucked mints all the way there –

Two at a time.

Terry ran through the lobby into the bar.

Diane was sitting on a high stool with her legs crossed. She pushed the vodka and tonic towards him. She put her right hand on the inside of Terry's right thigh. She said, 'I'm afraid the ice has melted. It went all warm and wet.'

Terry Winters took off his glasses. Terry put them in his jacket pocket. He smiled.

Diane leant forward. She whispered, 'Fuck me before dinner. Upstairs. Now.'

Terry nodded. He said, 'Without me, they'd be bankrupt already.'

Diane rubbed her fingers over his lips. She said, 'You talk too much, Comrade.'

The Mechanic needs time to think this through. Space. He drops Jen off at her sister's. Goes in with her just to make sure. He picks up the dogs from his mother's. Goes back to his. Theirs. He makes a couple of calls. Makes sure he'll be rid of the Rover first thing tomorrow. He has another shower. Another drink –

The Mechanic lies on his bed. Their bed. He switches on the news –

'An elderly woman has been found brutally murdered in the Shropshire countryside. The seventy-nine-year-old rose grower and anti-nuclear campaigner was –'

They will want answers. Then they'll want silence.

she shouts. You're all bloody blind. I get up from table. I say, Do you want a lift in? Listen to you, she laughs. How long you think you'll be able to keep car? I say, They give us petrol money – Aye, he'll pay you when you picket for him, she says. I shake my head. Do you want a lift in or not? He going to pay your tax, your MOT? He going to pay for your tyres, your radiator? You'll have driven it into ground before he's finished with it. You'll be no bloody use to him then. See how much he pays you then – Bugger her. I put on my coat. I go outside. I get car out of garage. I sit in drive for a bit. She doesn't come out – Bloody bugger her. I set off into Thurcroft. Go down Welfare. I'm very early. I wish I'd put my name down for either days or nights now. Not fucking afternoons. Pete comes in. Asks if I fancy going into Doncaster with him. Coal House. Too right, I do. Get there just before eight. There are only a couple of coppers. *Krk-krk.* Hundred-odd of us – Parkas. Kagools. Boots. Trainers – Coppers on their walkie-talkies. *Krk-krk.* Shitting it. NCB staff turn up about quarter-past to half-past eight. Police everywhere now. There's usual shoving. Shouting. Scuffles. Most of NCB staff take one look and go home. One–nil to us. Pete and me drive on over to Bentinck – Reality. Windows down. Roadblock fucking City. *Krk-krk.* Have you heard what I was telling them other lads? Pete shakes his head. No, he says. I have not – We know you are peaceful, says copper. But if you carry on you'll be arrested because you're liable to cause a breach of the peace. What? says Pete. So if we just drive on towards colliery, then we'll be arrested? Aye, says copper. You will. So don't bother. **Day 22.** Bred into them, John is saying on A18. They're not Union men. Never have been. You've seen their houses. Their cars. Remember me dad telling our Kevin, Work down there and you'll end up a scab – Rich like, but a scab. That was fifteen, twenty year back. They're all, Fuck you, I'm all right Jack, says Tony. Always have been – Fucking incentive schemes, says Michael. Made it worse. Remember that fucking ballot? John laughs. They

were completely outvoted. Cunts just ignored result and went their own sweet fucking way as usual. Now them same cunts want another vote, says Michael. Long as it suits them, says Tony. If it didn't, they'd just sod us anyway, says John. Bred into them. I say, Aye-up. Company. Fucking hell, says John. Not again. I pull over. I wind down window. *Krk-krk.* Where you going? Fishing – Fuck off – That's not very nice, says John. I don't give a shit, says copper. You're pickets and I want to know where you're going? I say again, We're off fishing. Get out, he says. I get out – Driver's licence – I hand it over. Rest of you, out, he says. John, Tony and Michael get out of car. Two other coppers come up. One of them takes down registration. Other takes keys out of ignition. He goes round back, opens up boot. You got a warrant to do that, have you? asks Tony. Why? asks copper. Got something to fucking hide, have you? I think they have, sir, says one with his head in my boot. He stands up, six small logs in his arms. One with driver's licence in his hands, he's shaking his head. Now what have we here? he asks. They look like offensive weapons to me. I look at him and smile. He throws my driver's licence down on road. You've got ten minutes to get back to Yorkshire, Mr Daly of Hardwick – Or what? asks John. Or you're all fucking nicked. **Day 25.** Cath wants to go over to her sister's. She lives just outside Lincoln. Place called Branston. It's a straight run down A57. We get on road after breakfast. I want to try to get there and back before National starts. We pass Shireoaks and are just by first turn off into Worksop when I see all cones across road. Them parked up in a lay-by. *Krk-krk.* Crowbars and cameras out. *Smile.* They wave us over to side. Fuck. Fuck. Fuck. He taps on glass. I wind down window. Where you going? Lincoln. Why? See her sister. Where you live? Hardwick. Where's that? Just back up there. Near Thurcroft, says Cath. What you do? You what? Your job? I'm a miner. Are you now? he says. Thurcroft? I nod. Working, are you? What's that to you? He shakes his head. Turn your vehicle around, he says. What?

The Fourth Week

Monday 26 March – Sunday 1 April 1984

Theresa Winters woke Terry up. She had made him porridge. Scrambled eggs on toast. She stuck the kids in the back of the car. Half asleep. She dropped him at the station.

Terry stood on the platform. He stamped his feet. He rubbed his hands together. He had a first-class seat on the first train down.

The train was ten minutes late.

Terry found his seat. He ordered coffee. Breakfast. He checked his files:

National Coal Board vs National Union of Mineworkers: NCB High Court action against the NUM's pension-fund investment policy.

Terry checked his notes:

Union constitutionally opposes investment of funds overseas and in industries that compete with coal.

He checked his sums:

£84.8 million annual contributions from members; £151.5 million from the NCB; £22.4 million in pensions and £45.2 million lump-sum payments to be paid annually; £200 million for investment.

The President would be representing the Union. Himself. The President would be conducting their defence. Personally. The President would be waiting for Terry. Himself. The President would be counting on Terry –

Personally.

Terry put away the file. He picked up the complimentary copy of *The Times*:

More miners join strike as pickets increase; BSC cutbacks 50% at Scunthorpe; Miner found hanged –

Terry felt sick. Terry looked at his watch. Terry changed carriages –

Terry sat at a table in second class as the train pulled into King's Cross.

Terry Winters knew they would be waiting for him. Watching him.

'These people need our help,' says the Jew again –

'They are putting concrete blocks and metal poles across their roads. They are smashing their windscreens and slashing their tyres. They are urinating in plastic bags and throwing them at these people as they try to go to work.'

Neil Fontaine nods. He keeps his eyes on the motorway.

'Nottinghamshire, Derbyshire, Lancashire, Leicestershire – these are the places where we shall win this war.'

The Mercedes leaves the M1 at Junction 21.

'These are our people, Neil. These are their places.'

Neil Fontaine follows the police cars to the Brant Inn at Groby. He parks among the TV vans and the Transit vans. He opens the back door for the Jew.

The Jew gets out of the car. The Jew takes off his aviator sunglasses. He says, 'What a charming little place, Neil.'

Neil Fontaine nods. He holds open the saloon door of the Brant Inn –

The room is packed with Union Moderates and police, TV crews and reporters –

Lights. Cameras. Action:

'My name is Stephen Sweet,' shouts the Jew. 'I am here to help.'

The court had adjourned for the day. The President to his fortieth-floor flat in the Barbican with Len and the ladies. The rest of them back to their rooms at the County. They were all watching the news on the telly in Terry's room. They were all laughing at the sight of the Union Right –

'Some bloody secret meeting,' roared Paul. 'Look on Sam's fucking face, eh?'

'Couldn't organize a piss-up in a brewery, that lot,' said Mike.

'Talking of breweries,' winked Dick. 'We're wasting valuable drinking time.'

Terry switched off the telly. Terry stubbed out their cigarettes again.

They all went down to the Crown & Anchor for old times' sake.

Dick drank pints of half-and-half and told the stories –

Drunken stories from different times.

Industrial and labour correspondents in and out all night –

Just like in the old days. Different days.

Terry sat in the corner with his vodka and tonic and paid for their drinks. Tomorrow the President would ask him what they had done last night –

The President would smell it on them and Terry would tell him.

The Mechanic sleeps with the curtains open. The dogs in the garden. He watches the news five times a day. Buys every different paper they have. He cuts out the stories. Sticks them in a scrapbook. He phones Jen at her sister's. Every hour. On the hour –

The Mechanic is waiting for their call –

The call comes. The voice says, 'You owe us.'

'Like fuck I do.'

'Really?' says the voice. 'Well you've got four grand of our money and we've got a front-page murder that's costing us a further five grand a day to clean up. Now does that sound fair to you, Dave? Does it? Really?'

'I warned you about Schaub,' the Mechanic says. 'Only got yourselves to blame.'

'Not quite,' says the voice. 'We can think of three or four other people.'

'Are you threatening me?'

'Dave,' says the voice. 'If we were threatening you, you'd be tied up watching us feed your dogs' cocks to your wife –'

'Fuck you. Fuck you. Fuck you.'

'Finished?' asks the voice. 'Now listen –'

The Mechanic hangs up.

The President had not come to ask for help. He did not want help. He did not need help. The President had not come to beg. He did not want charity. He did not need charity. The President had come only to hold them to their word. To have them keep their promises. Honour their pledges. The President had come only to collect. To collect what was his –

From the steel men. The lorry drivers. The railwaymen. The seamen –

The promise and the pledge to cease all movement of coal –

By road. By rail. By sea –

To cut off the power stations. To shut down the steel works –

The whole country.

This was what he had come to collect and the President meant to collect it.

The Union took over the TGWU. They ordered tea. They ordered sandwiches. They listened to the report. The daily update:

Thirty-five out of one hundred and seventy-six pits still working; tail-backs on the M1 and A1 as pickets took revenge on the roadblocks; fresh trouble at Coal House; arrests at three-hundred-plus.

The President was in his court suit again. The President was impatient –

'This case is going to go on for ever,' he said.

'But we knew this,' said Paul.

'For ever!' he shouted. 'While the Right are up there plotting and scheming.'

'You're taking on too much,' said Dick.

'Ballot. Ballot. Ballot,' said the President. 'That's all I ever hear.'

'We shouldn't be down here,' said Paul. 'We should be up where the fight is.'

'We've been set up,' whispered the President. 'Set up.'

'Let me take care of the pension problem,' said Terry.

The President looked up at Terry Winters. The President smiled at Terry. He said, 'Thank you, Comrade.'

There was a knock at the door. One of the President's ladies came in. Alice said, 'They're waiting for us.'

'No,' laughed the President as he rose to his feet. 'We're waiting for them –

'Waiting for their unconditional support; for the movement of all coal in the British Isles to be blacked –

'Then we cannot lose,' said the President.

Everybody nodded –

Kiss me.

'Not one single piece of coal will move in the whole country without our say so. We will picket out every pit. We will close down every power station and steelworks.'

Everybody nodded –

Kiss me in the shadows.

'We will bring the government to its knees. We will make her beg.'

Everybody nodded –

Kiss me, Diane.

'We cannot lose,' said the President again. 'We will not lose! We shall not lose!'

Everybody stood up. Everybody applauded –

Kiss me in the shadows –

Everybody followed the President. Down the corridor. Down to business –

Kiss me in the shadows of my heart –

To victory.

Neil Fontaine leaves the Jew in his suite at Claridge's. He drives back to Bloomsbury. Back to his single room at the County. Neil Fontaine hasn't been here in almost a week. He checks his mail. His messages –

Just the one.

Neil Fontaine goes up to his room on the sixth floor. The door with the extra lock. He takes off his shirt. He washes his hands and face in the sink. He puts on a clean shirt. He opens the wardrobe. There is a blazer in a polythene bag –

Just the one.

Neil Fontaine puts on the blazer. He locks the two locks. He goes down the stairs. He walks past the bar and out into the night. He takes a cab to the Special Services Club. Neil Fontaine hasn't been here in almost a year –

'Really?' asks Jerry Witherspoon. 'Has it been that long?'

'Election night,' nods Neil.

'Night to remember and all that,' smiles Jerry –

Jerry pushes away his dessert. Jerry lights a cigar. Jerry smokes in silence –

Jerry knows people upstairs. Upstairs pass jobs down to Jerry. Jerry owns Jupiter. Jupiter Securities pass the jobs down to Neil. Neil takes on the jobs –

The little jobs. The sudden jobs. The cut-out jobs –

Neil knows people downstairs. People under the stairs. Under the floorboards.

Jerry finishes his cigar. Jerry pushes away the ashtray. Jerry leans forward –

'Bit of a night to forget in Shrewsbury by all accounts,' says Jerry.

Neil Fontaine waits.

Jerry lifts up his napkin. Jerry pushes an envelope across the table-cloth –

Just the one.

Neil Fontaine takes the envelope. Neil Fontaine stands up –

Jerry smiles. He says, 'Don't let one lapse in judgement become a habit, Neil.'

Neil Fontaine takes a taxi back to Bloomsbury. He walks down towards Euston. He goes into St Pancras. He sits in the pew. He bows his head. He says a little prayer –

Just the one –

Bring her back.

It was April Fool's Day and it was snowing outside. Terry Winters lay in the double bed. He could smell Sunday lunch. He could hear the kids fighting. The little tempers rising. The little fists flying. The President had been fuming too. The President had been raging. The Iron and Steel Trades Confederation had very predictably denied him. Betrayed him! The President demanded revenge. The President would be on *Weekend World* again today. The President would let the whole world know what he thought of those who would deny him. Those who would betray him, his members and their families. Judases. Terry turned over in the double bed. He looked at his brief-case with the broken strap. The one he never used now. The papers piled up on the dressing table. Terry got out of the bed. It was cold. He put on his slippers. His dressing-gown. He went across to the bathroom. His cock was sore when he pissed. He flushed the toilet. He washed his hands. His face. His hands again. Terry went back onto the landing. He switched on the light. He pulled down the ladder to the loft. He climbed up the ladder. He looked into the loft –

The two suitcases standing in the shadows –

Kiss me.

Insurance. April Fool's Day, 1984.

You heard. You can't do this, says Cath. We're going over to my sister's. Not today, love, you're not. Why not? says Cath. Why can't we? I have reason to believe that you're liable to cause a breach of the peace. You can't do this, says Cath again. Turn your vehicle around or you'll be arrested. I start car. Martin, she says. He can't do this. I say, Yes he can. Yes, he bloody can – *We warmed your houses. Your kitchens and your beds* – **Day 30.** They think they're being clever. Well, so do we. Don't tell Cath what I'm up to. I sit in dark with curtains open. Van pulls up about four. Builder's sign on side. Ladders on roof. They give me a pair of overalls. Off we set. Back roads all way. Get into Mansfield with time to kill. Park up down a side-street. Sit in back. Quiet as mice, we are. Half-eight CB wakes us up. Take off our overalls. Jump out back of van. Follow Pete to Notts HQ. Come round corner, see we aren't alone. About five hundred of us, all told. Fair few of them and all. And police. *Krk-krk.* Their delegates are making their way inside. We start up – Judas. Traitor. Scab. Judas. Traitor. Scab. Judas. Traitor. Scab – Five hours it goes on. Then word comes out: hundred and eighty-six to seventy-two against. Wankers. They'd have let a train driver be sent home for respecting an NUM picket line. They'd let a train driver be suspended for respecting an NUM picket line. They'd let a train driver be sacked for respecting an NUM picket line – NUM picket lines they cross with not a second thought for anything but brass in their own pockets. Fucking wankers. Get back to van and they've done every bloody tyre, haven't they. Stanley knife. Left us a Polaroid photograph of front of van and registration number under windscreen wipers. *Smile.* Pete's name, address and telephone number on back in black pen. He just shakes his head. Calls a local garage. They send a tow truck. Half-nine by time I get home. Cath's already in bed. Thank Christ – *We drove your dreams. Your cities and your empires* – **Day 31.** Nottingham again. Silverhill for a change. Just outside Sutton in Ashfield. Geoff shows his face. Take two other lads with us in his car. Tim and Gary. Stay on A61 past Chesterfield, out of Nottinghamshire. Park up on Derbyshire side. Walk to pit through farms and fields. Proud of ourselves. There's six blokes stood at gate as we come up to Lane. We're still on public footpath. From distance they look like they're our lads. They're not though – They're fucking plainclothes. We get to end of footpath. What you up to, lads? they ask us. I say, We're having a walk on a public footpath. Go any further and I'll arrest you, says one. I say, For what? Behaviour likely to cause a breach of the peace. I say, Look, we just want to go over and stand by gate and talk to them that'll stop. If you step off this path, he says, I'll arrest you. I say, All right, you come and stand with us at gate. I've told you once, he says, I'll arrest you. I say, But we've got a right to go and stand over there and tell people our opinion. Not going to stop anyone who doesn't want to stop. But we have rights too. I've told you, he says. Now fuck off. Geoff walks past them onto road. Fuck this, says Geoff. Arrest him, says copper. Another plainclothes goes up to Geoff. What's your name and address? Geoff Brine, says Geoff Brine. From Todwick. I'm arresting you then, Mr Brine, for obstructing me in the course of my duty, says plainclothes. What? Geoff laughs. Plainclothes puts his hand on Geoff's shoulder. You heard. Geoff shrugs off man's hand. There's no need for that, says Geoff. Which van you want me in? Plainclothes points down road. That one, he says. This Inspector comes over. What's going on here? he asks. They tell him. He looks at other three of us. Take them all, he says. I say, What? Obstruction, says Inspector. **Day 32.** Mansfield Nick. There's a funnel of coppers from van to station. They're taking photos of us. *Smile.* I keep my head down. Get that bastard's head up, says biggest one of them. They can't. Pull his hair, he says. They pull my hair. I keep my head down. Grab my nose. They put their fingers up my nostrils. I move my head from side to side. Right, you bastard, says big one. He punches me in face. Top of my nose. Between my eyes. Tears come. They put my head in an arm lock. Force my head

The Fifth Week

Monday 2 – Sunday 8 April 1984

The committee breaks up. The Jew comes out of Downing Street. Neil Fontaine opens the back door of the Mercedes for him. The Jew gets in. He picks up the car phone.

Neil Fontaine drives across the Thames. The Jew is still on the phone –

'Play it long and cool, then pay them off. No common cause. No second front.'

The Jew is talking trains. The Central Electricity Generating Board. Deals –

Deals, deals, deals –

Deals and secrets –

Secrets, secrets, secrets –

Secrets and deals.

Neil Fontaine spots the man sitting on a bench up ahead. The man is wearing a blue belted raincoat. He is reading the *Financial Times.*

Neil Fontaine pulls up in the shadows of Battersea Power Station. He leaves the Jew sat in the back of the car. He walks towards the bench. The man looks up from his newspaper –

Neil Fontaine remembers his lines. He asks, 'What kind of dog have you lost?'

The man remembers his. He replies in a foreign accent, 'A Yorkshire terrier.'

Neil Fontaine nods. The man stands up. They walk in silence over to the car.

Neil Fontaine opens the back door of the Mercedes. The man gets in.

The Jew moves over. The Jew says, 'Join us.'

Neil Fontaine drives back across the Thames. The Jew practises a little Polish. The man in the back whispers in English. The Jew closes the partition with his driver –

Neil Fontaine switches on the radio. He can hear every word.

*

The Mechanic goes to work. He opens the garage up. Puts the radio on. Gets changed. The Mechanic drinks a cup of coffee. He works on the Allegro. Finishes it. Calls the owner. The Mechanic has another cup of coffee. He works on the Capri. Gearbox. MOT next week. The Mechanic doesn't have the part. He goes home. Lets the dogs out. Puts a can of soup on. The Mechanic makes a sandwich. He eats lunch. Watches The One o'Clock News. *Reads the paper. The Mechanic washes up. He goes into Wetherby for the part. Back at the garage for half-two. Finishes the Capri. The Mechanic starts on the Lancia. He stops at half-six. Gets changed. Locks the garage up. The Mechanic goes home –*

It is a war of nerves.

Jen is asleep. The dogs in the garden. The Mechanic goes into the lounge. He puts a record on low. Sade again. The Mechanic pours a brandy. He sits on the sofa in the dark. The curtains open. Just the lights on the stereo. The Mechanic watches them rise and fall through the brandy in the glass. He has got ten grand in the bank. This house paid off. The garage ticking over –

The Mechanic thinks about things. Thinks about the things he has done –

The supermarkets. The post offices. The Mechanic opens his eyes. He looks up –

'Penny for your thoughts,' says Jen –

She is stood in the doorway in one of his T-shirts. She is beautiful.

'They're not worth it,' the Mechanic tells her –

It is a war of nerves and there will be casualties.

The Jew is beaming. He says, 'You know, Neil, I practically wrote that speech for her.'

Neil Fontaine keeps his eyes on the A616.

The Jew is repeating himself. He says, 'I believe the police are upholding the law; they are not upholding the government.'

The Mercedes comes to a roadblock outside Creswell. Neil Fontaine pulls over. He winds down the driver's window –

'Good morning, sir,' says the young policeman. He is not local. He is nervous. 'I'm afraid I'm going to have to ask you the nature of your business in Creswell today.'

'Don't be afraid,' says Neil Fontaine. 'The man in the back is Mr Stephen Sweet. Mr Sweet is here to meet the Assistant Chief Constable.'

'Sorry to have inconvenienced you, sir,' says the policeman.

'Don't be sorry, either,' says Neil Fontaine. 'You're just following orders, son.'

Neil Fontaine winds up the window. Neil Fontaine drives into the village –

What's left of the village –

There are over sixty Transits parked along the main street. Police everywhere. Their dogs barking and snarling at the Mercedes. No civilians on the streets –

Just debris. Rubble. Glass under the tyres of the car –

The village camouflaged in smoke.

Neil Fontaine parks beside a white saloon car outside the church hall. He gets out of the Mercedes. He walks through the police into the hall –

The hand-drawn posters for jumble sales and keep fit, judo and the Boy Scouts.

Another policeman a long way from home stops Neil Fontaine at the door.

Neil Fontaine says, 'I have an appointment with the Assistant Chief Constable.'

'Neil!' shouts the Assistant Chief Constable across the hall. 'Neil Fontaine!'

John Waterhouse, Assistant Chief Constable of North Derbyshire, greets Neil. The two men shake hands among the folding chairs.

John Waterhouse says, 'I didn't realize you were working for these people now.'

Neil Fontaine shrugs. He says, 'Just short term.'

John Waterhouse says, 'Could be long term, the way things are going.'

'Let's just hope it's not permanent,' smiles Neil Fontaine.

John Waterhouse nods. He says, 'So where is your man? This Stephen Sweet.'

Neil Fontaine points at the door. He says, 'He's in his car.'

'What on earth is he doing sat out there? Bring him in, for heaven's sake, man,' laughs John Waterhouse. 'Don't leave him out there like a lemon.'

'Mr Sweet wishes to talk with you in his car,' says Neil Fontaine.

'What?' says John Waterhouse. 'Don't be ridiculous, Neil.'

Neil Fontaine smiles at the Assistant Chief Constable. He gestures at the doors. Neil Fontaine says, 'Mr Sweet insists.'

John Waterhouse, Assistant Chief Constable of North Derbyshire, rolls his eyes. He follows Neil Fontaine outside. Neil Fontaine opens the back door of the Mercedes –

The Jew says, 'Assistant Chief Constable, do join us.'

John Waterhouse gets into the back of the car.

Neil Fontaine closes the door. He sits in the front. He switches on the radio:

'– must tell you, she is very, very, very disappointed in you,' the Jew is saying. 'The Prime Minister wishes – insists even – insists there be no repetition of such scenes. No repetition whatsoever. And she has asked me to make that very plain to you.'

'I'm afraid the situation on the ground –'

'The situation on the ground is completely unacceptable,' interrupts the Jew –

The Jew leans forward. He taps on the partition. Neil Fontaine lowers the radio –

'Drive slowly through the village to the pit, if you would please, Neil.'

'Certainly, sir,' says Neil Fontaine. He starts the car. He turns the radio back up:

'Just look at the place,' the Jew is saying. 'Windows smashed, cars wrecked, homes daubed in paint, telephone poles brought down, barricades erected, fires started –'

'Mr Sweet, there were one thousand pickets and –'

'Please, we know very well how many bloody pickets there were,' says the Jew. 'We also know how many arrests there were. Or were not.'

'I can assure you –'

'Mr Waterhouse, nineteen arrests and the cancellation of the night-shift fail to assure either the Prime Minister or myself of anything. There were sixty arrests in Babbington last night and not a fraction of the damage I see here.'

John Waterhouse takes off his cap. He runs his hand through his hair.

The Jew puts his arm round the Assistant Chief Constable. The Jew tells him, 'Never again must this happen, John.'

John Waterhouse dries his eyes. He blows his nose.

'Never again,' says the Jew. 'Never again.'

The Assistant Chief Constable nods.

*

They'd taken apart Terry Winter's office. Everything in it. Every-thing –

The carpet off the floor. The cabinets. The bookcase. The desk. The telephones. The chairs. The blinds. The lights –

Everything but the portrait off the wall –

It had been Terry's idea.

These were paranoid times at the Headquarters of the National Union of Mineworkers. Even more than usual. The press and televi-sion coverage was almost all hostile and negative. Even more than usual. Every question returned to the issue of a national ballot and democracy –

Democracy. Democracy. Democracy –

Even more than usual.

Terry took three aspirin. Terry picked up his files. His calculator.

He walked down the corridor. He didn't take the lift. He took the stairs up.

Len Glover frisked him at the door. Len told him to leave his jack-et outside.

Terry took off his jacket. Terry went inside –

Just the plastic chairs and the plastic tables remained. Melting –

The heating on full. The lights all on.

Terry drew the curtains.

The President looked up. He whispered, 'Thank you, Comrade.'

Terry nodded. He took his seat at the right hand of the President. He listened –

No ballot. No ballot. No ballot –

Listened to the schemes and the plots. The counter-schemes and the counter-plots:

'Without Durham,' said Gareth, 'the Moderates haven't got the numbers.'

'You rule it out of order,' said Paul. 'We'd get twelve–nine our way. Possibly thirteen–eight.'

'The simple-majority proposal is going to derail them anyway,' laughed Dick. 'They'll agree to hold a Special Delegate Conference just to buy themselves more time.'

'Then come the SDC,' said Paul. 'Then we'll have them.'

'I'll talk to Durham,' said Sam. 'I'll make sure they deliver for us.'

Everybody looked up the table. Everybody looked at the Pres-ident –

'Then it's decided,' said the President.

Everybody smiled. Everybody clapped. Everybody patted each other on the back.

'There's just one more thing,' said the President –

Everybody stopped clapping. Everybody stopped smiling.

The President stood up. The President stared around the room. The President said, 'They are opening our post. They are tapping our phones. They are watching our homes.'

Everybody nodded.

'This we knew. This we had come to expect from a democratic government.'

Everybody nodded again. Everybody waited.

'What we didn't know and we didn't expect is that we also have a mole.'

Everybody waited. Everybody shook their heads.

The President looked around the table. The President said, 'A mole, Comrades.'

Everybody shook their heads again. Everybody looked down at the table.

The President nodded to Bill Reed. Bill Reed stood up. Bill edited the *Miner* –

Bill Reed stared at Terry Winters as he said, 'Contact of mine, very well placed. Told me they're boasting they've got someone on the inside. Here and in Barnsley.'

Everybody else stared at the table. Their hands. Their fingernails. The dirt there –

Terry Winters stared back at Bill Reed –

Bill Reed said again, 'They've got someone, Comrades.'

Bill Reed sat down.

The President said, 'I need strategies. I need ideas.'

Terry coughed. He said, 'It could be disinformation. Create mistrust. Paranoia.'

The Tweed next to Dick said, 'And so could that remark, Comrade.'

Mike Sullivan raised his hand. He said, 'Do we have any actual proof?'

The President stared at Mike. The President said, 'We have proof, Comrade.'

Everybody looked up. Everybody waited.

'The proof is on the face of every policeman on every picket line,' he shouted. 'The smile that says, *We knew you were coming* –

'*We knew you were coming before you even did!*'

The battle for a ballot is as relentless as the Union's refusal to hold one. It is the one battle in this war that the Jew is prepared to lose. The Jew knows where the war will be won. Where the real battles lie. The real struggle –

For hearts and minds. Bodies and souls –

The Jew waves the *Sun* around his Sheffield suite. The banner headline –

UNION'S REAL AIM IS WAR!

The Jew opens another bottle of champagne. The Jew types another article –

Another *Sweet Piece*.

Neil Fontaine leaves the Jew to his hangover and his hallucinations –

Neil Fontaine has his own struggles. His own battles. His own war –

Neil Fontaine drives out of Sheffield. He turns off at the first motorway services. He watches the café. He waits. He stubs out his cigarette. He gets out of the Mercedes. He walks across the car park. He goes up the stairs into the restaurant.

The bastard sits down opposite the Mechanic. The bastard says, 'Nice tan, David.'

'Where is she? Where's my wife?'

Bastard puts a packet of cigarettes on the table. Bastard says, 'Safe enough.'

'Where?'

Bastard lights a cigarette. Inhales. Exhales. Bastard shakes his head.

'Fucking bastards. Fucking cunts.'

Bastard nods. Bastard says, 'Yeah, yeah, yeah.'

'What do they want?'

Bastard holds up three fingers. Bastard says, 'The diary. Julius Schaub. Silence.'

'I don't have the bloody diary and I don't want to know where fucking Schaub is. But I never talk. You know that. Never.'

Bastard stubs out the cigarette. Bastard says, 'I'll tell them what you said.'

The Mechanic puts an envelope on the table. 'Give them that when you do.'

'What is it?'

The Mechanic taps the envelope. 'The four grand they paid me.'

'It's not about the money, David. Ever. You know that.'

The Mechanic pushes the envelope towards the bastard. The cunt –

'I want my wife back,' says the Mechanic. 'I love her, Neil. I love her.'

The nightmares have returned. Neil Fontaine dreams of the skull. The skull and a candle. He wakes in his room at the County. The light is still on. He sits on the edge of the bed. The notebook in his hand. He picks apart the night. Puts the pieces back together his way. He stops writing. The notebook to one side. He stands up. He opens the dawn curtains.

Jennifer Johnson turns over in the bed. She says his name in her sleep –

There are moments like this.

Neil Fontaine stands at the window. The real light and the electric –

There are always moments like this.

up. *Smile.* They take their photo – Next! They take my wallet, my watch, my wedding ring, my belt and my shoe-laces. They put me in a cell. They leave me here for about three hour, maybe four. I sit on floor with my knees up. My arms on my knees. My head on my arms. They come and take us to an interview room. There are two of them. Both plainclothes – One old. One young – They don't speak. Old one goes off somewhere. Leaves me with young one. He doesn't speak. Then old one comes back. He sits down. How did you get to Silverhill? he asks me. We drove. Whose car? Geoff Brine's. Where is it? We parked it in Tibshelf. Other side of M1. How did you get there? Down A61. He nods. What's your Cath think of all this, then? he asks me. You what? Your wife? he says. Your Cath? She support you, does she? What's that got to do with anything? Well here you are nicked, while she's working two jobs to put food in your face and beer in your belly – just so you can go out breaking the law. I ask, How do you know this? Who you been talking to? He smiles. Suppose, not having kids, he says, you don't have same commitments rest of us have, do you? I don't answer him. Young one leans forward. Why is that? he asks. I look at him. I say, Why is what? Is it you or is it your wife? he asks. What? That can't do the business? I look at him. I shake my head. He smiles. He winks. Suppose you must have a fair bit of spare cash? says old one again. Not having any kids. I say, You after a loan, are you? He laughs. He shakes his head. Not me, he says. But your mate Geoff might be. Debts he has. Hire purchase. Mortgage. Two kids. Won't be long before he's cap in hand at your door. Unless he does go back to work, says young one. Old one nods. He will, he says. That's why he wants a ballot. How about you? asks young one. You want a ballot? Course he does, says old one. He loves democracy, does our Martin. He voted Tory last year. Well fancy that, smiles young one. Here we are, three good Tories having a nice little chat in a police station. I say, I didn't vote at all. Old one laughs in my face. Liar, he says. No,

I'm not. Yes, you are. No, I'm not. You are, he says. You must be. Because I've been told not to charge you. Been told to release you. I say, You're lying now. He shakes his head. You're lying, I say. I know you are. Stay here if you like, he says. I don't care. I stand up slowly. He nods. Pete Cox is waiting outside for you, he says. Take you home. I go to door. They smile. They wave. Whatever it is you're do-ing, says young one. Keep up the good work. Pete drives me home. Drops us off. I don't invite him in. Thought there might be fireworks. I open door. House is quiet. I go into kitchen. Cath isn't here. **Day 36.** There's no talking to her. She either shouts and carries on or lies on bed and cries. Picket line's a bloody relief and that's saying something this week. Babbington was a mass picket. Two or three thousand. Massive shove. *Krk-krk.* Load of arrests. *Smile.* Cameras out again. Pete told us to keep at back after what had happened at weekend. Today it's Agecroft over in Lancashire. Tomorrow it'll be Sheffield for big meeting. No sign of Geoff. Pete says he got bail but has to keep out of Notting-ham. His wife hit roof and all. Poor bas-tard. There are about six hundred by time we get over to Agecroft. Doesn't look to be that many police but they're pulling anyone who swears or shouts Scab – Use of threatening words and behaviour. About half-eleven they start turning up for afternoon shift. Inspec-tor lets six lads stand at gate and talk to them that'll stop. Not one fucking stops. Same as Nottingham. That pisses everyone off. Lot of pushing then. Plan is to make a human wall across road. Have a bit of luck at first but then cop-pers get their act together and that's that then. Few punches. Few arrests. Scabs go in. Lads have a go at an ITN camera crew on way back to cars. Be different after tomorrow. **Day 37.** Sirens and chants all day – Arthur Scar-gill, Arthur Scargill, we'll support you ever more. We'll – support – you – ever – more. It's supposed to be just four men from each colliery in Yorkshire coalfield. Fat chance. Not today – No ballot. No sell-out – Time to see who's who. Four thousand lads ringing St James's tower block – Arthur's Red

The Sixth Week

Bastards. Dark side of a bloody and a fucked-up moon. The Mechanic drives through the night. North to South. Fucking bastards. The dogs in the back. He comes into Worcester with the dawn. He parks outside the bungalow. He goes up the drive. He bangs on the door –

Keeps his finger on the bell.

'Who is it? What do you want?' someone shouts from inside.

'I want to speak to Vince.'

'He's not here.'

'Where is he?'

There are whispers behind the door. Someone says again, 'Who is it?'

'His mate, David Johnson. I need to speak to him. It's important.'

The door opens. His wife and teenage son stare out. They shake their heads.

The Mechanic asks them again, 'Where is he?'

'He's gone,' says his wife. 'Left us.'

'Where?'

She shakes her head. She says, 'Ask Joyce bloody Collins.'

The Mechanic nods. He says, 'Thank you.'

She slams the door.

The Mechanic goes back down their drive. He gets into the car. He drives over to Diamond Detectives. He parks among the minicabs. He sticks the radio on. He waits –

Hands holding the steering wheel –

Tight.

Half-past eight, Joyce pulls up in her Fiat. She gets out. She opens the office up. She goes inside. She puts the lights on.

The Mechanic turns the radio off. He gets out of the car. He walks past the cabs. He goes into their office –

Joyce is filling an electric kettle at the sink in the back.

The Mechanic doesn't knock. He says, 'Where is he?'

She turns round. She drops the kettle in the sink. She starts to cry.

'Where is he, love?'

'I don't know,' she cries. 'He's gone.'

The Mechanic puts an arm round her. He sits her down behind one of the desks. He asks, 'When?'

She has her elbows on the desk. Her head in her hands. She says, 'Last week.'

'What happened, love?'

She pulls her hands down her face. She says, 'Men came.'

'And?'

She swallows. She says, 'They turned the place upside down. They hit him.'

'They took him away?'

She says, 'No.'

'He ran?'

She nods. She looks at him. She says, 'This is about Shrewsbury, isn't it?'

The Mechanic puts a finger to his lips. He walks over to the telephone sockets and disconnects them. He goes over to the filing cabinets and goes through their files. He finds the three files that he wants. He goes over to the desks and goes through the drawers. He finds two sets of keys, a packet of cigarettes and a box of matches. He walks over to the window. He looks up and down the street. He points at the door –

She nods. She dries her eyes. She goes outside.

The Mechanic stands behind Vince Taylor's desk. He lights a cigarette. He drops it in the bin. He watches it burn. He picks up Joyce's handbag. He goes outside. He gives Joyce her bag.

She asks, 'Where are we going?'

The Mechanic puts his finger to his lips again. She nods again.

They walk down past the cabs. They get into his car –

The dogs are barking.

The Mechanic locks all the doors. He checks both mirrors. He looks at his watch. He starts the car.

'Where are we going?' asks Joyce again.

'Find Vince.'

There were times when Terry Winters thought he had bitten off more than he could chew. More than they would swallow. More than he could stomach. Two coke hauliers had begun legal action against the South Wales Area's secondary picketing of the Port Talbot steel-works. South Wales had sought legal advice from Terry. *Click-click.* Terry said he'd have to call them back. Terry took an aspirin. And another and another. The Board's action against the Union's management of the Pension Fund was concluding. The President was counting on victory from Terry. Terry hadn't the balls to tell him. Terry took another aspirin. Terry threw the empty container into the bin beside his desk. He missed. He put his head in his hands. There were still forty-eight hours before the Executive met. Terry didn't think he could stand much more of this. The tensions. The suspicions. The machinations. The talk of ballots. The rumours of moles. The whispers of coups. The silence and the fear. Nobody spoke in the corridors. In the lift. On the stairs. Everybody locked themselves in their offices. People were summoned by one word on the telephone. No reason given. People went upstairs to stand before the President's desk. No small talk. People were given their instructions. Nothing on paper. People went back to their offices. No questions asked. They locked their doors. They sat at their desks –

Guilty monks, thought Terry. The lot of them.

Terry looked at his watch. The abbot would be waiting.

Terry went upstairs –

No Len on the door. Len was inside. Terry hung up his jacket. He knocked once. He went inside. The Conference Room was still stripped. The curtains drawn again. Terry mumbled his apologies. He took his seat at the right hand. He stared at his fellow friars –

Most didn't know if it was light or dark outside. They'd been up here so long.

Paul stopped speaking. Paul sat down.

The President stood back up. The President said, 'Comrades, as you are all aware, over the course of the next week this office will take over the control and the deployment of all picketing for the entire British Isles. It will also take full responsibility for ensuring the blockade on the movement of all coal or alternative fuel within the British Isles. All local requests for the support of our brothers and sisters within the trades union movement must also be made to this office. To provide the support the areas and branches require, the office will be staffed twenty-four hours a day, seven days a week. The Yorkshire Area is preparing a list of volunteers to help us meet the necessary staffing demands. The question of internal security and the degree to which our communications have been compromised remain a problem. To that end, the Chief Executive has some practical, short-term measures that can be implemented with immediate benefits in our fight to preserve jobs and pits. Comrade –'

The President sat down again.

Terry stood up. Terry said, 'Thank you, President. I have drawn up a code that will allow the areas and branches to contact us here at the Strike HQ using our existing telephone lines and numbers. I intend to reveal the code to you here and now, though I would ask you to write nothing down but rather to commit the details and instructions of what I am about to say to memory. On returning to your areas you are to brief the panels verbally and in turn instruct the panels to brief their local branches in the same manner. I repeat, nothing is to be written down. I shall now reveal to you the code –

'Pickets will henceforth be referred to as apples. I repeat, apples –

'Police are to be referred to as potatoes. Repeat, potatoes –

'Henceforth, branches will be requested to supply X number of apples based upon Y number of potatoes at a given site. Likewise branches can request extra apples from HQ in response to superior numbers of potatoes. Our brothers and sisters in the NUR are henceforth to be known as mechanics –

'I repeat, mechanics –

'Members of the NUS are henceforth plumbers. Repeat . . .'

They turn off the main road. They drive through the industrial estate. They come to the fence. The gate. The old USAF sign –

There is a resprayed Escort parked up.

'What would he be doing here?' asks Joyce.

The Mechanic opens his door. He lets the dogs out. He says, 'Waiting for me.'

They get out into the cold. The rain.

'Where is he?' she asks.

The Mechanic pushes open the gate. He says, 'This way.'

They walk across the rough ground towards the airstrip. The old control tower.

Joyce cups her mouth in her hands. She shouts, 'Vince! It's me, Joyce!'

They keep walking.

'Vince,' she shouts again. 'We just want to talk. That's all. Come on –'

The dogs are barking. The Mechanic and Joyce stop walking –

Vince Taylor is coming down the steps of the control tower. He is pointing a double-barrelled shotgun at them –

'Vince,' the Mechanic says. 'There's no need for that.'

Vince walks towards them. He says, 'Shut up. On your knees. Both of you.'

They kneel down on the ground –

It is wet. It is cold.

Vince points the shotgun at their chests. He says, 'Hands on your heads.'

They place their hands on their heads –

It is raining and the dogs are barking.

Vince puts the barrel of the shotgun under his chin. He pulls the trigger.

There are roadblocks on the routes in and out of Sheffield. There are checkpoints on the streets of Sheffield city centre. There are private security guards here on the hotel doors. There are big miners down to protect and serve their big leaders in the dining room of the Royal Victoria Hotel. They put their hands on the Jew's chest and ask him his business. The Jew laughs and tells them his business *is* business. He is here *because* he means to do business –

The Jew is wearing his leather flying-jacket.

Neil Fontaine asks them to take their hands off the Jew and to step to one side. The big miners take their hands off the Jew and step to one side. The Jew thanks them. The Jew goes from breakfast table to breakfast table introducing himself to the big leaders from Durham, Northumberland and Cumberland, from the Midlands, Lancashire and Derbyshire. He urges these moderate men, these weak and cowardly men, to become extreme men, to be strong and brave men today –

Thursday 12 April 1984 –

Today of all days.

The big leaders from the Midlands, Lancashire and Derbyshire smoke cigarette after cigarette, the big leaders from Durham, Northumberland and Cumberland drink cup after cup of tea. Then these moderate men, these weak and cowardly men, make their excuses and leave the Jew to sit alone among the breakfast tables with their full ashtrays and their empty cups –

The Jew is wearing his leather flying-jacket. The Jew means war now.

The Jew retreats upstairs to the temporary war room of his Sheffield suite –

He paces the carpet. He strikes the poses. He barks the orders –

The windows to open. The sun to shine in. The curtains to billow.

Neil Fontaine opens the windows to the sun, the wind and the world outside:

Three thousand striking miners ringing their National Headquarters. Two thousand policemen watching fruit and cans rain down on the Nottinghamshire leaders.

Neil Fontaine calls room service. The Jew wants wine with his lunch –

Their President ruling the Right's demand for a national ballot out of order.

Neil Fontaine calls room service again. The Jew wants another bottle of wine –

Their National Executive proposing to reduce the 55 per cent majority required for strike action to a simple majority and to convene a Special Delegate Conference.

The Jew drinks bottle after bottle. The Jew lies on the double bed –

Their President leaning out of an upstairs window with a megaphone to tell the mob below, 'We can win provided we show the resolution we did in 1972 and 1974.'

The curtains fall. The sun goes in. The hotel windows are closed –

'Easy. Easy. Easy,' chant the mob on the dark streets of Sheffield.

The Jew puts pillows over his head. The Jew shakes. The Jew sobs.

Neil Fontaine picks up another empty bottle. He rights another upturned table.

The Jew gets up. The Jew wobbles about amid the wreckage of his hotel suite. He is panting. He is drunk. He is morbid –

'These are the dreadful hours, Neil. The dreadful hours of his shameful war –

'He has his army, Neil. His Red Guard. The Shock Troops of Socialism –

'But where are our soldiers, Neil? The soldiers who will fight this war with us, who will win this war for her –

'Oh, she has placed so much faith in me, Neil. So very, very much –

'And I have failed her, Neil. Failed her so very, very miserably –

'She expects so much, Neil. So very, very much –

'And I must deliver, Neil. Deliver her victory –

'Victory, Neil. Victory –

'I promised her victory, Neil. Promised her nothing less . . .'

The Jew falls back onto his bed. He is sobbing. He is drunk. He is moribund.

Neil Fontaine picks up the Jew's bedding from the carpet. He draws the curtains. He puts a blanket over the Jew. He tucks him in –

'Easy. Easy. Easy –'

He wishes him sweet dreams. He kisses him goodnight.

She's still screaming. She's still shaking. She's still trying to wipe his blood from her clothes. From her hair. Her face. The dogs going mental in the back –

They're on the A49 outside Ludlow. A Little Chef up ahead –

The Mechanic turns into the car park. He switches off the engine. He grabs her –

Joyce stares at him.

The Mechanic holds her by her shoulders. He says, 'You got family?'

She chews her lips in her teeth.

The Mechanic squeezes her hard. He says, 'Have you got any family, Joyce?'

She stares.

The Mechanic says, 'Who?'

'My son,' she says.

'How old is he?'

'He's nine.'

The Mechanic asks, 'Where is he now?'

'School.'

'Where's school?'

'Worcester,' she says.

The Mechanic looks at the dashboard clock. He says, 'What time's school finish?'

'Quarter to four,' she says.

'Who picks him up?'

'Me or his dad.'

'His dad?' the Mechanic asks. 'Where's his dad?'

'It's Vince,' she says. 'Vince is his dad.'

The Mechanic sits back. He watches a young couple come out of the Little Chef –

He watches them run from the rain, run for the cover of their car.

Joyce squeezes herself between her legs. She says, 'What am I going to do?'

'Go pick your car up,' the Mechanic says. 'The police will be waiting for you.'

'They'll have found him already?'

'No,' he says. 'But I set fire to the office when we left.'

She starts to cry. She starts to shake again.

'Just think of your boy,' he tells her. 'Think of him and you'll get through this.'

She wipes her eyes with her hand. She nods. She says, 'What shall I say?'

'You haven't seen Vince since last week. He's been depressed about his marriage. You went into the office this morning. Vince wasn't there. You tried to find him. There was no sign. You came back to the office. Fire.'

She starts to cry again. She says, 'I'm covered in blood. They'll never believe me. They'll think I set fire to the office. Think I killed him.'

'There's no blood on you, love,' the Mechanic says. 'No blood on you.'

One day they won. The next day they lost –

The Judge said the President had not been acting in the best interests of the three hundred and fifty thousand beneficiaries of the Pension Fund. The Judge ruled the President was in breach of his legal duty. The Judge ordered the President to lift the embargo on overseas investments. The Judge threatened to dismiss the President from the management committee of the fund, if he did not comply with his orders.

Terry Winters hailed a cab outside the High Court. Five of them squeezed inside. The President on the backseat in the middle. Flaming. Furious. Terry looked at his watch. They weren't going to make the four o'clock train. The President wiped his face with his handkerchief. He hated London. The South. Terry turned to look over the driver's shoulder up the road. Nothing was moving. The President gently touched his hair. He said, 'That's British justice.'

Everybody nodded.

Terry Winters looked at his watch again. Terry Winters had to think of an excuse. The President straightened his tie. His collar was wet. Terry wound down the window. The radio in the car next to them was playing pop music loudly. The President reached across Terry and wound the window back up. He sat back in his seat, touched that hair. He said, 'I'm disappointed, but not surprised.'

Everybody nodded.

Terry Winters put his briefcase on his knee. He opened it and searched through it. The President was watching him. Terry looked at his watch. He searched through his briefcase again. The President leant forward. He said, 'What is it, Comrade?'

Everybody nodded.

Terry Winters looked at his watch again. Terry checked his case again. Terry said, 'I think I must have left one of the files at the court. You'll have to let me out.'

Everybody nodded.

Terry stopped the taxi. He got out. He gave Joan the fare and the tickets. He said, 'Don't worry about me. Don't wait for me.'

Everybody nodded –

Everybody except Paul. Paul shook his head. Paul watched him go –

Disappear again.

He buys some dog food. A can opener. Bread. Water. He pulls over in a lay-by. He feeds the dogs. Lets them run in the field. He sits in the car with the door open. He eats the bread. Drinks the water. He takes out the three files. He reads them. Then burns them by the side of the road. He whistles. The dogs come. They jump into the back of the car. He puts the can opener in the glove compartment. He closes the door. Turns the key –

The Mechanic knows where Julius Schaub will be.

Guard. Provisional wing of Labour & Trade Union Movement – That's us. Brought in three thousand police from across country. *Krk-krk*. Stuck them in army camps. Can't stop us, though. Not today – No ballot. No sell-out – Time to see who's bloody who. Banners. Placards. Jackets. Badges – *Victory to Miners*. Pete and me hop on top of a pair of giant bins so we can see them arrive. Tell when it's Ottey or one of them lot. Cans and fruit start flying. They grab Ray by his collar. They shake their fists in his face. Henry pulls him away – Scab. Scab. Scab. Scab. Scab. Scab. Scabs – Chants and sirens. Helicopters. Then word comes down from top – Ballot proposal from Leicestershire is out of order. Special Delegate Conference next Thursday – King Arthur comes out onto steps. Salutes all lads. Lads go mental. They pass him a megaphone. Can't hear a word he says – Easy. Easy. Easy. Easy – Chants. No more sirens. Not today – No ballot. No sell-out – Arthur's Red Guard. That's me. I'll support you ever more. **Day 41.** This is first time we've sat down, shared a meal in a week. You know that? I say, I'm sorry, love. I wish it wasn't like this. It's just, you know – No, I don't know, Cath says. I put my knife and fork down, not hungry. I do know you're living in cloud-cuckooland, she says. I do know that. Cath, please – Cuckoo-land, the lot of you. Bloody lot of you. Look – You think she's going to give up, do you? They've been planning this for years, you've said so yourself. For years, Martin. I say, We can win. Like Arthur says, if we show same resolution, we – Listen to yourself, Martin. *Arthur?* You've never met the bloody bloke. You're like some daft teenage lass with a crush on some bloody pop star or someone. I leave my plate. I stand up. I walk over to sofa. I put on television – Torvill and fucking Dean again. Cath comes in front of sofa. She switches off television. She says, I'm warning you. I'll not stick around and watch you throw everything away again. Once was enough, thank you very much. I get up. I go into kitchen. I open back door. I go out into back garden. I stand in rain where conservatory was going to be. I

have a cigarette. *We fuelled your fears with our raven-wings* – I open my eyes. I can hear phone ringing. I go back inside. I pick it up. *Click-click*. It's Pete. Front door slams. **Day 44.** Sheffield – all day. Fucking worth it, this, though. Result we get. Feels like we're bloody getting somewhere now. Feels like victory – Simple majority. No ballot – Sixty-nine to fifty-one. Notts told they're officially out – officially scabs if they're not. King Arthur taking charge of things himself. By scruff of neck. Fight to finish. To victory. Just like before. Time to celebrate. Not going to let her rain all over it either. We stop in Sheffield drinking. Miss coach back. Massive fight in pub next to station. Scab bastards. Chairs flying. Glasses. Police wading in. *Krk-krk*. Hide under pool table like in a fucking film or something. Taxi back to Thurcroft with Pete and Big Tom. Keep drinking – all on Pete's tab. Welfare. Hotel. Club. Hotel. Welfare. Club. Walk home again. Clear my head. She's put something against bedroom door. My gear in spare room. Thomas Cook brochure in about a million pieces on floor. She must have cancelled holiday. I sit down on carpet with my back to wall. Head on my knees. Good Friday tomorrow. **Day 46.** Lads are fucking seething. So much for so-called Triple bloody Alliance. Nobody wants to see other blokes put out of their jobs – But they're taking piss as far as we're concerned. ISTC begged – Fucking begged. Deal had been to send Scunthorpe fifteen thousand tons a week to keep their furnaces in good nick. To be moved by rail. Loaded only by British Steel drivers. From Cortonwood, Bullcliffe Wood, Dinnington and us – To help them out. That was deal – Not to be bleeding working at over 50 bloody per cent. Fucking bollocks, that is. We tell Pete to tell Barnsley we don't want them to have it – Bastards. But they've done their deal. Fucking pisses everyone right off. **Day 47.** Easter Sunday. I knock on bedroom door again. I say, We need to talk, love – Go away. Come on, Cath. We can't go on like this – Go away. Please, love – Go away! she shouts. Can't just lock yourself in there all day. Come on just – Go away,

The Seventh Week

Monday 16 – Sunday 22 April 1984

Terry couldn't keep up. He was exhausted. Diane was too much for him. She was insatiable. He fell over onto his back. He was out of breath. He hurt. She rolled on top of him. She mounted him. She rode him. He groaned. He moaned. She smiled. She laughed. He cried out. She screamed. He came. She lay beside him. He had his eyes closed. She took his cock in her hand. He opened his eyes. She stroked his cock. He closed his eyes again. She whispered, 'You got a codeword for him, Mr Chief Executive?'

The traffic out of London is a nightmare. Roadblocks at junctions. Helicopters overhead. Sirens. The Jew sits in the back of the Mercedes. He gets his updates on the car phone. He orders flowers for the dead policewoman's family. Flowers to mark the place where she was slain. Felled by a single shot from the Libyan People's Bureau in St James's Square, South West One.

Neil Fontaine fiddles with the frequencies on the radio:

'– pursuing its domestic policy, the government relies on the aid of the security service which cynically manipulates the definition of subversion and thus abuses its charter so as to investigate and interfere in the activities of legitimate political parties, the trades union movement, and other progressive organizations. Bettaney's solicitor went on –'

Neil Fontaine changes channels again. He puts his foot down on the motorway.

The Jew looks out of the windows of the Mercedes. He gets excited as they approach Sheffield again. He talks of the body politic. He talks of the soul politic –

She has given him new orders –

New orders from the New Order –

New orders to follow. New orders to give.

Neil Fontaine has his own orders –

Old orders.

*

Terry knew the President blamed him. The situation was extremely dangerous and nobody dared predict what would happen next. The families would not be starved back. Troops could be used to move coal stocks –

The greatest good for the greatest number.

The situation was extremely dangerous and the President blamed Terry. Blamed him for everything. Terry had told the President he'd take care of it –

Take care of everything. Terry had told the President they would win –

They had lost.

Terry put his forehead against the window of his office. Terry closed his eyes. Terry knew the President blamed him. Blamed him. Blamed him –

Back to the Big House for Terry.

The phone on the desk rang again. It never fucking stopped –

South Wales called him at least twice a day with questions about the injunction. *Click-click.* They were not alone. Legal questions. Financial questions. Endless fucking questions –

It pissed him off –

Terry had done what he had to do. Terry had done his job –

Why couldn't they?

Terry thought this would be Clive calling again. Clive Cook called constantly. Clive confused the codes. Clive forgot the codes. Clive ignored the codes. Clive cried –

'I don't know how much more of this I can take.'

Terry Winters thought Clive Cook might well have been a very poor choice.

Terry picked up the phone. *Click-click.* He said, 'The Chief Executive speaking.'

'Terry? Thank Christ for that. It's Jimmy. I'm trying to get hold of the President. No one will tell me where he is. What's going on?'

'Not allowed to give out information over the phone. New directive.'

'Fucking hell, Tel. This is urgent. You seeing him?'

'I'd like to tell you, but then –'

'Look, just listen. I'm down in London. We've just come out of a JPA meeting. The Board have just told us they're willing to sit down with you all. Talk. Face to face. No messing about. I'm trying to set something up for next Tuesday –'

'What's to bloody talk about? He was on *Weekend World* saying they should use troops to move stocks. Told Jimmy Young he'd got more constructive things to do with his time than talk to us. There's Tebbit all over the papers talking about denationalization. You'd be wasting the President's time, Jimmy –'

'Terry, listen. No compulsory redundancies and they'll drop their initial timetable. That's a fucking climbdown in anybody's book. It's a victory for us.'

'Us?'

'For the whole movement. For the NUM and NACODS. For the President.'

'What do they want?'

'I've got a letter from them saying what I just told you. But they want a response. And they want it as soon as possible. Then we'll talk about setting the time and the place. But I do need to speak to the President.'

Terry drummed his fingers on the desk. He said, 'Get their letter to me by courier. I'll make sure the President sees it –'

'He'll thank you, Terry.'

'I'll ensure you have our response by the end of the day,' said Terry. 'Personally.'

'You're a hero, Comrade,' said the man from NACODS. 'A real hero, Terry.'

Terry put down the phone. Terry stood up. Terry smiled to himself –

Terry knew the President blamed him. Blamed him for everything –

But not for long.

Good Friday will be the Führer's birthday. Ninety-five years old –
Happy birthday, Uncle Alf.

Ten days of feasting and festivities until the finale in the Walpurgisnacht fires –
The rehearsals will have already begun.
The Mechanic drives through Evesham onto Cirencester, across to Stroud and up to Cheltenham. This is the heart. The secret heart. The dark heart.
The Cotswolds. The Norfolk Broads. The West Coast of Scotland –
These are the places. The secret places. The dark places.
The Mechanic looks for the signs. The secret signs. The dark signs –
He finds them. Remembers.

This is the place. The secret place. The darkest place –

The Estate. The Big House –

Wewelsburg.

He parks well away. Lets the dogs out. He goes to the boot of the car. Takes out the rucksack. He puts it on. Whistles. The dogs come back. He feeds them. Locks them in the car. The windows open just a crack. He walks through the fields. The streams –

He comes to the trees. The leaves. He sits in the tall grass. He waits –

Is she sleeping. In the dark? Is she waking. In the light?

He watches the back of the house. The grounds through the binoculars –

The marquee is up. The fairy lights on.

It'll be night. Darker still soon –

The generals in the house with their Wagner and their Bruckner under the portraits of Robert K. Jeffrey and A. K. Chesterton, the troops drunk in the grounds singing their songs about nig-nogs and wogs under the Fylfot and St George bunting –

Just because you don't see it, doesn't mean it's not here –

And he'd be here somewhere.

The Mechanic watches. The Mechanic waits –

The music stops. The rehearsal starts –

The doors from the house to the grounds are opened. The trolley is wheeled out. The fake swastika cake revealed. Ninety-five unlit candles –

The birthday boy with the party knife in his hand –

Uncle Adolf played by Julius Schaub, a.k.a. Martin Peter Cooper.

The Mechanic gets the car. The dogs.

Terry couldn't keep up. He was exhausted. Christopher and Timothy were too fast for him. They were incorrigible. Louise fell over on the flagstones. She started to cry. She looked around for her daddy. Terry stopped chasing after the boys and the football. He walked back across the lawn. Louise pointed at the graze on her knee. Terry bent down. He kissed it better. He picked her up. He held her. Theresa came out of the house. She was carrying a tray of barley water. Ice clinked in the glasses. She looked at Terry –

She didn't speak. She never did. Theresa Winters just smiled –

He didn't speak either. He never dared. Terry Winters just smiled back –

He winked at his wife. He was going to amaze them all.

*

64

Last week was a dress rehearsal for the main event. The aperitif for today's main course. Neil Fontaine has dressed for this dinner in a donkey jacket. He helps the Jew into his –

NCB on the back.

The Jew stands in the middle of his hotel suite in the donkey jacket. He says, 'When in Rome, eh, Neil?'

'I'm afraid so, sir.'

'Chop-chop then,' says the Jew. 'Let's not miss their Nero and his games.'

Neil Fontaine escorts the Jew downstairs. They walk through the hotel lobby. They step out into the bright Sheffield sunshine.

The Jew puts on his sunglasses. He looks up at the helicopters.

Neil Fontaine leads the Jew through the deserted backstreets. Towards the noise. Neil Fontaine leads him to the Memorial Hall. Towards the chants –

This is what the Jew has come back to see:

The Special Delegate Conference of the National Union of Mineworkers.

Seven thousand men on the streets. One single message on their lips –

Their badges and their banners:

No ballot.

The Jew waits in the shadows. Neil Fontaine stands behind him.

The Jew watches the crowd. The Jew listens to the crowd –

Listens to their cheers. Their thunderous cheers.

The Jew watches the speakers. The Jew listens to the speakers –

Speech after speech from speaker after speaker –

Against the government. Against the police. Against the state. Against the law.

The Jew listens to their reception. Their thunderous reception –

Not for the Labour Party. Not for parliamentary opposition. Not for democracy –

But for extra-parliamentary opposition. And for their President.

They have their victory again and their President has his –

His victory. His victory speech:

'I am the custodian of the rulebook and I want to say to my colleagues in the Union that there is one rule, above all the rules in the book, and that is when workers are involved in action –

'YOU DO NOT CROSS PICKET LINES IN ANY CIRCUM-STANCES.'

The Jew listens. The Jew watches –

He watches their leader lauded. He watches their delegates disperse –

He watches the men move on –

To bottles. To stones. To attack the press –

The banks of photographers. The mass of TV crews.

To attack the police and the police attack back –

The pub fights and the snatch squads.

The Jew in the shadows. Neil Fontaine behind him.

It is Thursday 19 April 1984 –

Maundy Thursday –

'But this is not Britain,' whispers the Jew. 'This is another Nuremberg.'

'The fuck is this, Winters?'

Terry looked up from his figures. Paul Hargreaves was standing before his desk. Len Glover in the doorway. Paul holding out a piece of paper –

A letter. *The* letter.

Terry put down his pen. He took off his glasses.

Len stepped inside. He closed the door.

'Is there a problem, Comrades?' asked Terry.

Paul banged the letter down onto Terry's desk –

'Yes there's a problem, *Comrade*,' he said. 'The fucking problem is you.'

'Have I done something wrong?' asked Terry.

Paul stared at him. He tapped the letter. He said, 'You changed this.'

'Did I?' asked Terry. 'Did I really?'

Paul reached across the desk to take hold of Terry. Len pulled him back –

'What do you mean, *did I*?' shouted Paul. 'You know fucking well you did. You're such an arrogant bloody prick, Winters. Arrogant and –'

'Then I apologize,' said Terry. 'I apologize to both of you, Comrades.'

Paul made another lurch towards the desk. Len held him back –

'It was a fucking opportunity and you fucking killed it,' screamed Paul. 'Dead. There's nothing now. No meeting. Nothing. I hope you're fucking pleased with yourself, *Comrade*. Dead in the water. Nothing. Fucking satisfied now, *Comrade*?'

'I made a mistake then,' said Terry. 'I thought the President said pit closures and job losses were not negotiable. I thought I was simply restating our position. I'm sorry.'

Len let go of Paul. Paul stared at Terry Winters –

Terry smiled at Paul Hargreaves. Terry smiled at Len Glover –

Len shook his head. Len opened the door. Paul pointed at Terry –

Paul said, 'I'm on to you, Winters.'

Martin! Please – Go away, will you? I hate you! I lean my head against door. I say, I'm sorry, I – Just leave me alone for God's sake, she screams. Leave me alone! I walk down stairs. I get my jacket. I drive into Thurcroft. I go into Welfare. They're looking for people to go and stay in Nottingham for a couple of days at a time. I have a few drinks and I put my name down. **Day 50.** Harworth. By half-ten we're starving. There's a gap in crowd. Head off down a side-street with Little John and Keith. We go into this newsagent's that's got some sandwiches and pies. Got a couple of sausage rolls and a can of pop in my hands when police come in – Three of them. White shirts. No numbers. Met – *Krk-krk.* What you fucking doing in here? Buying a sausage roll and a can of pop. No, you're fucking not. Get out. I haven't paid. You got no money, scum. Get out. But – You fucking deaf as well as thick. Fucking out. Bloke behind counter just stands there. Gob open. We put stuff back. Keith turns to bloke behind counter. Sorry, he says. Shut up and get out, says tit-head. We walk outside – They push us in back. Across road. Now, they say. Pick up them feet. We start over road to field where everyone's being penned in. Police three deep around them. Miles from scabs and gate. Nearly there when this big shout goes up. Lads are charging towards police with a bloody cricket screen. Police counter-charge. Screen goes straight into about half a dozen of police. Lads scatter. Run over tip at back. Hundred or so police haring after them. Rest of lads push forward – Fences go down. Folk grab posts – We're just stood there on road behind police line. Police vans coming up behind us. Lorries for pit. Scabs. Scuffles. Stones coming over top – Fuck this, says Little John. We head back down side-street. Turn around. No one behind us. We go in shop again. Bloke behind counter shakes his head. Pick up a sausage roll and a can of pop each. Pay for them double-quick. Go outside and walk off back towards pit – Pitch fucking battle now. Ten thousand men kicking the living fuck out of each other – Like something from bloody Middle Ages. Dark Ages. Three of us

just stand there – Mouthfuls of sausage roll. Shitting fucking bricks. **Day 51.** I phone Pete first thing. Tell him I'm a non-runner. Truth is I don't fancy it. Not after yesterday. I put breakfast TV on – talking about troops moving coal stocks again. Cath comes down. Stands behind sofa. Not a word. I switch it off. She goes into kitchen. I follow her. I walk over to her. I put my hands round her waist. I say, I'm sorry. She nods. I kiss her hair. I say, Let's go up to Whitby this weekend. She shakes her head. She's crying. We can't afford it, she says. I turn her around. I say, Can't afford not to. Kip in car if it comes to it. She smiles. First time in a long time. **Day 52.** Pete called late last night, asked if I was up for it today. Told him I still felt bad. Tell from his voice he didn't believe us – I don't care though. Done practically every bloody day since it fucking started. Nerves are in shreds. Don't even switch on television now. Rather spend day in garden. Least Cath is happy. Have tea ready for when she gets in. Sausages and Smash. Lovely. Go up to bed early, ready for tomorrow. Top of stairs, telephone goes again. I think, Bugger it. Let thing bloody ring. But Cath goes down. Martin, she says. It's for you. I come back down stairs. I say, Who is it? She's got her hand over receiver. Mr Moore from colliery, she says. I take phone from her. I say, This is Martin Daly. Cath doesn't move. She stands there, watching my face. I listen to him. I say, I don't know who told you that. Stands there, watching my face. I say, They were wrong. Stands there – Yes, I tell him. I know where you are. Goodnight to you. Watching. *You threw us in a pit.* I hang up. **Day 53.** We set off early. Drive up to York. Avoid Ferrybridge. Drax. Them places. Go through Malton. Pickering. Over North York Moors. Beautiful. Lovely pub lunch. Fresh air, windows down in car. Can smell sea fore we see it. Hear gulls. Turn to Cath. Her handkerchief out. Tears down her face – Mine too. *You showered us with soil.* **Day 54.** We hold hands. We walk up to Abbey. Find path. We walk to edge. Look over – The sea. The cliffs. The sky. The sun – I want to jump. Take her with me. Fall –

The Eighth Week

Monday 23 – Sunday 29 April 1984

The skull. The candle. The clock and the mirror. Neil Fontaine moves across the floor. The carpet. The towels and the sheets. The light across the wallpaper. The curtains. The fixtures and the fittings. The shadow across the bone. The face. The hands and the hair. The boots across the room. The building. The town and the country –

Jennifer moves across the bed. The pillow. His name in her dreams.

She wakes in the light –

We bury the ones we treasure –

The door is locked. Neil gone again.

His head falls forward. Schaub is unconscious. Tied up.

The Mechanic goes over to the sink. He rinses his right hand under the cold tap. He puts the plug in the hole. He fills the basin. He soaks his knuckle in the sink.

His head moves. Schaub groans.

The Mechanic pulls out the plug. He dries his hands on a small towel. He walks over to the telephones. He picks up one of the receivers. He dials the number.

Julius Schaub moans.

Neil Fontaine sits in the Mercedes and reads the papers –

Their President claiming CEGB coal stocks will last only nine more weeks. The TGWU threatening to call a national docks strike if dockers are sacked for supporting striking miners. Their President refusing to meet the Board to discuss the rescheduling of pit closures. The Board launching their back-to-work campaign today.

Neil Fontaine tears out two small stories from the inside pages –

He puts them in his pocket. He saves them for later.

The War Cabinet dissolves. The Jew comes out of Downing Street.

Neil Fontaine holds open the door.

The Jew gets in the back. He says, 'The Club please, Neil.'

'Certainly, sir.'

Neil Fontaine drives to the Carlton Club. He opens the back door for the Jew.

The Jew looks at his watch. He says, 'Three o'clock please, Neil.'

'Certainly, sir.'

Neil Fontaine leaves the car close to the Club and walks along to Charing Cross. Neil spots Roger Vaughan. Roger spots Neil Fontaine. Neil follows Roger Vaughan down the Strand. Roger turns left down a small alley. Neil Fontaine is right behind him. Roger Vaughan goes into the pub. Neil sits down at a table in the corner. Roger orders the drinks. Neil Fontaine lights a cigarette. Roger Vaughan brings over two drinks –

Fresh orange for Neil, double Scotch for Roger.

Roger Vaughan sits down –

Roger runs Jupiter Securities for Jerry. Jerry is worried about Neil. Neil must meet Roger –

Roger smiles. Roger says, 'Well?'

'It's in hand,' says Neil Fontaine.

Roger stops smiling. Roger says, 'Been quite a flap upstairs. You know that?'

'These are difficult times for all of us,' says Neil. 'Bad times.'

Roger shakes his head. Roger says, 'Not a good time to screw up. For any of us.'

'They didn't find anything,' says Neil. 'Johnson would have said.'

Roger sips his drink. Roger says, 'Just a question of their silence then, isn't it?'

Neil takes out the envelope. He puts it down between the two drinks. He says, 'He asked me to give you this.'

Roger picks it up. He opens it. He looks inside. He puts it down. Roger laughs. 'How very trusting. Really believes he can just walk away, doesn't he?'

'Hand in hand,' says Neil. 'Into the sunset.'

Roger finishes his drink. Roger says, 'Love will always let you down.'

Neil pushes his drink away. Neil waits.

Roger stands up. Roger asks, 'How is dear Jennifer these days?'

'Hungry,' says Neil.

Roger puts a hand on Neil's shoulder. Roger says, 'Always lets you down, Neil.'

*

70

The President stood up behind his desk. Stood up in front of the huge portrait of himself. He walked round to where Terry was sitting. Handed Terry a tissue, hand on his shoulder. The President said, 'People make mistakes, Comrade. It's what makes them human.'

Terry blew his nose. Terry dried his eyes.

'I believe you had the best interests of the movement in your heart, Comrade.'

Terry sniffed. Terry nodded.

'This time you are forgiven, Comrade.'

Terry stood up. Terry said, 'Thank you, President. Thank you. Thank you –'

The President walked back behind his desk. Back in front of the portrait.

Len held open the door for Terry –

'Thank you,' said Terry again. Terry went downstairs for his coat –

Terry Winters knew he was on a short leash.

Terry got his coat. Terry took the lift down to the foyer –

They were waiting for him.

Terry sat in the back of the car between the President and Paul –

Joan up front with Len.

They drove to Mansfield. They parked near the Area HQ. They parted the crowd –

No one said a word.

They went inside. They walked through the room. They sat at the top table –

Ray spoke. Ray said, 'Get off your knees –'

Henry spoke. Henry said, 'You are mice, not men –'

Paul spoke. Paul said, 'You are on strike officially –'

Then the President spoke to them. The President scolded them. The President shouted, 'YOU DO NOT CROSS PICKET LINES!'

They got up from the table. They walked through the room –

There was no standing ovation. No applause. No songs. No autographs. Not here.

A man got up from his seat. A man rushed forward –

He pushed past Terry. He pushed past Len. He poked the President in the chest. He said, 'You impose this strike on these members and I'll take you to court.'

'Sit down, Fred,' said Henry. 'Making a bloody fool of yourself.'

The President looked at the finger on his chest. He looked up into the man's face. The President smiled. He said, 'See you in court then, Comrade.'

The helicopter is in the shop. The Jew needs Neil to drive him down to his Suffolk pile; *Colditz*, as it's known to everyone who has ever been there. Everyone but the Jew –

Neil Fontaine knocks once on the door of the Jew's fourth-floor suite at Claridge's. Neil steps inside. The Jew is on the phone in the middle of a dark sea of maps and plans. He is saying, 'She fears a cave-in on Nottingham's part. Fears he has the initiative . . .'

Neil Fontaine gathers up the maps and the plans. He puts them in the briefcase.

The Jew hangs up. He looks at Neil. He shakes his head.

Neil Fontaine hands the Jew a file. He says, 'Spot of reading for the journey, sir.'

The Jew opens the file. He scans the cuttings. He arches an eyebrow. He smiles. He says, 'Why, thank you, Neil.'

Neil Fontaine takes the briefcase and a small overnight bag down to the Mercedes.

They set off for Colditz.

The Jew reads the cuttings aloud. The Jew strokes his moustache. The Jew smiles. He lowers the partition ten miles out of London. He is excited. He can see possibilities. He says, 'Interesting, Neil. Perhaps you should pay a personal visit to these people. These places. Assess the potential. The possibilities –'

Neil Fontaine nods. He says, 'Certainly, sir.'

The cunt sits down. The cunt hands him a folded copy of today's Times.
The Mechanic opens it. There is an envelope inside. He opens it –
There is a Polaroid inside; Jen sat on a chair holding the same paper.
The Mechanic stares at the photo.
Cunt lights a cigarette. Cunt inhales.
The Mechanic puts the photo in his pocket. He says, 'Where is she?'
Cunt exhales. Cunt shakes his head.
'Did you tell them what I said?'
Cunt nods.
'What did they say?'
Cunt holds up two fingers. Cunt says, 'One down. Two to go.'
'I fucking told you, I don't have the diary. It wasn't there.'

Cunt stubs out the cigarette. Cunt says, 'I'll tell them what you said.'
The Mechanic takes out the key. 'I found Schaub. Now I want my wife back.'
Cunt shakes his head again. Cunt holds up two fingers again.
The Mechanic drops the key onto the table. 'I want her back, Neil.'
Cunt picks up the key. Cunt stares at it.
'I love her,' says the Mechanic. 'I always have and I always will.'
Neil Fontaine shakes his head. Holds up two fingers. For the last time.

The Jew asked for a list from the Chairman of the National Coal
Board. The Chairman approached the Home Secretary. The Home
Secretary gave the list to the Chairman. The Chairman handed the
list over to the Jew. The Jew passed the list on to Neil Fontaine –

Neil Fontaine likes lists. Neil keeps lists. He loves lists:

Lists of lawyers. Lawyers who might help miners. Miners who
might help –

Neil Fontaine parks on Ripley high street. Neil Fontaine opens the
door for Fred. Fred Wallace gets out of the car with his armful of
books and papers. Neil Fontaine and Fred Wallace walk into Reid &
Taylor. They have an appointment to see Dominic Reid. Fred Wallace
is nervous. He is not sure this is the right thing –

In his heart.

Neil Fontaine is worried too. He is not sure these are the right men
for the job.

Dominic Reid comes out to greet them. His hand out. He is young.
Perspiring. Neil Fontaine rechecks his list. They go through into the
office. They sit down.

'Mr Reid,' says Neil Fontaine. 'This is Fred Wallace. Fred Wallace is
a miner. He works at Pye Hill Colliery. Or at least he'd like to work.
As I'm sure you're aware, Fred and the majority of his Nottinghamshire colleagues voted to reject strike action in support of the
Yorkshire miners –

'However, the leaders of the Nottinghamshire Area NUM have
gone against the wishes of their members. The leaders have declared
the area to be officially on strike. They have instructed the membership not to cross picket lines –

'Fred has just one simple question for you,' says Neil. 'Haven't
you, Fred?'

Fred Wallace nods. Fred Wallace asks the young lawyer, 'Is this
strictly legal?'

The sky. The cliffs. The sea – Never go home again. Never again. **Day 56.** Back to reality. Pete called when Cath was at shops – I can't sit at home. Hide in garden. He knows that. Knows I've bloody tried. Even rang redundancy hot line. Told Cath I'd see what they had to say. But I can't do it. Daren't tell her I'm going back on tour – Arthur's Army. Break her heart again – But when I'm here, I wish I was there. When I'm there, I wish I was back here – Fuck. Know where I am today, though – This was always going to be bad. Notts Area are meeting in Mansfield. NCB have given all scabs day off – Full pay with coaches laid on to make sure they show up and let Chadburn and Richardson know they want to scab on. Fucking wankers. Sheffield isn't having any of this. Lads are to go in – Send scabs back where they come from. That's plan. Everyone knows it. Press know it. TV know it – Police fucking know it. Get as far as Pleasley. Far as anyone is going today. Thousands of lads standing about. Milling around. Police fucking everywhere. On foot. In cars. Vans. Coaches. Helicopters. Even got a fucking plane up there. Bloody works. Letting everyone know they're here too. Giving it out to anyone who tries to get into centre of Mansfield. Few lads go down old railway line. Police set dogs on them. Lads throw stones. Police crack heads. Rest of us just stood about. Milling – Top men from Union arguing with this Inspector. Waste of bloody breath as usual. They've got their orders for today. No miners in Mansfield – Only scabs. Scabs with their Adolf Scargill placards. Scabs singing, We're off to work tomorrow. MacGregor's mates on their NCB coaches with their thirty pieces of bloody silver in their deep fucking pockets. Proud of themselves and all – Scum. **Day 57.** Feels different now. Big change. Tempo and tempers rising. Fucking Creswell again. Scabs just walking in. Bold as fucking brass. No shame. There's a big push – Hard. Bloody. Knuckle. Police charging us – Hard. Bloody. Leather. Boots coming from all over. Men run – Scatter. Out of breath. This way and that. I follow Pete over a fence. Through a hedge. Onto cricket pitch. Police on our heels. Across pitch. Some lads hiding in pavilion. Police steam straight in. Haul them out. One lad on floor. Six of them and one of him. Skin exposed. Police dishing out leather – Gloves. Truncheons. Boots – Pete goes back over. I follow him. Lad on pitch isn't moving. Police still dishing it out. Pete picks up one of deckchairs. I do same. Pete charges coppers. I do same. Pete's chair breaks over one copper's back. I throw mine. They turn on us – We run. They chase us – We run. Over fence – We run. Hedge – We run. Onto road – We run. Keith's car coming up lane – Pete and me waving. Keith pulls up – We get in. Police spitting – Shaking their fists. Keith foot down – Shitting bricks again. **Day 63.** No fucking end in sight. Folk have gone through their savings now. Them that had any. Holidays cancelled. Stuff taken back to shops – Nothing from social. Nothing from union – Lot of muttering. Pete calls us to order. Tries to – I don't give a monkey's what panel says, shouts Keith. Bloody waste of our time. We're getting nowhere, says Tom. Nowhere but nicked, shouts someone from back. Power stations, says Keith. It's only way. Talking rubbish, someone else says. It's all bloody bollocks, says another. They got fucking mountains piled up. Keith turns round. Let's hear your suggestion then, he says. Pete's got his hands out in front of him. You're in T-shirts yourselves, he says. I stand up. I say, What about British Steel? Scunthorpe? They're taking piss. They keep asking for more coke. They don't need it. Mate of mine who works at Anchor, he says it's a con. Keith and John nod. Room nods. How is it a con? asks Pete. Lad told us, you don't keep a furnace ticking over. Doesn't work like that. When they were all out, they just bunged it full of coke and shut top. Let in as little air as possible. He reckons it lasts for months like that. Room shakes their heads. Shooting ourselves in bloody foot, someone says again. It's our fucking coal they need. Us and Cortonwood. Picket them, less reason to buy it from us in first place. Good luck to them, shouts a bloke from back. Three years ago we were voting to

The Ninth Week

Monday 30 April – Sunday 6 May 1984

Wait. Wake. Can't. Sleep. Can't. Wake. Wait. Can't. Sleep. Can't. Wait. Wake. Can't. Sleep. Can't –

The record on the stereo. The money on the table. The Polaroid in his hand.

Wake. Wait. Can't. Sleep. Can't. Wait. Wake. Can't. Sleep. Can't –

The Mechanic switches off the stereo. The Mechanic counts the money again.

Wake. Wait. Can't. Sleep. Can't –

It's not enough.

Wake. Wait. Can't –

The Mechanic stares at the money. The Mechanic stares at the Polaroid.

Fuck them. Fuck them all –

The Mechanic picks up the phone. The Mechanic calls Dixon –

Paul Dixon laughs down the line. Paul Dixon says, 'Well, well, well –'

Hands holding the receiver –

'Look who's come crawling back to his Uncle Paul.'

Tight –

'How the mighty have fucking fallen.'

Upstairs downstairs. In one minute. Out the next. In, out. In, out. They shook Terry all about. This way. That way. Here. There. And everywhere –

Rally. Rally. Rally. Meeting. Meeting. Meeting –

Speech. Speech. Speech. Talk. Talk. Talk –

The Chairman said one thing. The President said another –

Forever reacting. Never acting –

The Chairman said the strike could be defeated with the support of Nottingham. The President said the strike could be won without the support of Nottingham –

You say hello. I say goodbye –

Goodbye, goodbye, goodbye –

Terry slipped his leash. Terry had his own plans.

Terry drove straight down from Sheffield. Clive Cook down from Barnsley. Desmond Toole straight up from Kent. Gareth Thomas up from Cardiff –

They met in the Leicester Forest Service Station.

Terry was early. Desmond on the dot. Clive late –

Gareth pissed off. Tired from the drive. He hated all this cloak-and-dagger shit.

'I'm sorry,' said Terry. 'The President insists we take the utmost precautions.'

Gareth pushed his tea away. Gareth said, 'They want damages.'

'How big are these firms?' asked Desmond.

Gareth shook his head. Gareth said, 'Not big at all. Ten wagons at most.'

'What about their lawyers?' asked Terry.

'Local,' said Gareth. 'From Neath.'

'How much they after?' asked Clive.

Gareth looked at Terry. Gareth said, 'Fifty grand.'

'It'll be contempt if you picket again,' said Desmond.

'Then sequestration,' said Clive.

Gareth nodded. Gareth tapped the table. Gareth looked at Terry again –

Terry stared back at him. Terry said, 'Did you do the things I asked, Comrade?'

Gareth nodded again.

Terry looked across the table at Clive and Desmond. Terry said, 'Comrades?'

Desmond Toole nodded. Clive Cook bit his nail –

Bit his nail and said, 'You know I fucking did.'

These men are hard. Think they are –
  Territorials. Reserves.
These men have debts. Think they have –
  Southern Nazis. London hooligans.
These men stare at the walls. The briefing-room walls –
  The OS maps. The aerial photographs.
These men read the words on the wall –
  Internal Defence and Development. Stability Operations.
These men sit. These men wait.
  The side door opens. The Brass step inside. Dressed in black. Their hair

cropped. The Brass walk to the front of the room. Put their leather cases on the table next to the OHP. The Brass take out their files. Three big pens. Markers. The Brass turn to the board behind them. The Brass write down two words –

Counter Insurgency.

The Brass replace their pen tops. The Brass look up at these men before them –

These hard men. These men with debts.

The Brass look from these men to this one man at the back –

This one hard man. This man with debts. David Johnson –

The Mechanic.

'Welcome home, soldier,' say the Brass. 'Welcome home.'

Neil Fontaine is at the bridgehead; the Mansfield HQ of the Nottinghamshire Area NUM. The Prime Minister has taken up the Jew's suggestion. The Minister for Energy has taken up the Prime Minister's suggestion: the Board has taken up the Minister's suggestion. The Board has given every miner in Nottinghamshire the day off with full pay and a bus ticket into town on an NCB coach for a demonstration –

A Right to Work demonstration.

Miners from Derbyshire and Yorkshire who planned a counter-demonstration have been turned back in their thousands at the road-blocks on the borders –

The *scabs* have had a police escort. There are seven thousand of them here –

Just two thousand strikers penned in on the sports field behind the HQ –

Penned in by horses. Penned in by dogs. Penned in by pigs:

Hundreds of Hampshire policemen have been flown in aboard a Boeing 737. From Hurn to East Midlands airport. Billeted in Nissen huts. Paid time and a half –

Tax free –

To stand with thousands of local policemen. Three deep in human walls –

Human walls to keep miner from miner. Striker from scab –

Neil Fontaine walks among them. He takes photographs for the Jew:

The people. *His people.* Their protest. *His protest.* Their placards. *His placards –*

Adolf Scargill. Nottinghamshire miners have a lot of bottle. Right to Work.

Neil Fontaine takes notes for the Jew. He listens to their *leaders*. He hears:

'– you are the only friends MacGregor has got –

'– it's about time you acted like bloody men –

'– showed your solidarity with other miners.'

He takes notes. Records their response. Hears:

'– resign –

'– traitor –

'– we're off to work tomorrow. We're off to work tomorrow. Off to work –'

Neil Fontaine hears –

Possibilities.

Neil Fontaine leaves Mansfield. He drives up the M1. Onto the M62 –

Eastbound. Maps out. Notes –

Possibilities.

Neil Fontaine passes Ferrybridge. Turns off at Goole. Takes small roads through Scunthorpe. To Immingham Dock. He parks. He walks about. He takes photographs. Notes. He listens. He hears –

Possibilities.

Neil Fontaine gets back in his car. He drives back through Scunthorpe. He comes to Flixborough. To Gunness. He parks. He walks about. Takes more photographs. Notes. He inhales. He smells –

Possibilities.

Neil Fontaine gets back in his car. He follows the lorries back down to Sheffield. He comes to the black chimneys. To the giant ovens. He parks. He walks about –

He listens. He hears. He inhales. He smells. He watches. He sees –

Railways. Roads. Slag heaps. Disused workings –

He sees land. Space –

Open space.

He closes his eyes. He remembers. He opens his eyes. He sees –

Batons. Shields. Horses. Dogs. Dust. Blood –

Victory.

Neil Fontaine has his notes. His photographs. His plans. His battle-plans –

The Jew will have his victory –

Here.

Neil Fontaine stands in the telephone box. Neil Fontaine makes the call –

The Jew is at his suite on the fourth floor of Claridge's.

'This place is called what again?' asks the Jew.

Neil Fontaine stares out at the possibilities. Neil Fontaine says, 'Orgreave.'

Training days. They march him across moorland. Put bags on his back. Handcuff him to the next man. Walk him through the days. Warminster and Sandhurst accents in the rain. Whispers in the rain. Echoes. Training nights. They sit him in the back of Transits. Put bags on his head. Handcuff him to the next man. Drive him through the night. Camberley and Latimer accents in the dark –

Whispers in the dark –

Echoes.

The Brass give him a cell. Make him Team Leader. Two thieves and a rapist from the Army of the Rhine. Military Prison. Time off the block for a bit of bad behaviour back in Blighty. Remission. Parole. Early doors –

Whispers. Echoes –

The Brass give his team photographs. The Brass sit them down at the top table. The Brass yawn. His team stare. The Brass pick their noses. His men scratch their balls.

The Brass give his team videos. The Brass sit them down before the big screen. The Brass yawn. His team watch. The Brass bite their nails. His men crack their knuckles.

The Brass give his team orders. The Brass open the door. The Brass yawn –

His team leave. The Brass wave –

The Mechanic and his men gone.

Dick was still in Scotland. Everyone else on the top floor. Terry Winters took the stairs. Two at a time. Late again. Terry hung his jacket outside with all the others. He knocked once. He went inside. He mumbled his apologies –

The Tweeds and the Denims stared. The Tweeds and the Denims muttered.

Terry took a seat by the door.

Joan was standing at the front. Joan saying, '– thirty-eight arrested at Wivenhoe. Twenty-one at Harworth. Better news from Lancashire. Only two pits there now working. We calculate that a hundred and twenty-one pits are out, forty-nine still producing some coal. President –'

Joan sat down.

The President stood up. He said, 'Thank you, Comrade. I have agreed to attend next Monday's May Day rally in Mansfield. However, Monday week, there will also be a Union family rally in the town. The Areas and Panels will be notified today. Coaches will be provided to ensure every branch is represented. Chief Executive –'

The President looked down at Terry. Everybody looked down at Terry –

Terry looked down at his calculator and his files. Terry blushed. Terry looked up. Terry said, 'That is correct, President.'

The President waited. The President said, 'And the Local Council, Comrade?'

Terry nodded. Terry said, 'All the necessary approval has been granted.'

The President waited. The President said, 'Anything else, Comrade?'

Terry shrugged his shoulders. Terry shook his head. Terry said, 'No.'

The President said, 'Thank you, Comrade. The final items on the agenda are the General Secretary's statement on behalf of the Vice-President on the situation regarding the local agreements with the ISTC and transport unions. No doubt you are all aware that BSC have intensified their use of scab road haulage to maintain deliveries and coal stocks at their plants. The General Secretary will then also make a brief statement of his own in regard to coal stocks at CEGB sites. General Secretary –'

Paul stood up. He was looking at Terry.

Terry looked back down at his calculator. He had pressed 77340734.

He turned the calculator upside down –

Terry smiled. Terry closed his eyes –

Chickens, the lot of them. The Tweeds. The Denims –

Headless chickens, the lot of them.

Terry didn't panic. He just did it. Terry didn't read the forms the Council sent him. The small print. He just signed where he had to sign. Signed what he had to sign. Terry didn't listen to the things the Council asked for on the phone. The guarantees. He just agreed with what they said. Agreed to what they said. Terry didn't question the terms the coach firms wanted. The prices. He just accepted what they said. Accepted everything. Terry knew the important thing was that the President got what he wanted –

Britain's biggest ever trade union demonstration –

That he got what he wanted. Next Monday in Mansfield. The biggest –

The phone was ringing. Terry opened his eyes –

He was back downstairs. He was back in his office. Back behind his desk.

Terry picked up the phone. *Click-click.* He said, 'Chief Executive speaking.'

'Bill Reed here,' said Bill Reed. Bill edited the *Miner* –

Terry had stopped smiling.

He knows she's hurting. In the backs of Ford Transits again. No windows. Transit stops. They put bags on their heads again. No eyeholes. He closes his eyes in the dark. He knows she's hurting. The doors open. They take them out of the Transit. The air is cold. They march them across the tarmac. Up steps. Onto seats. Doors shut. Motors start. Engines. Helicopter engines. Up they go. He closes his eyes. He knows she's hurting. Down they come. Motors stop. Doors open. Down steps. Across tarmac. The air cold. Keys turn. Doors open. The air old. Down corridors. Doors open. Keys turn. They stop. They take the bags off their heads. He opens his eyes. He blinks. Stares –

Bare bulbs. Bunk beds. Blankets. Kit bags –

Barracks.

Doors slam. Keys turn –

The Mechanic closes his eyes again –

He knows Jen is hurting. Knows he is not there for her –

Not yet.

support them – To save them. They get no coke, they got no job. They got no job, we got no job, someone else shouts. Keith turns round. Divide and rule, he shouts. That's what she bloody wants. Fucking stick together. That's only way there is – Stick together, someone laughs. Tell that to fucking Nottingham. Tell them your fucking self, snaps John. Never seen you down there. Should do more for them, Pete says. Them that are out down there, they need all help they can get. All help we can give them. Keith nods. We need everyone on picket line, that's what we need, says Keith. All of you. Room goes up. Big shouts – Fuck off! Shut up! Need to stop yapping about it. Need to start dishing it out – Petrol money isn't going to get us a new radiator, is it? Pete shakes his head. Pete stands back up. This is getting us nowhere, he says. Bloody nowhere. **Day 65.** John's driving. Following Pete's piece of paper again. What he's written. Talk is all of gangs and squads – Hit squads. Super squads. Scab squads. Intercept-or squads – Lads getting hidings from gangs of off-duty coppers – Squaddie gangs. Scab gangs – Like after Sheffield. Police had just waded in. Taken anyone in town centre after dark – Beaten fuck out of them. Nicked them – Tried that shit earlier, says Keith. Be no fucking Sheffield left now. There's rumours that scabs are giving names of blokes on strike in Notts to police. Their addresses. Police giving names to these hit squads. Hired hands. Lads getting ambushed. Wives getting dirty calls when their men are out picketing. Heavy breathing – I've told Cath to keep chain on when I'm out – Be Yorkshire next, says Little John. Mark my words. Get through again. Creswell again. Police waiting. Cameras out. *Smile.* Stick us out of road. Scabs go in – Waving. Smiling – Bastards. We shove. Shout – That's all we do. All we fucking can do. They're in and we're out. That's it. Head back to cars. Police waving bye-bye – Smiling. Fucking bastards – Wasting our bloody time down here, says Keith. Never going to change their bloody minds. Be better at power stations. Trent wharves. Pay off would come then. You'd soon see.

Day 68. Bad dreams again – *We lie among corpses. Thousands of them. We are parched. Drowned in blood. Stained armour. Fallen crowns. We lie among corpses. We listen to the field beneath us. Worms coming. Slugs. Rats. Little bloody footprints across cold white skin. We lie among corpses. We look up at the sky. Clouds coming. Rain. Crows – One lands on me. Struts upon my chest. Cocks its head. It goes for my eye* – I wake up. Bad dreams are mine – All mine. Here we go. Here we go. Here we go – **Day 69.** Mansfield rally today. Most of wives have come – Cath too. She wanted to. Lot of blokes have brought their kids and all. We've got on coach. Right laugh it is. Lot of songs. Banter. Come to Leisure Centre. We get off coach – What a sight. Must be thirty thousand easy. Banners as far as you can see – From Scotland. Wales. Lancashire. Derbyshire. Kent and Yorkshire – By bus. By van. By car. By foot – Here to their Heartland. Not to intimidate them. Not to bully them – Here to shame them. God smiling on us too. Baking-hot sunshine. We march through town centre behind our banner. Heads held high, lot of us. Heads high with pride. Hand in hand with Cath. Kids sat on front of banner. Ice creams. Local folk out to welcome us. Clapping us. Cheering us from rooftops – Roaring us on. No scabs and their wives. None of Maggie's Storm-troopers. Not a helmet in sight. Just thirty thousand ordinary, decent men, women and children. Twelve noon we come back to Leisure Centre. Can't get near platform. But we can hear them. Tony Benn. Dennis Skinner – We can cross frontiers we have never dreamed of. We can not only stop pit closures – we can have Socialism. Fantastic every one of them. Cath clapping. Cheering. Chant goes up for Arthur. Who people want. One name – Arthur, Arthur, Arthur, Arthur, Arthur, Arthur – I look over at Cath – Clapping. Cheering. Chanting with best of them. And he's magnificent. Magnificent – You have got a union leadership who are prepared to lead until we win, and win we will – She looks at me. She squeezes my hand. She has tears in her eyes. Tears in mine – Good ones, for a change.

The Tenth Week

Monday 7 – Sunday 13 May 1984

Bill Reed and the President went way back. Bill Reed knew the President from Woolley. Bill Reed knew the President from Barnsley. Bill Reed had been the President's candidate. Bill Reed had got the job. Now Bill Reed edited the *Miner*, the Union's paper.

Bill Reed put down his cup. Bill Reed said, 'Think it's fair? Us donating our salary to the hardship fund? I'm not on strike. I'm working twenty-four hours a day, me.'

'What do you want, Comrade?' said Terry.

Bill Reed nodded. Bill Reed said, 'This contact of mine, very well placed. Remember he told me they'd got someone inside Huddersfield Road?'

Terry said nothing. He stirred his coffee –

Anticlockwise.

Bill Reed leant across the table. Bill Reed said, 'I know who it is, Comrade.'

Terry stopped stirring his coffee. He put the spoon on the saucer.

'Did my homework on this feller at Manton,' said Bill Reed. 'Feller who's organized the vote down there. This Don Colby?'

Terry took a sip from his coffee. He put the cup back down. He shook his head.

Bill Reed smiled. Bill Reed said, 'Turns out you and Don have a mutual friend.'

Terry said nothing. Terry waited –

Bill Reed smiled. Bill Reed said, 'Clive Cook.'

She had got the Jew and Neil Fontaine on a private flight up to Prestwick. Not Glasgow. Her car was there to meet them. Drive them straight to Motherwell –

Neil Fontaine sat in the front with the driver. The Jew in the back with the Brass. The Strathclyde Brass briefed the Jew about the day's events at Ravenscraig. *The Craig.* The events at Hunterston –

The lorries. The horses. The injuries. The arrests. The photographs. The numbers.

The Brass told the Jew one thousand pickets had already gathered at Hunterston –

The Jew rubbed his hands. The Jew wanted to be where the action was –

And the action was now steel –

Steel, the New Battlefield.

The Jew watched the horses charge. The pickets fall or fly –

The Jew applauded. The Jew thanked the Brass. The Jew had seen enough. It was home time –

Neil Fontaine opens his eyes. He watches the lights come up from down below. Nothing too good for her friends. Private night flight back: Prestwick to East Midlands. The Jew in the cockpit. The Jew in the co-pilot's seat. The Jew waving his licence about. The Jew with his hands on the controls. Neil Fontaine with his stomach in his mouth. Touchdown. More applause. Handshakes. Another private car waiting on the tarmac –

Nothing too good for her friends –

Nothing too good for his friends either; the Jew's new friends:

The link-up of friendship.

The Jew has hired the upstairs room of a modern pub –

The Green Dragon. Oxton. The middle of nowhere.

The Jew has laid on beer and sandwiches. The men arrive in dribs and drabs. They shuffle in. They stand in the corners. They drink heavily –

They don't touch the sandwiches.

The Jew moves from man to man. The Jew introduces man to man –

Fred, this is Don. Don, this is Fred. Fred is from Pye Hill. Don is from Manton. Fred, this is Jimmy. Jimmy, this is Fred. Fred is from Pye Hill. Jimmy is from Lea Hall –

Jimmy, this is –

The link-up of friendship.

They form small groups. They stand in the corners. They drink heavily –

They don't touch the sandwiches.

They whisper about this branch and that branch. Behind their hands about this secretary and that secretary. Under their breath about this solicitor. That solicitor –

They stand in the corners and talk about right and wrong. They drink heavily –

They don't touch the sandwiches.

They are the Nottingham Working Miners' Committee –

The Secret *Nottingham Working Miners' Committee.*

Terry called Clive Cook from a payphone. Terry spoke in code. Terry set it up –

Dawn. Woolley Edge Services.

Terry was early. Clive was late –

Clive got out of his car. Clive wore sunglasses. Clive crossed the car park –

Clive said, 'I don't think I can take much more of this, Comrade.'

'Get in,' said Terry. 'You might not have to.'

Terry drove down little roads and little lanes. Terry drove to Bretton Park –

Down by the lake, they sat down. Terry said, 'Bill Reed called me.'

'How very unpleasant for you,' said Clive.

Terry grabbed Clive by his coat. Terry said, 'For you actually, *Comrade.*'

'What?' said Clive. 'What are you talking about?'

Terry pulled Clive closer. Terry whispered, 'Bill says you're Special Branch.'

Clive pushed Terry away. Clive swung at Terry. Clive missed Terry –

'Fuck you!' screamed Clive. 'Fuck you for getting me into this, Winters!'

Terry shook his head. Terry said, 'I'm just telling you what Bill said.'

'You believe him,' cried Clive. 'You fucking believe him! You fuck-ing –'

Terry walked over to Clive. Terry put his arms round Clive.

'I've only been doing what you told me to do,' sobbed Clive. 'That's all.'

Terry squeezed Clive tight. Terry said, 'I know that, Comrade. I know –'

'Now I'm finished,' wept Clive. 'Because of you and that drunk bastard.'

Terry held Clive. Terry said, 'I'll talk to the President for you.'

*

They lift weights. They run. They wrestle. They shower. The Brass break them into their cells. Their teams. The Brass give them photographs. Maps. The Brass give them instructions. Uniforms. The teams change into their brand-new boiler suits. They sit on their beds. They crack their knuckles. They grind their teeth –

The Brass give them pills. The Brass make them wait.

The Transits come as the sun sets. Ten of them. Back doors open –

The teams get into their Transits. They sit in the backs with their helmets on –

They drink. They listen to music: Ace of Spades *on loud.*

The Transit carrying the Mechanic and his team stops. The doors open –

The Mechanic and his men get out. They walk into the centre of town. They come to the Robin Hood. They stand outside. They grind their teeth –

And wait.

Their targets come out. Easy to spot with their badges on. Their stickers –

They've had a few and all, these striking miners.

The Mechanic asks them, 'Where you lot going, then?'

'Home,' the strikers tell him.

The Mechanic and his men step aside.

The strikers start up the road.

The Mechanic and his men follow them.

One striker at the back is very drunk.

The Mechanic catches him up. He pushes him. He trips him up –

Slaps him on the back of his head.

The drunken striker stops.

The Mechanic grabs him. Throws him to Team Member A –

A pushes him to B. B pushes him to C. C gives him back to the Mechanic –

The Mechanic and his men laugh. The Mechanic throws him over to A again.

The rest of the strikers are watching. One of them comes back down the road –

'Please let him go,' he says. 'He's done nothing. He's just drunk.'

The Mechanic tears the yellow sticker off this man's sweater. He folds the yellow sticker up –

The man just stands there, this striking miner. Just watching the Mechanic.

The Mechanic grabs this striker's head. His hair. He twists this striker's head –

The Mechanic pushes the yellow sticker up the man's nostril.

The rest of the strikers come piling back down the road –
The Mechanic and his men have their truncheons out –
Ready.

Terry looked out of the hotel window. Terry shook his head. Terry said, 'I feel terrible.'

'Why?' asked Diane. 'From what you've told me, you did the right thing.'

Terry said, 'But Bill Reed trusted me. I went behind his back to the President.'

'Congratulations,' laughed Diane. 'He needed to know. You had to tell him.'

Terry tightened his towel. Terry said, 'Bill Reed's going to be after my blood now.'

'You worry too much,' said Diane. 'He's an old drunk. Now come back to bed.'

Terry said, 'But he's one of the President's oldest and closest friends.'

'Never change, do you?' laughed Diane. 'Now, please. Come. Back. To. Bed.'

Don Colby sits in the back of the Mercedes outside Manton Colliery. Don is nervous. Don is scared. Gutless. Don wants to quit. Don looks at the Jew. Don shakes his head. Don says, 'I haven't the numbers.'

'I know you haven't,' smiles the Jew. 'But the men of Manton are scared. *Intimidated.* The important thing is not the victory. The important thing is the *fight*. To be *seen* to fight. For the men to *see* someone stand up and *fight*. Someone who is *not* scared. *Not* intimidated. Someone with *guts*. Someone who is made of *steel*. Someone *special*. Today that someone is *you*, Don –

'*You!*'

Don Colby raises his shoulders. Don Colby puffs out his chest. Don Colby nods.

'The day *is* coming,' says the Jew. '*Our* day is coming, Don.'

Don Colby beams. Don Colby opens the door.

'Remember, Don,' shouts the Jew. 'The Prime Minister knows your name.'

Trench warfare. The NEC had agreed to postpone branch elections for the duration of the strike. Hand-to-hand combat. The NEC had also discussed new disciplinary measures. Internecine –

Manton Colliery in South Yorkshire had held a branch meeting to discuss a possible return to work. The men had voted to stay out. But the result wasn't the point. The point was they'd had to have a vote in South Yorkshire –

The Heartland.

The President was out on the picket lines. The President was down in Parliament. The President was here. The President was there –

Taking no prisoners. Showing no mercy –

The President was everywhere –

Terry picked up the thank-you card on his desk –

The same painting of the Battle of Saltley Gate which hung in reception.

Terry thought the President might have forgiven him. Truly trust-ed Terry again. But there were rumours sweeping the building –

Talk of talks. Talk of meetings. Talks about talks. Meetings about meetings.

The President had said nothing to Terry Winters. Terry still not truly forgiven. Not truly trusted again –

Still out of the loop.

Terry sighed. He walked over to the big windows. Immediately the phone rang.

Terry picked it up. *Click-click.* He said, 'Chief Executive speaking.'

'Terry? It's Joan here. Can you come upstairs?'

'Now? This minute?'

'Is there a problem?' she asked. 'Bad time?'

Terry shook his head. He said into the phone, 'No, no. But is some-thing wrong?'

'Why do you always think that?' laughed Joan.

Terry hung up. He went back over to the window. Bit his thumb-nail until it bled. Terry wrapped it in his handkerchief. He squeezed it –

Tight.

Terry put on his jacket. He locked his office door. He walked down the corridor. He went upstairs. He knocked on the President's door –

Terry waited.

Len Glover opened the door. Loyal Len nodded.

Terry went inside.

The President was on the phone. His back to the room –

Joan pointed at the seat next to Paul. Paul looked away. Terry sat down.

'– know where they stand. They know where we stand,' the President was saying. 'There is no change in our position. If there is a shift on their part, then fine. Let's meet. We'll listen to what they have to say. But they know very well what we have to say. Know what we want. What our membership want –'

The other phone rang. Joan picked it up. She handed it to Paul.

Terry took his right hand out of his jacket pocket. He opened up his handkerchief. He looked at his bloody thumb. He stuck it in his mouth. He sucked it. He looked up.

The President had finished on the phone. So had Paul –

Everyone was staring at Terry again.

Paul said, 'Paper cut, Comrade?'

Terry took his thumb out of his mouth. He put his hand back in his pocket.

Paul sighed. He held out four files. He said, 'You're going to need these.'

Terry took the files in his left hand. He said, 'Why? What –'

'Comrade,' said the President, 'I need you in Paris with me next week.'

Terry stared at the President. The portrait behind him. Terry nodded.

'It's short notice,' said Joan. 'Is there going to be any problem with your family?'

Terry Winters shook his head. Terry said, 'My family are no problem.'

Day 70. *Put us in the ground* – Wake up. Lie here – Lie here smiling. Feels like it was all a dream. Good one for a change – What a day. Cath opens bedroom door. Come downstairs, she says. Quickly, love. I sit up. I reach for my cigarettes. Quick, she says. It's on telly. I follow her down stairs. I sit on sofa next to her. I put cigarette to my lips. Television has pictures of Mansfield. Pictures of King Arthur looking like Adolf bloody Hitler. Right hand raised in a Nazi salute. Pictures of broken windows. Smashed-up cars. Lads throwing bricks and bottles. Lads fighting with police. Police bleeding. Police on stretchers – I throw cigarette on carpet unlit. I get up from sofa. I switch it off. Liars. Cath is crying. Bloody liars. **Day 75.** Bad dreams are Cath's tonight – *To drown. To suffocate* – Keep us both up. That and rain. **Day 78.** Orgreave – First day. Bad from get-go. Lot of knuckle on both sides. Thirty of us from Thurcroft. Sixty-odd from Maltby and Silverwood. Outnumbered pigs for once – One convoy of trucks. Motorcycle outriders. Range Rovers. Seventy mile an hour. No stopping them – Someone picks up a stone. Someone throws it through a windscreen – Then that's it. It's begun. **Day 80.** Orgreave – They stick on an extra convoy. Jack and Sammy come down. No talking to drivers. Non-union as usual. Eighty mile an hour. Motorcycle outriders. Range Rovers. Half of South Yorkshire force out to help them in. Command posts. Cameras on roofs. *Smile.* Bloody works. Bad as Met for dishing out knuckle. Worse because they're local. Know you. Get too near front you get a hiding – Black eyes. Stars. Broken noses. Ribs. Blood from your ears. Your teeth – Big push starts up. I go forward. Feet off ground. Into front. Into a fist. Take a punch – Here we go. Here we go. Here we go – I go down. Hard. Someone picks us up. I go backwards. Feet off ground. I fall backwards. Blokes all over me. I crawl out – Black eyes. Stars. Broken nose. Ribs. Blood from my ears. Teeth – Fuck me. They've got us in field again – Penned in. Like fucking animals – Lorries come up road. Lorries go in. Ninety mile an hour – No stopping them. Cowboys.

No talking to them – Lorries come out. Lorries go off – Loaded. There were a thousand pickets up at Anchor today. Thousand fucking lads stood at wrong end. Pigs had set us up. Lorries had gone in Dawes Lane gate. Hundred of them lads here with us and we'd have had them today, says Keith. I say nothing. He's dreaming. I look back down hill at place. Horrible – Chimneys and storage tanks. Black and ugly. White smoke and motorway – Bloody nightmare, this place. I hate it. Fucking hate it. **Day 84.** Pete opens envelope. He looks up. He nods – Orgreave. We go out to cars. We get in. It's that fucking close we could walk it. I'm in with Keith and Tom. There's room for one more. Pete tells us to hang on for stragglers. We watch rest of them set off. Twenty minutes later a lad comes into car park. He gets in with us. Off we set. It's just gone eight when we arrive. Union have got blokes with maps and loud-hailers waiting. Directing you. Telling you where to go. Where they want you. Most of lads from Thurcroft are down Catcliffe end. They send us up Handsworth end. Police are helpful, too – Park here. Park there – We go down a side-street. Get out. Go up top field. End of High Field Lane. Walk down towards front. Must be five thousand here. Easy. Arthur himself again. Every man matched, copper for miner. Miner for copper. Stormtroopers stood five abreast. Ten abreast. Fifty abreast – Five deep. Ten deep. Twenty deep. Land fucking black with them again. Marching up and down. Up and down. On bloody double. Like it's drill time – Like they're fucking soldiers. Not coppers – Their gaffers bark orders. Try to corral everyone. Push us about. Not so fucking helpful now – Go here. Go there. Shut it, scum. Stand here. Stand there. Fucking shut it – That game. Half on one side of road. Half on other. Stick us lot in front of Rother Wood. Hear they've already let dogs loose on them down Catcliffe end. Maybe it's our lucky day for once. Loud-hailers crackle. Roar goes up. I look at my watch – It's nine o'clock. Two mile off in distance, twenty lorries are coming up road. I can see them – them and police escort. Lot of shoving now – Push.

The Eleventh Week

Monday 14 – Sunday 20 May 1984

The set-up. The trigger effect. The wheels in motion. The chain reaction. The solution –

Neil Fontaine sets it up –

The final solution.

Waiters wheel in the trolleys. Waiters lay out the plates. Waiters serve the spirits. The Poles are hungry. The Poles take from the silver plates. The Poles drink the spirits –

The Poles are here to offer their coal.

The Poles watch Neil Fontaine pin maps to the board. The Poles watch him use red drawing-pins to mark the sites. The Poles watch Neil Fontaine introduce the Jew –

The Jew is here to accept their offer. Here to sign the blank cheque from her.

'Gentlemen,' says the Jew. 'I am here to tell you all is in hand.'

But the Poles are worried about pickets. The Poles are worried about dockers.

'Gentlemen, worry not,' says the Jew. 'Our intention is to avoid either foe.'

Neil Fontaine points at a red pin on the map. Stuck in the map. In Gunness.

'Thank you, Neil,' says the Jew. 'This will be our secret little sanctuary.'

But the Poles ask questions about the Employment Acts. About the law –

'Our friends in Sheffield need distractions,' says the Jew again. 'Not causes.'

But the Poles are still worried about the pickets. Still worried about the dockers.

'Worry not,' says the Jew again. 'We have our distraction planned.'

Neil Fontaine points at another red pin on the map. Stuck in the map. Stuck in –

'Thank you, Neil,' says the Jew again.

The Poles offer their coal –

The Jew accepts their offer. The Jew fills in the blanks on her cheque.

The Poles are happy. The Poles clean their plates. The Poles drink toasts –

The Poles leave with the cheque and all the bottles they can carry.

Neil Fontaine looks at his watch. It's stopped. He taps it. It's started –

Time slips.

It stops again. It starts again –

Neil Fontaine used to love her, too.

The Jew turns to Neil with his glass raised. The Jew puts down his glass –

'Heavens above,' says the Jew. 'You don't look at all well, Neil.'

'I'm fine, sir.'

'Really?' asks the Jew. 'How are you sleeping these days?'

They lift weights in the morning sun. They run. They wrestle. They shower. The Brass break them back into their cells. Their teams. The Brass give them maps. Instructions. Fresh clothes. They change into their jeans and their boots. They sit on their beds. They crack their knuckles. They grind their teeth –

The Brass give them more pills. Rationed. The Brass make them wait.

The Transits come as the sun sets. The Mechanic and his team sit in the back. They drink. Listen to music: White Riot *loud.*

The Transit stops. The Mechanic and his team get out. They walk through the centre of Mansfield. They come to the car park. They come to the coaches. They come to the bricks. The bottles. There are kids. Kids with their mums and their dads. His team pick up the bricks. The bottles. They throw the bricks. The bottles. The dads charge. Big men. Soft and drunk. Red from the sun. The Mechanic and his team charge. Big men. Hard and wired. Black from hell. There is fighting. Fists and boots. Boots and bottles. The dads go down. The Mechanic and his team stay up. Helicopters overhead. Sirens. Police car doors. Batons. His team walk away. Through the police. Back into the centre of town. Into the market place. The pubs. They buy drinks. They look for badges. They look for stickers. The Mechanic spills drinks. The Mechanic picks fights. His team take it outside. They fight. Fists and boots. Boots and bottles. The badges go down. His team stay up. Leave the badges on the pavement. In the road. The sirens come. The badges don't give up. The badges make Sieg Heil salutes. The police beat them again. The police arrest them. The Mechanic and his men walk into the next pub and the next and the next. They look for badges. Look for stickers. Spill drinks. Pick fights. Take it outside. Fight. Fists and boots. Boots and bottles. The stickers go down. His men stay up. Leave the stickers on the pavement. The sirens come. The stickers chant, 'Section 5. Section 5.' The police beat them again. Arrest them –

Breach of the Peace.

Neil Fontaine has a busy day. He drives North with the Jew. He drops the Jew in the car park of the Green Dragon. The Jew is here to meet with the Working Miners' Committee. Neil Fontaine drives further North –

First stop Gainsborough.

Neil Fontaine looks at his watch. Taps it. Twelve noon. He takes the briefcase off the passenger seat. He gets out of the Mercedes. He walks across the forecourt towards the Portakabin –

The door opens. A middle-aged man in a suit appears –

'Mr Parish?' asks the man.

Neil Fontaine squints into the sun. He says, 'Yes.'

'Brendan Matthews,' says the man. 'Nice to be able to put a face to the name.'

Neil Fontaine shakes the man's hand. He says, 'John Parish. How do you do?'

'How do you do?' says Brendan Matthews. 'Step this way.'

They walk up the white wooden steps into the Portakabin. A young woman is talking on a telephone at a school desk. They go through into Brendan Matthews' office –

'Can I offer you something to drink?' asks Brendan Matthews.

Neil Fontaine raises a hand. He says, 'I'm fine. Thank you.'

Brendan Matthews unlocks a filing cabinet. He takes out a large manila envelope. He hands it to Neil Fontaine. He says, 'These are the photocopies of their licences.'

Neil Fontaine takes out the photocopies. He flicks through them.

'I know you'll obviously want to do your own checks,' says Brendan Matthews. 'But I'm confident these men will meet your needs.'

Neil Fontaine opens his briefcase. He asks, 'How many are there?'

'Fifty, as requested.'

Neil Fontaine puts the manila envelope inside his briefcase. He takes out another large envelope and fifty smaller plain brown envelopes held together with a rubber band. He hands the fifty smaller envelopes across the desk to Brendan Matthews. He says, 'These are retainers of five hundred pounds for each man.'

'Thank you very much,' says Matthews.

Neil Fontaine hands him the large envelope. He says, 'This is a deposit for the transport. The wagons are to be covered with Corporation stickers, which will be with you by the end of the week. Further payment will then be made when we are certain of the dates and the numbers. The men are to be paid in cash on a daily basis.'

'Hundred quid a run?' asks Matthews.

'There and back,' says Neil Fontaine. 'Two runs a day with a completion bonus.'

'That's good money,' says Brendan Matthews.

Neil Fontaine smiles. He says, 'You want to give me a copy of your licence?'

'It's a pleasure doing business with you, Mr Parish,' laughs Brendan Matthews.

Neil Fontaine and Brendan Matthews shake hands and say their goodbyes.

Neil Fontaine leaves Gainsborough. He drives to Scunthorpe. To Anchor –

To the furnaces. To the Queen Mary.

Neil Fontaine looks at his watch. It's stopped. He taps it. It's started –

Time slips, like a furnace.

It stops again. It starts again.

Terry felt the tide had turned. The Mansfield rally had been a magnificent occasion –

A triumph. A show of strength –

Just as Terry had planned.

Terry felt his own stock had risen. His own star back on the rise –

Yesterday, Mansfield. Today, Paris. Tomorrow, the world –

Just as Terry had planned.

Theresa packed Terry an overnight bag. Shirt. Vest. Pants. Socks. Razor. Toothbrush. Towel. She stuck the kids in the back of the car. Half asleep. She drove him to the station. They kissed him goodbye.

He got the Manchester train. Taxi to the airport. The President and Joan were at check-in. They didn't acknowledge him. He didn't acknowledge them. The President was calling himself Mr Smith. He was wearing a hat. Sunglasses. They were not to speak to each other until Paris –

The flight took one hour.

There was a big car waiting at Charles de Gaulle. The President took off his hat. His sunglasses. He sat in the back between Terry and Joan. Pierre from the MTUI sat in the front with the driver. They went straight to their big modern offices in East Paris. They met François and Jean-Marc. They had good coffee. They talked about the dispute. The prospects for peace. Then the President and Joan went off with Pierre and François for the meeting with their international comrades –

The French, the Polish and the Australians.

Terry was sent upstairs to meet with Claude. They discussed international law. They discussed international banking. They discussed legal strategies. They discussed financial strategies. They discussed law firms. They discussed private banks. They discussed clauses. They discussed routes. They discussed lawyers. They discussed accountants. They discussed fees. They discussed funds. They discussed perjury. They discussed penury. They discussed sequestration. They discussed bankruptcy –

The meeting took two hours.

There was another big car waiting to take them to a late lunch at Chartier. They sat at the long tables. The waiters wrote their orders on the paper table covers. The President had the chicken and chips. A salad. The house red.

Terry Winters had the same.

The President leant across the table. He touched Terry's arm. He raised his glass. The President said, 'There'll be no more scab coal from Europe, Comrade.'

Terry raised his glass.

The President shouted, '*Vive la Révolution!*'

The President loved Paris. *Revolutionary City*. Second only to sacred Leningrad. *Holy City*. The President loved the bread. The cheese. The good coffee. The red wine. The President carried Zola everywhere. *Germinal*.

Terry had a copy too. He couldn't get into it –

Terry threw it across the hotel room. He hadn't slept. He couldn't –

The President and the fucking Frogs had bloody left Terry in town after lunch. The President and Joan had had their own plans for the rest of the day. The evening –

Plans in which Comrade Terry had not been included.

Terry sat up in his single bed. Terry could see the rooftops of Paris. The pigeons. He called Theresa. *Click-click.* The kids. He said he'd be home tonight. Terry hung up. He called Diane. She wasn't there. Terry wished she was here. He went to the bathroom. He touched himself. He shaved. He washed. He went downstairs.

Pierre and François joined the Union for breakfast. The President ate croissants. He drank hot chocolate. Terry asked for toast and a pot of tea. Then they checked out. Pierre and François drove them back to the MTUI offices. They had informal meetings. They made informal plans. They ate another late lunch together. Pierre drove out with them to Charles de Gaulle.

The flight took one hour.

They were back in Manchester for half-five. The President put on his hat again. His sunglasses. Len was there to meet them. They didn't offer Terry a lift –

They weren't going his way.

Terry said he'd see them in London. Terry took the train home. It was raining.

Today is the day. The first of many days. The start of the action. The start of many actions. Neil Fontaine parks behind the Law Courts. Fred Wallace sits in the back with his two mates and the Jew –

Today is their day in court. Their first of many days.

Fred is here to issue writs against his own Union, at both area and national level. Fred will first argue the strike in the Nottingham Area is not official. Fred will then argue the instruction to strike does not have to be obeyed. Fred will also threaten to issue further writs if the local branch elections are postponed –

These are expensive arguments for little men in cheap suits –

Frightened men.

Neil Fontaine switches on the signal. He listens to the Jew rally his troops –

'They stalk your streets while you work. Terrorize your women. Your children. They daub your houses in paint while you sleep.

Break your windows. Slash your tyres. Kill your pets. They watch your windows to see when your lights go on. Force you to dress in the dark. Watch your doorways and drives to see who works and who strikes. How long before the arson starts? Before your women are assaulted? Your children? These are the same men who would have you thrown out of your own Union. The same men who are using your own subs which you have loyally paid – and continue to pay –

'To intimidate you! You!

'This is why you are here today. This is what you are here to stop –

'Intimidation. Corruption.'

Neil changes channels. He listens to the Home Secretary make the same speech. Listens to the Home Secretary announce the formation of special squads to counter the intimidation in the pit villages of Nottinghamshire and Derbyshire –

Intimidation squads.

Transit van. Boiler suit. House to house in Nottingham. Bringing out the dead scared. Twenty Yorkshire men still lodging down here with the striking families. Picketing pits. Twenty men still staying with the families on Thorney Abbey Road. In their gardens –

In tents. In caravans.

The Mechanic sits in the Transit van. In his black boiler suit. He watches the pickets leave the tents. The caravans. Watches the pickets go into the Jolly Friar. Watches them leave the worse for wear. Watches the pickets buy their bags of chips. Watches them stumble back to Thorney Abbey Road. Watches them thank their hosts. Wish them goodnight. Head into the gardens –

Their tents. Their caravans.

It is gone midnight.

The Mechanic and his team get out of their Transit. They go up the drive of number 52. Round the back. Into the garden. There is an orange tent pitched on the lawn. There are two pickets inside. They are asleep. The Mechanic picks up a child's bicycle. The rest of his team pick up some garden tools. Garden ornaments. Garden furniture. The team look at their leader –

The Mechanic nods.

They throw the objects onto the top of the orange tent. The pickets inside wake up. The pickets shout. Moan. The pickets try to get out of the tent. Thrash around –

The Mechanic and his team jump up and down on the tent. On the pickets inside. The pickets shout. The pickets scream –

They cannot get out.

The Mechanic nods again –

His team drag the tent out of the back garden. They drag it round to the front. Down the drive. They throw the tent and the pickets into the back of the Transit –

Lights going on up and down the street. Curtains opening. Faces at the windows.

The Mechanic and his team get in the back. The Mechanic bangs on the partition. The Transit sets off. The pickets tangled up inside the tent. Poles and ropes everywhere –

The pickets struggling to free themselves –

The Mechanic and his team punch them. They kick them. Beat and batter them –

The pickets shouting. The pickets screaming. Moaning and pleading.

The van stops. The Mechanic opens the back doors. His team jump out –

The Mechanic and his men drag the pickets out. The pickets wrapped in the tent –

They fall onto the ground at the side of the road.

The Mechanic and his men pull the orange tent off the pickets. They drag them round to the front of the van –

The two pickets are in their twenties, dressed only in their underpants and socks –

They are dirty, bloody and bruised –

One of them has pissed himself.

They blink into the headlights of the van.

The Mechanic and his men step forward. They punch the pickets. Bridge of their noses. Kick them. Their balls. The Mechanic and his men put bags on their heads. Tight. Handcuff their hands behind their backs –

Tighter –

They march the pickets to the side of the road. Lie them face down in a ditch –

They cover them with yellow Coal not Dole *stickers.*

The Mechanic nods. His men get back into their Transit.

The Mechanic stands by the side of the road. He looks at the two pickets face down in the ditch in their underpants and socks –

Bags on their heads. Badges on their bodies. Handcuffed.

The Mechanic takes two Polaroid photographs.

It starts to rain.

The Mechanic jumps down into the ditch. He takes off their handcuffs –
Whispers in their ears, 'Stay out of Nottingham.'

Neil Fontaine takes the back roads. The lanes. He comes to the bridges. The roadblocks. He slows. He pulls over. He shows the necessary papers to the private security guards. Neil Fontaine comes into Flixborough. The Trent Wharves –

It is a beautiful sight, glorious –

The checkpoints. The helicopters. Stopping and searching –

Twenty-four hours a day. Seven days a week.

The ships in the port. The wagons on the dock. Unloading and loading –

Twenty-four hours a day. Seven days a week –

Coal.

Neil Fontaine parks the Mercedes. He walks across the car park.

She is waiting for him. She exhales. She smiles. She says, 'Congratulations.'

'The drivers need helmets,' says Neil Fontaine. 'The windscreens need grilles.'

'Never change, do you?' laughs Diane Morris. 'Never satisfied, are you?'

Push. Push. Push. Push. Push. Push – Police ten deep. Holding – Thrust. Thrust. Thrust. Thrust. Thrust. Thrust. Thrust. Everyone shouting – Scab. Scab. Scab. Scab. Scab. Scab. Few stones coming over. Hands up. Coats up. Shields up – Brick coming. Lorries go in – Folk go down. Folk go under. Folk get lost. I get pulled back. Fall back. I get pulled up. Picked up – It's Keith. He shakes his head. We go back in. Five minutes later another lot of lorries come up road – Push. Push. Push. Push. Push. Push. Push – Thrust. Thrust. Thrust. Thrust. Thrust. Thrust. Thrust – Scab. Scab. Scab. Scab. Scab. Scab. Scab. More stones – Brick coming. Lorries inside. Gates shut. Lines break. Snatch squads of six coppers charge out. Piling in – Thrust. Thrust. Thrust. Thrust. Thrust. Thrust – Blue helmets. Visors down. Short shields. Round shields. Truncheons out – Hidings on both sides – Snatch squads taking as many prisoners as they can – Taking them hard – By their hair. By their throats. By their balls – Chaos. Bloody fucking chaos – Someone chucks a smoke-bomb. Fire-crackers. Thunder-flashes. Explosions. Red smoke everywhere – Then out come fucking horses. First time I've seen them up close. Six at a time. Visors down. Batons swinging – Kill you if they could – And they could. They fucking could – We run. We scatter – Half through wood. Half up hill – Into fields. Into open – Lads stopping to pick up sticks. Stones. Spars. Anything they can – I don't stop. Horses don't stop either – Straight into field after us. Open ground – Snatch squads behind horses. Transits behind snatch squads – Under blue skies. Across green fields – Fuck. I keep on running. Don't stop till I get up near Asda – Till I hear them banging. Banging their truncheons on their shields as horses trot back and lorries leave – Leaving us to blood. To bodies. Burials. *Under the ground.* **Day 85.** My car today. I ask Pete for somewhere else. He looks at me. He shrugs. He opens envelope. He shakes his head. He holds it up. He shows it me – *Orgreave.* I tell him, It's a waste of time. Fucking side-show. That's what it is. He nods. He says, Fuck them. Try Bent-

inck. I say, Thanks, Pete. I go and get Keith and John. Lad called Stevie says he wants to come in with us. Set off. Get on M1. Radio on: *Footloose.* Everyone dead chuffed to be going somewhere else. Even if it's back to bloody Bentinck. *Wake me up before you go-go.* Halfway down motorway it comes on radio Arthur's been nicked up at Orgreave and pickets have invaded NCB HQ in London. Barricaded themselves in. Hung *Free Arthur Scargill* banners from windows. Mood in car changes. Radio goes off. Come to Junction 28 and it's like police Transit van of year contest. Very helpful, they are – Try Junction 31, lads, they tell us. That's where action is. Orgreave – They'll let you go to Orgreave. No problem. They'll even give you directions. Fucking escort – Make bloody sure you get there. There and only there – Nowhere else. I look at Keith. He shrugs. Stevie sticks his head between front seats. I want to go, says Stevie. Let's go. I look at Keith again. He nods. I look at clock – Gone ten. Probably missed all drama. I go round junction. Set off back way we came. Come off at Junction 31. Take Retford Road. Head back to Orgreave. There for about eleven. Park by another pub called Plough. Place packed. Rammed. Have a pint. Talk all about Arthur. What they've done to our Arthur. Talk all about revenge. Payback. What we're going to do to them. Word is lorries will be back between half-twelve and one o'clock. I look at my watch again. Time for another pint. And another. Dutch fucking courage. Gets to half-twelve and we head back out. Bright sunshine. Start up towards main entrance. Stormtroopers having none of that. Sieg Heil. Herd us all up to top field. Lot of lads are already up there. Not as many as yesterday. Most are sat about in sun. Shirts off. Packs of cards. Cans of cheap ale. Look like a load of tomatoes, that red. Be able to spot a scab by paleness of his skin. There's a game of football going – Skins and shirts. Then game stops – Police boots march up road. Four abreast by us. Twenty deep down by gate – Lorries must be coming. Everyone pushes forward. Towards truncheons and shields. Full-length

The Twelfth Week

Monday 21 – Sunday 27 May 1984

The Transits come at midnight. His team sit in the back. They drink. Listen to music: Under Cover of the Night. *Loud. Deafening –*

Their Transit stops. The Mechanic and his team have their bags packed. Ready. Their tools. The paint. The Mechanic and his team go from street to street –

House to house. Scab to scab –

In the last street. The last house. The last scab. They tip paint over the scab's dog. Put the empty cans through his windows. The lights go on –

The Mechanic and his men shout. They run –

The Transit picks them up.

In the back. They drink. Laugh. Listen to music: Breaking the Law –

The Transit stops. The Mechanic and his team have their bags. Their tools –

They do the padlocks. Do the chains. Bentley Brothers – Hauliers.

Through the yard. Tools out. The Mechanic and his men set about the trucks –

The windscreens. The brake pipes. The tyres –

Back to the Transit –

More drink. More laughs. More music: Smash It Up –

Transit stops. Bags. Tools. Padlocks. Chains. NCB Property.

Through the pit yard. Set about the offices. The windows. The doors. Anything –

They smash it up –

The Transit comes back for them as the sun rises. This tour finished.

The Transit drops the Mechanic near his mother's house.

He picks up the dogs. Heads home. He has a shower. A drink. He lies on the bed. Their bed. He switches on the news. Switches it off again. He gets up. Into the lounge –

He puts on a record. Sade. Turns it off again. He sits on the sofa in the dawn –

The curtains shut. His eyes wide open –

The money on the table. The Polaroid –

He knows she's hurting. Knows he is not there for her. Knows –

The Chairman was ready to meet. The Chairman was not. The President ready to meet. The President not. Preconditions. No preconditions. Set agendas. No set agendas –

The talks were on. The talks were off. The talks on. The talks off –

The talks on again.

Everyone went South with the President. Everyone but Terry –

Terry left to wait by the phone. To wait for the call. The word.

Terry did his homework. Two piles of big files on his desk. One pile of accounts. One pile of actions.

The phone rang. *Click-click.* It was the President. The President for Terry –

The talks were off again. The Chairman was a liar. Everyone was a liar –

Terry was to chair the morning meeting. The President hung up.

Terry gathered his files. His homework. He went upstairs –

They were waiting for him. They were waiting for news –

Terry had no news. No one told him anything –

So Terry told them things they already knew –

The Board in Derbyshire had sent out personal letters to every miner in the area but just sixty men had gone back; ten thousand still on strike. Lancashire had suspended one thousand members for crossing official picket lines. The President of Kent had been remanded in custody for nine days for breach of bail conditions.

Mike Sullivan raised his hand. Mike asked, 'Is it true a Nottinghamshire miner nailed himself to his own fucking floor in protest over the scabs at his pit?'

The phone rang. Nigel picked it up –

Click-click.

'Tell them we're in a meeting,' said Terry.

Everyone laughed. Everyone but Nigel. Nigel shook his head –

It was the President. The President for Terry –

The President wanted Terry. The President needed Terry –

Now. In London –

Terry dropped the phone. Dropped everything. Left Mike in charge –

In charge of everything.

Terry caught the first train down. First class –

It was a *big* day. The talks were scheduled to happen –

Huge. The Nottinghamshire High Court action was set to be heard too –

Terry took a taxi to the hotel. Through the revolving doors. Up the stairs –

Enormous. Terry knocked on the door. Terry walked into the hotel room. Everyone looked at Terry. Everyone but the President and Paul. Terry looked at Joan –

Joan shook her head. Joan whispered, 'Kent won't lift the picket of Hobart House. The President won't cross a picket line. The Board won't change the venue –

'The Prime Minister won't let them.'

Alice Keyes picked up the phone. *Click-click.* She put her hand over the phone. She said, 'President. It's Yorkshire.'

The President took the phone from her. He said, 'Comrade?'

Terry looked round the hotel room. People came in and people went out again. Took away cups and saucers. Brought in papers and files.

'They're liars,' shouted the President into the phone. 'Liars! Tell them, no way.'

The President hung up. The President gestured to Len Glover. Len came over. The President whispered in Len's ear. Len walked over to Paul. Len whispered to Paul. Paul nodded. Paul got up. Paul left the room.

Alice picked up the phone again. *Click-click.* Put her hand over the phone again. She said, 'President. It's Yorkshire again.'

The President took the phone back. He said, 'Comrade, I don't care if their whole bloody plant goes up. They're not having another single piece of coal from us. Not one. Not while they continue to ride roughshod over every agreement we come to.'

Joan picked up the other phone. *Click-click.* Joan said, 'President. Kent –'

The President put down one phone. He picked up the other. He said, 'Comrade?'

The dogs in the back of the car. The Mechanic takes the A1 down to Leeds. He pulls into the car park. He leaves the dogs in the back. He walks across to the transport café –

Paul Dixon is already here. The table facing the door and the car park.

The Mechanic sits down opposite Dixon.

'Nice work, Dave,' says Dixon. 'People are very pleased with you.'

The Mechanic says, 'Always nice to be appreciated, Sergeant.'

Paul Dixon puts an envelope on the table. He pushes it over to the Mechanic.

The Mechanic opens it. He smiles. 'Very nice to be appreciated, Sergeant.'

'Lot more where that came from,' says Dixon. 'Way things are going.'

The Mechanic smiles again. He says, 'Good. I need the money.'

'Not planning to retire to the sun again, I hope?' asks Dixon.

The Mechanic looks up from the envelope –

Paul Dixon is staring at him. The dogs barking in the car –

'No,' the Mechanic says. 'Home is where the heart is.'

Neil Fontaine lies in the dark with the curtains open. Neil Fontaine thinks about alchemy; the transmutation of base metal into gold –

He looks at his watch. He taps it. It is five-thirty in the morning –

The telephone rings.

Neil Fontaine picks it up. He listens –

'There's been an explosion. Major slip in one of the furnaces.'

Neil Fontaine hangs up. He looks at his watch again. Taps it. He makes two calls. Hangs up again. He takes his blazer from the wardrobe. Puts it on. He checks the windows. The corridor. He leaves the room –

Leaves Jennifer sleeping in his bed, the living and the dead.

He takes the stairs. Goes outside. He hails a cab to the garage. Gets the Mercedes. He drives to Claridge's. Picks up the Jew.

They head North. The fast lane. The Jew on the phone.

Neil Fontaine comes off the M1 at Junction 33. Heads down Sheffield Parkway. He goes round Poplar Way. Onto Orgreave Road. Down Highfield Lane –

They are here –

Orgreave.

They park. The Jew gets out of the Mercedes. His binoculars round his neck.

Neil Fontaine leads the Jew to a concrete-roofed bus shelter. Neil Fontaine helps the Jew up. They stand on top of the bus shelter. The Jew looks through his binoculars. The Jew sweeps the landscape. The Jew can see Catcliffe and Treeton. Handsworth and Orgreave. The Jew can see the cornfields and the slag heaps. The fences and the trees. The Jew can see the River Rother and the Sheffield–Retford railway. The roadways and the motorway –

The Jew can see a white Range Rover approaching.

Neil Fontaine helps the Jew down. They walk over to meet the Range Rover.

South Yorkshire Brass gets out. Handshakes. Smiles. Nods.

The Jew leads the way. They inspect the apron where the convoys will line up. They walk across the road to the old chemical factory. This is the base of their operations. Their command post. They climb dirty stairs up to the third floor. The ladder to the roof. They walk out into the sunlight. The Jew hands the Brass his binoculars –

The Brass surveys the scene. He lowers the binoculars. He bites his lip. He says, 'What if they succeed? If we can't keep the place open? Like Saltley?'

The Jew looks at the Brass. He asks, 'Do you want to be the next Derek Capper?'

The Brass shakes his head.

The Jew gestures at the empty fields. The Jew points at the road. The Jew says, 'Look at this place. You can open it. You can close it. Your decision. Your discretion –

'Just make sure you have enough men –

'The right men, too. Real men. Hard men. Not dilettantes.'

The Brass nods. The Brass says, 'Thank you.'

'She is counting on you,' says the Jew. 'The nation is.'

The Brass shakes the Jew's hand. He hands back the binoculars. He leaves.

The Jew watches the white Range Rover through his binoculars. He lowers them. He is smiling. He is laughing. He turns to Neil –

'Well done,' says the Jew. 'Well done indeed, Neil.'

Here. He. Goes –

The Mechanic through the automatic doors. Hits the alarms. Chaos –

Up the supermarket aisles to the office. Through the office door –

The secretary stands up. 'No! Please God, no –'

Punch to the security guard. He goes down –

Slap for the secretary. Down and she's out –

Kick to the guard and he stays down –

The Mechanic drags the manager across his desk by his hair –

Puts his face to the safe and shouts, 'Open it!'

Manager hesitates. Hit with the handle of the pistol. The manager opens it –

The Mechanic kicks his legs from under him. Manager falls flat on his face –

'Stay that way,' the Mechanic tells him. 'And live.'

The Mechanic fills the bag. Just the cash. Takes the money and he runs –

Down supermarket aisles. Through automatic doors. The chaos and he's gone –

Just. Like. That.

There had been calls all night. There had been talks all night. There had been deals. Concessions. Favours. Kent lifted the picket. The word went out. The talks were back on. Calls were made. Plans. Strategies. Meetings about the meeting. Talks about the talks. Face to faces about the face to face. Everyone was here –

Everyone was going to be there –

The entire National Executive. Their entire staff. Fifty people.

The President addressed his troops. The President laid it out. The President said, 'Listen to them; let them have their say. Then they will listen to us; let us have our say. But there can be no negotiation. Because there can be no closures. No redundancies –

'So there is nothing to negotiate. Nothing!'

Everyone cheered. Everyone applauded. Everyone followed the President –

Ten cabs to Hobart House.

Terry paid the drivers, all ten of them.

They pushed through the press. They went inside. Straight upstairs –

The Mausoleum.

Room 16, Hobart House, Victoria:

Bright lights, smoke and mirrors –

The orange anti-terrorist curtains still drawn. The matching carpet and the wall-length mirrors. The tables round the edge of the room. In the middle –

No man's land.

The Board at the top end; everyone else down at the bottom –

Seventy people –

Sixty-eight people sat in silence as they listened to the Chairman –

To the Chairman tell them that everyone agreed it was the Board's job to manage. Tell them that everyone agreed the Union had no plans to interfere in that job. That everyone agreed on how much coal had to be produced. Everyone agreed they could not continue to lose money. Agreed pits had to close for reasons of safety. Had to close for reasons of exhaustion. That everyone agreed pits had closed for reasons other than safety or exhaustion in the past –

That pits always had done. That pits always would.

Sixty-nine people sat in silence as they watched the President take his fingers from his ears and shake his head –

Sixty-nine people listen to the President tell the Chairman that pits had always closed for reasons of safety. That pits had always closed for reasons of exhaustion –

Always had. Always would –

But pits had never closed for reasons other than safety or exhaustion –

Never had. Never would –

Not Polmaise. Not Snowdon. Not Herrington. Not Bullcliffe Wood – Not Cortonwood. Never –

Ever. Ever. Ever –

'Does everyone agree on that?' the President asked the Chairman.

The Chairman stood up. The Chairman said, 'No comment.'

It is a war of nerves. There have been casualties. Prisoners taken. Hostages to be freed –

The dogs in the garden. The Mechanic opens the door. He goes into the lounge –

He has company.

Neil Fontaine is sat on the sofa in the dark with a brandy. Sade on low – A Polaroid on the glass table.

Neil lights a cigarette. Inhales. Exhales. Neil holds up two fingers –

'Fuck you,' the Mechanic shouts. 'Fuck you. Fuck you. Fuck you.'

'Finished?' asks Neil.

The Mechanic shakes his head. 'I haven't got her fucking diary.'

'You haven't looked, David,' says Neil. 'You haven't even fucking looked.'

'I don't know where to fucking look and neither do you.'

'Girl could be forgiven for thinking you don't love her. Not like you say you do –'

'Fuck you,' the Mechanic screams. 'Fuck you! Fuck you! Fuck you!'

Neil finishes his drink. Neil stubs out his cigarette. Neil stands up.

'Where are you going?' the Mechanic says. 'I want her fucking back!'

'You don't have the diary,' says Neil. 'You won't help me. I can't help you.'

'I don't know anything about the fucking diary!'

'Just a question of silence, then,' says Neil. 'Yours? Or hers?'

The Mechanic picks up his holdall. He puts it on the glass table. Opens it –

'What's in there?' asks Neil. 'Your heart?'

The Mechanic shakes his head. 'Twenty-five thousand pounds in cash.'

'David, David, David,' says Neil. 'Would it were so simple –'

'I love her,' the Mechanic says. 'Never say I don't, Neil. She's mine now –'

'It's not my decision,' says Neil. 'Not my choice.'

It is a war of nerves. There have been casualties. There will be reparations. Ransoms to be paid –

A price.

ones. Stones coming over. Lads getting hit. Folk shouting to pack it in with stones. I pull my T-shirt over my head, like that's going to fucking help. I get swept right down to front. Then carried back again – Like a fucking horrible sea. Helmets flying up. Truncheons. Sticks. Stones. Broken bones. Blokes go down. Boots all over them. Then lorries are in and everyone falls back. I start to walk away. To look for Keith or John. Everyone else making their way off road when – Shit. Fucking horses charge – I head for wood. They won't follow us in here, I think. They fucking do. Wood's only about fifty bloody metre wide and all. I come out other side and there's a wall of a thousand fucking coppers with their truncheons out – Fuck me. I turn back – Horses still coming. I try to get up a tree. They're swinging with their batons. Hitting anyone they can get. I jump down. Run. Horses still coming. Bastards on foot with shields and truncheons behind them. Batons drawn and ready. I come out other side of long grass. Brambles. I'm at embankment. I jump down. Land badly. My ankle fucking kills. End up on railway. Bloke tearing down line towards us – Shit. Train's fucking coming – I scramble off line. Look up banking. Hundred fucking coppers banging their shields. Beckoning for us to come back up and have a go – Cunts. Fucking cunts – Train goes past. I cross line. Head up other way. Get to Rotherham Road. Lot of lads here – Split heads. Cracked ribs. Broken limbs. Bloody – Mates nicked. Beaten. Lost. Everyone fucking angry. Fucking furious. Things bastards have done to them. Completely unprovoked. Lads you've never met before telling you to get back down there. Give them what they're fucking asking for. Fucking hiding they've got coming – To pick up bricks. Fence poles. Milk bottles. To make a trap – Few blokes get some wire and string it between these telegraph poles. They come up to where I am. Tell us to go down lane. Throw stones at bastard pigs. Then leg it back up here. I go down with about fifty or sixty other blokes I don't know from Adam. I stand there in front of shields. Truncheons. I throw stones.

Ranks break. Out come horses again. Eight of them – We run. Fucking run – Wire gets one of riders. Bang! Down he goes – Hard. Onto road – Everyone turns back. Hundred lads heading down on him – Hundred of their lot coming back up for him. I can see his fucking face beneath his visor – White in terror. Thought of his own death. Here on this road. In this place – And I wish him dead. I do. I wish him and all his kind dead. Every last bloody one of them. Dead – But he gets up. He runs. He gets away. Escapes – I watch him get up. I watch him run. I watch him get away. Escape – Taste of salt in his mouth. Taste of salt in mine – Fear. Fucking fear – I spit. I spit and I spit. My stomach knotted – Lads have got a fucking Portakabin from somewhere now. Put a match to it – Smoke everywhere. Next news they've got one of telegraph poles – Running down hill towards police lines with it. Like a fucking battering-ram – Not enough of them though. Thing drops to ground – Starts to roll away. Police go for it – Get hold of it. Rest of them all banging on their fucking shields again – Applauding their mates as all lorries leave again. Loaded – **Day 87.** Orgreave. Fucking Orgreave. Here we go. Here we go. Here we go – Here I go down. Here I go under. Here I get lost – I get kiss of life and a fractured fucking skull. **Day 89.** They keep us in for observation. Daft bastard fell off a ladder, that's what Pete tells doctors. Fell off a ladder and down stairs. They send us home after twenty-four hours. Bag of bandages. Load of pills. Plenty of rest. Doctor's orders – Rest. Sleep. Rest. Sleep – I lie here in our big bed. In our room. Our house. I lie here and I watch shadows on our ceiling. On our walls. Our bedroom door – It's been three months. Three fucking months – Lifted. Threatened. Beaten. Hospitalized. Broke in every fucking sense – I lie here and I listen to rain on our windows. To her tears – I turn over. I look at her – Her hopes. Her fears – All our hopes. All our fears – I close my eyes. Tight – *Under the ground, we brood. We hwisprian. We onscillan. Under the ground, we scream* – I open my eyes. Wide – She's not finished with us. Not finished with any of us.

The Thirteenth Week

Monday 28 May – Sunday 3 June 1984

These were bad days. The deliberate and inevitable failure of the talks. The predictable and inevitable success of the Board and their stooges in the High Court –

The High Court had overruled the President. The Court had overruled the NEC. The Court had instructed the Nottinghamshire Area to hold their Union elections now. The Court had upheld the Nottinghamshire miners' right to work. The Court had ruled there was no basis to call the strike in Nottingham official –

Bad days, worse weeks –

The Court also held the Union liable for all costs from the Pension Fund case. Terry had not mentioned this to the President. Terry was waiting for the right moment –

Now was not the time –

The Board had just called the President on the phone. *Click-click.* Their Deputy Director of Industrial Relations. He'd gone on about the Queen Mary furnace at Scunthorpe –

The threat to life. The threat to limb.

He'd begged the President for more tonnage out of Orgreave. He'd pleaded with the President to help them relieve this potential pressure point –

The President put down the phone. He stared at the faces round the table in the Conference Room. He repeated the Deputy Director's last three words –

'Potential pressure point.'

The President smiled. Everybody smiled. He nodded. Everybody nodded –

The President turned to Alice and Joan. He said, 'Get me Barnsley.'

Neil Fontaine stands on the dock in the rain. He looks through the showers at the ships and the lorries. He watches the ships unload. The foreign words on their sides. The foreign flags on their masts. The foreign seamen on their decks. He watches the lorries load up.

The stickers across their sides. The grilles on their windscreens. The drivers in their motorcycle helmets.

Neil Fontaine leaves Humberside and Lincolnshire. He drives in circles through the lawless Yorkshire borderlands with Nottinghamshire and Derbyshire. The back roads. He passes the reserves parked up in their buses and their vans –

Suddenly Neil Fontaine brakes hard. He swerves across two lanes. Lands in the lay-by –

Roundheads lead their horses across the road. Bloody. They are beaten. In retreat. The steam rises from the backs of their horses to meet the rain. To wash away the battle.

Neil Fontaine blinks. He starts the car. He pulls out of the lay-by. Back to Orgreave –

Neil Fontaine has orders for the South Yorkshire Brass on the passenger seat. Signed orders from her. Sealed by the Jew. To be hand-delivered –

Mass arrests. Serious charges. Restrictive bail conditions –

This is what she wants. This is what she'll get –

She always gets what she wants.

Neil Fontaine stands on the roof in the rain. He looks through his brand-new binoculars at the allied forces. He watches the horseboxes unload 32 police horses; the Transits unload 2200 officers in 96 PSUs. He looks through his brand-new binoculars at the enemy hordes. He watches the President of the National Union of Mineworkers. He watches him walk alone down the hill –

The grey trousers. The black anorak. The navy baseball cap. The rain in his face –

Neil Fontaine has him in his sights.

The scabs had won their right to scab. Official. Legal. But no one seemed to care. Notice. Only Terry. The focus had switched. *Orgreave.* Everything was Orgreave now. Everything had to be done to close Orgreave. It would be the Saltley Gate of this dispute. The turning point. It was a matter of pride. Three miles from the Union's headquarters. On their own doorstep. Matter of history. The Orgreave coke supplied Anchor. *Anchor.* The steel complex at Scunthorpe which had been the scene of the Little Saltley of 1974. The President reminded everyone it was his success here in 1974 that had brought down Heath and the Tories. It was a matter of destiny –

His destiny –

The President had done it once. The President would do it again –

This time he would do it alone. This time he had no choice.

The ISTC at Rotherham had refused to black the Orgreave coke.

The President ranted. The President raved –

The President couldn't tell the difference between union and management –

Management and government –

Government and police –

Police and –

Terry looked up from his calculator. Paul Hargreaves was staring at him again.

Must not sleep. The days of the week are seven pits. Fifty days without her.
Fifty nights. Routine now. This loss. These minutes. These hours. These
days –

The telephone is ringing –

Fifty days. Fifty nights. Must not sleep. Seven pits –

The Mechanic answers the phone.

They pick him up at Scotch Corner. Black Transit. Four in the back.

They give him a donkey jacket. Stickers. Badges. A sports bag –

Smoke-bombs. Fire-crackers. Thunder-flashes –

Ball-bearings.

They drive him down to Sheffield. They drop him in a suburb called
Handsworth.

He walks up Handsworth Road. Police everywhere.

There are a couple of Union men stood about in stickers and badges with
a clipboard and a loud-hailer. They call him over. They ask him, 'Where you
from?'

'Selby,' he tells them.

They say, 'Straight up road. Mind yourself now. Pigs are dishing it out.'

The Mechanic nods. He heads up the road –

Disappears from view. Disappears into the war –

Man can lose himself in a war. Man can disappear –

Bide his time. Lie low. Pick his moment. To advance or to retreat –

The decision his. The choice –

Lucky man, lost.

The President was black from the battle. He sat at the end of the table.

Maps before him. There had been over 2000 pickets; 84 arrests; 69 in hospital; 1000 tonnes moved.

Paul was in his suit. Terry in his suit. Mike in his.

Joan put a cup of tea down on the table next to the maps. The President was writing notes on scraps of paper. Putting the scraps in envelopes. Putting the envelopes in his pocket. He spoke as he wrote. Spoke about Saltley and Grunwick. Mao Zedong and Che Guevara. Chile and Bolivia –

Spoke of the thousands that would come tomorrow.

'The Board want to talk,' whispered Paul in his ear. 'Talk concessions.'

The President looked up. He nodded. He smiled. He said, 'I bet they bloody do.'

'What do I tell them?' asked Paul.

The President put his baseball cap back on. He said, 'Tell them we'll be there.'

Paul picked up his papers. Paul left the room.

The President stood up.

Len said, 'They'll arrest you if you go back there.'

The President adjusted his baseball cap. The President nodded.

Len asked, 'Will you go easy then, or do you go hard?'

'Hard,' said the President.

Neil Fontaine stands outside the door to the Jew's suite on the fourth floor of Claridge's. He listens to the telephones ring and the laughter rise inside. The corks pop and the glasses chink. The bottles break. He waits for them to stagger out. To stick twenty-pound notes in the top pocket of his blazer. Run hands through his hair and pat him on the back. Neil Fontaine stands outside the Jew's suite on the fourth floor of Claridge's and misses how the angels sing –

The lighting of the corridor. The shadow on the wall –

His wings –

Neil Fontaine stands outside the Jew's suite. He listens to the devils –

Inside.

Monk Fryston, North Yorkshire. Terry and Paul sat in the hotel lobby and waited. Tommy from the Board tried to make small talk. Did they want a quick game of pool to kill the time? A game of pool in a posh hotel while their members were being beaten. Their members were being nicked. Their members were being charged –

Their President lifted. Their President arrested –

Their President jailed.

Terry and Paul shook their heads. They looked at their watches –

Everyone had had enough.

The police had had enough; the police wanted the Board to go back to court –

For injunctions.

The Board had had enough; the Board wanted to talk conciliation –

Concessions.

Everyone had had enough. Everyone except the President –

They were on the verge of the greatest industrial success in post-war Britain!

The President and the Prime Minister –

Insatiable, thought Terry. The pair of them. Terry looked at his watch again –

The President had been bailed. Len and Dick gone to pick him up –

Len and Dick to drive him straight here. Then the talks could restart.

Paul got up. He went to use the telephone.

Terry looked at Tommy. Tommy winked. Terry looked away, out of the window –

The President's car was coming up the drive.

Terry stood up. Terry went out to the hotel steps. Tommy followed him.

The President got out of the car. He looked up at Terry. He looked up at Tommy –

The President put his wrists together. He held them up in invisible cuffs –

He said, 'Great Britain – 1984.'

PART II

Two tribes

June – August 1984

The Panel, Silverwood – I was a delegate from Thurcroft Strike Committee; delegate took his orders from South Yorkshire Panel at Silverwood; South Yorkshire Panel took its orders from Yorkshire Area Strike Co-ordinating Committee at Barnsley, along with other three Yorkshire panels; Strike Co-ordinating Committee took its orders from National Co-ordinating Committee in Sheffield. In theory – Fat fucking chance. It was a bloody mess – Fuck him, shouted Johnny. It's a waste of time and manpower – Johnny, Johnny, said Derek. He's President of bloody Union – I don't give a shit if he's Queen of fucking Sheba. He's wrong – Unity is strength, Comrade. Unity is strength – Aye, Johnny nodded. And blind bloody loyalty is sheer fucking stupidity. Lads in Notts are under more pressure than us. That's where we should fucking be. Even if we did close Orgreave, wouldn't mean anything. We won't win without Nottingham. We can't – Johnny, Johnny – Nottinghamshire and power stations. That's where we should be. Not hitting same place every bloody day. Just plain daft, that. Banging your head against a brick bloody wall. Surprise them. One day here. One day not. Keep them guessing. Not us, though. Like an open fucking book, us lot. Derek turned to me. Derek said, You tell him. Make him see sense, Pete – But I had my fingers in my ears. My eyes closed – I'd had world on my back for thirty years. Thirty years I'd carried it. We all had – That was what we did. We were miners – Not pickets. Not thugs. Not hooligans. Not criminals – *We were miners. The National Union of Mineworkers* – Trade unionists and miners. Thirty years I'd carried it, but I'd carry it no more – Not for likes of MacGregor. Not for likes of Thatcher – It was time to put it down. Put it down and stand – In lines. Under sky – Black and blue. Shoulder to shoulder – But I'd come down to Panel each day for one. I'd sit in this hall and listen to them argue toss about this pit or that – Power stations or depots. Wharves or offices – I'd get our envelope. Our orders – Be back at **Welfare** for five at best. Never less than fifteen folk waiting for a word – I'd try to sort them out.

Do what I could – Then I'd open envelope. Orders – Work out cars. Minibuses. Vans. Ring round. *Click-click.* Have drivers in for eight. Tell them who was in with who and have them meet us all back at Welfare for two in morning. Give out instructions. Maps. Petrol money. Quid for going. Send them on their way – Young lads, most of them. Send them on their way to places they'd never been until three month ago. Places where they'd stand about without direction – Without guidance. Leadership – Send them on their way to get beaten or nicked. *Krk-krk.* Or bored to death – Same with afters. Same with nights – Then back I'd go again next day and Barnsley SCC would sit there and ask Panel why more weren't out picketing and **Silverwood Panel** would come back and ask us delegates why more weren't out picketing and Thurcroft delegate would tell them why more weren't out picketing – Because they got nicked. *Krk-krk.* Because they got beaten. *Krk-krk.* Because they'd got no leadership. Because they'd got no money. No strike pay. No nothing – So they were working other jobs to feed their wives and kids. Why fuck did they think more weren't out picketing? Pete, Pete – Don't Pete, Pete me, I told them. I had one of mine knocked unconscious last Friday at Orgreave. Mate of mine called Martin Daly. He was purple in face. Fucking couldn't find a pulse. Eyes in top of his head. Thought he was dead. This fucking copper hadn't given him kiss of life, he might be. Three times he give him it. This same copper tells me not to take him to hospital in Sheffield or Rotherham because he'll be nicked. Had to drive him all way up to Donny. Kept him in overnight. I went round his house to see him couple of days ago. His wife stands at door with pan of boiling fucking water – That's what she thinks of us. This bloody Union. This fucking strike – I got my jacket. I stormed out – Back again next day like. Every day – **Panel.** Lads had been going back into Nottinghamshire all week. Some of them staying over a couple of nights. Been going well – Yorkshire Gala on Saturday and Sunday – but it was all

The Fourteenth Week

Monday 4 – Sunday 10 June 1984

Neil Fontaine pulls out into the traffic. Claridge's to Downing Street. The sky is grey. Sirens wail. Armed police stand on every corner –

Ronnie's riding into town.

The Jew is in the back. *In the saddle.* The Jew is ranting –

'They think they're winning,' he shouts. 'They actually think they're winning.'

The Jew waves newspapers around the backseat –

'And these clowns believe them,' he laughs. 'They actually believe them.'

The Jew throws his head back. Puts his hands through his hair –

'So will the bloody Board,' he moans. 'And so will half the fucking Cabinet.'

Neil Fontaine stops at the end of Downing Street.

The Jew sighs. He reaches for his aviator sunglasses and a large white umbrella. He takes a deep breath. He is here to set the record straight –

'Wish me luck, Neil,' he says.

'Good luck, sir.'

Neil Fontaine watches the Jew disappear into Downing Street –

The War Cabinet.

He looks at the clock in the dashboard. He starts the Mercedes –

He takes a deep breath of his own. He has his own records to set straight.

Jerry and Roger are side by side in the dining room of the Special Services Club. They are looking at christening photographs.

Neil Fontaine sits down. He glances at the photographs. He recognizes faces –

Famous faces in private places.

Roger puts the photos in an envelope. He licks it shut. He looks up at Neil.

Jerry drums his fingers on the white linen tablecloth. Jerry leans forward. He says, 'It isn't getting any less complicated, is it, Neil?'

Neil Fontaine doesn't say anything. Neil Fontaine waits.

Jerry leans back –

Roger leans forward. Roger places his hands on the table. Roger stares up at Neil. 'Unfortunately,' he says, 'despite all your protestations, Jerry and I still do not share your conviction that our friends failed to find anything.'

Neil Fontaine waits.

'However,' says Jerry, 'it would appear the panic upstairs has abated. A touch.'

'A touch,' repeats Roger. 'For now.'

Neil Fontaine waits.

Jerry watches Neil Fontaine's face. He drums his fingers on the tablecloth again. He says, 'Roger and I feel now would be a good time to draw a line under certain . . .'

'People,' says Roger.

Neil Fontaine waits.

Jerry says, 'No more loose ends, Neil. Please?'

'Present company excepted, of course,' adds Roger.

Neil Fontaine stares back across the tablecloth into their eyes –

Their endless lying, lidless fucking eyes –

Neil Fontaine smiles at Jerry and Roger. Neil Fontaine says, 'Of course.'

Jerry says, 'Roger and I do feel the Mechanic has served his purpose.'

'Dixon is not going to be very happy,' adds Roger. 'We know that.'

Neil Fontaine shrugs. Neil Fontaine says, 'The policeman's lot.'

Jerry laughs. He lifts up his napkin. He pushes an envelope across the tablecloth –

Roger puts a hand on it. He stops it. He taps it –

'Both of them,' he says. 'Hand in hand into one last sunset.'

Neil Fontaine nods.

'Both of them,' Roger repeats. 'No loose ends, Neil.'

Neil Fontaine nods again. He picks up the envelope. He stands up. He stops now –

'Aren't we all forgetting someone?' he asks.

Jerry raises a hand. He makes a hook. He says, 'Leave the Tinkerbell to us.'

'Jerry and I are very fond of our fairy friends,' adds Roger, with a wink.

Neil Fontaine stares back at them. Neil says, 'He can hear things.'

'We know that,' laughs Jerry. 'It's his bloody job, Neil. Why we hired him.'

Neil Fontaine smiles. Neil Fontaine bows. Neil Fontaine leaves them to it –

He gets the car. He looks at the clock. He leaves for Downing Street –

The War Cabinet dissolves –

Neil Fontaine holds open the door.

The Jew gets in the back. The Jew shakes his head.

Neil Fontaine sits behind the steering wheel. He looks into the rearview mirror –

Muscles strain. Leather. Teeth snarl. Chains –

'Call off the dogs,' says the Jew. 'Call off the dogs, Neil.'

Malcolm Morris drank instant coffee. Malcolm Morris smoked duty-free cigarettes –

Malcolm Morris watched and Malcolm Morris listened –

'– pick us up by Asda. What he said. But did he? Did he heck as like –'

Every minute. Every hour. Every day. Every week. Every month –

Malcolm Morris went to his office. Malcolm Morris worked at his desk –

On the fourth floor opposite NUM Headquarters, St James's House, Sheffield –

'– scab on her knee was as big as a plate, it was. Should have heard her –'

Every minute. Every hour. Every day. Every week –

The lenses leered. Smile. The tapes turned –

Cameras clicked and recorders recorded –

'– I tell you, Rita. I see more of him on telly than in our own home –'

Every minute. Every hour. Every day –

The shadows on the screens. Smile. The whispers in the wires –

The stake-outs and the phone-taps –

'– Orgreave, they reckon. Big push again, Bomber said. Boots on –'

Every minute. Every hour –

'– thinks he must have been Special Branch. Paint-stripper. Lot of it and all –'

Every minute –

Every single minute of every single hour of every single day of every single week on the taxpayer's clock –

Operation Vengeance.

*

Skull. Candle. Clock. Mirror. Neil Fontaine moves across the floor. Carpet. Towels. Sheets. Starlight across the wallpaper. Curtains. Fixtures. Fittings. Shadow across bone. Hands. Hair. Boots across the room. Building. Town. Country –

She doesn't move.

Neil Fontaine sits in the dark with one curtain open. He thinks about legerdemain; the sleights of hand and the juggling –

He looks at his watch. He taps it. It is two in the morning –

Today the Jew will get his reward. The Prime Minister has promised.

Today the Jew will meet the President of the United States of America –

The Prime Minister has promised. This will be his reward –

The London Economic Summit. The D-Day celebrations –

With the world watching –

The Prime Minister has promised (and she always keeps her promises).

The telephone rings –

Neil Fontaine gets up. He picks up the phone. He listens. He hangs up –

Jennifer sits up in the bed. Jennifer says, 'Forgive me, Neil. Take me back. Kill him –'

Skull. Candle. Clock. Mirror. Neil Fontaine moves across the floor to the bed. Carpet. Towels. Sheets. Light across the wallpaper. He holds her. Curtains. Fixtures. Fittings. Shadows across their bones. He kisses her. Hands. Hair. Loves her –

There are always moments like this.

He dresses. He leaves. He takes the fast lane North –

He has his other promises to keep. Orders to give. Instructions. Hand-delivered –

Now is not the time, the day or the hour –

The world watching.

But the time, the day and the hour will come –

The world not watching.

Neil Fontaine comes off the motorway at half-past seven. He parks the Mercedes. He walks through the gathering pickets to the old chemical factory. He goes through the police lines into the command post. He has his binoculars. The envelope.

The South Yorkshire Brass looks up. He says, 'Christ, what now?'

Neil Fontaine smiles. He hands him the envelope –

The Brass opens it. He takes out the letter. He reads it. He shakes his head –

'Patience,' says Neil Fontaine. 'Patience.'

Neil Fontaine leaves him to it. He goes up to the roof. He raises the binoculars. He sees the horse-boxes. The kennels. The Transits. The PSUs –

He hears the hooves. The barking. The tyres. The boots –

Fresh from Creswell.

Radios crackle. Signals are given. Arms linked –

Ready.

The pickets move down the road to the field –

The lorries are coming.

Neil Fontaine watches them speed along the top road. Watches the pickets push. The police line hold. The lorries inside.

Neil Fontaine puts down the binoculars. He turns to leave –

'*We'll support you. We'll support you. We'll support you ever more (ever more) –*'

Neil Fontaine raises the binoculars again –

'*We'll. Support. You. E-ver. More!*'

The President of the National Union of Mineworkers is coming down the road. Grey trousers. Black anorak. Baseball cap –

Neil Fontaine has him in his sights again.

All the President's men clap. They cheer –

Salute their Communist Caesar.

Neil Fontaine smiles –

For those about to die.

Diane got out of bed. Diane found her knickers in the sheets. Diane put them back on. Her bra. Her tights. Her petticoat. Her blouse. Her skirt. Her jacket.

Terry sat up. He looked at his watch. He had an hour before the train to London. Theresa and the kids thought he was already there. Gone down last night. For the march –

The first major Commons debate. The lobby of Parliament –

The Home Match with the Met.

Terry had booked the coaches. Made the arrangements. Paid the prices –

London. Wakefield. Orgreave.

'That's all he thinks I'm good for,' Terry said. 'Booking bloody buses.'

Diane came back over to the bed. She sat down on the edge. She kissed his cheek.

Terry said, 'When will I see you again?'

Diane put her hand beneath the sheet. She held his cock. She smiled.

Terry lay back. He closed his eyes. He said, 'When?'

Diane went under the covers. She kissed his cock. She sucked it.

Terry said, 'I've got a lot of money, you know? We could just –'

She reached up. She put her finger to his lips.

The Jew calls Neil Fontaine at the Victoria Hotel again. It is the very middle of the night. The Jew is lonely. The Jew is bored. The Jew is depressed. The Jew is drunk –

He has been mixing his drinks; equal parts bravado and dread.

The Jew boasts about the success of the Derbyshire High Court action. Brags that the Nottinghamshire elections will rout the Militants –

Bravado.

But the Jew worries that it will all have been in vain. Fears the Board and the Wets will seek to use the Employment Acts –

Dread.

The Jew tells Neil Fontaine the Board are due to meet the Union again. Today. This time in Edinburgh. As far away as they can get. The Jew knows he's been cut out. After all he's done. The Jew senses a cave-in. A climb-down –

Beer and sandwiches at Number 10.

The Jew talks about Cabinet leaks. Talks about Wets. He says they are scared. Scared by the sight of ten thousand miners marching through the streets of London –

By the headlines in the *Daily* fucking *Mirror* –

The leaks about government intervention in the railway pay dispute.

They will betray her. These neophytes. These proselytes.

But the Jew is ready –

Ready to defend her. To save her. To send her victorious –

Victorious.

The Jew wants Neil back down in London –

ASAP.

Neil Fontaine opens his eyes. He tells the Jew he'll see him on Monday. Not before.

The Jew sulks.

Neil asks the Jew about the President of the United States. The Summit. D-Day.

The Jew gushes. Neil Fontaine yawns –

He hangs up on the Jew. He checks out. He gets the car. He goes for a drive –

A job to do.

Neil Fontaine turns into the car park of the café. David Johnson is already here. Two big dogs in the back of his car.

Neil Fontaine signals for him to follow.

David Johnson starts his car. The dogs in the back –

The two cars head South.

Neil Fontaine winds down the window. Puts on the radio –

Ronnie goes home; the GLC Jobs Festival; England beating Brazil in Rio.

Neil Fontaine switches off the radio. Winds up the window –

Two cars. South.

Junction 14. Newport Pagnell. Milton Keynes –

Two cars.

Slip-roads. Side-roads. Back roads –

A cul-de-sac.

Nice houses. Detached houses. Barratt houses –

Safe houses for the unsafe.

Neil Fontaine parks in the drive. David Johnson parks on the road. Neil Fontaine gets out. He locks his door. David Johnson gets out. Locks his –

The dogs in the back –

David Johnson follows Neil Fontaine up the drive. He follows him inside –

They stand in the hall. The holdalls in their hands. The handguns in their belts.

The air smells old. The codes for Belfast and Derry are written above the phone.

David Johnson says, 'Where is she? Where's Jen?'

Neil Fontaine swallows. Neil Fontaine closes his eyes –

There are skulls. Mountains of skulls. There are candles. Boxes of candles –

'Your silence? Or hers?' asks Neil Fontaine. 'It's your choice, David.'

about collapse of talks now. Looked like it'd go all way to winter – Thatcher on TV talking no surrender; Heathfield saying it was stalemate; Board wanting to hold its own bleeding ballot – That's why they'd scuppered talks, said Tom. Fucking planned it that way – They'll go back to High Court now, said Derek. Mark my words – Everyone nodded. Everyone knew – He's going to want one last push before they do, I said. Derek nodded. Derek said, Lads won't like it. But if he says go, they'll go – Last fucking time then, said Johnny. Last fucking time I go there – Everyone nodded again. But everyone knew – National Executive were in session in Sheffield. They were set to end all dispensations – No secret meetings. No secret deals. No sell-out – Not that we gave a shit; we ran South bloody Yorkshire. No one else, Johnny was shouting over chat. And that goes for more than just steel – Everyone nodded. But everyone knew where we were going – **Orgreave**. I looked round Welfare. Lads knew what it was going to say before I even opened frigging envelope. There were sixty-odd of us. Every one of them nodding. Big Tom came in. He said, Few thousand already up Handsworth end. It's on radio. So off we set – Half-five. Didn't take us long to find out what was happening. Lads were waiting for us at fence. Thought they were CID because this one bloke had a walkie-talkie. *Krk-krk.* Keith and Sammy were ready to give him a thump. Turned out he was from Doncaster area. He got out his map. Got on his walkie-talkie. Idea was we were to occupy frigging plant – He didn't know how, like – But that was plan. Being local, we told him best way was to march ourselves round back of old tip and over top. Drop down right into plant. So that's what we did – Bloody look on faces of security guards and coppers that were there – Shit themselves. *Krk-krk.* Just this one bloke who fancied his chances. Said he was going to set his dog on us. We told him to piss off. But he only went and let dog loose, didn't he? Big one and all. Dog come running at us. This one lad Steve, one of ours – he just stuck up his foot. Kicked dog in head. Dog went down.

Dog was dead. Fucking killed it – Just like that. But we were in – Inside fucking plant – and for that one sweet bloody moment we were here and they were there – and we were winning. *Winning.* We had fucking plant. We were holding them on tip, too. Dust going up. Folk black as pitch. Bobbies head to toe in stuff. *Krk-krk.* Dawn coming up with it – Beautiful one it was, too. Right hot one – But that was end of it. No fucking clue what to do next. Doncaster lads went for pump house. All wagons that were there. Rest of them ready to go toe-to-toe with boys in fucking blue – but they'd fucked off to get their riot gear. *Krk-krk.* Back in a bit with big sticks and their kits – Bits of wood, all we had. Like waiting to get kicked and nicked – Big push or a few hundred more and we'd have had them. Had them bastards. No messing. Shut plant – Won day. Then and only then, like – But there was no support. No big push – No sense waiting to be clobbered or collared either. So we walked. Headed back up Treeton Lane onto Orgreave Road – First lorries coming off Parkway and past us as we went. I looked at my watch again: eight-fifteen – Massive roar. Big noise went up – First lorries were in. It had started again – Lads had heard they were using dogs to mop folk up. Stragglers left back in villages – Lads wanted to join main body up Handsworth end. It was where Our Arthur was – *Our Leader. Our King* – Safety in numbers. That's what they wanted – What police wanted, too. They marched us south down onto Highfield Lane – Police cordon across road. They broke to let us through. Told us to join thousands they'd penned in up at Handsworth end of lane – What a sight that was. Thousands of us – They'd laid on buses from all over: Kent, Notts, Wales, Durham, Newcastle, Scotland – Parked them up in centre of Sheffield. Then they'd all walked out to Orgreave – Thousands and thousands of us. Like Saltley Revisited – Everyone marching out here. Traffic at a standstill – Police were a sight themselves, mind. Thousands of them and all. Got their own buses, too – Fifteen different forces, they reckoned – Big black sea of

The Fifteenth Week

Monday 11 – Sunday 17 June 1984

Operation Vengeance. Imported from Ulster. Updated for Yorkshire.
Computer recording equipment activated by voice-imprint, the speaking of
selected words, the coincidence of individual listed or unlisted telephone
numbers, and the combinations of telephone numbers and/or area codes.
Recordings filed and cross-referenced with terminal surveillance records on
all employees of the National Union of Mineworkers, their families, friends
and known sympathizers. This included, but was not limited to, the home
phone numbers of all members of the National Union of Mineworkers; the
home and office phone numbers of the owners of all vehicles logged in note-
worthy circumstances *in the Yorkshire, Nottinghamshire and Derbyshire*
coalfields; all public telephones in the Yorkshire, Nottinghamshire and
Derbyshire coalfields. Information cross-referenced with data from the
Department of Health and Social Security, the Inland Revenue and the
Union, company and personal bank accounts of the above via two hundred
and fifty terminals nationwide. The movement of all persons and assets
could be further tracked by GCHQ Cheltenham in tandem with NSA C-
group network via the Morwenstow and Menwith Hill stations –
    Operation Vengeance. Imported from Ulster. Updated for Yorkshire –
    By Malcolm Morris –
    '– picked them until they bled –'
    Malcolm Gordon Morris, forty, government fairy –
    Tinkerbell.
    '– told her, leave them bloody scabs alone. Would she? Would she –'
    For the collection of words –
    The air full of them. Everywhere. Heard but not seen –
    Expressions. Assertions. Declarations. Statements. Utterances. Assever-
ations. Designations. Locutions. Affirmations. Pledges. Promises. Guarant-
ees. Assurances. Commitments. Reports. News. Information. Accounts.
Intelligence. Advice. Tidings. Greetings. Phrases. Secrets. Passwords.
Catchwords. Watchwords. Shibboleths. Signals. Calls. Signs. Counter-
signs. Codes. Commands. Orders. Announcements. Enunciation. Proclam-
ations. Pronouncements. Judgements. Rows. Polemics. Quarrels. Feuds.

Altercations. Contentions. Debates. Arguments. Shouts. Questions. Answers. Responses. Facts. Figures. Messages. Interactions. Interplay. Intercourse. Transmissions. Connections. Contacts. Intercommunications. Communications. Interchange. Notifications. Telling. Discussion. Articulation. Rhetoric. Vocalization. Dialogue. Discourse. Speech. Comment. Remark. Observation. Opinion. Critique. Wisecrack. Prattle. Conference. Confabulations. Chatter. Rumours. Gossip. Hearsay. Tattle. Scandal. Suggestions. Hints. Undertones. Murmurs. Grumbles. Mumbles. Whimpers. Lies. Cries. Whispers. Talk –

'– sent up the horses, brained us, knocked shit out of us, to disperse us, he said –'

Talk. All talk. Nothing but talk –

Language. The air full of it. Everywhere –

'– ruptured blood vessels in his chest which caused a massive accumulation of –'

Words and –

'– blood around his heart –'

Death.

Terry was out of the talks again. Terry took another aspirin. Fuck them –

One day in. The next day out. In. Out. In. Out. Piss Terry all about. Fuck them –

Fuck them. Fuck them. Fuck them –

It was a waste of petrol anyway. Terry knew that –

Terry had seen the so-called shopping list: the settlement of the pay dispute; early retirement; a shorter working week; extra holidays –

The President thought the Chairman was on the ropes. Terry didn't –

Terry had just finished reading the interview with the Chairman in today's *Times*. The Chairman had described the President as a *Dr Jekyll and Mr Hyde character*.

A waste of petrol. A waste of breath. Terry could read their minds –

The Board were winning the legal actions; they were getting men back in Derbyshire day by day; the scabs unseating the pro-strike delegates in the Nottinghamshire branch elections. The government were further cutting off benefits one by one; they were saying they had coal enough until the New Year –

Repeatedly.

A waste of petrol. A waste of breath. A waste of time. It was up to Terry –

Terry Winters would save the day. Terry packed his briefcase. His papers and his pens. His facts and his figures. He locked up his office. He checked the door –

Fuck them all.

There was a Denim in the lift. He said, 'Missed you on the march, Comrade.'

Terry put his finger to his lips. He whispered, 'Union business, Comrade.'

The Denim looked at Terry. The Denim raised his eyebrows.

Terry tapped the end of his nose. He winked at him (glad it wasn't a Tweed) –

Fuck him. Fuck them all.

Terry got his car. He drove out to Huddersfield Road. He'd left it too long –

Clive had kept phoning. Kept leaving messages. Never using the code.

Terry parked outside the headquarters of the Yorkshire NUM. Terry went inside. Terry went upstairs. Terry knocked on the door of the Yorkshire Area Finance Officer. Terry didn't wait. Terry went straight in –

Clive Cook looked up. Clive shook his head. He said, 'Fuck –'

Terry put his finger to his lips again. He said, 'Walls have ears, Comrade.'

Clive shook his head. He got his coat. He followed Terry down the stairs –

Clive and Terry went for a walk. They found a bench in the sun.

Clive said, 'Me and Gareth have been talking. We're worried . . .'

'What about?'

Clive sighed. He said, 'The money. What do you think we're worried about?'

'I don't know,' said Terry. 'The strike? The hardship? The legal issues . . .'

Clive said, 'People are beginning to ask questions.'

'And that's exactly why we've done what we've done,' said Terry.

Clive said, 'These are our own people asking the questions. Not just Bill Reed.'

'Let them ask.'

Clive held out his hands. Clive said, 'So what do we tell them?'

'You tell them to ask me,' said Terry. 'That's what you tell them.'

'The President knows what we're doing?' asked Clive. 'Supports us?'

Terry leant into his face. He said, 'Who got Bill Reed off your back, Comrade?'

'But who put him on my back in the first –'

Terry poked Clive in his chest. Terry said, 'Who? Who was it, Comrade?'

Clive Cook closed his eyes. Clive Cook nodded.

Terry stood up. Terry said, 'The battle hasn't even begun yet, Comrade.'

Clive opened his eyes. Clive looked up at Terry. Clive said nothing.

'They're laying traps,' said Terry. 'Setting out the bait. But I'm ready for them.'

Clive stood up now. Clive sighed. Clive said, 'I really fucking hope you are.'

'Trust me,' said Terry Winters, his hand on Clive Cook. 'Trust me, Comrade.'

Clive shook Terry off. Clive headed back to the office.

Terry watched him go. Terry banged his head against the trunk of a tree –

The stupid things he said.

Go, go, go, go, go –

'We are on target for more and more conflict.'

Edinburgh down to Sheffield. Sheffield out to Rotherham –

The Clifton Park Hotel, Rotherham –

Cole said, 'This is the place the press have been using for Orgreave.'

'Place is tidy, then?' Malcolm asked him.

Cole flicked through the notes on his lap. He said, 'Bar the Conference Suite.'

Fuck. Malcolm looked at his watch. He put his foot down –

Go, go, go, go –

Car park.

Go, go, go –

Reception. Register. Key. Twin room for one night.

Go, go –

Lift. Corridor. Door. Key. Door open. Room.

Go –

Bed stripped. Linen in the bath. Cases open. Floor plans out. Headphones on –

Malcolm looked at his watch.

Go. Door. Corridor. Keys out. Inside –

Malcolm looked at his watch.

Plant one. Plant two. Plant three. Plant four –

Grid one in place. Test signal to first receiver. Check –

Malcolm looked at his watch.

Plant five. Plant six. Plant seven. Plant eight –

Grid two in place. Test signal to second receiver. Check –

Malcolm looked at his watch.

Toilet –

Plant nine. Plant ten –

Ante-room –

Plant eleven. Plant twelve –

Grid three in place. Test signal to third receiver. Check –

Malcolm looked at his watch.

Outside. Corridor –

Plant thirteen. Plant fourteen. Plant fifteen. Plant sixteen –

Grid four in place. Test signal to fourth receiver. Check –

Malcolm looked at his watch.

Go out –

Out, out, out –

Past the Board and the Union in the corridor. Room service –

'I would not trust him if he told me the time of day.'

And Malcolm Morris was gone –

Back to their twin room. Cole with the cases open. Headphones on. Thumb up –

Tapes turning. Static. Recording –

The sounds of bags being unpacked. Chairs scraping. Voices:

'– just at the outset, that the train leaves at –'

'– kindly address all your questions to the President –'

Silence. Static –

Malcolm touched his headphones. Watched dials. Checked levels. Equipment –

For ten minutes. Static. Silence. Then:

'– our membership, we ask for the withdrawal of pit closures and job losses –'

'– nope.'

Chairs scraped. Bags packed. Doors opened. Slammed shut –

Static. Silence. Tapes ending –

Silence.

Cole looked at Malcolm. Malcolm looked at Cole. They shrugged their shoulders. Took off their headphones. Packed their bags –

Boxed tapes for drop boxes. Cole the cleaner for today. Malcolm off the clock –

He drove home. Radio off. Silence. He put the car in the garage. He went inside –

The house quiet, but not quiet enough.

Malcolm drew the curtains. He sat down on the sofa. He rolled two large pieces of cotton wool into two small balls. Placed them deep inside his ears. He wrapped his head in bandages. He closed his eyes –

Silence. Sleep. Dreamless sleep. Silent sleep –

Dull sleep. Dying sleep. Dying silence. Dull noise –

The telephone ringing –

Malcolm Morris opened his eyes. He unwrapped the bandages. Took out the cotton-wool balls.

He pressed buttons. Picked up the telephone –

'Late night?' *asked Roger Vaughan.*

Malcolm sat up. He double-checked –

The wheels were turning. Wheels within wheels. The tapes recording.

Malcolm said, 'Aren't they all?'

'We've got a shopping list for you.'

'How many?'

'Watches, not radios,' *said Roger.* 'Two, if you have them?'

'Presents, are they?'

'Birthday.'

'What colour wrapping-paper do you want?'

'Green.'

'For when?'

'As soon as you can.'

'I'll be in touch.'

'Good man,' *said Roger.* 'Jerry and I will be waiting.'

Malcolm hung up. He stopped the recording. Pressed rewind. Stop. Play –

He listened again. Pressed stop again. Rewind. Stop –

Malcolm took out the tape. He found a case and wrote on the tape and its box –

RVPSN/MM/150684.

He put it somewhere safe.

Malcolm looked at his watch. He looked at the alarm clock. They were both fast –

He washed and shaved. Dressed. Made two cups of instant coffee. He ate cereal. Toast and marmalade. He drank the other cup of coffee. He put on a tie. Picked up his briefcase. His car keys. He locked the house. Backed the car out of the garage. He locked the garage. Drove to work –

Harrogate to Sheffield.

He sat at his desk. He drank instant coffee. He smoked duty-free cigarettes –

And Malcolm Morris listened –

His hands over his ears. His headphones. Eyes closed. Head splitting –

Every minute of every hour of every day of every week of every month –

He heard it. Heard it coming. Coming near. Nearer and nearer. Now –

The traffic erupting. The dials turning. The levels rising. Deafening –

Noise.

Something was happening. Happening again. Happening near. Happening now –

The wheels turning. The tapes recording –

Death –

A Kellingley picket crushed to death by a lorry at Ferrybridge power station –

Silence.

The Jew has got his reward. The Jew has an office in Hobart House –

Full steam ahead with the legal actions. Individual legal actions. No more talks –

Except of victory.

Neil Fontaine carries the boxes up from the Mercedes. He sets them down on the office carpet –

Derbyshire. Lancashire. North Wales. Notts.

The Jew's secretary takes the files from the boxes. She puts them in the cabinets. Chloe is new. Black. Beautiful. She started today.

A man in an overall is unscrewing a name-plate from the door. It is old. Finished.

Men in suits pace the corridors. They scowl. They slam their office doors –

The Jew doesn't care. The Chairman doesn't care –

The Chairman is an American. From Glasgow.

The Jew wants to be an American, too. From Suffolk.

They get on like a house on fire, the Chairman and the Jew –

They love Capitalism and Opportunity. They hate Communism and Dependency. The Freedom of Cash versus the Slavery of Coin –

The United States of Free Enterprise.

The Jew spins round in his new leather chair –

A house on fire.

It will be dark when the Jew and Neil Fontaine begin the drive North –

The world asleep.

The Yorkshire Miners' Demonstration and Gala Day, Thornes Park, Wakefield –

In the Year of the Strike to Save Pits and Jobs.

Malcolm Morris marched from Wakefield city centre –

Behind the brass bands and the branch banners. The families and their friends. The kids with their stickers. Their mums in their T-shirts –

Women Against Pit Closures.

He followed the miners and the majorettes down to the park –

Sunshine and skin; beer tents and boxing rings; side-shows and singing. This year's Coal Queen contest had been cancelled. Just the fancy dress –

First prize to Dusty Bin (for putting scabs in); Maggie got fourth –

'– Out. Out. Out. Maggie. Maggie. Maggie. Out. Out. Out –'

There must have been a thousand plainclothes police and security personnel here. Everywhere Malcolm looked; wearing wires; talking into their collars and their cuffs –

Just like Malcolm –

Malcolm stood in the marquee. Pressing buttons. Making tapes. Recording –

The speech and the speeches; the speaking and the speakers.

'– a fight to the finish and it is not going to be a white flag – it is going to be a victory for the White Rose –'

Dennis. Ray. Jack. Hamlet without the Red Prince –

But Arthur would be here tomorrow –

Malcolm too. He moved on. Back to the post –

To sweat in a mobile on some industrial estate. PSUs playing cricket outside. Helmets for wickets. Truncheons for bats. Heads down. Out of sight –

134

Pit villages burning. Police stations stoned. Sieges and mass arrests in Maltby –

Payback. Playback. Payback. Playback –

Everything felt wrong. Bad –

Thunder. Heat. Static. Death. Noise. Ghosts –

Saltley. Orgreave. Saltley. Orgreave. Saltley. Orgreave. Saltley –

Worse coming –

Vengeance.

Head on his desk. Eyes closed. Headphones off. Fingers in his ears –

But the tapes didn't stop. Nor the dreams. The echoes –

Miners and their wives. Their kids. Their brass bands and their banners –

Their badges –

Victory to the Miners. Coal not Dole –

Surrounded by spies –

Spies like Malcolm.

Desk. Eyes. Phones. Ears. Tapes. Dreams. Echoes –

A miner and his wife. Their two sons. Their two placards –

I Support My Dad – Me Too.

Surrounded by spies –

Like Malcolm.

Fingers out. Eyes open. He was awake at his desk –

Malcolm stopped the tape. He pressed rewind. Pressed stop. Play –

The sound of sobbing –

Under the ground, the echo.

them. Riot shields up. Crash helmets on. Right across road and over two whole fields. Three double ranks. Six to seven yard apart. Four deep behind each shield. To left and right there were snatch squads. Further right still they'd got cavalry ready. To left were dogs. Helicopters above us. Reserves stretching back three hundred yard. More vans and buses parked up in lanes. They must have been bloody hot. Boiling. TV was here, too. Fucking couldn't keep away, could they? – None of us could. Everywhere you looked – You looked and you knew. Knew there was going to be a lot of bloody hurt today – It was now or never. Everyone knew that. Now or never – Lines had been drawn. Lion's mouth was open – Now or never. Bloke side of me said, Wish I'd wore me boots – Now: half-nine – Lorries coming back out. Loaded up. Police fucking drivers. Royal Corps of Transport. HGV licences still fucking wet – Saluting as they left. Two fingers – Us trapped right in middle of push. Meat in sandwich we were. Bloody truncheon meat – Fucking big push from lads now. T-shirts and skin hard against Perspex and leather – Jumpers round our waists. Faces against their shields – Truncheons coming over top of shields. Ribs and shins struck in the ruck. Ribs and shins – Fuck me. Bricks and sticks over top of us. Bricks and sticks – Fuck. It had started again all right. Fuck me it had – Black. Blue. Bloody. All the colours of war – Then police line gave. Ground moved – Like Doomsday. End of fucking world – Hooves tasted earth. The hooves bit. The hooves chewed. The hooves ate fucking earth – Here they came. Here they came. Here they came – Noise of it all. Boots and stones. Flesh and bones – There we went. There we went. There we went – Smell of it all. Earth and sweat. Grass and shit – Noise. Torn flesh and broken bones – Stink. Piss and puke. Shit – Taste as I hit ground. Salt. Dirt. Blood – I tried to stand. I tried to turn. I did stand. I did turn and CRACK – I saw stars not comets. CRACK – He'd felled me. This copper – *Listen to the voice*. Ground was hard – *The voice saying, Follow me.* Sun right

warm – *Follow me*. Lovely on my face – My father used to take us as a lad to many of fields from Roses and Civil Wars: Wake-field. Ferry Bridge. Towton. Seacroft Moor. Adwalton Moor. Marston Moor – Picnics in them fields. Flask of tea in car if weather was against us – Photograph of me somewhere, squinting by Towton memorial on a Palm Sunday. Snow on ground – He was dead now, was my father. Ten year back. I was glad he was, too. Not to see me in this field. Here – Orgreave. South Yorkshire. England. Today – Monday 18 June 1984. Sun on my face. Blood in my hair. Puke down my shirt. Piss on my trousers – I was glad he was dead. I closed my eyes. *Forgotten voices. A lost language. A code. Echoes* – Like funeral music. Drumming was. They beat them shields like they beat us. Like we were air. Like we weren't here – Here. Now – I opened my eyes. I tried to stand. To turn my head – Three coppers were carrying this other copper back. He was a young lad this one. Helmet off. His nose too. Looked like he'd stopped a brick. They passed me. They saw me – First one turned back. He swung his truncheon – I ducked down. Hands over my head – But he was gone. I picked myself up. Fast. Didn't know where I was really. I just started walking away. Through field from where all police were. Fast as I could. Then I heard them again – Them hooves. Them boots – I legged it. Ran for my bloody life. Mouth full of salt. Heart pounding ten to dozen – Thousands running with me. Jumping walls and fences. Like Grand National – That one white horse charging down on us. Bastard with his baton out again. Half lads over embankment. Down banking onto train line – I was lucky. Horses went back down hill. Left us be – I'd managed to get top-side of Highfield Lane. Like half-time up here – Most folk seemed to have headed up this way and on to village. But some had stripped off for sun. Bit of a lie down for a few minutes. Others had other ideas. Taken all bricks off walls ready. All way up road on both sides of lane. Talk was how Arthur had gotten a hiding. They said he'd walked police lines first thing. Told them what he

The Sixteenth Week

Monday 18 – Sunday 24 June 1984

Terry had sat with his office door open all Sunday night. He had watched them stagger back from the Wakefield Gala. A few of them had had to be carried in. They had stuck them in rooms where the President wouldn't look. He was still in Wakefield –

Rallying the troops.

Terry had kept the office door open all night. He had listened to them making their plans. Listened to them talk about the death of the picket at Ferrybridge. The siege of Maltby. The police reprisals. They were waiting for the President –

Their general.

'Comrade –'

Terry looked up. The President was stood in the doorway. He was wearing his baseball cap. Len and Joan were standing behind him. They were carrying maps. Plans –

Battle-plans.

'Comrade,' said the President, 'we're going to need more envelopes.'

Terry nodded. He opened his bottom drawer. He took out the requisition forms. He completed the order. He initialled the forms. He stood up. He walked over to the door. He handed them back to the President.

'Thank you, Comrade,' said the President and passed the order to Joan.

Terry watched the President walk away down the corridor –

To his tent and to his dreams.

Terry closed his office door. Terry had his own plans. His own dreams –

Soon it would be dawn: Monday 18 June 1984.

'Have you ever, ever, seen anything like this before, Neil?'

Neil Fontaine shakes his head. He never, never, has seen anything like this before:

The Third English Civil War.

Neil Fontaine closes his eyes. He never, never, wants to see anything like this again.

'Thank you, Brixton,' shouts the Jew. 'Thank you, Toxteth.'

Tell the world that you're winning –

The morning after the day before:

The miner was cowering. The miner was wearing just a pair of jeans and trainers. The miner had his shirt tied round his waist. His back to the car. His palms up –

The policeman had a shield and a helmet. The policeman had a baton.

The policeman hit the miner with his baton. Hit him –

Again. Again. Again. And again –

The TV showed the policeman hit the miner.

The President watched the TV. The President touched the back of his neck –

The President said, 'These bastards rushed in and this guy hit me on the back of the head with his shield and I was out.'

The President had spent the night in Rotherham District Hospital.

The police had cheered as he'd been taken to the ambulance.

The nation was outraged –

Not by the assault on the miner. Not by the assault on the President. No –

The TV had lied again. They had cut the film. They had stitched it back together –

Stitched up the Union with it –

Miners threw stones. Miners hurt horses. Miners rioted –

'*– the worst industrial violence since the war –*'

Police defended themselves. Police upheld the law. Police contained the riot –

That was it.

The lorries had emptied the place of coke. The miners had lost –

That was it.

Meanwhile, Nottingham had continued to produce coal. The power stations power.

'*The President of the National Union of Mineworkers slipped off the top of the bank and hit his head on a sleeper,' said the Assistant Chief Constable of South Yorkshire. 'He was not near a riot shield. The officers with the riot shields were on the road and he was off the road. They did not come within seven or eight yards of him.'*

The President was a liar. The President had lost –

That was it –

End of story. Finished.

The President switched off the TV. The President went upstairs.

The National Co-ordinating Committee was meeting in the Conference Room –

For the first time –

Today was the hundredth day of the Great Strike to Save Pits and Jobs.

Terry picked up the phone. *Click-click.* He had tears in his eyes. In his dreams –

Tell the world that you're winning –

The hundredth day.

Malcolm listened to the tapes. He played it all back. Listened to the tapes. To them pay it all back –

'If a highwayman holds you up, it is always possible to avoid violence by handing over to him what he wants.'

EVERY WOMAN'S GOT ONE –

'– shields up –'

[– *sound of body against Perspex shield* –]

'– breach of line at middle holding area. Request –'

BUT MARGARET THATCHER IS ONE –

'– heads –'

[– *sound of rock hitting Perspex shield* –]

'– field operatives be advised horses imminent –'

DE DEE DEE DEE –

'– take prisoners –'

[– *sound of police truncheon against body* –]

'– DSGs D and E to Main Gate –'

DE DEE DEE DEE.

'– bodies, not heads –'

[– *sound of police truncheon against body* –]

'– Zulus in retreat. MP 4 and 5 stand down –'

HERE WE GO –

'– can't throw stones if they've got broken arms –'

[– *sound of police truncheon against body* –]

'– target is wearing white T-shirt, blue jeans and distinctive hat –'

HERE WE GO –

'– on then, fucking hit him –'

[– *sound of police truncheon against body* –]

'– officers down at topside holding area. MP 6, please respond –'

HERE WE GO –

'– fuck off back where you come from –'

[– *sound of police truncheon against body* –]

'– prisoners to be restrained in vans until further notice –'

HERE WE –

'– Commie bastards are going to lose and so is that bald bastard Scargill –'

[– *sound of police truncheon against body* –]

'– exceptional DSG B. Exceptional. Drinks are on us –'

HERE –

'We are going down the royal road in this country that Northern Ireland went down in 1969.'

Malcolm listened to the tapes. He played it all back. The tapes never stopped. Listened to her –

The Union burying another one under the ground today –

Pay it all back (but she would never, never, never stop).

They were playing Shostakovich upstairs again. Loud again. The Seventh Symphony. *Leningrad.* Terry Winters had his head in his hands. There were now five separate legal actions:

Lancashire. North Wales. North Derbyshire. Nottinghamshire. Staffordshire.

The Tweeds knocked on his door –

Day and night they knocked –

'This is serious, Comrade,' they told him, day and night.

Terry agreed. Terry said, 'But everything is in its place.'

They left the door open –

The Denims in the corridor. Arms folded. Backs to the wall –

Day and night they watched Terry Winters –

It was not Leningrad. It was Stalingrad.

Terry slammed the door. He walked to the window, forehead against the glass –

How long has it been?

They had buried another yesterday. Terry had put on his best black funeral suit. Had told Theresa he was off to Pontefract. Told the President and the Tweeds he had to work out the implications of the legal actions against South Wales. Then he'd gone to Hallam Towers. He had taken off his best black funeral suit and fucked Diane in the Honeymoon Suite –

'They've left me with no choice,' he had told her. 'No choice at all.'

They had cut him out –

'Because I've never worked in a pit. Because my father wasn't a bloody miner. Because I've never been a Communist. Because my father was never a Communist. Because I'm not working class. Because I'm from the fucking South. It makes me laugh. It really does. Their talk about equality. Fraternity. Socialism. You can hardly breathe in the place. It's that snotty. Egotistical. Solitary –'

Diane had kissed his left ear. She had licked his ear. She had sucked it. She had bitten it. She had held it in her mouth. Then she had moved down his cheek to his mouth. She had kissed his bottom lip. She had licked his lip. She had sucked it. She had bitten it. She had held it in her mouth. Moved down his neck to his chest. She had kissed his left nipple. She had licked his nipple. She had sucked it. She had bitten it. She had held it in her mouth. Down his stomach to his cock –

'Looking for something down there, are you, Comrade?'

Terry opened his eyes. Terry turned from the window to the door –

Paul Hargreaves held out an envelope. He said, 'Happy reading, Comrade.'

Terry took the envelope. He opened it. He read the letter. Read the words –

YOUR FUTURE IS IN DANGER –

Terry looked up –

Paul had gone. He had left the door open again –

The Denims in the corridor. Arms folded. Backs against the wall –

The Shostakovich shaking the ceiling.

Terry put his head back against the glass. Terry closed his eyes again –

'They have left me with no choice,' he had told Diane again. 'No choice at all.'

thought of them – He'd marked their cards. They'd marked his – Put him in Rotherham Hospital. Beaten up Jack Taylor down Catcliffe end and all – Least lads had given ITN a good kicking. They'd get their revenge at 5.45 mind – Knew Mary and our Jackie would be watching. Knew it wasn't over yet, either – There were young lads wanting to get on with it. Lads on about making petrol bombs. Police had got guns, they said. Back of them vans. Be tear gas out next, they said. Rubber bullets. Paras – *Bloody Monday*, that's what this is. Bloody Monday – Don't know why I fucking stopped there. I was that bloody knackered from all running, though. So fucking hot – I should have kept walking, though. But then it all started up again. For last time – Blokes were throwing brick down at police line. Line broke again. Out came horses. Short shields behind them. Hundreds of them – They weren't stopping, either. Not this time – They were here to clear field. To take bridge and take road. Hold them both – Knuckle and boot for anyone in their way. Batons out – Barricades going up. Vehicles dragged out of this scrapyard. Set alight. Thick smoke. Cars burning. Tyres. Thick smoke all over place. Barricades looked like hedgehogs, that many spikes sticking out of them. Hand-to-hand fucking combat. Coppers had bridge. Coppers tried to hold bridge. Coppers couldn't. Missiles falling through sky on them from out of scrapyard. Coppers heading off back down road behind their shields – Lads all cheering. Not for long, like – Coppers regrouped. Mass charge again – Horses. Men – That fucking white horse back for more. Bastards – Up Highfield Lane. Pushing us right back over bridge all way down Orgreave Lane – But then I saw this one young lad. This one young lad who'd got left behind – He was walking about alone in field. Blood from his head. White with shock, he was – Let's go get them, he was shouting. Give them a good sorting. Let's – He was alone in field. God deaf and far from here – Horses still coming. Sticks out – I went back for him. I grabbed hold of him. I took him back over bridge with me. I ran into vil-

lage with him. I sat him down behind this garden hedge; old couple stood at their window just watching us. Lad turned to me. Looked at me. He said, I won't go back down pit again. I won't, you know. I'll not work down there no more. I won't do it. I want to go home now, please. I want to go home – I got out my handkerchief. I tried to stop blood from his head. He put his hand out towards us. He touched my mouth. He had blood on his hand – He said, What happened to you, like? I put up my hand. I touched my mouth. I'd got blood on my hand. No front teeth. I looked down at myself. My shirt was ripped. Strap of my watch was broken. Face stepped on and crushed. My father's watch it was and all. Shoes split open. Trousers ripped at bottom. Felt a right big bruise across my back. Ribs and my shins. Cuts and marks all over me. I stood young lad up. I said, Best get you home, hadn't we? I walked us away through all people – Police. Pensioners. People with Asda carrier-bags full of shopping. Like it was all normal – Ambulance drivers effing and blinding at policemen. Blokes being brained in front of them. Beaten up behind their houses. In their gardens. Their alleys – Up by truck company there were a bloody ice-cream van. This one bloke just sat having a fucking ice-cream. Like it was a day out – Back up road you could still see smoke. Black, bitter smoke from cars and tyres. Police just watching us go. Behind their visors. Two of them waving tenners at us. Bye-bye, I thought. I'll not see thee again. Not where you're going. Not where you're going – Been a week tomorrow. Bloody long one and all. I'd spent most of it looking at ceilings. **Bedroom.** Dentist's. Welfare. One time I did go out in open air was for Joe's funeral. Beautiful and sad day, that was. There was a coach laid on, but that were full by nine. So Little Mick took Keith Cooper and their Tony with us in his car. No sign of Martin again. Met up with coach in **Knottingley**. There were eight thousand easy. Put me in mind of Fred Matthews. His funeral in 1972. He'd been killed on a picket outside a power station and all. Keadby. Been

The Seventeenth Week

Monday 25 June – Sunday 1 July 1984

It is flesh time in the corridors and toilets of Westminster. The Jew whistles *Waterloo*. They pat him on the back. They shake his hand. The Jew says:

'Four thousand men in one hundred and eighty PSUs. Forty-two mounted police. Twenty-four dog handlers. Spotters in among their men. Helicopter and military surveillance. Regiments in reserve. One hundred arrests. Countless injuries inflicted –

'Orgreave was a battle; they are right to call it that. Because it is a war –

'But it was a battle we won. And it is a war we shall win.

'Our finest hour to date, gentlemen. Our very finest yet. Rugeley power station alone received one thousand and twenty-eight deliveries of coal that day and –'

The Jew stops mid-flight. The corridor has cleared –

There is a fresh hand on the Jew's back. A word in his ear. Then the hand is gone.

The Jew rushes into the toilets. He comes out again. He's not whistling –

He smells of vomit.

Neil Fontaine fetches the car.

Malcolm Morris drove down to London. To Hounslow. This was the place where they'd built the village. The place where they trained their divisional support groups. Their mounted police –

In Hounslow.

Malcolm found his plastic pass inside his clothes. He handed it to the officer at the metal gates. The officer took it inside a sentry hut –

Malcolm waited in the car with the radio on –

I Won't Let the Sun Go Down on Me.

The officer came back with his pass. The gate went up. Malcolm was inside again.

He drove past the stables. The kennels. The barracks –

He could hear them banging their shields. Practising.

He turned into the village –

Pitsville, UK –

Two rows of mock-redbrick houses either side of a strip of road with an estate of mock-grey semis behind them. Malcolm watched the mounted police and the snatch squads drilling by a row of mock shops. Boarded-up shops. Charging –

NATO helmets on. Staffs drawn –

Men in donkey jackets and yellow stickers ran. Loudspeakers on street-corners barked orders. The horses stopped their charge. The horses cantered back –

The men were banging their shields again. Training.

Roger Vaughan was parked in the mock car park by the mock pub –

The Battered Ram –

Roger waiting today. Not Jerry.

Malcolm parked. He got out. Shut the car door.

Roger got out of his car. Roger said, 'I've been waiting, Malcolm.'

Malcolm walked round the back of his car. He opened the boot. Took out the Slazenger holdall. He placed it on the tarmac. He closed the boot. Picked up the holdall again. He walked over to Roger. Handed him the holdall.

Roger took it. Roger said, 'Two?'

Malcolm nodded.

Roger said, 'Wrapped in green?'

Malcolm nodded again.

Roger took out an envelope from his coat. He handed it to Malcolm.

'Wrapped in red, white and blue?' asked Malcolm.

Roger smiled. Roger said, 'There was one other small matter, Malcolm . . .'

Malcolm waited.

Roger said, 'That business in Shrewsbury?'

Malcolm waited.

Roger said, 'Jerry and I would be very grateful if we could have the tapes.'

'The tapes were destroyed,' said Malcolm.

Roger stared at him. Roger said, 'Is that right?'

Malcolm nodded.

Roger sighed. Roger said, 'That's a shame, Malcolm. A very great shame.'

'Standard procedure,' said Malcolm. 'In compromised operations.'

Roger said, 'The operation in question was not subject to standard procedures.'

'But it was compromised.'

'In your opinion.'

Malcolm turned to go. He said, 'I don't like loose ends, Mr Vaughan.'

'Neither do we, Malcolm,' shouted Roger after him. 'Neither do we.'

Malcolm turned back. He said, 'I hope that wasn't a threat, Mr Vaughan?'

'No, Malcolm,' said Roger. 'That wasn't a threat.'

The Jew paces his fourth-floor suite. The Jew wants to get his show back on the road. Back to the front line. Back among his new-found friends. And foes. Fighting the good fight. The Jew is tired of the offices and the corridors of the capital. Tired of the handshakers and the backstabbers. Tired of the good news/bad news brigade –

The Jew asks Neil for another cup of tea. He says, 'Did you speak with Frank –'

'Fred?' says Neil.

The Jew blinks. The Jew says, 'Did you speak with him or not, Neil? Yes or no?'

Neil Fontaine closes the suitcase. He says, 'Briefly.'

'And how is life with our hero?' asks the Jew. 'The John Wayne of Pye Hill?'

'He thinks the pit managers and local police are talking people out of returning –'

'What?' screams the Jew. 'What? Tell me you are joking with me, Neil.'

'To avoid bloodshed.'

The Jew throws his cup against the wall. He screams again, 'What?'

Neil Fontaine nods.

The tea runs down the wall. The tea drips onto the carpet.

The Jew looks at Neil. The Jew shakes his head from side to side –

Neil Fontaine nods again.

'Remember what she once said, Neil?' asks the Jew.

Neil Fontaine waits for the words of wisdom from the wise –

'A criminal is a criminal is a criminal,' says the Jew. 'Remember, Neil?'

Neil Fontaine nods now.

'The good news?' asks the Jew. 'Please tell me there is good news, Neil?'

'The strike in Lancashire is about to be ruled unofficial by Justice Caulfield up in Manchester; their delegate decisions at their area conference will be meaningless; their hands tied. The Union won't be able to discipline members who cross picket lines; the Union won't be able to instruct members not to cross picket lines; the Union won't be able to call the strike or the picket lines official –'

But it is not enough –

'There is still talk, though, of a return to court by the likes of British Rail and Steel. Rumblings at the Board, too. The Cabinet.'

The Jew nods. The Jew asks for a fresh pot of tea. The Jew picks up the phone –

The railways will stop tomorrow and certain newspapers not appear –

The Jew shouts down the phone again:

'No, no, no. Use their own domino strategy against them. Take the individual area ballots that went against a strike and use them to beat the National Union. These actions – these actions from within – these will be the very key. The key to victory –

'How many more times must we go over this?

'Further action from British Rail, from British Steel, from the Board itself, will only be detrimental to the overall strategy. The nation perceives this dispute to be about the assault and intimidation of ordinary men who simply want to go to work but who are being prevented and frightened by the vicious hooligan thugs of an extra-parliamentary hard left –

'Assault and intimidation are a matter of criminal law not industrial legislation. The individual actions by members against their own Union underline this perception –

'OK? OK?'

The Jew throws the phone against the wall. The Jew closes his eyes –

The broken telephone lies on the damp carpet in a pool of cold tea.

Neil Fontaine puts the Jew's suitcase and briefcase by the door. He says, 'Sir?'

The Jew opens his eyes. He looks at Neil Fontaine. The Jew smiles. He says, 'Neil, there are two separate paths for them to choose now; they will either choose the way of the ballot or, better yet, they won't. Either way, the courts can really roll now –

'Really, really roll now, Neil.'

The Union was alone in an upstairs room in Congress House. There was still no support. Just a few sandwiches. The Union was on its own. Isolated –

'I remember we gave that bastard an oil lamp back in 1980,' said the President. 'He had tears in his eyes. Tears in his eyes because of support our lads had given his lads. Our lads who would rather salvage used steel in old workings than touch any scab steel. Now they sit by sea in Scarborough and their conference applauds the striking miners. Gives us a bloody standing ovation. Promises of moral, financial and physical support. Then they go back to their plants and their offices and handle scab coal and scab coke. There'd have been no need for Orgreave if they did for us what we did for them. Bastards. Bloody bastards. Thank Christ for the railwaymen –'

There was a knock on the door. The President stopped speaking. Terry stood up. He opened the door –

It was just Stan with more sandwiches.

Roll up. Roll up. The carnival is back on the road. Roll up. Roll up. The Border Country. Derbyshire and Nottinghamshire. Roll up. Roll up. For this week only –

The fear. The misery.

The Mercedes tours the coalfields with a convoy of pressmen and television vans. The Jew takes them to Bolsover. To Creswell. To Warsop. The Jew shows them the places where gangs of men with wooden sticks wrapped in barbed wire rampage and maraud at night –

Intimidating. Threatening.

Roll up. Roll up. The Jew introduces them to Bolsover Bill. Bill has had his waste pipes blocked. Bill's house was flooded as a result. This happened to Bill because Bill chooses to work. The Jew tells them that there have been fifty-six attacks upon homes. Ninety-five vehicles damaged –

The intimidation and the fear.

Roll up. Roll up. The Jew introduces them to Creswell Chris. Chris was attacked outside the Top Club. Chris had his leg broken. This happened to Chris because Chris chooses to work. The Jew tells them that there have been sixty-two cases of physical assaults upon men and their families –

The threats and the misery.

Roll up. Roll up. The Jew introduces them to Warsop Wendy. Wendy's cat was covered with paint. Wendy's cat is blind now. This happened to Wendy's cat because Wendy's husband chooses to work. The Jew tells them there have been countless cases of attacks upon the pets of working miners and their families –

Of fear and misery. Intimidation and threats.

Roll up. Roll up. The Jew leads the carnival on through the Scab Alleys –

Suddenly Neil Fontaine brakes hard. He swerves to the side –

Cavaliers struggle with the broken wheel of a wagon. Purple-frocked men bark orders in the rain and the mud. Crosses around their necks. Rings on their fingers –

Neil Fontaine blinks. He starts the car. He glances in the rearview –

The Jew is staring at the back of Neil's head. The Jew is watching Neil.

Roll up. Roll up. Finally the Jew brings the carnival to the village of Shirebrook. The ringmaster leads them with their cameras and their pens up the garden path to the home of Stuart Tams –

The late Stuart Tams.

Mrs Tams shows the gentlemen of the press and the Independent Television News their boarded-up windows, each covered with one single painted word –

Scab.

'They were getting at the kids,' says Mrs Tams. 'That's what hurt him the most. He tried to tell them of the hardship he was facing. They would not listen to him. They spat at him. They turned their backs on him. They had been his mates. His colleagues. He bottled everything up. He kept putting off discussing financial matters. He would just go upstairs. He sat in his bedroom alone for long periods. Then the telephone calls started. Nine times they called. They were against our daughters. That was it then. Stuart was put in a position where he had to decide whether to continue to put the children through this ordeal. Stuart chose not to. Stuart chose –'

The Jew puts his arms around Mrs Tams. The Jew glances at the garage –

The press take their photographs. The press shoot their story.

'The men who made the telephone calls threatening violence against a twelve-year-old and ten-year-old girl are cowards. Murderers,' says the Jew. 'They are not fit to stand side by side, shoulder to shoulder, with miners such as Stuart Tams. They are a disgrace to the great tradition of mining and mining folk.'

Mrs Tams nods.

The ringmaster leads everybody back down the garden path to stand out on the street. To stand before the skinny hedge and the boarded-up windows covered with that single painted word –

Scab.

The Jew introduces Fred Wallace from Pye Hill –

'Fred is the spokesman for the Nottinghamshire Working Miners' Committee. He is here to help any miner, regardless of his area. Here to help any miner who wants to work but is denied that right by his own Union. Any miner who is intimidated and threatened. Any miner's wife who is intimidated and threatened. Any miner's children who are intimidated and threatened. Fred is here to tell you that you are not alone. That what happened here to the Tams family will never again happen –

'Never!' shouts the Jew. 'You are not alone.'

Fred Wallace nods.

'Fred would also like to add that the Nottinghamshire Working Miners' Committee will compensate any miner for any act of criminal damage or vandalism to his person, property or vehicle which occurs as a result of his determination to exercise his right to work, if that miner does not himself have insurance,' says the Jew.

Fred Wallace nods again.

'My name is Stephen Sweet,' says the Jew. 'I am here to help.'

ten thousand that day. Put me in mind of my father and all – Marched with my father that day. He'd be retired now if he were still alive. He'd still march for Joe, though – Banners were out and bands. Arthur, Jack and all lads. Half of us with black eyes and bandages. Piper playing *Flowers of the Forest* in a right strong wind. Service were at Pontefract Crematorium. It lasted an hour. Then Arthur spoke. He said, We owe it to memory of Joe Green and David Jones to win fight to keep pits open, jobs secure and our mining communities intact, and make no mistake – We are going to win. Magnificent, Arthur was. Needed to be – They weren't going to charge that TV Copper. *Krk-krk*. Talk Union might take out a private summons against bastard. He were only one of many, like, but he were one they caught. One they caught on camera, lathering this young lad with his truncheon. That was Great Britain in 1984 for you – Policeman could belt living fucking shit out of an unarmed, shirtless kid on national television and get away with it. Not only that, whole of state jumped to his defence – But if a bloody miner, who had served this country, man and boy for thirty year, if he wanted to stand on a picket line and persuade another man to help him defend his job, his family, his community, his whole way of life, then they'd nick you and charge you – 3444 of us since start of March. Probably a few fucking more today and all – Back on active service. **Coal House** again. NCB's Regional Office, Doncaster. Not all lads were impressed. Older blokes especially – Just lasses that work there, said Joey Wood. Tall Paul nodding, too. He said, Going to look bad on telly – Fuck telly, said Brian. It always looks bad on fucking telly. I said, If you don't want to go, go direct to Harworth for half-eleven – Few of blokes nodded and stayed put. Rest of us went out to cars and vans. Drove straight up to Doncaster, no problem. There for quarter to eight. Parked down a back street. Made us way to Coal House. Not many stormtroopers today. *Krk-krk*. Them that were there looked a bit shocked when we all rocked up. Made them-

selves into a police wall for scabs to hide behind. Only enough of them to reach from Police Station to Court House, which was where lads had chased first lot of office scabs they'd come upon. Half-eight scuffles started. Then reinforcements arrived from RAF Newton or Lind-holme or wherever it was they were hiding them this week. Now wall stretched from Court House to doors of Coal House. Nine o'clock and scabs set off – Big push from all lads. Load of bricks thrown at Coal House windows – Lot of lasses who were scabbing had got bags over their faces. Lot of them crying and shaking. Running as fast as they could, like – Not very nice for them. All abuse they got – Then this fucking policeman went through a plate-glass window. That was that then. Load of arrests after that – Sixteen windows broken. Eleven cars damaged. Thirty-seven people assaulted. One thousand pickets – Bloody pointless. Drove back to **Welfare**. Queue of folk waiting for us as usual – Bills. Debts. Bills. Debts – Bloody DHSS. YEB. Same as fucking usual – They were talking about discipline, **Panel** were – NEC were proposing a new national disciplinary rule. Rule 51 – It was a way to clamp down on acts detrimental to Union, meaning Notts mob mainly, though it could be anything: breaking strike by crossing picket line; leaking documents; anything – There was a lot of anger about our own discipline, too. Discipline on our own side – Disobedience. Things that had happened at Coal House – SCC had been dead against it. Lads had still gone – Pissed a lot of folk off, that had. Then there was still anger about Orgreave; Scholey, vice-chairman of BSC himself, he'd been on box saying Orgreave was only a diversion so they could bring in what they needed through Immingham and Trent Wharves. But here we were still arguing toss about whether to picket place or not. I'd heard enough – Enough to last me a lifetime – I stood up. I took out piece Mary had cut from paper. Notes we'd made from news. MacGregor's told his area directors that a long strike was preferable to an early settlement, I said. Now how's that

The Eighteenth Week

Monday 2 – Sunday 8 July 1984

Malcolm Morris and Alan Cole drove down from Euston to Buckingham Palace Road –

The Rubens Hotel. A few steps up from the Clifton Park Hotel, Rotherham –

The job was the same, though.

They parked and used the tradesman's entrance at the back of the hotel. Introduced themselves to the in-house security and the men from the Met. The talks were to be in one of the larger rooms on the second floor. The Board would have the room to the right. The Union the room to the left. Everyone had a chuckle at that.

The man in charge of in-house security handed over two sets of keys. He said, 'The keys to the room on the left. The keys to the talks.'

Malcolm handed back the keys to the room on the left. He shook his head.

'We know what King Arthur's going to say,' Cole told everyone. 'Big Mac, though, now that man's a law unto himself. Law unto himself.'

In-house security put the keys to the room on the right into Malcolm's hand.

Malcolm picked up the cases. He stood up. Left.

Cole followed him back out into the corridor. They took the service lift up to the third floor. Room 304. The room above the talks.

Cole said, 'I'm sorry, Chief.'

Malcolm opened the door. Locked it after them. 'Just can't keep it shut, can you?'

Cole sighed. He closed his eyes. Nodded and said again, 'I'm sorry.'

Malcolm looked at his watch. He drew the curtains. Switched on the lights. He stripped down the double bed. Handed the linen to Cole. Cole dumped it in the bath. Malcolm took the mattress off the bed. Leant it against the curtains. He opened up their cases on the base of the bed –

They laid out their equipment. They set it up. They looked at their watches –

Malcolm put on his overalls. He picked up the smaller case. Took the stairs –

Room service –
On a silver plate.

The Troika had gone to the Rubens Hotel for the talks. Everybody else was left to wait. Divide their time between Congress House and the pub. Pace the corridors. Cross their fingers. Pray at a table in the bar at the County, if you were Terry Winters –

Pray that both sides wanted a deal. That a deal could be reached –

That Terry could be saved.

Terry nodded to himself. Terry thought the President knew the time was right –

There was no Triple Alliance any more. No support. No stomach for it.

Terry nodded again. Terry thought the Chairman knew the time was right, too –

There'd been only seven hundred responses to the Chairman's letter. The huge NCB adverts running in the papers this week looked like a waste of taxpayers' money –

Money –

Terry closed his eyes. Terry bowed his head. Terry said his prayers.

'Your lips are moving, Comrade.'

Terry opened his eyes. Terry raised his head. Terry said another prayer –

'First sign of madness that, Comrade,' said Bill Reed. 'Talking to yourself.'

'What do you want now?' asked Terry.

Bill Reed put an envelope down on the table. Bill Reed said, 'Gotcha, Comrade.'

Malcolm drank instant coffee. Malcolm smoked duty-free cigarettes –

Malcolm watched and Malcolm listened –

Every minute. Every hour. Every day. Every week. Every month. Every year –

The shadows and the whispers. In his thoughts and in his dreams –

Hotel doors. Hotel doors slammed –

I want you I want you I want you now –

Hotel beds. Hotels beds creaked –

I love you I love you I love you for ever –

Hotel headboards. Hotel headboards banged –

I have you I have you I have you here –
Hotel walls. Hotel walls shook –
I hate you –
Blood on hotel walls and hotel floors, hotel beds and hotel doors –
Malcolm opened his eyes. He unwrapped the bandages. Took the cotton
wool out of his ears. Bloody and wet –
Malcolm put on his headphones –
'I HATE YOU!'
Every single minute of every single hour of every single day of every sin-
gle week of every single month of every single year of his whole fucking life –
The ghosts without. The ghosts within –
Operation Vengeance –
Public and private. Personal.

The Jew hasn't been to sleep. He's too anxious. He doesn't wait for
the doorman or Neil. He opens the back door of the Mercedes himself. He fidgets on the backseat –

He wants to tighten the screw further –

He rambles on about Enterprise Oil. The GLC. The House of Lords –
About loose screws.

He is wearing his dark blue pinstripe suit, his pale blue shirt with
a white silk tie –

He has a boot full of pale blue notes to donate to his true-blue
secret cells –

'Our men have control of the Nottinghamshire Area Council,' the
Jew boasts. 'We have our bridgehead now, Neil. The intimidation
stops here.'

The car phone rings. The Jew pounces. Listens –

'What?' shouts the Jew into the phone. 'What?'

Neil Fontaine looks into the rearview mirror.

The Jew hangs up. He bangs on the partition. He wails, 'Stop the
car, Neil!'

Neil Fontaine pulls over onto the hard shoulder. He switches on
the hazard lights.

The Jew gets out. The Jew paces the verge –

Neil Fontaine joins him.

The Jew looks up. He says, 'Be a pal and pass me a coffin nail, Neil.'

Neil Fontaine hands the Jew a cigarette. He lights it for him.

The Jew inhales. He coughs and he coughs. The Jew exhales.

Neil Fontaine watches the Jew choke again.

The Jew throws away the cigarette. The Jew says, 'There's a dock strike, Neil.'

Neil Fontaine nods. Neil Fontaine knows.

'She wants answers, Neil,' says the Jew. 'Heads.'

Neil Fontaine nods again. Neil Fontaine knows –

The Jew coughs. The Jew spits. The Jew clambers back into the back of the car.

Neil Fontaine starts the car. Puts his foot down –

One spark –

The Immingham bulk terminal out over the use of unsupervised non-scheme labour to unload iron-ore pellets at a registered port –

The Jew opens his window. The Jew screams into the road and the wind –

'This is a disaster. An absolute, utter disaster. Exactly what we didn't want, Neil. This is a second front. A second bloody front. Exactly what he wanted –'

Neil Fontaine has a slight smile on his face. The road rising –

The one spark –

The lorries would work round the clock for forty-eight hours to move at least half the Immingham stockpile to the Scunthorpe steel works –

Neil Fontaine nods. Neil Fontaine knew a set-up when he saw one –

This was a set-up.

Neil Fontaine stops before the gates and the guns and winds down his window –

Neil Fontaine says, 'Mr Stephen Sweet to see the Prime Minister.'

The officer speaks into his radio.

Neil Fontaine glances into the rearview mirror. The Jew is sweating again –

His pinstripe soaked.

The officer steps back from the car. The officer gestures at the gates –

The guns rise. The gates open.

Neil Fontaine starts the car.

'Doubt she'll be in a very good mood,' says the Jew for the third time.

Neil Fontaine drives slowly over the gravel. He parks before the front door.

There is no one here to meet the car today –

Neil Fontaine has to open the back door of the Mercedes for the Jew.

The Jew gets out. The Jew goes up to the front door –

The door opens.

The Jew turns back to look at Neil. The Jew nods. The Jew gives a little wave –

The Jew has tickets for Wimbledon. The final –

The Jew planned to take Fred, Don and James. Their special treat.

Fred, Don and James will have to go on their own now –

The Jew is due out on the real centre court today –

And he has left his aviator sunglasses and his panama hat on the backseat.

Neil Fontaine starts the car again. He parks in the empty garage. He sits in the car. He can smell the exhaust fumes. He can hear the peacocks scream –

Neil Fontaine is thinking of Vincent Taylor and Julius Schaub –

One spark, he thinks. *That's all it ever takes –*

David Johnson and Malcolm Morris –

One spark to burn the whole thing down –

Jennifer Johnson.

Malcolm took the weekend off. He drove North. He ate dinner at Da Marios on the Headrow in Leeds. Deep-fried garlic mushrooms. Lasagne. A bottle of the house red. He smoked two cigarettes. He finished with coffee. Drove home to Harrogate. He put the car in the garage. He went into the house. Picked up the post. The papers from the mat. He left his briefcase in the hall. Took off his tie. He made a cup of instant coffee. He went into the lounge. Drew the curtains. He switched on the lights. The stereo. He went over to the shelves. The many shelves which lined every wall of the room. He took down the double-cassette box of Jeff Wayne's The War of the Worlds –

Malcolm opened the box. Two cassettes inside –

He took out the first cassette. Tape 1. *He put it in the stereo.* Side A.

Malcolm unwrapped his bandages. Took the cotton wool out of his ears –

He lowered the volume. He adjusted the tone. He pressed play –

The Eve of the War *started. Four minutes later* The Eve of the War *stopped –*

There were other noises on the tape now –

Other noises from other rooms. Other rooms, other sounds –

The wheels turning. The wheels within wheels –

The sound of a door opening. The sound of footsteps coming –

Malcolm pressed stop. Forward. Stop –

Silence. Just the silence. Pregnant –

Two bloody wet cotton-wool balls in his hands, Malcolm pressed play –

Screams. Just her screams –

Stop. Rewind. Stop. Play. Malcolm played it all back –

Over and over and over –

Stop. Rewind. Stop. Play. Again and again and again.

preferable when it's costing them an arm and leg? Because he's worried that any settlement now would breakdown again when stocks were still low. That's why. So I say we take his warning as a piece of bloody good advice. I say we push for a return right now. Keep overtime ban on. Mend some fences. Build our bridges back with Nottingham. Triple Alliance. Rest of movement. Clear some debts. Then, *Bang!* Hit bastards hard, right before Christmas. They won't be able to last long then, I'm telling you. I sat back down. David Rainer nodded. He said, Not up to us, though, is it, Pete? So who is it up to then? asked Johnny – But there were no answer to that. That was why we all knew bloody answer. That was why. Martin Daly came round **ours** tonight. Thought they'd put you in Middlewood, I said. He didn't laugh. He shook his head. He said, You don't know half of it – Fair enough, I said. How's your Cath? Not bad, he said. What about you? Looks like it hurts – Only when I breathe, I said. He laughed. He shook his head again. He said, Bloody state of us, eh? I said, Not just us, lad – Right there, he said. Pint going to hurt, is it? Not if you're buying. He laughed again. He stood up. He said, Best get our straitjackets on then, hadn't we? Ended up in **Hotel**. I could tell Martin weren't keen. Talk at tables was what you'd expect – They go on about uneconomic pits and then they spend sixty-five million quid a week on police, compensation costs to industry, alternative power and lost income tax. Sixty-five million fucking quid. Every week. That's nigh on ten million fucking quid a day. It's been over a hundred days. Hundred days at ten million quid a day. Never spent a bloody penny round here before. Think about it, said Billy. Ten million quid a day for a hundred days. Fucking hell, she must really hate us. Really fucking hate us – I was nodding. Everybody was – That fucking letter, Danny said. Wish I'd never opened bloody thing. Should've fucking burnt it like Keith did. *Dear Colleague, Your future is in danger. Everybody will lose – and lose disastrously. Your savings will disappear. The industry will be butchered. Twenty or* *thirty pits in danger of never reopening. Join your associates who have already returned to work. Sincerely, Ian MacGregor. Your future is in danger?* Little Mick nodded. Who does that Yankee bastard think he is? I'm sat there reading that fucking thing with a black eye and two fucking broken ribs. I know my future is in fucking danger – In fucking danger from him and her and their fucking boot-boys – That's who my future's in fucking danger from – I was nodding. Everybody was – You saw photo on front of *Miner*? That bloke were an army sergeant driving that police van during London march – Khaki shirt. Sergeant stripes. Badges. Insignia. The lot – Clear as fucking day. I'm telling you, that weren't first time, either. That were never just police at Orgreave. Never. Not in a month of fucking Sundays. Not a number on any of them, were there? I know I didn't bloody see one. Army, that's who they were. Fucking troops. Light relief after Northern Ireland. Light relief. 1926 all over again – I was nodding. Nodding and watching Martin at bar. Bar and dartboard. Bloke at table got out his photocopy of Ridley Plan. Revenge, he said. That's what this is. Revenge – I nodded. Everybody nodded – I'd had enough, though. I stood up. I went outside. I needed some fucking air. Our Jackie had left a sandwich out for us when I got back – Two slices of Mighty White. Margarine. Packet of cheese and onion crisps – Bloody crisp sandwiches again. I ate it and went up. Mary was asleep. I checked alarm clock. Put on my pyjamas. Got into bed. Lay there looking up at ceiling. It was midnight. Had to be bloody up again in an hour and a half. Didn't want to sleep, though. Ruined even that, hadn't they? I couldn't remember a single bloody dream I'd had before strike. Now I couldn't close my eyes for more than five minute fore I had them open again – Shitting bricks. Sweating like a bastard – *Total darkness. I can touch my nose with my finger and still not see my finger. Hear hammering on metal in distance. Or was it here? Near. Here with smell of wood. Mice. Then hammering stops. Mice are gone. There's a different noise. Different*

The Nineteenth Week

Monday 9 – Sunday 15 July 1984

Christopher, Timothy and Louise were about to break up for their summer holidays. Theresa Winters thought the children should go down to Bath to stay with her mum and dad, at least for a couple of weeks. Terry thought Theresa should go too. Theresa was hurt. How would she be able to help him if she went down to Bath? How would she be able to support the strike? Help the women's action groups? Did he not appreciate the cuttings she took from the papers, the videos she made from the news? Did he not want her to assist the welfare groups? Did he not want her to attend the Women Against Pit Closures Conference at Northern College next Sunday? Theresa had stopped washing the frying pan and the grill. She was staring at her husband. Her hands wet. Christopher, Timothy and Louise had stopped eating their cereal. They were staring at their dad. Their mouths open. Terry Winters looked down at his newspaper. He pushed his glasses up his nose. His mouth moved –

'I'm sorry,' he told them. He stood up. He left them –

Terry Winters went to work.

Terry spent most of the day organizing the hand-delivery of confidential envelopes to the finance officers on each executive committee of each separate area. These envelopes contained individual sets of instructions; the individual sets of instructions to his latest master plan –

His greatest masterstroke –

Instructions to authorize with immediate effect the payment in full to all non-elected employees of the Union (Regional and National) their entire salary for fiscal 1984/85. Instructions to suspend the collection of rents on any properties owned by the Union (Regional and National) for the duration of fiscal 1984/85. Instructions to transfer the deeds and titles of properties owned by the Union (Regional and National) to the tenants of the properties concerned for the duration of fiscal 1984/85. Instructions to suspend repayments to the Union (Regional and National) of loans made by the Union (Regional and

National) to employees for the duration of fiscal 1984/85 –

Each instruction a masterstroke –

Each instruction divesting the Union of its assets at national and regional level, pre-empting the possible sequestration of funds while simultaneously ensuring the loyalty of its employees in its darkest of hours –

The darkest, darkest of hours yet to come.

Clive Cook called Terry back within an hour. *Click-click.* Just like he always did. Just like Terry knew he would. Clive used the telephone in his office at Huddersfield Road to call Terry at St James's House. *Click-click.* Just like he always did. Just like Terry knew he would. Clive failed to use the codes. Just like he always did. Just like Terry knew he would –

Just like Bill Reed had said Clive would.

Terry listened to Clive's questions. Then Terry said, 'Just fucking do it, Clive.'

Terry hung up. Terry stood by the phone. Terry picked it up again –

Click-click.

Terry hung up again. Terry walked backwards down the stairs. Terry went out.

Terry called Diane back from a phone box in the station. He'd dreaded this call. He'd gone over it tens of times in his head. Hundreds. He knew it had to be said –

Had to be done.

Terry picked up the phone. *Click-click.* He dialled their room. Listened to it ring –

Listened to Diane say, 'It's all very 007 is this, Mr Chief Executive Officer.'

'These are very dangerous times,' said Terry. 'I can't see you any more.'

'What?'

'I am under surveillance. I am being tailed and I am being bugged.'

'What are you –'

'If they found out about us, they could use you against me. Against the Union.'

'What are you talking about, Terry?'

'They've bugged our offices,' he said. 'Our houses. All our phones –'

'What on earth does that have to do with us? Our relationship?'

'It can't go on,' said Terry. 'I can't see you any more. It's over.'

These are the hours Neil knew had to come –

The recondite hours.

He wants to be believed. Not to be deceived. His messages received –

The Jew naked on the carpet of his suite. The Jew shouting, 'There is no crisis.'

He clutches his cock in both hands. He quotes Hayek –

'Crucial truths,' whispers the Jew. 'Crucial battles, Neil.'

Neil Fontaine drags the Jew into the bathroom. He throws him into the cold bath –

Neil watches the Jew thrash –

His white limbs and his red chest.

He listens to the Jew scream –

His right fingernails scratching at his left breast, tearing it open.

Neil changes the water. He runs the hot tap. He fetches the Jew's rubber duck –

The Jew soaks among the suds until he is clean and sober again –

His wounds almost healed.

It is here that the phrase comes to him. He often thinks about that war in the bath. It was where the Jew first came in –

The Jew's *grande entrée* –

She had been surrounded then by apostates and apologists, cowards and caitiffs. Milksops to a man. The Jew had ridden a coach and horses through that dastardly pack.

The Jew had walked straight up to her and introduced himself with the words, 'The British public wants you to stick it to Johnny Dago, ma'am.'

The Jew had been right too. The Iron Lady had conquered the Tin-Pot General. The Jew would be right this time too. The Iron Lady would vanquish King Coal –

It was time again to break out the coach and horses.

This the hour Neil knew had to come –

The occult hour.

He wants to be admitted. Not to be rejected. His membership accepted.

The Jew drips bloody water across the carpet of his suite. The Jew says to Neil, 'The enemy within.'

*

All hands on deck. The Dock Strike was national. Notts strikers had occupied the Mansfield committee rooms, preventing the Area Council meeting to mandate their representatives to oppose the introduction of the new disciplinary rule at this week's Extraordinary Annual Conference. The talks between the Union and the Board had resumed in Edinburgh. The Troika had taken with them a written draft of an agreement on which they would be prepared to settle.

These were the days. The best days yet –

The President had left Terry Winters in charge at Strike HQ –

'To hold the fort,' he had told him.

Terry stayed at the office all night. He had had the staff enlarge photocopies of the draft agreement. He had them pinned to the Conference Room walls. He stared at them. He watched TV. Ceefax. Oracle. He paced the carpet –

He waited for the telephone call.

His eyes began to close. He sat down in the President's chair. He –

– is sat in a tall chair made of gold in a dim room made of dull walls. He wears a white cassock with a purple shawl. His head is shaved, his hands bejewelled. The room begins to turn. The chair falls. Terry –

Opened his eyes, his face white with shock, his breath black with –

'Comrade,' said the Tweed again. 'Telephone.'

Terry stood up. Terry rubbed his face. Terry took the phone. Terry said, 'Hello?'

'Rise and shine, Comrade Chief Executive,' said the voice of Paul Hargreaves.

Terry rubbed his face again. Terry looked up. Terry looked around –

There were four Tweeds standing over the President's desk.

Terry said into the phone, 'What news, Comrade General Secretary?'

'Cautious optimism,' said Paul. 'That's the phrase for today.'

'Let us hope it bears fruition,' said Terry. 'Our members are counting on you.'

'Yes, yes,' said Paul. 'Thank you very much. The President and the Vice-President have asked if you would prepare a draft agenda for the pre-conference NEC meeting tomorrow. There is every chance we will be back in Sheffield by six.'

Terry nodded. Terry said into the phone, 'You can rely on me, Comrade.'

'Let *us* hope so,' said Paul. 'Because the President would also like you to prepare an additional item for the agenda on the possible legal challenges from the Nottinghamshire action against Rule 51.'

'I can tell you now,' said Terry. 'If and when the scabs get the High Court decision they want, we could well be in contempt even holding a conference, let alone debating the rule itself.'

'But will they come after us?' asked Paul. 'And can we withstand it if they do?'

Terry looked back up at the Tweeds. Terry looked down at the phone. Terry said, 'They will come after us as soon as they can, that's certain. But we have taken the appropriate and necessary measures. We are ready for them.'

'Let's hope so,' said Paul again. 'The President will be heartened by your words.'

'Good luck, Comrade General Secretary,' said Terry. 'We are counting on you!'

'Goodbye, Comrade Chief Executive,' said Paul Hargreaves.

Terry Winters put down the phone –

There was clapping from the doorway to the Conference Room.

The Tweeds turned round. Terry looked up –

'Fuck 'em all,' shouted Bill Reed. 'And fuck you all, Comrades.'

The Norton Park Hotel, Edinburgh. The talks had failed. The Chairman blamed semantics over the third category of pit closures. The President blamed the third hand –

'The third ear more like,' laughed Cole.

Malcolm Morris pressed rewind. He pressed stop. Play –

'– paragraph 3c is a demonstration of positive negotiations –'

'– we just added one word, that's all –'

'– there is not much between us –'

'– just added one word, that's all –'

'– but beneficial is not acceptable –'

'– then you will have to think of another word –'

'– someone better go get us a bloody thesaurus then –'

'– just one word, that's all –'

'– we could not sell that to the lads –'

'– I am too old for victories –'

'– you have the Prime Minister's ear, Mr Chairman –'

'– just one word –'

'– we have to find a formula that takes us beyond March 6 –'

'– it's in your hands –'

'– all the guidelines and safeguards protect you – not us –'

'– one word –'

'– we have stopped running and we cannot be chased any further –'

'– it's now up to you.'

Malcolm pressed stop. Rewind again. Eject.

'Love is a battlefield,' laughed Cole again.

Malcolm labelled each cassette. Each spool. Put the copies into separate boxes. The boxes into the express-delivery pouches. The spools into the brief-case –

He closed the door behind them. They took the stairs –

Heartache to heartache. Room to room. Wall to wall –

Behind private walls in private rooms, the private heartaches of public demons –

Malcolm and Cole had their headphones back on. Tapes turning again –

'Whatever we do to them, whatever action we take, they've still got a job.'

'We won't work with scabs.'

'We'll have no fucking choice.'

'Lads won't have it.'

'Lads won't have a job, then.'

'It's unacceptable.'

'It's unacceptable but it's now the bloody policy of the fucking Coal Board. They've set us a trap and we've walked into it. Doesn't matter what we say or do now. Means we've lost Nottingham for good –'

'Means we've lost full stop, President.'

'Does it heck mean we've lost.'

'See sense, man. Course it bloody does. Nottingham will keep working. Nottingham will keep producing fucking coal. We can't call strike official in Nottingham. We can't order them to respect picket lines. Can't take action against them if they don't. And now, if we do take away their membership, Board will still let them work –'

'They're scabs.'

'Aye, they're scabs and they'll always be scabs – so they'll keep working no matter how long we stay out. In a word, we're fucked now.'

'It's time to settle, President. Settle now and keep this Union together –'

'He's right –'

'Lads won't go for it.'

'Lads always listen to you. Lads will hear you now. Lads will see sense.'

'Take it, President. Take it now. Take it just for now.'

'I can't.'

'They've said they'll withdraw bloody closure programme –'

'Verbally.'

'Verbally, orally, whatever. Them five pits will be kept open. It gives us victory.'

'Does it heck.'

'It can be made into one. They've backed down. Pits will be kept open.'

'Not kept open. They said they'll be subject of further considera-tion –'

'Joint consideration –'

'But for how long? Won't be like before. Old procedures won't be there –'

'President, President, there'll be time for talk –'

'And how bloody long will it be before they stop talking and start closing –'

'But we'd have kept our powder dry, while we still had powder to keep dry.'

'It's just one word, President.'

'It's one word, aye. It's retreat. It's carte-blanche to do what the hell they want. There's never been a third category before. They've set no parameters for exhaustion of reserves. The government is insisting on that word. *Because* it's carte-blanche –'

'But they've got that anyway now. Now closed shop's out the win-dow –'

'Seam exhaustion, and that's it. Safety grounds. Geological grounds. That's it.'

'It's time to take what's on the bloody table, man. Take it to the lads –'

'Not now! Not bloody likely. Now is the hour –'

The tapes ran. They ran and ran. The wheels turned. Turned and turned again –

The private heartaches of public demons, in private rooms between private walls –

Headphones off. Suitcases packed. Cigarettes. Coffee. Goodbyes –
The drive South again. The wheels in motion (the wheels within wheels) –
Trucks full of troops being deployed. Lorryloads of shaven heads –
'– there is in no sense a crisis –'
There were curfews in English villages. There were curfews on English estates –
'– no state of emergency –'
Fitzwilliam. Hemsworth. Grimethorpe. Wombwell. Shirebrook. Warsop.
'– a touch of midsummer madness –'
 York Minster had been struck by lightning. York Minster was burning –
'– acts of God –'
Malcolm Morris stood among the crowd of ten thousand people at the Durham Miners' Gala and listened to the speeches –
'– we will at the end of the day inflict upon Mrs Thatcher the kind of defeat we imposed on Ted Heath in 1972 and 1974 –'
The spectres. Rising from the dread. The rectors. Raising up the dead –
The old ghosts, without and within –
Malcolm Morris spied Neil Fontaine parked in a lay-by in a black Mercedes –
England was a séance, within and without.

The SDC had passed the rule change to discipline anyone responsible for actions detrimental to the interests of the Union. The SDC had passed the disciplinary rule change with a two-thirds majority and in defiance of a court injunction.

Terry made the call. Terry used the code. Terry drove up to Hoyland –

Terry was late. Clive Cook was already parked behind the Edmund's Arms.

Terry walked over to the brand-new Sierra. Terry tapped on the passenger door.

Clive gestured for Terry to get in.

Terry shook his head. Terry walked away.

Clive jumped out of his new Sierra. Clive shouted, 'Where are you going?'

Terry went back over to stand by his car. Terry waited –

Clive ran after him. Clive grabbed him. Clive said, 'What is it? What's wrong?'

'I've spoken to Bill Reed.'

Clive let go of Terry. Clive sighed. Clive said, 'What did he want this time?'

'I know everything.'

Clive blinked. Clive said, 'Know what? He's a fucking liar and a drunk.'

Terry pushed Clive against the car. Terry ripped open Clive's shirt – Pulled up his vest.

Clive Cook was shaking. Clive Cook was sobbing.

Terry tore the microphone off his chest. The micro-recorder off his back.

Clive Cook slid down the side of the car –

'They pay me fifty quid a day,' Clive Cook wept. 'Fifty quid. Monday to Friday. A grand a month. Tax free. Just to tell them what they already know.'

Terry threw the equipment onto the ground. Terry stamped on it – *Repeatedly.*

Clive Cook looked up at Terry Winters. Clive Cook said, 'I'm sorry, Comrade.'

Terry grabbed him by his hair. Terry spun him across the car park.

Clive Cook fell on the floor. Clive Cook lay on the ground. Clive Cook smiled –

'I'm the one you're meant to find,' he laughed.

Terry spat on him once. Terry got into his car –

Terry went back to work.

sound now. Hooves. Horses' hooves. I start running. Running and running – Like a bastard. A bastard – Shitting bricks. Sweating buckets – I stared up at bedroom ceiling. I was thinking about my father – How my father died. How my father lived – Then alarm went off and I jumped. They said talks were going well. They said there was a dock strike in offing – It was a bloody beautiful day and all. Felt like we were winning – Then I got down **Welfare** and saw queue. Be double if it weren't for Women's Action Group and Welfare Rights folk – It was still out door, like. Knew what half of them were going to say before they'd even opened their gobs and all. Arthur Larkin was back about his compensation claim; Paul Garrett's wife had had another run-in with YEB; John Edwards was still being given runaround by DHSS; and Mrs Kershaw would want to know why Mrs Wilcox had got two cans of beans in her food parcel and she'd only got one and did I know that some had got a bag of potatoes and others hadn't? And, while she was here, what about all them tins from Poland. How was that fair? I nodded and wrote down what she said. What they all said – I didn't say I knew her husband was working cash in hand on a building site in Chesterfield and that was why he never went on a picket. Didn't say I knew he'd be first on mesh bus when they started it here. I just nodded and wrote down what she said. What they all said – Didn't say there were folk ten times worse off than them. Folk that never came down here. Folk that never asked for anything. Folk that said thank you when you did see them and gave them something. Folk that didn't tell us what we already knew – That we were unprepared. That we were badly organized. That things were going to get worse – Folk whose bloody addresses we didn't even have. Faces we couldn't remember – You're not even bloody listening, are you? shouted Mrs Kershaw. Typical. Bloody typical. I nodded and I wrote it down – Day of Jitters, they were calling it down in London. Not up here, they weren't – Not at **Sheffield University**. The Extraordinary Annual Conference – High

Court or no High Court, we were still here – Here to say you cannot break ranks to our collective disadvantage. Here to accept Rule 51 with a two-thirds majority. Here to say sod state interference. Sod pit closures. Sod scabs – And sod her. King Arthur stood up and we all stood up with him – Through the police, the judiciary, the social security system, he said. Whichever way seems possible, the full weight of the state is being brought to bear upon us in an attempt to try to break this strike. On the picket lines, riot police in full battle gear, on horseback and on foot, accompanied by police dogs, have been unleashed in violent attacks upon our members. In our communities and in our villages, we have seen a level of police harassment and intimidation which organized British trade unionists have never before experienced; the prevention of people to move freely from one part of the country, or even county, to another; the calculated attacks upon striking miners in streets of their villages; the oppressive conditions of bail under which it is hoped to silence, discourage and defeat us – all these tactics constitute outright violation of people's basic rights. So to working miners, I say this: Search your conscience – Ours is a supremely noble aim: To defend pits, jobs, communities and the right to work, and we are now entering a crucial phase in our battle. The pendulum is swinging in favour of NUM. Sacrifices and hardships have forged a unique commitment among our members. They will ensure that the NUM wins this most crucial battle in the history of our industry. Comrades, I salute you for your magnificent achievement and for your support – Together, we cannot fail! We will not fail! We were stood with him – Stood by him. Stood for him – Shoulder to shoulder we were all stood. And they must have been able to hear applause and cheering in Downing Street – The new war cry: *Here we are* – TGWU had voted to extend their strike to all ports. *Here we are* – Pound had collapsed. *Here we are* – Billions had been lost in stocks and shares. *HERE. WE. ARE* – I drove down to **Annesley** before Panel today. Took

The Twentieth Week

Monday 16 – Sunday 22 July 1984

Neil Fontaine stands outside the door to the Jew's suite on the fourth floor of Claridge's. He listens to the Jew whimper and whine in his dreams. He listens to him weep and wail. Neil Fontaine stands outside the Jew's suite on the fourth floor of Claridge's and wonders where the angels are tonight. Those better angels, their wings tonight –

The lights out. The shadows long –

The scars across his back.

Neil Fontaine stands outside the Jew's suite. Neil Fontaine listens to the summer –

Inside.

'– at the time of the Falklands conflict, we had to fight the enemy without –'

Malcolm Morris had found Clive Cook first –

He was sitting in the road outside the telephone box in Hoyland.

Clive was a mess. His shirt open. His buttons gone –

He was pissed. Frightened.

'I'm fucked,' Clive had kept saying. 'I'm fucked! Fucked! Fucked! Fucked!'

Malcolm got Cole to take Clive's car. Malcolm stuck Clive in the back of his. Gave him a lager –

To keep him pissed.

Malcolm drove him down through Mexborough and Doncaster to Finningley –

Eyes in the rearview mirror, ears bleeding.

Malcolm took Clive into the barracks –

Light inside, dark outside. It was night now, and that was good –

Things changed in the night. Things always looked different in the morning.

Clive woke in the room with the mirror. In a change of clothes.

He said, 'I want to go home now. I want to go back home.'

'OK,' said Malcolm. 'I'll get the car.'

But before Malcolm reached the door Clive had remembered –

Clive said, 'No, wait. I don't –'

'What?' said Malcolm.

Clive looked at him. Clive said, 'I don't want to go home any more. I'm fucked.'

'Relax,' Malcolm told him. 'She'll be here any minute. Then everything will be all right.'

Clive nodded. Malcolm nodded, too. Clive smiled. Malcolm smiled back –

Clive said, 'That's good. That's very good. Diane will make things better.'

'– but the enemy within, much more difficult to fight, is just as dangerous to liberty –'

Neil Fontaine picks up the Jew in the small hours. The Chairman and the Great Financier carry the Jew down the stairs from the flat in Eaton Square and out to the Mercedes. They have been drinking jeroboams again. The Jew demands that Neil pin black cloths over the inside of the windows in the back of the car. He demands that Neil play the elegy from Tchaikovsky's *Serenade in C for String Orchestra, Op. 48*. He demands that –

Neil Fontaine does ninety up the M1 with the Jew asleep on the backseat –

Neil Fontaine likes to drive North through the night. To hurtle into the new dawn. To meet the light head on –

The Jew wakes in the black of the back. He is disorientated and has a hangover. He taps on the partition. Neil Fontaine lowers the glass.

The Jew says, 'Where on earth are you taking me, Neil?'

'Oxton, sir.'

The Jew struggles to remember why on earth Neil would be taking him to Oxton.

'Grey Fox, sir.'

The Jew slumps back in his seat. The Jew sighs. The Jew says, 'Quite.'

Neil Fontaine turns off the Tchaikovsky.

The Jew sits forward again. The Jew says, 'Can we stop somewhere, Neil?'

Neil Fontaine exits the M1 at the next services –

Leicester Forest East.

Neil Fontaine parks the Mercedes among the lorries and the coaches.

'Please tell me you've brought my flying-jacket, Neil,' says the Jew.

Neil Fontaine nods. He says, 'Along with a complete change of clothes, sir.'

'You're a national treasure, Neil. A national treasure.'

'Thank you, sir,' says Neil Fontaine. He gets out of the car. He opens up the boot. He takes out a small suitcase and the worn leather flying-jacket with the blood-spotted collar. He closes the boot of the car. He opens the back door of the Mercedes.

The Jew steps out into the sunshine. He has found his sunglasses and his panama.

Neil Fontaine points. He says, 'I believe the toilets are that way, sir.'

'Very good, Neil,' says the Jew.

Neil Fontaine hands him the small suitcase.

'Thank you, Neil,' says the Jew.

Neil Fontaine watches the Jew cross the car park of the Leicester Forest services. The Jew is wearing a cream tuxedo cut short in the manner of a hussar, with a gold brocade front and matching epaulettes. His jodhpurs are tucked into his riding boots. He takes off his panama as he enters the toilets.

Neil Fontaine lights a cigarette. Neil Fontaine waits.

Five minutes later the Jew reappears in his flying-jacket and his chinos. He hands Neil the small suitcase and his panama hat. He puts his aviator sunglasses back on. He caresses his moustache. He stretches. He breathes in deeply through his nose. He slaps Neil on the back. He says, 'What's the ETA, Neil?'

Neil Fontaine checks his watch. He taps it. He says, 'Under an hour, sir.'

'Let's press on then, Neil,' says the Jew. 'Our people are waiting.'

Neil Fontaine says, 'Certainly, sir.'

The Jew gets in the back of the Mercedes. Neil Fontaine closes the door.

They drive on to Oxton –

The Green Dragon.

Neil Fontaine holds open the door of the pub for the Jew. They go up the stairs to the first floor. There are two men sitting at a table in the corner. One of them has prematurely grey hair. He is wearing sunglasses. Both men stand up as the Jew approaches –

The man from the *Mail* says, 'Stephen Sweet meet Grey Fox.'

The Jew shakes hands with the man with the prematurely grey hair. The Jew says, 'Do I call you Grey or Mr Fox?'

Grey Fox shrugs his shoulders. He says, 'Whichever you want. It's just a –'

The Jew holds up his hand. The Jew says, 'Or how about just plain Hero?'

This Grey Fox has turned a deep red. He takes off his sunglasses.

The Jew sits him down. The Jew says, 'You are the bravest man I've ever met.'

The man from the *Mail* nods. He says, 'The bravest man in Britain.'

Grey Fox shakes his head. Grey Fox says, 'I'm just an ordinary man who –'

The Jew squeezes his hand. The Jew says, 'You are a far from ordinary man, sir. You are an extraordinary man. Please, I want to know everything. Tell me your story, Grey Fox. The story of the Bravest Man in Britain –'

The Jew and Grey Fox sit side by side at the table in the corner of the upstairs bar of the Green Dragon public house in Nottinghamshire.

Grey Fox doesn't drink. The Jew does –

'Hair of the dog that bit me,' he says. 'Now, please, tell me everything –'

'There was no one you could turn to,' says Grey Fox. 'The branch officials were on strike. You couldn't go in on the nightshift because they'd brick your house or worse. Richardson – our leader – came down to Welfare and he called us scabs. Told us all to stop scabbing. I thought, What-the-bloody-hell-is-this-world-coming-to when this man who is our elected representative comes down to our Welfare and tells us, the men that pay his wages, tells us that we are scabs? I was offended, Mr Sweet. Offended and afraid because folk didn't know who to turn to. But I thought there must be hundreds like me –'

The Jew is leaning forward. He hangs on to the words of Grey Fox –

'The areas were like islands though. Isolated from one another. Some pits were cut off. Rumours were going round, that was all we heard. I wanted to bring people together. Then at Mansfield on May 1, I got the chance. I got the chance to make a difference. I gave my name and number out to people on slips of paper. That night the phone started ringing and it's never stopped since –'

The Jew nods. His eyes are full of tears –

'Then again, I've always said, and I still say, if fifty per cent were out and it was official, then Grey Fox would be one of them.'

Grey Fox stops speaking.

The Jew is drying his eyes. He is wiping the tears from his cheeks.

Neil Fontaine stares at Grey Fox –

Grey Fox looks back.

Neil Fontaine smiles at him –

Carl Baker, 35-year-old blacksmith and father-of-two from Bevercotes Colliery. Carl Baker, the former small businessman, now of 16 Trent Street, Retford –

Carl Baker smiles back, because he is a nice man –

He is a very nice man, but Carl Baker already has his doubts. And his doubts will become regrets. His regrets will bring blame. Blame will bring bitterness –

Then Carl Baker won't be a very nice man any more.

'Will you please excuse me?' he says. 'I need to use –'

'I think it's downstairs,' says the man from the *Mail*.

'Would you like Neil to go with you?' asks the Jew.

Carl Baker looks at Neil Fontaine. He shakes his head. He says, 'No, thanks.'

The Jew smiles. He nods. He stands up to let Carl Baker out.

Carl Baker puts his sunglasses back on. He goes downstairs for a shit –

'That's his fourth today,' says the man from the *Mail*.

The Jew turns to the man from the *Mail*. He says, 'Well done, Mark.'

Mark from the *Mail* laughs. He says, 'My pleasure. Now, about the –'

The Jew raises his hand. He says, 'Neil will take care of the details.'

Neil Fontaine hands Mark from the *Mail* a piece of paper and a pen.

Mark from the *Mail* looks down at the notepaper. He looks up at Neil Fontaine.

'Your name, branch, sort code and account number, please,' says Neil Fontaine.

Mark from the *Mail* nods. He writes quickly. He hands the note back to Neil.

Carl Baker comes back upstairs. He sits back down. He takes off his sunglasses.

'You really are a hero to me,' says the Jew. 'And not just to me and the thousands of terrified miners who want to work and are too intimidated to leave their families and their houses, but you'll also become a hero to millions of ordinary people throughout this country and around the world who are sick and fed up of the bully-boys and the Black Shirts, the Socialists and the skinheads –

'Have you ever seen *On the Waterfront* with Marlon Brando?' asks the Jew.

Carl Baker shakes his head. He says, 'I don't think that I –'

'See it,' says the Jew. 'See it, because it's you.'

Carl Baker looks at the Jew. Carl Baker looks confused.

The Jew takes out his chequebook. He says, 'How much do you need, Carl?'

Carl Baker looks at Mark from the *Mail*. Carl Baker says, 'He knows my name –'

'Soon everyone will know your name,' winks the Jew.

Carl Baker puts his sunglasses back on. Carl Baker clutches his stomach.

'People are crying out to hear a name like yours, Carl,' says the Jew.

They had breakfast across the road from the County. There was only the one table today. Terry was going to the High Court later. The Troika back to the Rubens for more talks. Dick and Paul just played with their food. They had to be at the Rubens Hotel in an hour. There was supposed to be confidence going into these talks. The Dock Strike was solid. There was obvious panic in Downing Street and Fleet Street. There was no rise in the rate of men returning to work. This was supposed to bring confidence. But there was none. The friends Terry Winters had on the inside of Hobart House (and there were many these days), these friends from the other side suggested the Board would withdraw the March 6 closure programme –

Not for nothing, though.

But the Union had only nothing to give. Nothing further they could take, either. The EAC had made that clear. Crystal. Their hands were tied. Dick and Paul stood up. Terry paid the bill.

Dick and Paul had gone when Terry came out of the café. Terry hailed a cab. Terry got in the taxi. Terry asked the driver to take him to court. The driver smiled and dropped him at the High Court.

Terry sat in the public gallery of the Crypts. He listened to Sir Robert Megarry declare their new disciplinary rule 51 unlawful. Null and void. Terry left the High Court. He ate a ploughman's lunch in the pub across the road. He bought an *Evening Standard* –

There was no news. They were still talking –

Thirteen hours they talked. Back and forth. Back and forth. Back and forth for thirteen hours. Thirteen hours. Back and forth. Back and forth. Back and forth for thirteen hours –

Terry in the bar. Terry on the bog. Terry on the phone. Terry on his knees –

Back and forth for thirteen hours. Then they stopped.

It was midnight when they got back to the County. The press and television tried to follow them inside. Doors were slammed in their faces. The Troika took off their jackets. They collapsed in the armchairs –

There was silence.

Paul went to the toilet. Joan asked for some tea and sandwiches to be brought up –

'Fuck cups of tea,' said Dick. 'I've drunk enough bloody cups to last me all year. I want a proper fucking drink.'

The President had his head right back. His eyes closed –

It was a long march home from here –

There was the wet trail of a tear from his eye to his ear.

The nightmares are recurrent. Neil Fontaine dreams of skulls. Many, many skulls. Skulls and candles. He wakes in their room at the County. The light is still on. He sits on the edge of their bed. The notebook is in his hand. He picks apart the months. Puts the pieces back together his way. He stops writing. The notebook to one side. He stands up. He opens the dawn curtain.

Jennifer thrashes in their bed. She screams his name in her sleep –

There are only moments like these now –

Neil Fontaine stands at the window. The real light and the electric –

The summer angry. The enemies within –

A scar across the country.

Keith, his cousin Sean and his mate who was staying with them. We were hitting Nottingham every day now – Linby. Moor Green. Every pit we could – Dayshift. Afters – Often as we could. Many as we could – Annesley a lot. Best way there was straight down M1. Junction 27 – No roadblocks today, either. Few spotter cars on hard shoulder. *Krk-krk.* Plainclothes mob on bridges with their cameras and stuff. That was all – Think they just wanted to see how many of us they were dealing with after Orgreave. Take down names and car registrations – Keith said he'd started getting silent phonecalls first thing of a morning. Reckoned it was just to see if he was in. Sean's mate Liam said, That's what they do with IRA in Northern Ireland. To keep tabs on them. If they don't see a face about for a bit, they know something's up. Big job coming – I put on radio for rest of way. *Two Tribes* – Must have heard that bloody song ten times a day now for weeks. Ought to make it bloody National Anthem, said Sean. It was early when we got to pit. Load of coppers, though. *Krk-krk.* White shirts, too. Fucking Met. Scum. Bloody lot of them. Arrogant scum and all – Do this. Do that. Don't do this. Don't do that. Fair few lads were arriving now. Maltby mob. Dinnington. More of our lads. Big Knob drove up to where we were stood around in cowfield. Got his notebook out ready. Head darting about like a bloody pigeon. Right, he said to us. Where are you men from? I told him. I said, We're from Yorkshire. Are you indeed? he said. Indeed we are, I said. Right then, he said. Get back in your vehicles and fuck off back to Yorkshire. I said, That's not very nice language, Inspector. No, he said. And if you don't move, you'll hear more of it in Lincoln Jail. That was when it started up. Like a bloody dance. Us quite prepared to play it to death – Him threatening us with this, that and other. This time, though, Keith had only gone behind bastard's back and taken fucking keys out of his car. Chucked them over hedge into next field. Mad bastard. I thought we best be off now. I said, Right, Inspector, you've made a good point there. We'll get on our way

now. Big Knob couldn't keep smug bloody look off his face. Right proud he was. Probably thought they were going to give him Queen's Medal for Bravery or something. Us lot just trying not to laugh – Keep a straight face. Not give game away – Me, Keith and other two headed back to our car. Rest of lads did same. I made sure we all drove off past him. And there he was, going through his pockets. Keith wound down passenger window. He said to him, What's up with thee? Never you mind, shouted Knob. Keith said, Not lost your keys, have you? Think police would set a better example than that, said their Sean – Everybody laughing. Laughing all way back to Thurcroft – All way back to another fucking letter from bloody Board on us mats. Must have had some fucking time and brass to spare, that bloke. That fat fucking Yankee bastard – This was a dangerous time. Talks were over. Board busy telling us how pit faces were in danger of collapse. Telling us how coal stocks would last well into next year. Telling us how sixty thousand were still working. Telling us how we needed a ballot. Telling us in their personal letters. Telling us in their telephone calls. In their home visits. Their vendettas. Their lies. Derek said, Lads are itching for more mass pickets – Shirebrook give them taste back last week, said Tom. **Panel** were nodding. Johnny said, Get rusty if they don't – Few of mine are saying they'll only turn out if it's a mass picket, I said. David Rainer nodded. He said, Barnsley are hearing same – How many are going out on a usual day, David? asked Johnny. David looked at his notes. He shook his head. He said, Under four thou' – And how many of them make it to target? said Derek. David sighed. He said, About half on a good day – What about if it's a mass picket? How many turn out then? asked Johnny. David said, There were ten thou' at Orgreave, easy – Not counting coppers' narks, I said. Folk nodding. Johnny said, More mass pickets it is, then – Babbington. Creswell. Them types of pits, said Tom. Derek said, Lads will be happy. Just itching for another crack – **Babbington** it was. This where strike was for today

The winds rattled the wires up here. The chatter distorted. The conversations displaced. The voices disembodied. The guards scared the ghosts in here –

Diane put a cigarette to her lips, a lighter to her cigarette.

Malcolm Morris waited.

She inhaled, her eyes closed. She exhaled, her eyes open.

On Menwith Hill, he waited.

'Don't let it happen again,' she said. 'Don't ever let it happen again, Malcolm.'

Malcolm nodded.

She stubbed out the cigarette. She put a hand to his ear. She kissed his forehead.

Malcolm Morris shut his eyes until she'd almost gone. Her smell still here –

The Free World.

All at sea again. The Dock Strike had collapsed. Negotiations with the Board suspended. Mrs Thatcher and her Cabinet back on the attack. The miners now Britain's enemy within. The President a Yorkshire Galtieri –

There was a war on, declared *The Times.*

Terry Winters had his head pressed against the glass of the window in his office, exhausted. Terry and Theresa had driven Christopher, Timothy and Louise down to Bath yesterday. They had stopped for lunch with her mum and dad. They had said goodbye to the children. Then Terry and Theresa had driven back to Sheffield. He had kept the radio on all the way home. He had dropped Theresa off at the end of the drive. Then he had gone back to work. Terry hadn't seen his wife since then. Terry had slept downstairs last night. Theresa had already gone when he got up –

The Women Against Pit Closures Conference.

He opened his eyes. He looked up at the bright blue Sheffield sky –

Always light, never dark.

He turned back to his desk. To the piles of files. The mountains of –
The telephone was ringing.

Terry picked it up. *Click-click.* Terry said, 'Chief Executive speaking.'

'Hello, Chief Executive,' she said. 'Guess who?'

Terry swallowed. Terry said, 'How did you know I'd be here?'

'Where else would you be?' she laughed. 'With your wife?'

Terry sat down. Terry stood up again. Terry said, 'I told you, we're finished.'

'We're not finished,' she whispered. 'We've not even begun.'

Terry said, 'I don't know what you're talking about.'

'It's our anniversary on Tuesday.'

Terry shook his head. Terry said, 'No, it's not.'

'I was just thinking about that first night, sitting here alone, brushing my hair –'

Terry's mouth opened. Terry swallowed again.

'I'm still holding my hairbrush, Terry. I'm still thinking about you –'

Terry's mouth –

'I want you –'

Terry –

'Don't make me use the handle again, Terry. Please don't make me –'

Terry sat down under the portrait of the President –

'Please don't make me –'

The walls began to turn. The chair began to fall –

'Please –'

Terry said, 'Where are you?'

Back to base. Back to Sheffield. To drink more instant coffee. To smoke more duty-free cigarettes. To stare at rows and rows of huge reels turning. To stare at the strips and strips of gaffer tape turning on those reels. To stare at the names and the places turning on that gaffer tape –

1OF CON.RM #1–4

1OF GENTS –

9F LADIES –

8F PRES. OFF #1–4

8F PRES. OFF O/L #1–4

7F TW OFF #1–2

The names and the places, the tapes and the reels recording it all –

Every single resonance and reverberation of every single sound in every single room on every single floor of every single building the Union used –

St James's House. The University. The Royal Victoria. Hallam Towers –

To be numbered, dated and copied. Transcribed and collated. Analysed, interpreted and debated –

In pitch. In tone. In note –

This beautiful, ugly noise. This heathen cathedral of sound –

Renovated and repainted for Yorkshire, but conceived and borne of Ulster –

By Malcolm Gordon Morris, government fairy, the original Tinkerbell, then thirty:

May 1974, Ulster – the Ulster Workers' Council Strikes combined mainland industrial action techniques with homegrown paramilitary intimidation to bring the Province to a standstill. The telephone-intercept system known as Pusher (Programmable Ultra and Super-High-Frequency Reception) was failing to provide the necessary information as key figures rightly assumed their phones were being tapped and so spoke only in codes in the privacy of their own guarded homes. Malcolm Gordon Morris, government fairy, the original Tinkerbell, then just thirty, bounced microwaves off the windows of their offices and their homes to monitor the vibrations of the glass in order to reproduce and record the conversations taking place within –

In pitch. In tone. In note –

Those beautiful, ugly noises. Those heathen cathedrals –

The timbres in which Malcolm lived and lost himself. Hid and hurt himself.

Malcolm unwrapped his bandages. He took the cotton wool from his ears –

He picked up the headphones. He switched channels –

Hallam Hotel Room 308 #6 –

Doors would slam. Beds creak. Headboards would bang. Walls shake –

He put on the headphones. He closed his eyes. He turned up the volume –

'– I want you, Terry. I have you, Terry –'

He listened to their words –

'– Now fuck me, Terry. Fuck me –'

Blood in his ears. Headphones against the wall. Malcolm screamed –

'I hate you! I hate you! I hate you!'

*

Neil Fontaine sits before the dawn in the Mercedes in the car park of Woolley Edge service station. He is here to watch. He is here to wait –

This is what Neil Fontaine does –

Before the dawns he parks in the dark in service station car parks.

This is what he has always done –

He parks. He watches. He waits for –

Possibilities.

The Celica arrives at half-past seven. Five minutes later the Sierra pulls in –

Neil Fontaine watches –

Don Colby and his best mate Derek Williams get out of the brand-new Celica. They walk over to the new Sierra. They are wearing low hats and dark glasses. They have a shopping list. Don gets into the Sierra. Derek waits by the boot. He is nervous. Unstrung –

The clock in the dashboard of the Mercedes ticks. Neil Fontaine waits –

Don Colby gets back out of the Sierra. Don has a pile of documents in his arms.

The Sierra reverses out of the parking space. The Sierra leaves at speed.

Don Colby and his best mate Derek Williams get back in the brand-new Celica.

Five minutes later the Celica leaves Woolley Edge services –

At speed.

Neil Fontaine gets out of the Mercedes. He walks across the car park to the phone. He makes two calls –

Neil Fontaine tells the first voice: 'Presents were exchanged as planned.'

He hangs up.

Neil Fontaine tells the Jew: 'This time for real.'

Jerry Witherspoon was smoking a cigar at his table. He was waiting today. Not Roger.

Malcolm Morris sat down.

Jerry smiled. He said, 'And how are we today, Malcolm?'

'I don't have the tapes,' said Malcolm. 'If that's what this is about?'

Jerry stubbed out his cigar. He leant forward. He smiled. He said, 'We know.'

'Good,' said Malcolm. 'I just wanted to get that out of the way.'

Jerry smiled again. He said again, 'We know.'

'So what is it I can do for you, Mr Witherspoon?'

Jerry sat back. He said, 'Roger and I would like to borrow your eyes and ears.'

'I'm afraid the price has gone up.'

Jerry said, 'Whatever you feel is fair, Malcolm. They are your eyes and ears.'

'Who?'

Jerry lifted up his napkin. He pushed an envelope across the table. 'Him.'

Malcolm opened the envelope. He stared at the photograph inside –

He looked back up at Jerry Witherspoon.

Jerry nodded. Jerry said, 'Love will always let you down, Malcolm. Always.'

– Nowhere else. Not Hobart House. Not St James's House. Not Shirebrook. Not today – Today it was here. Here in Babbington – Here and only here. Here where camera crews were. Here where aggro was. Here where strike was. *Here* – South Nottinghamshire. Our own enemy within – Mass picket at last. Lads on both sides of road. *Here* – and I wished I wasn't. *Here* – I was at back with Ken when it all wheeled round. Put us down at front – *Listen to voice.* Massive shove, massive – *Voice saying, Follow me.* Had them halfway across road, traffic stopped – *Follow me.* More police running up to shove us back, clear way for snatch squad – Scabs just walking and driving in. Like nothing was going on – Like nothing was wrong. Bounders. Traitors. Bastards. Scab. Scab. Scab – They went in hard, snatch squad. Fucking hard on this one lad – Five on to one. Trail of blood told you where they'd taken him. Must have given them taste for it too, because they were all going in hard now. Hard after anyone they could – Hard until they got their seventy arrests or however many it was they were after today. Mission accomplished – That was it, then. That was strike over for today – Be somewhere else tomorrow. Not here – Hobart House. St James's House. Creswell – Not Babbington. Not tomorrow – Tomorrow it'd be somewhere cameras were. Where aggro would be. That was where strike would be – Not here. Not tomorrow – Been out twenty week now. Twenty bloody week. Fucking hell. Our Jackie made Sunday lunch today. Been a while since we'd had one. Proper one, like. Not sort of thing you said when you went down **Welfare**, either. Blokes looked at your dinner medals to see what you'd had. One too many roasts down you and folk would think you were scabbing or out robbing – And they'd sooner you were out robbing. Better that than other – Some of older blokes buying us drinks again today. They were glad of company and we were glad of pint. Listen to their stories of 1926 and who'd done what then; who'd scabbed and who'd not. Richest folk in village nowadays, pensioners and some of them on dole. I was in toilets when Keith came in. He said, Seen anything of Martin? Not since start of month, I said. Keith nodded. Keith said, No one's seen him – I might have a drive up there then, I said. Keith shook his head. He said, There's no one about – What about his Cath? I asked him. Keith shook his head again. He said, Jacked her job in, I heard. Fucking hell, I said. You don't think they've flit? I don't know, Keith said. Thought you might. Why? I asked – Not seen hide nor hair of him, I said. Or her – Maybe they've just gone away for a bit. Holiday or something? said Keith. I looked at him. I said, They take Scotch Mist, do they? Lunn Poly? No, he said. I doubt they do. I said, These are dangerous times, Keith. Be careful what you say. Be careful what you think. There were a few festivals on down in **London**. Yorkshire Area were laying on coaches. Demand was such that we'd had to stick on a few more. Mary and lot of lasses were off in fancy dress as usual. Should have seen bloody state of them. Boost to morale, though, so they said. Loaded up our buckets and badges, our begging bowls and flat caps and off we set. Ironic really, it must have been only time it had bloody rained all month. Been glorious weather. Now it was pissing it down. Pissing it down all fucking day and all. I was stood at **Jubilee Gardens**. Must have been a hundred bloody buckets. Every branch here, plus mob from GLC. Only good thing that happened all day was when this one coloured lad come past. He stops. He looks at all buckets. He takes out his wage packet from his pocket. He opens it up and pulls out two pound notes. I thought, That's decent of you. But then he only goes and sticks the two quid back in his pocket and drops his whole bloody wage packet into our bucket – His whole week's wages. Bar two pound – It made me think, that did. There were no coloured people in Thurcroft and there were them that were right glad about that. I wished they'd been here to see that – But I was same; grew up thinking that blacks had a chip on their shoulder and that Irish were all bloody nutters. I didn't think that now, I tell

The Twenty-second Week

Monday 30 July – Sunday 5 August 1984

The National Executive Committee had rejected the Board's offer. The Special Delegate Conference had been recalled for August 10. It was set to run and run –

It was cap-in-hand time to Congress House. Almost –

The Denims and the Tweeds were staring at Terry Winters.

The President had just asked, 'Will it be jail or fines, Comrade?'

'Fines first,' said Terry.

The President said, 'And how much do you think the fines will be?'

'For contempt? Fifty thousand plus costs,' said Terry.

The President said, 'And what steps will they take to recover it?'

'The court will set a deadline of twenty-four to forty-eight hours for payment.'

The President said, 'And when that passes?'

'They'll appoint sequestrators to take over the Welsh assets.'

'Who?'

'Price Waterhouse,' said Terry. 'Who else?'

The President nodded. The President said, 'But everything is in place?'

'Everything is in place. Everything is set. Everything ready.'

The President stood up. The President put his hand on Terry's shoulder –

Terry looked up into his eyes. Terry smiled.

The President said, 'Unity is just around the corner, Comrade.'

'Unity and strength, Comrade President,' said Terry.

The President left the room for the meeting.

Neil Fontaine drives the Jew North again. The Jew closes his eyes in the back of the car. Neil Fontaine switches on the radio in the front and the back of the Mercedes –

'*– there is no going back. There is no surrender. We will fight and we will win – or we will die in the attempt –*'

Neil Fontaine glances in the mirror. The Jew opens his eyes in the back of the car. Neil Fontaine switches off the radio in the front and back of the Mercedes –

This time for real.

The Jew holds court with the people from the court. The legal eagles of Newark. The Jew talks about the individual. The individual's resistance. The resistance of the cell. The cell's resilience –

'But I digress,' says the Jew. 'Forgive me, gentlemen.'

Grey Fox, Don Colby and Derek Williams stare blankly at the Jew. Dominic Reid sweats.

Piers Harris touches the huge pile of Union documents on his desk again. He says, 'This is quite a trove you men have amassed.'

Don Colby and Derek Williams smile, proud of what they have become.

'But does the trove contain the treasure we seek?' asks the Jew.

Piers Harris nods. He says, 'I would think so. Don't you, Dominic?'

Dominic Reid wipes his forehead with his handkerchief. He nods too. He says, 'Looking at the inventory of the documents the men have obtained, there does appear to be some real meat here.'

'Meat for the traps,' says the Jew. 'Bait.'

'Anything else you need,' says Don Colby. 'You just let us know.'

The Jew applauds. The Jew says, 'This mole of yours is certainly a busy bee.'

'He knows it's the right thing to do,' says Don Colby. 'The right thing.'

'It's certainly a brave thing to do, too,' says the Jew. 'One really dreads to imagine what the Red Guard would do to the poor creature should he ever be unmasked.'

Everybody imagines. Everybody nods –

Grey Fox puts his sunglasses back on. Picks his underpants out of his arse.

The Jew claps his hands. He says, 'To the battle-plan. Piers, if you would –'

Piers Harris stands up. He walks to the blackboard. He picks up a piece of chalk. 'Through the very great endeavours of the Chairman and Stephen on our behalf,' he says, 'Justice Megson is set to hear the orders a week on Friday. It is unlikely anyone from either the Yorkshire or National Union will be in court. Therefore, there will be an adjournment to allow the Union time to prepare their case. But –'

Derek Williams is fidgeting. Derek Williams puts up his hand.

Piers stops. Piers smiles. Piers says, 'Yes, Derek?'

'Will we have to be in court a week on Friday? Me and Don?'

Piers looks over at the Jew. Piers sits down –

The Jew says, 'Neil has made reservations for yourselves and your wives to travel down to London on Thursday and for you all to spend two nights at the –'

'Westbury Hotel in Mayfair,' says Neil.

Derek and Don whistle. Derek says, 'What about the kids?'

'We'd like them to spend the week at Bridlington or some place,' says the Jew. 'With their grandparents or some other relatives or friends.'

'It's going to cost a pretty penny is all this,' says Don.

'But worth every pretty penny,' says the Jew. 'If it brings you both piece of mind during your stay in London.'

Grey Fox takes off his shades and says, 'Folk are going to know who they are.'

Don, Derek, Piers and Dominic all turn to look at the Jew –

The Jew says, 'Folk already know, Carl.'

Grey Fox puts his sunglasses back on. He says, 'But there'll be cameras at court.'

'There are cameras everywhere,' says the Jew. 'In fact, the producers of TV-AM have asked if Don and Derek would be good enough to appear on their programme along with their lady wives.'

Derek looks at Don. Don nods. Derek nods. Don says, 'Aye, go on then.'

'TV-bloody-AM?' says Grey Fox. 'Whole bloody world will know who you are. Where you work. Where you live. Where you drink. Are you mental?'

Don shakes his head. Don says, 'Time for hiding's over, Carl.'

The Jew gets up. He walks over to Don Colby –

The Jew embraces him –

This time for real.

Dominic looks at Piers. Piers puts a finger to his lips. Piers winks at Dominic –

Dominic Reid went to school with Piers Harris. Piers is a member of the Newark Conservative Party. The Conservative Member of Parliament for Newark is married to the economics editor of *The Times*. *The Times* is often edited by the man who used to bully the little Sweet Stephen at Eton. *Mercilessly*. Because he was a Jew –

This is the way the world works. This small, small world.

Neil Fontaine drives the Jew South. The Jew closes his eyes in the back of the car. Neil Fontaine switches on the radio in the front and the back of the Mercedes –

'– *I am fed up of hearing of these movements to return to work by faceless men. They should stand up for what they believe and identify themselves –*'

Neil Fontaine glances in the mirror. The Jew opens his eyes in the back of the car. Neil Fontaine switches off the radio in the front and back of the Mercedes –

The Jew smiles. The Jew grins. The Jew chuckles. The Jew laughs –

Laughs and laughs and laughs.

The deadline expired at midnight. Terry Winters caught the first train down to Cardiff. He read books. Newspapers. He wrote notes. Letters. He did sums. Crosswords. It was a long journey. He took a taxi to the office of the South Wales NUM in Pontypridd. The office was in the Engineering Union building. The office was ringed by one thousand big men with moustaches and beards, baseball bats and badges. Terry got out of the taxi –

The big men stepped forward.

Terry said, 'Afternoon, gentlemen.'

'Who the fuck are you?' they said.

'I am the Chief Executive Officer of the National Union of Mineworkers.'

'Prove it.'

Terry Winters took his wallet out of his inside jacket pocket. He took out his card.

The big men gathered round the card. 'All right,' they said. 'Let him through.'

'Thank you,' said Terry. 'You are gentlemen and comrades.'

'No hard feelings,' they said. 'Thought you might be a sequestrator.'

Terry Winters shook his head. Terry said, 'They won't come down here.'

The big men shook their heads. The big men brandished their bats. They said, 'Just let them fucking try.'

Terry Winters nodded. Terry went inside the Engineering Union building. He took the lift up to the headquarters of the South Wales National Union of Mineworkers. He knocked on the door. He stepped inside –

Gareth Thomas was sitting on the floor next to a telephone. The office bare.

Terry Winters smiled. Terry said, 'Good afternoon, Comrade.'

'Have a seat, Comrade,' said Gareth Thomas. 'Oh sorry, there aren't any.'

Terry Winters smiled again. Terry said, 'It's the only way, Comrade.'

'So you say, Comrade,' said Gareth. 'So you say.'

'Has there been any contact with the sequestrators?' asked Terry.

Gareth stood up. He said, 'Our accountants in Cardiff have had a few calls.'

'What kind of information were they after?'

Gareth said, 'Names of our banks. Our auditors. And so on.'

'Did the accountants give them the names?'

Gareth shook his head. He said, 'Total non-cooperation, as you instructed.'

'Good,' said Terry. 'Very good.'

'So what happens now?' asked Gareth.

Terry said, 'They'll make the rounds of the banks and the auditors.'

'The banks will talk, won't they?'

Terry nodded. He said, 'They are obliged to.'

'Bastards,' said Gareth.

Terry nodded again. He said, 'They'll have set up a hotline to the judge, too.'

'That's convenient for them,' said Gareth. 'Lucky we've got nothing to take.'

'Yes, it is,' said Terry. 'And they know that, too.'

'Between fifty and a hundred grand a week,' said Gareth. 'Just on picketing. Almost a million and a half quid. If they don't sequestrate us, we'll be bankrupt anyway.'

'Nothing to worry about then,' said Terry.

Gareth walked over to the window. He looked down at the thousand men below.

'Just that lot,' he said. 'And they're not even going to see a sequestrator, are they?'

Terry shook his head. He said, 'They'll soon know exactly how much you had. Then they'll go after it through the banks and the courts. Try to find it and freeze it.'

Gareth turned back from the window. He nodded. 'Just like you said.'

Terry Winters looked at Gareth Thomas. Terry said, 'You did do what I said?'

Gareth Thomas nodded again.

'Good,' said Terry Winters. 'Then there really, really, is nothing to worry about.'

Gareth Thomas stared at Terry Winters. Terry smiled at Gareth –

The two men stood in silence in the empty office. Just a telephone on the floor between them –

Terry Winters said, 'Do you mind calling me a taxi back to Cardiff?'

'That's it?' said Gareth Thomas.

Terry Winters nodded. Terry said, 'I think so, yes.'

'You came all this way just to tell us not to worry?'

Terry nodded again. He said, 'The President wanted to show his support –'

'What about the money? Where's the cash?'

Terry looked at Gareth. Terry said, 'What money? What cash?'

'The bloody money you promised us to get us through this fucking mess!'

Terry said, 'I don't know what money you could mean, Comrade.'

'The money we fucking gave you!'

Terry held out his hands. He said, 'What money are you talking about?'

Gareth Thomas looked at Terry Winters. Gareth punched Terry in the face –

Terry Winters fell on the floor. His glasses broken. His nose bleeding.

Gareth Thomas spat at Terry Winters. Gareth Thomas walked out.

Terry Winters took out his handkerchief. Terry Winters wiped his face –

Blood and spit again.

The briefing at Gower Street was at ten. The usual maps and photographs on the walls. The one word and two numbers on the board:

Week 23.

The private door at the side opened. Forty faces followed her down to the front. Forty faces watched her stand behind the podium. Take her notes out of her briefcase. Her pen from her pocket. Her cigarettes –

Forty faces that wanted to fuck her. Again –

Malcolm closed his eyes until she'd finished. Until Diane had almost gone –

Her smell still here –

The New Order.

Malcolm went back to a different desk in a different office. He stared at the phone on the desk. The clock on the wall. He drank coffee. He smoked cigarettes –

And stared at the phone –

The car packed and ready to go.

Malcolm and Cole on stand-by –

Lot of secret talk about a lot of secret talks.

Malcolm sat at the desk. He stared at the phone. The clock. Drank another coffee. Smoked another cigarette and stared and stared and stared at the bloody phone –

The car packed. Ready to go.

Cole lay on the floor of the office. He had his eyes closed. His headphones on. The sound of National Radio 1.

Malcolm just sat there. Drinking and smoking –

And staring from the phone to the clock and back to the phone –

The car packed and ready to go. Fuck it –

Malcolm put on his headphones. He sat and still stared. But he listened now –

To them chatter – chatter – chatter –

'– I call on the British trade union movement to give total physical support to the NUM currently under attack from the government's anti-trade union laws –'

Chattering –

'– it has not penetrated the minds of this government and their judiciary that you cannot sequestrate an idea nor imprison a belief –'

Their ceaseless fucking chattering –

'– we will continue to operate, even if it means operating out of a telephone box –'

To them bicker – bicker – bicker –

'– she says she loves her country. For the sake of her country, she should go –'

Bickering –

'– there is only one word to describe the policy of the Right Honourable gentleman when faced with threats, whether from home or abroad, and that word is appeasement –'

Their bankrupt fucking bickering –

'– even in narrow financial terms, the three-hundred-and-fifty-million-pound cost of the strike represents a worthwhile investment for the good of the nation and that is before taking account of the wider issues in this debate –'

Ceaseless and bankrupt, endless and destitute –

Malcolm Morris wanted to cut off his ears. To put the pieces in an envelope –

Send her the envelope. First class. The scissors and a note –

Your turn, dear. For old times' sake.

Malcolm took off his headphones. Threw them across the room –

Cole was staring at him. The telephone ringing –

The voice telling them, 'Unity House, Euston Road –'

A date in the trees, their eyes and their ears among the branches and the leaves –

The Headquarters of the National Union of Railwaymen –

Just a hop, skip and a jump from here –

Malcolm put away the scissors. He stubbed out his cigarette –

Pressed record.

There were rumours of more court actions. Actions from within the Yorkshire coalfield. Lot being written and said about the Home Front now –

Terry watched Theresa Winters dump the frying pan and the grill in the sink. Terry watched Theresa squeeze Fairy Liquid onto the pan and the grill. He watched her run the tap until it was hot. He watched her pick up a Brillo pad. He watched her scrub and scrub the pan and the grill –

Slow. Slow. Quick. Quick. Slow –

Terry watched her put the Brillo pad back between the Fairy Liquid and the tap. He watched her rinse the pan and the grill under the tap. He watched her put the pan and the grill on the draining board. He watched her turn off the tap. He watched her pick up a tea-towel. He watched her dry and dry the pan and the grill –

Slow. Slow. Quick. Quick –

He watched her put the pan and the grill down on the worktop. He watched her dry her hands. He watched her put the tea-towel inside the washing-machine. He watched her put the frying pan in the cupboard above the fridge. He watched her put the grill back in the cooker. He watched her walk out of the kitchen –

Slow. Slow. Quick –

Out of the hall. Out of the house –

Out of their home in the suburbs of Sheffield, South Yorkshire.

you. Not after all I'd seen and heard – Them down here though, I don't know. Don't know what to think really. Lot of them gave a lot, but I don't know. Had a lot to give in first place. Like bloody Kent miners. They fucking pissed me off sometimes. First to tell you how hardcore they were – Militant through and through. Shoulder to shoulder. All that – But they didn't want their brothers-in-arms collecting down here, did they? Like London was their private bloody patch. Just theirs and rest of us could fuck off back to North. Right little gold mine it was for them and all. They only had two thousand men in three fucking pits and whole of London and bloody South to collect from. Be able to buy their pits soon, that much brass between them – Not like Yorkshire. Us that suffered most – Us that went out on picket. Picket, picket, picket – That were us. Not fannying about with fucking buckets. Having a chat with Red Ken on steps of GLC – Us out on picket lines getting our heads caved in. Beaten and arrested while our wives and kids went without. Curfews and roadblocks round our fucking houses and our villages – But I wouldn't have it other way round. I wouldn't want to be down here begging – That wasn't me. That wasn't any of us – Just would like a bit of their brass up our way for a change. But they could keep their bloody buckets – It said on front of our banner, *From Obscurity to Respect*. But part of me would come down here and feel like it ought to bloody say, *From Obscurity to Pity* – Because that was all it was for most of them. *Pity* – Not all of them. But a lot of them – Support the Miners. Stick your Southern quid in a Kent bucket to ease your bleeding conscience – But who fucking voted for her in first place? Who put me down here in bloody rain on streets of London with a plastic fucking bucket begging for their loose change? Crumbs off master's table? No one round where I bloody came from – No. It was all too easy for most of them down here – Different planet. Different world – Different country. Different class – They could keep it and all. Fucking keep it – My head had only just touched pillow

when there was a right loud banging on front door. That loud I thought it was riot squad. Mary stuck her head out of bedroom window – It was Keith. He must be drunk, I said – Mary shouted, He's asleep. He's got to be up again in three hour – Tell him he's got to be up now, said Keith. There's a mob of them gone up **Frank Ramsay's** – Fucking hell, I shouted. Hold on then. I'll be down. This had been brewing for a bit now. Frank Ramsay, Paul Banks and a couple of other lads had had short contracts over border in Nottingham at Bevercotes. Their contracts had run on for just first month of strike and lads here in village had turned a bit of a blind eye to them still working, because what they were doing were scabbing. But if they'd come out with rest of us they'd have got no benefits or nothing. They were all right and all. Known round village as good lads. Then their contracts had expired and that were that. Matter were finished with. But then last week, Board went and offered them permanent work – That was different. If they took them jobs they'd be taking jobs of blokes on Bevercotes picket line – That was same pit where that fucking Silver Birch twat worked and all. They'd be scabs same as him – It was wrong and they knew it. But they'd taken jobs and now they were going to have to pay price – Heavy one by sounds of it, too. Heavy one – Keith said, Frank were walking past Welfare and someone said something. There were words ex-changed. Lads got on about it inside and worked themselves up into a right lather – I bet they did, I said. I bet they did – Minute we turned into Frank's street we heard his window go through. Then shotgun – Fucking shotgun blast. Daft bastard had only gone and fired his twelve bore out the bloody bedroom window – Keith stopped car where we were. I got out. Frank was shouting, There's more where that come from. There's kids in here – Folk already moving off now though. Lad told me they were heading over to Paul Banks's house on next street. I wanted to go with them to make sure nothing else daft happened, but I was worried about Frank. I was worried coppers would come and shoot

The Twenty-third Week

Monday 6 – Sunday 12 August 1984

There is a full board meeting of the NCB today. The Jew has his invitation. He has been asked to address the Board by the Chairman. He knows the Board do not care for him. The Jew doesn't care. He is on the front line. Not them. He's fighting this fight. Not them. He's winning the war, not them –

'Help the Miners, yes,' says the Jew. 'But not him. Never. Not him. Never him. That one man's war has brought over five thousand arrests. Injured six hundred police and two hundred pickets. That one man's war has killed two of his own on the picket line. Driven to suicide many, many more. It has cost countless millions in damage to property. It has seen miner attack miner. Colleague attack colleague. Brother attack brother. It has led to threats of assault, rape and murder on the families of those that will not join this one man's war –

'Well, gentlemen, the time has come to fight back and I am here today to tell you that fightback has already started. Independent legal actions by ordinary working miners across the coalfields of Britain have begun. Collections by ordinary working miners to compensate the victims of intimidation and violence have begun. Committees of ordinary miners who want to organize a return to work have begun –

'These men are on the front line. They stand alone against one man's attempts to destroy the democratic rights of working-class people. If he succeeds and these men fail, this country fails too –

'The battle has been joined. The fightback has begun. If it is to be won, and won speedily, all who love and believe in freedom and democracy should do and give what they can financially or in any other way they see fit.'

Neil Fontaine claps long and loud. He says, 'Bravo, sir. Bravo.'

'To Hobart House, then,' says the Jew. 'To Hobart House, Neil.'

Malcolm didn't sleep because Malcolm didn't want to dream. He didn't want to dream because he didn't want to hear them –

Hear them in his dreams. Laughing. See them in his sheets. Fucking.

These were the nights from which he ran and hid. The days when he disappeared –

Checked into a hotel. Locked the doors. Drew the curtains –

Disappeared off the face of the Earth –

To lie deceived and defeated on hotel sheets. For nights and days like these –

These dark dog-days of August 1984.

Malcolm Morris lay awake in his room at the Clifton Park Hotel and watched the night retreat across the ceiling. The curtains. The shadows become sunlight. Malcolm lay awake in his room at the Clifton Park Hotel and wished that it were so –

That shadows became light.

Malcolm got up. Dressed. He checked out. Drove –

Dalton, Nottinghamshire.

He parked and sat low in the car and watched them arrive with their radios on –

'– I plan to come out into the open to prevent my friends from being hurt and intimidated by militant miners who are trying to identify Grey Fox through violence –'

He watched Carl Baker at the door of the pub between four large policemen –

'– I do not agree with the Board's pit closure programme but eighty per cent of striking miners want to go back to work –'

He watched him shake hands with each man who came to his meeting –

'– don't let this animal element, these left-wing bully-boys and their hit squads, don't let them destroy your lives. Call your mates, then call your pit manager –'

He watched him talk to the journalists and the TV crews with his sunglasses on –

'– let's all go back to work next Monday. Tell your wives to pack your lunch, then go to your pit and strike a blow for democracy –'

He watched him break down into hundreds of tears (a lifetime of fears to come). He watched Stephen Sweet put an arm around him –

A silent movie.

He watched their secret meeting break up before the cameras and the microphones. Their cars leave and the car park empty. He watched the police escort Carl Baker and Stephen Sweet and some journalists out to a police Range Rover.

Malcolm looked at his watch –

Fuck.

He started the Volvo. Drove back up to South Yorkshire. The A57 onto the A638 –

The Great North Road.

He passed through Retford and Ranskill. Noticed the Montego in the rearview –

Fuck.

The driver holding something to his mouth. Larger men in the front and rear –

Fuck.

Malcolm put his foot down. The car in front braked –

Fuck.

Malcolm swerved to the left. Into the hedgerow. Into the ditch –

Fuck.

Doors opened. Boots came –

Fuck.

Malcolm opened his door. He got out. Hands over his ears. But it was too late –

Fuuuuuuuuuuuuuuuuuuuuuuuuuuuuuuuuuuuuuuuuuuuuuuuuuuuuuuuuuck.

It never goes away. Tony Davies has left two messages for Neil Fontaine. They arrange to meet in the pub next door to the Kingsley Hotel on Bloomsbury Way. Tony is wearing a floral waistcoat under his stained linen jacket. Tony smells of sweat. Tony is a paedophile. Tony is a member of Nazi groups. Tony drinks double vodkas. Neil drinks a Britvic orange. They talk about the Olympics. They talk about Nigel Short. They talk about the weather –

'Too bloody hot,' says Tony. 'Unbearable. I need to get away. You too.'

Neil Fontaine stares at Tony Davies. Neil asks, 'What makes you say that, Tony?'

'I know about Shrewsbury,' he whispers. 'Very bad business. Very bad.'

Neil Fontaine keeps staring at Tony Davies –

The flowers and the stains –

Tony smiles. Tony points at Neil. Tony says, 'They're asking for names.'

Neil Fontaine picks up his Britvic. Neil Fontaine takes another sip from it.

Tony puts a hand on Neil's arm. Tony says, 'I can help you, Neil. I can help you.'

Neil Fontaine removes Tony's hand from his arm. He says, 'You're drunk, Tony.'

'Am I?' says Tony. 'Am I really? Well, so bloody what if I am?'

Neil Fontaine pulls him close. He whispers, 'You got something to say? Say it.'

'I want to know what you've done with my Julius?' says Tony. 'Where is he?'

Neil Fontaine puts his hand between Tony's legs. He grabs Tony's testicles –

Tony Davies sits in the corner of the pub and tries not to scream.

Neil Fontaine lets go of Tony's testicles. He says, 'Go back to your hole, Tony.'

Tony stands up. Tony runs out of the pub next door to the Kingsley Hotel.

Neil Fontaine picks up his Britvic. He finishes it. He stands up –

He follows Tony out of the pub next door to the Kingsley Hotel.

The Old Man was sick. He'd collapsed at the rally to commemorate the Tolpuddle Martyrs. He hadn't got up again yet. The Annual Congress was only three weeks away. The Fat Man had seized his chance. He took the train to Sheffield. The lift up to the tenth floor. The Fat Man wanted to see for himself. Hear for himself –

'The South Wales NUM accounts with the local Co-operative and Midland banks have all been frozen,' Terry Winters was telling him. 'The majority of their assets had already been transferred for safety, so the amounts involved are not great. However, they do include all recent donations and so we're hopeful we can argue in court that this money is then technically not the property of the South Wales NUM and should therefore be unfrozen. But, in the meantime, it leaves them on a day-to-day basis with no cash.'

The Fat Man turned to the President. He asked, 'The National Union cannot offer them any assistance? Short-term loans? Divert other donations?'

'Impossible,' said the President. 'Comrade Chief Executive, continue.'

'The National Union is itself desperately short of money,' said Terry. 'Our own assets were also transferred abroad at the start of the dispute. The substantial amounts of money we have received through donations and loans from other unions have, almost in their entirety, been used to alleviate hardship within the communities. There is no longer any finance available to assist areas with strike-related activities. This office itself requires well over one hundred thousand pounds a week to keep going, and by the end of October we will be unable to cover those costs –'

'Unless', said the President, 'the trade union movement comes to our aid.'

The Fat Man nodded. He picked up his TUC pen. He said, 'How about loans?'

'We've had loans,' said the President. 'We need total physical support –'

The Fat Man nodded again. He said, 'I know that. But what about interest-free loans from across the entire trade union movement? Not just the usual suspects.'

'It would show tangible physical support,' agreed the President.

'The loans would have to be shown to be secure,' said the Fat Man. 'And they would obviously have to be repaid.'

'Obviously,' said the President.

'And, *obviously*,' continued the Fat Man, 'they would have to be made in such a way as not to compromise the legal position of our members.'

The President looked over to Terry. He said, 'Comrade Chief Executive?'

'There's over eight million pounds of our assets overseas at present,' said Terry. 'These assets are untraceable and can therefore act as security for any loans received. If the loans themselves are made in the form of donations, then the legal position of the donor cannot be compromised should the National Union be subject to any future court actions in regard to our finances. At the conclusion of the dispute, our assets will be returned to Britain and repayments on the loans could then commence.'

The Fat Man stopped writing. The Fat Man put down his TUC pen again. He said, 'The assets are untraceable? You're absolutely certain of that?'

Terry Winters smiled. Terry Winters said, 'Of that I am certain.'

'There *is* another way,' said the President.

The Fat Man picked up his TUC pen again and asked, 'And what way is that?'

'Comrade Chief Executive,' said the President again, 'if you would –'

'The President has already submitted a motion calling for all-out support from the Trades Union Congress,' said Terry. 'Following last Wednesday's meeting with ASLEF, the NUS and the NUR, it was decided that we would add to our resolution a number of amendments – one of which is to demand a ten-pence-a-week levy from each individual member of each of the ninety-eight affiliated unions of Congress.'

The Fat Man put down his pen. He said, 'You're talking a million quid a week.'

'No,' said the President. 'I'm talking ten pence a week.'

The Fat Man shook his head –

There was silence on the tenth floor. Then footsteps –

Paul Hargreaves opened the door. Paul Hargreaves looked at Terry Winters –

The General Secretary stood and stared at the Chief Executive.

'What is it, Comrade?' asked the President. 'What's happened?'

'They've found and frozen the South Wales assets,' said Paul. 'All of them.'

The President turned to Terry Winters. The Fat Man turned to Terry Winters –

The whole room turned to Terry fucking Winters –

Terry shook his head. His head red. His head in his hands. His hands dirty –

His hands over his eyes –

His eyes full.

They've had a bit of a lie-in this morning have these would-be Working Miners. They have yet to come down to the lobby of the Mayfair Westbury and it is already well past ten o'clock. But they have had a busy week have these would-be Working Miners. They have been in court each day to hear their action against the Yorkshire Area of the NUM over the Union's failure to hold a ballot. They have been on television. They have been on the radio. In the papers. They are the men of the moment are these would-be Working Miners.

Neil Fontaine waits for them in a comfortable chair in the lobby of the Westbury while the Jew tries to keep Carl Baker patient.

'They certainly deserved their champagne,' the Jew is telling him.

Carl Baker shakes his head. He says, 'I could do with a glass or ten myself.'

'And you will have one, Carl,' says the Jew. 'As many as you want. Later.'

Carl Baker nods. He looks at his watch again –

The Jew has organized a lunchtime press conference for Grey Fox in the upstairs room of a pub near the High Court. Here Grey Fox will reveal himself to be none other than mild-mannered father-of-two Carl Baker from the Bevercotes pit. He will announce the launch of the *Carl Baker Fund for Democracy*. Then Carl will travel to the BBC and speak on *The World This Weekend*, after which the *Mail on Sunday* will accompany Carl on yet another tour of the pits and the villages of the British coalfields –

Carl Baker looks at his watch again. He says, 'I don't want to be late.'

'And you won't be,' says the Jew. 'You won't be.'

Carl Baker nods. He says, 'I think I need to use the bathroom again.'

The Jew and Neil Fontaine watch Carl Baker walk across the lobby in his tight pale denim jeans and his tight pale cotton jacket. He is going greyer by the minute. He has also grown a moustache since he first met the Jew. The Jew is flattered –

But Neil Fontaine is worried. He is not sure this is the right man. He tells the Jew, 'Fred Wallace called, sir.'

'And has the John Wayne of Pye Hill assembled his posse?'

Neil Fontaine says, 'They are all saddled up, sir.'

'Excellent news,' says the Jew. 'Will you make the necessary arrangements?'

Neil Fontaine says, 'Certainly, sir.'

The lift doors open. Don and Louise, Derek and Jackie step out. The ladies are laughing; their men carrying the suitcases.

The Jew stands up. The Jew says, 'Good morning. And how are we all today?'

The Working Miners and their wives all nod and smile.

'Good, good, good,' says the Jew. 'Now where has our friend Carl got to?'

Neil Fontaine stands up. He goes down to the Gents' –

Carl Baker is washing his face in the sink. He looks up at Neil –

His skin is grey. His eyes red. His tongue forked –

Neil Fontaine staggers back. Back from the sink. Back from the mirror.

Carl Baker dries his face with a paper towel. He says, 'Are you all right?'

'They're waiting for you upstairs,' says Neil.

Carl Baker puts the wet paper towel in the basket with the other wet paper towels. He follows Neil Fontaine back up the stairs and across the lobby. He says hello to Don and Louise, Derek and Jackie –

He smells of sick.

'Right then,' says the Jew. 'To the pub.'

Neil Fontaine holds open the doors for the Jew and his friends and their families. He hails a taxi for Don and Louise, Derek and Jackie. He gives the driver the name of the pub near the court. He hands him the fare in advance. He shuts the door of the cab –

The Jew and Carl wave them bye-bye.

Neil Fontaine holds open the back door of the Mercedes. Carl gets into the back. Neil Fontaine waits for the Jew to get in –

The Jew stops. He looks at Neil. He says, 'You don't look at all well, Neil.'

Neil Fontaine says, 'I'm fine, sir.'

'Really?' asks the Jew. 'How are you sleeping these days?'

him or something, him waving shotgun around like a bloody madman. I told him, Put gun away fore someone gets hurt, Frank – You want some and all, do you, Pete? he shouted down from window. I said, Don't be daft. It's not a bloody film, is it? This is real life – Fuck off, you and whole bloody lot of you – Fair enough, I said. I've tried. I walked back down path to pavement. I could hear them all over in next street. It sounded like they were giving Paul's car some hammer. I didn't blame them. You couldn't. Next news police van was coming down road. *Krk-krk.* Lads all walking back this way now. Police obviously didn't fancy their chances. But when I turned round I could see a load more vans coming down into village. *Krk-krk.* Be putting on riot gear in back – Lads started running. Me and all – I thought, Fucking hell, and I said to Keith, It's starting again – Never bloody ends, he said. Never bloody ends – **Panel** again. David Rainer nodded. He said, It's right. Tomorrow. Gascoigne Wood – There'll be civil war, said Johnny. Civil fucking war, that's what there'll be. I said, What you think we got now? Not a fucking picnic, is it? Johnny shook his head. He said, It'll be nothing compared to what's coming – He's right, said Tom. Will look like a bloody picnic next to this, I tell you – So what we going to do? asked Derek. What bloody hell we going to do about it? Does anyone know who he is? Tom asked. Johnny nodded. Johnny said, Name's Brian Green. Fucking electrician. I said, Has anyone from Kellingley or Barnsley spoken to him? Johnny said, He's a scab, Pete. First fucking scab in Yorkshire. What's point? Not until tomorrow, said David Rainer. Not until tomorrow, he's not – It was another one of them mornings when lads didn't need telling. Not after last week. I went up with Tony Stones, Mick Marsh and Lester. **Gascoigne Wood.** Just as dawn came up. That many pickets, there were tailbacks. Easy four thousand by eight o'clock. Easy. Most anybody had seen since Orgreave. Police out in force, of course. *Krk-krk.* Thousand of them. One. Fucking. Thousand – All for one bloke. One.

Fucking. Bloke. Five thousand folk on both side, gathered in a fucking pit lane, first thing of a morning, all because one bloody bloke wanted to sell his fucking soul. Take their scab shilling. I hoped he choked on it. Hoped he fucking choked. But you looked at all them coppers on all that overtime and you knew it was more than any bloody shilling and all. I stood there trying to work it out. How much it must have been costing them to get this one scabby bastard into that one pit to sit on his arse for eight hour. Say this for coppers, they're always quick enough to tell you how much they're on. How King Arthur had done more for police pay than any Home Secretary. Everyone knew they didn't get out of bed down South for less than a hundred quid a shift these days. There were a thousand of them easy, so that were a hundred grand straight off then. Just on police pay. Like Billy in Welfare said, She must really hate us. *Really fucking hate us* – And then shout went up. I got on my toes to get a good look at him. I couldn't see much, though – Raining fucking bricks as usual. Heavy weather – Just this blue taxi coming roaring up pit lane. Ninety mile an hour – Mass push. Lot of fucking scrapping. Helmets going up. Smoke coming off fields where lads had lit some bales – They got him in, though. They always did – Mick Marsh said there were two of them in back and all today. Lester bet other one was just a pig – Ten quid said so. Why they called him Lester – But how could you tell? Both scabs were sat in back of taxi with their jackets over their heads – Like real men. Them jackets would be on their heads for rest of their lives now – Fucking pressure they must have put on him, though. That first one. Felt for him in a way. Not that it was something you'd ever say, like – But who'd want to be him? That bastard. Only scab in Yorkshire. First scab in Yorkshire – What a thing to tell your kids. Your grandkids – There was Home Front. Then there was your own doorstep – And this was our own doorstep all right: **Silverwood** – Home of our Panel. Fucking war zone, what it was now. Like pictures of bloody Belfast or

The Twenty-fourth Week

Monday 13 – Sunday 19 August 1984

The wind rattled the wire. The question distorted. The torture displaced. The pain disembodied. The guard back to haunt the ghost –

Malcolm heard her inhale. Malcolm heard her exhale. Malcolm opened his eyes.

Diane said, 'They took your warrant card?'

Malcolm swallowed. Malcolm nodded.

She stubbed out the cigarette. She put a hand on his wounds. She kissed his ears.

Malcolm flinched. Malcolm cried.

Diane stood up. Diane said, 'Run, Malcolm. Hide.'

Malcolm closed his eyes until she'd gone. Her smell always the same now –

Disinfectant.

Theresa Winters had gone down to Bath to stay with her parents and the children. Theresa had said she would stay there until Terry apologized for all the things he had done. For all the things he had said –

The stupid things.

Terry dried his eyes. Terry said, 'I blame myself.'

The President stood up in front of the huge portrait of himself. He walked round to where Terry was sitting. He handed Terry a tissue. He put a hand on Terry's shoulder –

Terry looked up at the President. Terry said, 'Please don't blame Gareth.'

'I don't blame either of you, Comrade,' said the President. 'How could I?'

Terry blew his nose. Terry waited –

The sequestrators had seized seven hundred thousand pounds from South Wales. It would be held until the NUM leaders purged their contempt –

Terry's plans had failed.

'How could anyone,' continued the President, 'how could anyone possibly have foreseen the extent to which this government would manipulate the country's legal system in order to conspire against and crush the attempts of any trade unionist to save their job? How could you have foreseen that? You tried your best, Comrade –'

Terry sniffed. Terry nodded –

'But your best was not good enough,' said the President. 'Next time, Comrade?'

'Next time,' said Terry. 'Next time my best will be more than good enough.'

The President sat down in front of his portrait. He said, 'Then you are forgiven.'

Terry stood up. Terry said, 'Thank you, President. Thank you.'

The President did not look up from his desk.

Len held open the door for Terry. Terry walked backwards out of the room –

Terry went upstairs. He sat on his chair and looked around the Conference Room. Terry saw Bill Reed. Bill Reed winked. Terry looked away. Terry saw Samantha Green. Samantha was the Union's new solicitor. Terry smiled. Samantha looked away –

The President entered. Everyone rose –

The President was still fuming about the former Grey Fox –

'Least he's from Nottinghamshire,' shouted the President. 'Not a collier either, bloody blacksmith or something. Only done that for five year too. But I will say again, here and now, I don't want a single hair of his head touched.'

Everybody nodded.

'Not one hair,' said the President. 'But these other two –'

'Don Colby and Derek Williams,' said Paul.

'– these two are from Yorkshire. Bloody faceworkers at Manton –'

'Nottingham in all but name,' said Paul.

'They're Yorkshiremen,' said the President. 'They should know better.'

Everybody nodded again.

The President looked over at Samantha Green. He said, 'Love –'

'There are, in total, eleven orders now facing the Yorkshire Area,' she said. 'These *scabs* want a declaration from Justice Warner that the strike is not official in Yorkshire without a ballot. In some respects it's similar in nature to the actions brought against North Wales and the Midlands. Their lawyers are to argue that the 1983 Inverness Conference decision calling for action against any proposed pit closures was discretionary – not mandatory – and that this supersedes the 1981 vote, which, they argue, is too remote anyway. They have had help though –'

'Inside help and all,' said the President. 'Lot of it too –'

Everybody stopped nodding. Everybody looked back up the table.

'They have copies of the National and Yorkshire rulebooks. They have copies of the agendas and minutes for the past five area conferences, for the National and Area executive committees, and for the Yorkshire Strike Co-ordinating Committee. Not just minutes, actual verbatim reports.'

Terry Winters glanced across the table at Bill Reed. Bill Reed said, 'Who?'

'Huddersfield Road,' said the President.

Bill Reed said, 'I warned you.'

'Aye, you warned us,' said Dick. 'But you didn't give us a name, did you?'

Bill Reed smiled. Bill said, 'You want it on a silver plate, do you, Comrade?'

'I wanted more than gossip and rumour, aye,' said Dick.

Bill shook his head. He said again, 'I warned you, Comrade. I warned you.'

'Enough of this bloody bickering,' said the President.

Bill Reed tapped the table. Bill said, 'Here, here.'

The President looked at Bill Reed. The President looked around the whole room. The President said, 'Now is the time for action, Comrades. Action.'

Everybody nodded once again. Everybody clapped.

Terry Winters glanced back across the table at Bill Reed. Bill winked.

Terry Winters looked away. Terry looked over at Samantha Green –

Samantha was staring at Bill Reed –

Bill winked again.

'To your posts,' said the President. 'Be vigilant! Be valiant! Be victorious!'

Everyone applauded. Briefly. Then everyone ran for cover –

The Chairman wanted the President prosecuted for criminal conspiracy.

Terry took the lift back down. Terry stood between the Denims and the Tweeds. The Denims had their tobacco tins in their hands. The Tweeds their pouches –

'Fuck you, Stalin. Bugger you, Trotsky,' all the way down and out –

Terry walked through the lunchtime shoppers. Made his way across the precinct. He went into Boots. He wandered around the pharmacy. He looked at the pills and the medicines. He bought two hundred aspirins. Deodorant and mouthwash. He paid by cash. He went into W. H. Smith. He wandered around the newspapers and the magazines. He looked at the contents and the headlines. Reagan had joked about bombing Russia in five minutes. He bought every paper with a jobs section. Writing paper and envelopes. He went into Marks & Spencer. He wandered around the Men's Department. He looked at the shirts and the suits. He picked up a pair of socks –

'Not getting cold feet are we, Comrade?' asked Bill Reed.

Malcolm drove home to Harrogate. Fast. He left the car parked in the middle of the road. Doors open. He ran into the house. The lounge. He tore the cassettes off the shelves –

The War of the Worlds *into his pocket –*

The telephone ringing. Malcolm picked it up. Listened –

'Having a bit of a clear out, are we?' asked Roger Vaughan.

'What do you want?'

'Not forgotten already, have we?'

'Forgotten what?'

'Your eyes and ears, Malcolm,' said Roger. 'Your eyes and ears.'

'What about them?'

'We had a deal,' said Roger. 'Your eyes and your ears are ours now.'

Roll up. Roll up. The police have had to close part of Northgate. There are diversions. The Jew has brought the carnival to the streets of Newark. TV trucks and cars full of cameramen choke the town centre of Newark. The carnival has come to see the cash –

To smell it. To touch it –

The Jew stands downstairs in the reception area at the front of Robinson & Harris. He tips the contents of an oversized post-bag across the reception desk and hands the envelopes to the gentlemen of the press and the Independent Television News –

'Read them and weep, Adolf,' shouts the Jew. 'Read them and weep.'

Behind him stand Don and Derek; Don wearing his new Nottingham Forest shirt; Derek his new leather jacket –

'"Dear Don and Derek,"' reads the Jew. '"You are real heroes to me and all the other miners at our pit. We are only on strike because we are too scared of his Red Guard and South Yorkshire Hit Squad and what they would do to our wives and kids if we were to go into work. We think you are the bravest men in this country. We have not got much money, as you know, but here is over one hundred pounds that we want you to have. We hope you will win soon, so we can all return to work. Sorry we can't sign our real names, but we know you know why. Your friends and your fans."'

Pens scribble, cameras flash –

'And this one,' says the Jew. 'This one from a pensioner in Brighton who says, "Thank God that this country still has men like Mr Colby and Mr Williams to fight not only for their own and their mates' rights, but also for all the members of the public who are decent and hard-working like them, and who support them wholeheartedly –"'

'How much have the lads got so far, then?' ask the press.

Piers Harris steps forward. He says, 'To date, since the launch of the Ballot Fund, we have received over five hundred letters a day and a total of more than twenty thousand pounds.'

'Twenty thousand pounds,' shrieks the Jew. 'It just keeps flooding in. Pouring in. Pound notes from pensioners and schoolchildren, cheques for a hundred or for a thousand pounds from individuals and businesses.'

'How do you feel about all this, Don?' ask the press.

'It's fantastic,' says Don. 'Just fantastic.'

'Yes,' says Derek. 'It is fantastic.'

'Remember,' says the Jew. 'Their own homes are under twenty-four-hour guard. They are accompanied everywhere by members of the Special Branch. They are both heavily overdrawn and their mortgages have not been paid. Heaven forbid they should lose, this action could cost each man more than one hundred thousand pounds.'

'How do you feel about that, Derek?' ask the press.

'It would have been worth every penny,' says Derek. 'Every penny.'

'Yes,' says Don. 'Every penny.'

'But they're not going to lose,' shouts the Jew. 'Not with this kind of support from ordinary members of the Great British Public –

'The people of Great Britain won't let them lose!'

'What do you think of Carl Baker, the ex-Grey Fox?' ask the press.

Don and Derek look at the Jew. The Jew nods at Don and Derek –

'He has a lot of courage and integrity,' says Don. 'A lot.'

'Yes,' says Derek. 'A lot of courage and integrity.'

'OK, that's all folks,' shouts the Jew. 'Show's over for now.'

Neil Fontaine watches the gentlemen of the press and the Independent Television News leave the offices of Robinson & Harris. He watches them run back to their trucks and their cars with their headlines for their deadlines.

The telephone rings. The secretary says, 'Mr Sweet, it's Carl Baker for you.'

The Jew looks at Neil Fontaine. The Jew draws a finger across his throat.

Neil Fontaine takes the phone from the girl –

'Hello, Carl,' says Neil Fontaine. 'Mr Sweet is busy. Can I take a message?'

Malcolm showed the receptionist at the County his new warrant card and the receptionist showed Malcolm the register. Malcolm asked for Room 707 and the receptionist gave him a key attached to a long wooden stick.

Malcolm took the lift. He walked down the corridor past the bathrooms –

The rooms were empty. The rooms were quiet –

A black man pushed a vacuum cleaner down the corridor.

Malcolm came to Room 707. He unlocked the door. He stepped inside –

It smelt stale.

Malcolm hung the Do Not Disturb *sign on the outside handle of the door. He closed the door. Locked it. He took off his shoes. Placed them on the double bed. He walked across the room. Drew the curtains. He took a gauze mask from his trouser pocket. Put it on. He took off his trousers. Placed them on the bed. He took off his jacket. Placed it on the bed.*

Malcolm lay down on the floor between the bed and the door –

He turned his head to the left. His ear to the floor –

Malcolm closed his eyes. He controlled his breathing beneath the mask –

He listened –

No one home down below.

Malcolm breathed out through the mask. He opened his eyes –

Not today.

Malcolm took his shoes off the bed. Placed them by the door. He took his trousers and jacket off the bed. Hung them on the back of the door. He took the pillows, the blankets and the sheets off the bed. Folded them up and placed them inside the wardrobe. He lifted up the double bed. Placed it on its side. He picked up his case. Put it on the dressing table. He opened it. Took out a Stanley knife. He cut a large square out of the thicker carpet under where the bed had stood. Placed the square of carpet to one side. He cut a smaller square out of the underlay. Placed it to one side. He put the Stanley knife back in his briefcase. Took out a small brush. He dusted the floorboards clean. Put the brush back in his briefcase. He took out the stethoscope and the micro-recorder, the micro-tapes and the microphones. Malcolm laid them out. He set them up. He tested and adjusted them. He went back to the briefcase. Took out the envelope –

The photograph.

Malcolm Morris pinned the photograph to the wall of Room 707, the County Hotel, and lay on the floor and stared up into that face –

The ghosts without. The ghosts within –

The face of Neil Fontaine.

Beirut – Barricades across roads. Trees. Scrap cars. Tyres. Supermarket trolleys – David Rainer stood up with more bad news. He said, Board are saying seventeen went in today – Is that scabs or coppers in disguise? asked Johnny. Folk were nodding. I said, Know which pits, do we? Allerton-Bywater and Gascoigne Wood up there. Askern, Brodsworth, Hatfield and Markham Main in Doncaster area. Just Silverwood here, David read from his list. Folk were shaking their heads. Tom said, Thought Donny were solid? All part of their plan, said Derek. Board and police know them lads flying from those pits are hardcore. They've pushed them pits first so as to keep local lads busy – Lot of them blokes are stuck out in middle of nowhere, too, said Tom. Easy to get at them – Pressure they put on them is immense, said David. Folk were nodding again. I said, Talking to them. It's only way to help them – Help them? Johnny laughed. They're fucking scabs, Pete. How many more times? *They're as good as dead to us* – Be blackout curtains over **Welfare's** windows soon. That bad. I looked up – Built like a brick shithouse, he was. Not been down here before. Never been on a picket, either. Lads said he just sat about house or went up reservoir with his dog. His wife worked. Packing factory in Rotherham. Not as bad off as some, then. Two teenage kids at school, mind – But here he was. First thing after breakfast – Tears down both cheeks. Dog on a lead – Aye-up, Chris, I said. What's up with you, lad? It's about her, he said. Who? He pointed at his dog on lead. He said, Her – What about her? I said. I can't keep her. Can't feed her. RSPCA won't bloody take her – I looked at pair of them. I shook my head. I said, I don't know what – Thought you might know someone, he said. Bloody good dog, she is – I can see that, I said. But what – Don't want to just let her loose, he said. She wouldn't go, either. I know she wouldn't. Daft thing'd get hit by a car or something. I took her up reservoir last night. Had a bag with me. Few stones. Bit of rope. But I couldn't. I just couldn't do it – Chris, Chris, listen to me, I told him. If you came on picket with us, you'd get a

quid a day. Bill Blakey's will sell you a bag of bones for a quid. He looked up. He wiped his nose. He said, You don't want her, then? I bloody don't, I said. But I want you to come picketing. That way you can keep her. He wiped his nose again. He said, But I seen it on telly, Pete. It's not for me. I said, Looks worse than it is on TV. Nine time out of ten, nothing ever happens. Die of boredom most days. He shook his head. He said, That how you lost your teeth then, is it? Chris, I said, you'd be biggest bloody bloke there. He looked at dog. He said, I know that. That's why I don't want to go – I wouldn't let anything happen to you, I said. Not when I were with you. He looked up at me again, then back down at dog. He said, Just a quid? Unless there's anything left over from petrol and there will be, I said. Big bastard like you in car. He sighed. He said, I'll see you Monday then. I nodded. I said, I'll be waiting – Armthorpe. Askern. Bentley. Brodsworth. Easington. Hatfield. Silverwood. Wearmouth – Waiting for war to come to us – *Her war*. My war – Teeth woke me up again. Bloody hurt, they did. I didn't want to get out of my bed, though. Fucking week we'd had. Hardly been in house. I couldn't think last time I sat down for a meal with Mary and our Jackie – Mary was folding washing when I came **downstairs**. Jackie had gone to get us a paper. I made us all a pot. Jackie came back. Read bits of paper. Best news of week was Wednesday beating Forest three-fucking-one – Take that, you scabby fucking bastards, I thought – Mary said, What you grinning at? Nothing. She said, I saw Martin's wife yesterday. Cath Daly? I said. Where was that then? In town, she said. Centre of Rotherham. In precinct, wasn't it? Our Jackie looked up from her tea. She nodded. Did you speak to her? Just how's it going, Mary said. Usual – What did she say? Nothing – Mention Martin, did she? No – Keith thought they might have moved, you know? Mary shook her head. She said, What does he know about anything? I said, Might go up there after dinner – I got car out. Drove up to **Hardwick**. Parked outside their house. No sign of life. I knocked on

The Twenty-fifth Week

Monday 20 – Sunday 26 August 1984

The President sent Terry Winters and Mike Sullivan back to Huddersfield Road again. The President wanted them to find out what-the-bloody-hell-was-going-on-over-there. The President didn't trust Huddersfield Road at all now. Not one inch. None of them. The President was really, really fucking paranoid now –

They all were (they all said so). Everyone –

Dick and Paul. Joan and Len. The Tweeds and the Denims. Everyone –

Clive Cook was waiting on the front steps outside the Yorkshire Headquarters. Clive said, 'Good morning, Comrades.'

'Is it fuck,' said Mike Sullivan.

'You weren't expecting us, were you, Comrade?' asked Terry.

Clive Cook looked at Terry. Clive said, 'Should I have been?'

Terry and Mike Sullivan went through the arched doorway. Clive followed them. On the stairs, Clive asked, 'Is there anything I can help you with, Comrades?'

'You can show us where you keep your area minutes and agendas,' said Mike.

Clive shook his head. He said, 'They are all locked in the Area President's office.'

'And you don't have a key, I suppose?' asked Terry.

Clive shook his head again. He said, 'Of course not.'

'Who does?' asked Mike.

Clive stopped a step below Terry and Mike. He said, 'What is this, Comrades?'

'You have a mole in this building,' said Terry.

Mike nodded. He said, 'An enemy within.'

'So what are you two?' asked Clive. 'The Sheffield Inquisition?'

'Yes,' said Terry Winters. 'That's exactly what we are. Now find us the keys.'

Clive Cook walked back down the stairs. Clive Cook produced the keys –

Terry and Mike set to work; Clive Cook watched them –

Tear up plans. Budgets. Rewrite reports. Minutes –

Then Terry sent Mike out on another paper-chase and called Clive Cook closer. Terry ran his hands over Clive's chest. Across his back. Up and down his legs –

Terry pulled him closer still and said, 'I hope you're being a good boy, Clive.'

Clive put his arms around Terry. Clive put his head against Terry's chest –

Clive held on to Terry until he heard the footsteps –

The footsteps in the dark corridor.

Terry Winters got back to the office first. There would be no one here today. They'd still all be up at Gascoigne Wood. The Denims too. There to greet Brian Green –

The first Yorkshire scab –

The Home Front had opened up.

Terry had a long list of phone-calls to return. His old friend Jimmy at NACODS. The *Daily* bloody *Mirror.* Nearly every finance officer in the whole fucking Union. Terry took another three aspirins. He sat down under the large portrait of the President. He waited for the phone to ring. For her to call –

Please, please, please –

At five o'clock it rang.

Terry picked up the phone. *Click-click.* He said, 'Chief Executive speaking.'

'Hello, Chief Executive,' she said. 'Hope you missed me.'

Terry dropped the phone –

He did the stairs and the streets in five minutes. The drive in ten –

He ran through the hotel. Up the stairs. Through her door –

Terry dropped his pants –

Beds creaked. Headboards banged. Walls shook. Mouths cursed –

'My best was not good enough,' shouted Terry. 'Not fucking good enough!'

Diane reached over to touch him. To hold him –

Terry turned away. Terry said, 'I hate him. I hate him. I fucking hate him!'

'And I know, I know, I know you do,' said Diane.

'No, you don't,' shouted Terry. 'You've no idea. No one has!'

'Just tell me what you want,' she said. 'Tell me and I'll help you to do it.'

'Tell you what I want?' repeated Terry. 'You really want to fucking know?'

'Tell me,' she said. 'I want to know. I want to help you.'

Terry stood up. He held Diane's face in his right hand. He looked into it. He said, 'I want this strike to end. I want my marriage to end. I want to run away with you.'

'But where would we go?' she asked. 'How would we live?'

Terry said, 'I've told you, I've got money –'

Diane put her finger to his lips. She led him back to the bed. She sat him down. She said, 'Last week in Doncaster, I met a man who said he wanted to help –'

'Help who?' asked Terry. 'Help you?'

Diane smiled. She said, 'The Union, silly. I really think you need to meet him.'

The Jew has had Fred Wallace and Jimmy Hearn down to Claridge's for the night again. The Jew is keeping his options open. The Jew has some big plans for Fred and Jimmy. The Jew introduced Fred and Jimmy to Piers Harris and Tom Ball over breakfast this morning. Neil Fontaine drives the Jew, Fred, Jimmy, Piers and Tom to Hobart House. Don and Derek are waiting for them. The Jew has a conference room reserved and ready. The Jew leaves them to it. The Jew goes upstairs. The Jew knocks on the double-doors –

The Chairman of the Board.

Neil Fontaine closes the doors behind the Jew. He waits in the corridor outside.

The Jew coughs. The Jew says, 'It is a simple plan.'

The Chairman is listening –

'The emphasis now needs to be moved towards substantial, pre-arranged returns to work on the first shift of each Monday,' argues the Jew. 'At selected pits known only to ourselves and the police. Each area director agrees then to target just one pit per week, each with a set date for a mass return. This in turn allows us to release an ever-increasing weekly figure of the number of men going back to work. Reach fifty-one per cent and it's over and they know it.'

The Chairman is still listening –

'The situation in Yorkshire is quite different,' continues the Jew. 'The emphasis here should, for the time being, remain on isolated returnees. Their damage to local Union resources and morale are incalculable. The Union will be unable to picket pits outside Yorkshire, or at docks or power stations. Police resources can, therefore, also be concentrated on the areas we choose –'

The Chairman likes what he's hearing –

'The Back to Work campaign will be supported by Tom's campaign of local and national adverts, as well as our own continued legal campaign. These disparate campaigns and their various finances can now be brought under the single umbrella of the National Working Miners' Committee, which will be formally launched later this week. This will, at last, herald the birth of our union within a union. However, I'm afraid to say we will have to cut loose our Grey Fox, though Mr Colby and Mr Williams remain firmly on board and on course for a most helpful result.'

The Chairman claps. The Chairman likes what he's heard –

'Thank you, Stephen. Thank you,' says the Chairman. 'Unlike our adversary in the North, I am not a believer in overstatement. However, I have now a decided feeling that we have crossed a watershed. Until July I always felt as though we were sailing into a quite strong breeze. For the last few days there has been a period of calm. Now, after all these weeks, I can finally feel the wind on my back.'

The Jew leads the applause. The Jew says, 'Bravo, bravo.'

Neil Fontaine waits in the corridor outside. He watches men in suits storm out –

He watches them scowl and sulk. Them pace and then slam their office doors –

Them clean out their desks. Them write their letters of resignation –

Them screw them up. Them throw them at their bins –

But the men in suits always miss.

Neil Fontaine knows how they feel. The Jew has invited all his new friends and their families down to Colditz this weekend. They are to be awed by the affluence. Astonished by the abundance. The Jew will take them for spins in his private helicopter. Tours of the grounds in his golf buggy. Rides on his electric lawnmower. Punts on the lake. Billiards on his tables. Darts on the boards he has bought especially for their visit. He will let their kids play with his horses and his ponies, his dogs and his hawks, while their mothers and fathers eat and drink as much and as often as they like. Then they will sleep in his four-poster beds, wash in his porcelain sinks, and shit in his porcelain bogs, laughing behind his back at the outfits he wears and the things he says and does –

Neil Fontaine wishes the Jew wouldn't invite them.

He hates these working miners and their fucking families –

He hates this whole bloody strike and every cunt in it.

Neil Fontaine screws up his own letter of resignation. He throws it at a bin –

He misses by a mile.

It will be the death of him, thinks Neil Fontaine. This bloody strike –

The death of everyone.

Terry Winters parked in the Doncaster station car park. Terry locked up and left the car. He stood in front of the main station building. Diane picked him up at two o'clock. Diane drove them over the Don into Bentley and up the York Road. She parked outside a row of old terrace houses. They walked along the street to the little shop on the corner. It was an off-licence and newsagent's. Diane opened the door. Terry followed her inside. Behind the counter stood an Asian family. Diane pointed towards the middle-aged father of four. Diane said, 'Terry Winters, meet Mohammed Abdul Divan.'

Malcolm didn't hear them any more because Malcolm didn't dream. He didn't dream because he didn't sleep –

He lay on the floor between the bed and the door. His head to the left. His ear to the floor. He watched the night march across the carpet and the floor-boards. Up the four walls. The sunlight become shadow. He lay on the floor between the bed and the door and wished it was not so –

That light never became shadow.

Malcolm stood up. He took out the double-cassette box of The War of the Worlds. *He opened the box. The two cassettes inside –*

He took out the first cassette. Tape 1. *He put it in the recorder.* Side B –

He pressed fast-forward. Stop. He adjusted the tone. He lowered the vol-ume –

Pressed play and played it all back –

'– in again, if you don't fucking tell me where it fucking is –'

'– please. I can't breathe –'

'– just tell us where it is then, you old fucking slag –'

'– told you, it's not –'

'– come on, or you're going to make me –'

'– stop it, don't –'

'– you fucking like it, I know you –'

'– no, no –'

'– fucking love it really, you –'

'– no –'

'– put it back in, Granny –'

'–'

Between the bed and the door. Eyes closed. Head to the floor –

Malcolm listened to night march across the Earth. The world become dark again –

Between the bed and the door. The ears in his head. That bled and that bled –

O, how Malcolm wished it was not so.

He opened his eyes. He sat up. He went to his briefcase. He took out his scissors.

Downstairs a couple were fucking. Fucking and then fighting. Fighting and then –

Beds creaked. Headboards banged. Walls shook –

Reunited –

Neil and Jennifer. Jennifer and Neil. Terry and Diane. Diane and Terry –

Malcolm and his scissors. His scissors and his ears.

It was all about the numbers now. Not words. Numbers –

150 back last week; 170 this.

Numbers. Figures.

The President summoned them to the tenth floor. The President sat them down. The President told them what they already knew. What they had seen on TV –

First the bad news:

The latest Labour Party initiative had failed; the Board had said the Union must accept pit closures on grounds other than exhaustion; more scabs had started to work in Yorkshire; police had launched massive attacks on the communities concerned –

Then the good (always the good news last):

The men from NACODS were fuming with the Board; the Board weren't listening to them but the Union were; steel-workers had unloaded the Ostia, which dockers had blacked at Hunterston; last night TGWU dockers had

*voted 78 to 11 at their delegate conference to strike in support of the miners;
the TUC just around the corner –*

'Along with victory,' said the President. 'I am not going to the
Congress to plead. I am going to the Congress to demand – as one
trade unionist to another – the assistance of my brothers and sisters
in the trade union movement because –

'Comrades!' he shouted. 'Together we cannot lose. Together we
will not lose!'

The President put down his notes. The President began clapping –

The entire tenth floor got to their feet. The entire tenth floor
applauded.

Terry Winters cupped his mouth in his hands. He shouted, 'Here
we go –'

'Here we go. Here we go,' echoed the entire tenth floor. 'Here. We.
Go.'

Terry laughed. Terry wanted to dance on the desks of St James's
House.

Diane had shown him the way. The way out of all this –

Now Terry had a much better plan. Now. The best one he had ever
had. Ever –

Terry smiled –

He could not lose –

Terry had an erection. Now. The biggest one he had ever had –

Ever.

door. No answer. Had a look through their letterbox. Lot of post and what-have-you on other side of door. No sign of them, though. Had a bad feeling about it, did their house. Like it was a lovely day and all, but this place was all in shadow. Didn't know what to do for best. I walked across little front lawn they'd got. Put my hands over my face and stuck my nose to their windows. Looked in their front room. It was bare – Not a stick of furniture. Nothing. No carpet. No curtains – Everything gone. No dead bodies, mind. But it looked like Keith was right. For once – *Running and running. Deeper and deeper. Faster and faster – I turn corner. I go down. I wait for horses. Hooves. Batons. I look back – Water. Wall of fucking water bearing down – I run again. Deeper and deeper. Faster and faster – I look back up corridor. Water roaring down. Faster and faster – I see two blokes behind me. Water almost on top of them. Two blokes – One of them Martin. Other one my father –* It wasn't my teeth that woke me. I lay there in dark in **bed**, Mary beside us. Bloody sweating again, I was. Buckets. Thinking about my father – How he died. How he lived – I always did these days. These nights – Then I heard something. Like voices out back – I got up. Slippers on – Left lamp off. Didn't want to wake Mary – I walked onto landing. Had a good listen. I went down stairs. I walked down hall towards kitchen. Lights still off. I stood in kitchen. I looked out onto back garden. I could see something by shed – Like shadows out back. Moving about – I took a few steps back out of kitchen. I reached for hall light. Kept my eyes on back window. I switched hall light on. Then back off again – And I saw them run. Three or four blokes from by shed – Heard them knock over dustbin at side of house as they went. Effing and blinding – I ran back up hall to phone. I picked it up – *Click-click.* I dialled police – *Fuck.* I hung up – It probably was fucking police. Bastards – *Krk-krk.* Fucking bastards – I went back down hall into kitchen. Kept light off. I sat down at table. Kept my eyes open. I stared out window. Into night – Into dark. Into shadows – Lot of us had

been at **Kiveton** yesterday. Lot of us wouldn't forget that in a bloody hurry – Horses charging through old folks' gardens. That white horse there again – Horse got a scratch and public were up in arms. Felt sorry for it – Just horses. Horses and scabs – Poor blokes on these buses. Their startled faces behind wire cages welded to windows – Drivers with crash helmets. Pigs on back seat. Them sat on aisle side – But I knew them faces. Everybody did – Every pit had faces like theirs. Faces with little eyes that never met yours. Eyes that'd sooner stare at their boots or ground. Faces of a certain type, they were. Type that hated their work. Type that were out sick more often than not. Type that never pulled their weight. Type who always wanted Union to do this, that and other for them. Cowed and broken men before strike even began. Shirkers or gaffers' narks. Area managers and chief constables had leant on them hard. Broken them in two all over again – It wasn't pit managers' bloody idea. Pit managers knew them too well – Knew them of old. Knew what they were worth – *Nothing. Fuck all* – Just like this scab they'd got going in here at **Silverwood**. He'd have been fucking sacked years ago, if it wasn't for us, said Derek. Tom nodded. He said, That's thing that gets to me and all – But look at cunt now, said Johnny. Bold as fucking brass in his new V-reg – His time will come, I said. There'll be a reckoning. He knows that, too. Everybody nodded. Everybody said, Day will come all right – How about Monday? asked David Rainer. Arthur wants us all on front line – He would do, I said. He's addressing bloody TUC, isn't he? Talk of mass returns again, said Johnny. Look bad if a lot went in – I can't see it, said Tom. Not Monday. Everybody shook their heads. Everybody said, Not here. Not Monday – All same, said Derek. Best keep your eyes and ears open – Aye, said Johnny. There's always one – Everybody nodded again. Everybody knew he was right – Knew it was going to get worse. Much, much worse – Not this Monday. Not next – But it would. Had to. Because everybody knew. Knew one.

The Twenty-sixth Week

Monday 27 August – Sunday 2 September 1984

Jennifer puts on her shades. She runs her hands through her blonde hair and ties it back. She scowls at Neil Fontaine. She sticks out her tongue –

She says, 'You want a fucking picture, do you?'

Neil Fontaine gets up from the edge of the bed. The notebook still in his hand. The years in pieces on the floor. He opens the dawn curtain –

Jennifer slams the hotel door as she leaves –

Neil stood at the window. In the real light and the electric –

The very last moment like this.

The Jew isn't sleeping nowadays, either. He is too fearful of what the future holds. He doesn't wait for the doorman or Neil. He opens the back door of the Mercedes himself. He slams it shut –

'Downing Street,' he shouts.

'Certainly, sir.'

The Jew slumps in the backseat. The Prime Minister has cut short her holiday. The Prime Minister has cancelled her trip to the Far East due to the industrial situation. The Jew is embarrassed. The Jew shakes his head. He wants to hammer nails into coffins. He mumbles on about the danger in the docks. The TUC. The weak sisters of the Board. Bent nails and empty coffins –

'– I told her go. Leave everything to me. But those lascivious leeches begged to differ. Margaret, Margaret, you can't leave us. You mustn't leave us. Sterling is slipping, our shares are sliding, our ship is sinking. That's all they can ever think about, Neil. Feeding their own fat faces. Saving their own sorry selves. They have no conception, Neil. No conception whatsoever of the Big Picture. The War –'

The Jew is wearing the same clothes he wore yesterday.

'Two steps forward,' the Jew says to himself. 'One step back.'

Neil Fontaine stops at the end of Downing Street –

The Jew sighs.

Neil Fontaine opens the back door for the Jew. Neil says, 'Good luck, sir.'

The Jew stops. He looks at Neil Fontaine. He says, 'Thank you, Neil.'

Neil Fontaine watches the Jew disappear into Downing Street –

The Total War Cabinet.

He starts the car. He has his own steps to take –

Backwards and forwards.

Roger Vaughan drops three sugar lumps into his cup. He picks up the teaspoon. He stirs his coffee. He takes the spoon out of the cup. He knocks it twice against the rim. He puts the silver spoon down on the saucer. He looks across the table at Neil Fontaine –

Neil Fontaine is waiting.

'Fortunately,' says Roger, 'it would appear all our troubles will soon be over.'

Neil Fontaine is still waiting.

Roger Vaughan lifts up his napkin. He pushes the envelope across the cloth.

Neil Fontaine opens the envelope. He stares at the photo inside –

'He's been watching you,' says Roger. 'Listening to you. *Both* of you.'

Neil Fontaine starts to speak. To protest and to lie. To beg and to plead –

'There's no need for that,' says Roger. 'It's a blessing in disguise.'

Neil Fontaine looks down at the tablecloth. He closes his eyes –

There are mountains of skulls. Boxes of candles –

'He's waiting for you,' says Roger Vaughan. 'Expecting you.'

There were bandages upon the floor. Two small balls of cotton wool. Blood upon the blades. Blood upon his fingers. Malcolm opened the box. Two cassettes inside –

He took out the second cassette. Tape 2. *He put it in the recorder.* Side A –

He pressed fast-forward. Stop. He adjusted the tone. He lowered the volume –

Pressed play and played it all back (one last time) –

'– no, please, no, please, no, please –'

'– in here, that what you want –'

'– please, no, it's at the cottage at Llanymynech –'

'– shut up, it's too late –'

'– please don't, it's at the cottage, please don't, in the cottage, no –'

'– too late!' screamed Julius Schaub. 'Too late!'
'–'

*Malcolm lay on the floor between the bed and the door. In the spots of
blood. Head to the left again. In a pool of blood. His wounds to the floor. In
the sea of blood –*

These nights across the world. The shadows everywhere.

Malcolm lay on the floor covered in blood. Between the bed and the door –

He wished for day and he wished for light –

Head to the floor. In 1984. The knock upon the door –

Malcolm stood up. Malcolm listened –

*The sounds of the animal kingdom filled the room. The knock on the door
again.*

Malcolm walked over to the door. Malcolm touched the Emergency
Procedures –

Malcolm Morris wiped his eyes. Malcolm Morris asked, 'Who is it?'

'Room service.'

Between the bed and the door. In the shadows. In the night –

How he wished for day and wished for light.

It is the hour before dawn. Neil Fontaine parks at the junction of Gate
House Lane and Mosham Road. To the left is Finningley Airfield (disused). To the right Auckley Common. Doncaster straight ahead. The
Jew sits in the back with his army binoculars. He is dressed in combat fatigues. He is wearing his aviator sunglasses.

Neil Fontaine sees the headlights approach. He says, 'They're coming, sir.'

The Jew raises his sunglasses. He lifts up his binoculars.

Four sets of headlights come down Gate House Lane from the airfield.

The Jew watches them through his binoculars.

Four trucks turn left and head down the Mosham Road towards
Doncaster.

Neil Fontaine starts the car.

'Most impressive,' shouts the Jew from the back. 'Most impressive
indeed, Neil.'

The Mercedes follows the four trucks. Their brake lights in the grey
light –

The Mercedes loses sight of the lights in Doncaster. For now –

Neil Fontaine parks close to Rossington Colliery. The Jew with his binoculars. There are no scabs at Rossington. No scabs as yet. Just six pickets and a cardboard sign. Two policemen in their car. Neil Fontaine looks at his watch. He taps it –

Bentley. Hatfield. Armthorpe –

Neil Fontaine turns to the Jew in the back. He says, 'Any minute now, sir.'

The Jew takes off his sunglasses. He sits up. He looks through his binoculars.

Neil Fontaine looks at his watch again. He taps it again.

'Here they come,' says the Jew. 'Here they come, Neil.'

Neil Fontaine watches the pickets stand. The policemen get out of their car –

Neil turns to see the four trucks hurtle up the road and through the gates.

The pickets and the police run towards the trucks, then stop –

Pit managers come out of their offices, then back off –

Everybody staring, staring at the trucks –

The fifty men disembarking at the sound of a whistle –

Fifty men in camouflage jackets, boiler suits and balaclavas –

Fifty men with pick-axe handles, their leader in a baseball cap and sunglasses –

Fifty men setting about the yard at the sound of the leader's second whistle.

Neil Fontaine looks at his watch. He taps it. He looks at the Jew in the mirror –

The Jew watching through his binoculars from the backseat of the car –

Fifty men taking out the security cameras, the windows of the offices –

The cars and vehicles belonging to the NCB and their staff.

Neil Fontaine looks at his watch. He taps it. He looks up at the two policemen –

They are still hiding behind their car doors, still shouting into their radios.

There is the third sound of the whistle –

The men form columns. The men board the trucks. The first three trucks leave.

The team leader looks around the yard. The leader bangs on the side of the truck –

The last truck starts up. The team leader gets up into the cabin –

The leader takes off the baseball cap –

Long blonde hair blows across her face and shades as the truck accelerates away.

'Most impressive,' says the Jew again. 'Really most impressive, Neil.'

The NUM were on their way to Brighton. The fast lane –

'Comrades,' Dick had said on the phone. 'You have got to come tonight.'

The NUM had been summoned to account for themselves. The TUC were losing patience with the NUM and its president. That was what the TV was saying. Repeatedly. That was what the papers would say –

That was what made the President laugh. Made him really, really laugh –

'They accuse us of setting worker against worker,' he said. 'Accuse us!'

Terry and Paul were in the back with the President. Joan in the front with Len –

They all shook their heads.

'Is it our members who cross picket lines?' asked the President. 'Is it?'

Paul Hargreaves coughed. Paul said, 'It is actually, President.'

The President looked at Paul. The President bit his lip.

'Not our true members,' said Terry. 'Our true and loyal members, President.'

'Thank you, Comrade,' said the President. 'Thank you very much.'

Paul stared over at Terry. Paul raised his eyebrows. Paul shook his head –

Terry didn't care. Terry Winters was on a roll –

Terry had a three-point public plan (separate to his two-point secret plan). Terry had sold the President his three-point public plan (as he would later sell the President his two-point secret plan). The President liked Terry's three-point public plan (as he would later like his two-point secret plan). Terry was convinced of these things –

Two hundred and twenty miles later Terry was even more convinced.

The top men from the TUC were waiting on the steps of the Metropole Hotel –

The President shook their hands. Then the President led the way upstairs.

The meeting began at eight o'clock in the Louis XV Suite –

'This is a fancy place,' said the President. 'For some plain talk.'

The top men from the TUC smiled. The top men from the TUC waited.

'I am here for your total support,' said the President. 'Nothing less.'

Then the arguments and the accusations began. The spats and the squabbles.

Eight hours later, Terry Winters tore a piece of paper from his notebook –

Terry handed it to the President. The President read it. The President stood up –

'The National Union of Mineworkers demands Congress support our objectives of saving pits, saving jobs and saving communities,' said the President. 'The National Union of Mineworkers demands Congress campaign to raise money to alleviate the tremendous hardship in the coalfields and to maintain the Union, nationally and locally. Finally, the National Union of Mineworkers demands Congress make this dispute more effective and once and for all call upon all trade unionists to block the movement of coal and coke and the use of oil.'

The President sat back down to applause. The President winked at Terry Winters –

Terry Winters smiled back.

'It's been a very long night,' said the Fat Man. 'But I would like to thank the President of the National Union of Mineworkers for coming here tonight in advance of the Congress. I'd also like to thank him and all the members of his team for their help in finding this agreed form of words. I am certain these proposals will be implemented to the fullest extent after further discussions with the General Council and with the agreement of the unions concerned –'

No one was listening. The President in a huddle with Paul, Dick and Terry –

Terry Winters still smiling. Terry Winters on a roll –

The world his oyster.

Neil Fontaine lies in the dark with his curtains open in his room at the Royal Victoria. Neil Fontaine thinks about sortilege. He looks at his watch. He taps it –

It is three in the morning. The telephone rings three times.

Neil Fontaine goes upstairs. He knocks on the Jew's door. He knocks again.

The Jew shouts, 'I am her eyes and her ears.'

Neil Fontaine brings the Mercedes round. The Jew waits in his flying-jacket.

They take the A57 out of Sheffield through Handsworth, Richmond and Hackenthorpe. They turn down the Mansfield Road, then left over the M1 through the village of Wales and into Kiveton Park –

The slag heap and the colliery black and hard against the dawn and the sky –

The enormous, empty, endless sky.

The Jew worries he has lost touch. The Jew wants to be back where the action is –

'I am her eyes and her ears,' he says again. 'Her eyes and her ears, Neil.'

Neil Fontaine drives down Station Road. He parks at the junction with Hard Lane.

The Jew gets out. The Jew says, 'Keep out of trouble, Neil.'

Neil Fontaine watches the Jew march up Hard Lane across Hard Bridge –

Two thousand pickets and half the London Met here to meet seven fucking scabs.

Neil Fontaine drops his cigarette on the ground. He stands on it. Turns his boot.

The Met have their boiler suits and helmets on. Their horses and dogs out –

Neil Fontaine watches them charge through the village.

The Met want the pickets on the other side of the pit. The pickets won't go –

Neil Fontaine watches the sticks and the stones rain down –

The bones that always break and the names that always hurt.

The Met have attached metal grilles to the fronts of their Transits –

Neil Fontaine watches them sweep up and down the road.

Neil Fontaine has lost sight of the Jew again –

Fuck.

Neil Fontaine starts up Hard Lane towards Hard Bridge.

There is a hand on his arm. The voice in his ear, 'Hello, hello, hello.'

Fuck. Neil Fontaine turns round –

Paul Dixon is standing beside a mud-coated new Montego. He's in an old, dirty anorak, his jeans and size tens in need of a wash and a polish, too.

'Paul,' says Neil Fontaine. 'We really must stop meeting like this.'

Paul Dixon nods. Paul smiles. He says, 'People will start talking.'

'They always do,' says Neil Fontaine. 'They always do.'

Paul Dixon opens the door of the Montego. He says, 'That's people for you.'

Neil Fontaine looks back up the road. He shrugs. They both get into the car –

The Montego smells worse than the Allegro.

'You sleeping in this thing, are you?' asks Neil Fontaine.

Paul Dixon shakes his head. He says, 'Who says I'm sleeping?'

They watch police horses jump hedges and trample gardens.

'I thought you were NRC liaison,' says Neil Fontaine.

Paul Dixon shakes his head again. He says, 'Pit Squad.'

'Bloody hell,' says Neil Fontaine. 'Fuck did you take that for?'

'Bit rich coming from you,' says Paul Dixon.

Neil Fontaine shrugs again. He says, 'I'm just a driver-cum-dog's body.'

'Right,' says Paul Dixon. 'A dog's body. If that's what you say.'

Neil Fontaine looks at Paul Dixon. He says, 'That's what I say.'

Paul Dixon takes out a photo. He asks, 'And what would you say to her?'

Neil Fontaine glances at the photo –

Long, blonde hair, gaunt.

Neil Fontaine shakes his head. *Fuck.* He says, 'Never seen her before. Sorry.'

'I bet you are,' says Paul Dixon. 'I bet you are.'

Neil Fontaine closes his eyes. *Fuck. Fuck.* He says, 'Who is she anyway?'

Paul Dixon smiles at Neil. He says, 'Jennifer Johnson?'

Neil Fontaine opens his eyes. *Fuck. Fuck. Fuck.* He shakes his head.

'The lucky lady who married our mutual mate the Mechanic?'

'News to me,' says Neil Fontaine. 'Anyway, thought you told me Dave retired?'

Paul Dixon shrugs his shoulders. He says, 'Maybe permanently. He's missing.'

'Missing?' asks Neil Fontaine. 'Since when?'

Paul Dixon takes out another photo. He says, 'Since he met you in this photo?'

Fuck. Neil Fontaine glances at the photo. *Fuck. Fuck.* He shakes his head –

'You're talking to the wrong man,' says Neil. 'That's not me. I haven't seen him.'

Paul Dixon looks down at the photo again. He says, 'The camera does lie, then.'

'Can't trust anything these days,' says Neil Fontaine. 'Anything or anyone.'

Paul Dixon points up the lane. He asks, 'That go for him and all, does it?'

The Jew and another man are carrying another bloodied picket down Hard Lane –

Fuck. Fuck. Fuck –

Neil Fontaine opens the car door –

Never fucking ends –

Paul Dixon holds out the photo. 'Bad pennies, Neil. They always turn up.'

Neil Fontaine shakes his head. He slams the door on Paul Dixon, Special Branch –

FUUUUUUUUUUUUUUUUUUUUUUUUUUUUCK –

Bad fucking pennies.

PART III

Careless whisper

September – November 1984

Middle of night – *We hwisprian. We onscillan* – **Day 182.** There's no one here. Dead quiet. I walk up from village. Past Hotel. Police Station. *Krk-krk.* Sports Ground. Pavilion. Up Pit Lane. Green's on one side. Brickworks on other. I turn right before Villas and there she is – I stop. I stand here. I stare up at headgear and washer – Folk saw me now they'd think I was crackers. Middle of night. No one here – Just her and me. Bloody hell, says Pete. Look what cat's dragged in – All right, I say. Room for a little one? – Queer one, more like, he says. Fuck you been? I shake my head. I shrug. I say, Just needed to get away, you know? Pete nods. He says, Fair enough. You're back now. I nod. I say, If you'll have us. Don't be daft, he says. In with Keith and me and Chris here. I nod at Big Chris. I say, When did you start coming, then? Monday, he says. I shake my head. I say, Hope they're paying you bloody double – Are they fuck, says Keith. Less folk to split petrol money with though – Till bleeding Irish Rover returned, laughs Pete. Look, I say. We going to yap all day or we going to go fucking picket? Pete stands up. He says, The Big K here we come. I follow Keith and Chris back out to car park. Rest of lads have already set off. Pete locks up and off we go. Keith's driving with me and Chris squeezed in back, Pete fiddling with radio: Eighteen patients dead at Stanley Royd Psychiatric Hospital in Wakefield; Coal peace process on verge of collapse; Sterling at record low; Damage Squad arrest fifteen – Usual stuff. Usual day – Can't you find any bloody music? asks Keith. Pete reaches forward to dial again. He gives it a turn – *Agadoo.* Pete turns to us in back. He says, Bet you missed all this, didn't you? I nod. I say, Like a lanced boil. Keith laughs. He points out window. He says, Bet you missed them and all, didn't you? *Krk-krk.* I stare out at all police cars and vans parked up on hard shoulders of motorway. I say, No roadblocks, then? Not now it's on our own bloody doorstep, says Pete. No need. They know us. We know them. Keith takes us off motorway and through Doncaster onto A19 and up over M62 at

Eggborough onto A645, back to Knottingley and Kellingley Colliery – *The Big K* – Right modern super-pit, it is, like them up Selby. But it's a hard-line pit too. Like Sharlston and Acton Hall. It wasn't a hundred year ago that troops shot dead two miners and wounded sixteen at Featherstone. Lot of Scottish had come down to Kellingley in sixties and all – Hard to credit there'd be scabs round here. But there are – Super-pits breed super-scabs, says Keith. Mega-scabs. Lot of them here and at Gascoigne Wood and at Prince of Wales, they were dead against strike from start, says Pete. No stomach for it. Never on a picket, are they? It's where their bloody Panel is though, says Chris. Pete nods. Pete says, Not that that means anything. Look at us. Chris turns to me. He says, Hear about Silverwood, did you? I nod. Keith parks up in a field about two mile from pit gates. It's getting on for half-five now. Pit lane full of cars. It's a big picket – Horses and dogs are at back. I can smell them. Hear them – You all right? asks Pete. Been a while, I say. But I'm right. He looks at me. He says, What happened to you? Where did you go? I tell him, Sometimes you just don't want to be with anybody, do you? He nods. He says, How's Cath? She's right, I say. Mary said she saw her last week, Pete starts to tell me but then chant goes up – Here we go. Here we go. Here we go – Big push. Shove. Shout – Scab van and police escort fly through pit gates. Hundred mile an hour – Lads go down under weight. Lads out cold – Police hostile. Faces contorted beneath their visors, straps tight under their chins – I turn my back. I walk away – I wait for Pete, Keith and Chris. I see Chris first. White as a fuck-ing sheet. I call out to him. He comes over to where I am. I say, You all right, are you? He just nods. He stands by me. He waits for others. We don't say anything. Just watch – It's all over by half-seven. Lads start to make their way back to cars. Police pull few of them out and give them some hammer – Glove. Boot – Half an hour later, Pete and Keith come back and we set off back to Welfare. There's not much con-versation on way. Not much news,

The Twenty-seventh Week

Monday 3 – Sunday 9 September 1984

The best place to nick a car in Yorkshire is outside the Millgarth Police Station in Leeds. Has to be in the morning. Has to be a market day. Has to be a Ford. Has to be light coloured and has to be from the car park between the Kirkgate Market and the bus station. Have to be at least two of you as well –

The Mechanic and Philip Taylor are sitting in Phil's Ford Fiesta watching a woman lock her yellow Cortina. She checks the door handle. Twice. She walks past the Fiesta. She leaves the car park. She heads up towards Vicar Lane –

'Here we go,' says Phil –

Drum roll –

The Mechanic gets out of the Fiesta. He walks over to the yellow Cortina. He puts the key in the lock. He turns the key. The lock gives. He opens the door. He gets into the car. He closes the door. He puts the key in the ignition. He turns the key. The engine starts. He reverses out of the parking space –

Phil pulls out behind him.

The Mechanic goes round the roundabout in the shadow of the Millgarth Police Station, then takes the York Road up through Killingbeck and Seacroft all the way back to the garage –

Adam Young is waiting. Adam has everything ready –

He closes the garage doors behind them.

Two hours later the Cortina has a new coat of paint and a new set of plates.

Phil and Adam give the Mechanic a lift back to his mother's house at Wetherby –

The Mechanic says goodbye. See you later. He gets out –

Drum roll –

Here come the dogs. Down the drive. Tongues out and tails up. Fuck, he missed them. Missed his dogs. Back from being the only white face in the place. Back home from weeks and weeks of weed and wonder. Women and wounds. Back home. Where the heart is and all that. Lads in the car must think he's a bit on the peculiar side. See him here in his mother's drive with his dogs. But fuck it. Fuck them. Fuck them all. Dog doesn't stab you in your back. Dog doesn't break your heart. Dog just loves you –

Fucking loves you. So fuck them –

Fuck. Them. All.

The Mechanic waves to Phil and Adam in the Fiesta. He shouts, 'Stay free.'

And he means it –

Stay. Fucking. Free –

Free of everything and everyone.

The President preferred Scarborough or Blackpool. But he liked the Promenade at Brighton. The President walked from meeting to meeting along the seafront with Len and Terry. The President accepted the accolades and the abuse with the same smile. The people who wanted to shake his hand. The people who wanted to spit in his eye. The people who wanted an autograph for their wives. The people who wanted an apology for the violence. The President talked to them all. The President didn't hate the man on the street who kicked him up the backside. The woman on the pier who tried to push him into the sea. The President would talk to them all because the President blamed the press. Blamed the press for the letter bombs that came in the post. For the death threats on the phone. The meat pie in his face on the train. The elderly lady with the kitchen knife. The man with the axe at Stoke. The President would talk to them all –

The President would talk to anyone, almost.

The miners and their minders marched from the Curzon along to the Grand where Bill Reed introduced John James. John James wrote for the *Daily Mirror* –

The Miners' Mate –

The *Daily Mirror* which was now owned by Mr Robert Maxwell –

John James introduced Mr Maxwell of the *Mirror* –

Proprietor and *Editor-in-Chief*, holding court in his suite at the Grand Hotel.

Mr Maxwell of the *Mirror* lit a large cigar. He rolled up his sleeves –

Mr Maxwell of the *Mirror* said, 'Think of me as a human switchboard.'

The President stood up. He said, 'Then don't call us, we'll call you.'

The President, Paul, Joan and Terry walked out of the suite at the Grand Hotel –

The President had other fish to fry back at the Curzon.

Len called the lift. Bill Reed came running down the corridor –

Bill said, 'Comrades, Comrades, he only wants to help.'

'Help his circulation,' said Joan.

Bill shook his head. He said, 'You're wrong and you've offended him.'

The President turned to Bill. He said, 'He isn't what he seems, Comrade.'

Bill Reed shook his head again. Bill looked at Terry. He said, 'Terry?'

Terry shrugged his shoulders. He said, 'I don't –'

'You're all wrong,' shouted Bill. 'And you've made an enemy of a friend.'

The President turned back to Bill. He said, 'He was never a friend, Comrade.'

Len held open the lift doors. The President and the rest of them got in –

'Never a friend,' said the President again –

Bill Reed watched the doors close. Bill Reed said, 'But I was.'

The Jew likes Brighton. The Jew *loves* Brighton. The Jew had even lived here at one time; the time the Jew went bankrupt. The Trades Union Congress is a very good reason to be here again. The Jew has a large third-floor suite with a sea view at the Grand Hotel. Neil Fontaine is upstairs in a different room. Room 629. Under a different name. But Neil is never there. The Jew has an ever-open door to an ever-open bar. Here the Jew keeps thieves' hours with the Big Men from the unions of the New Right. These Big Men with their Bigger Minders who smoke cigars and drink spirits by the pint, who like to stake their subs in the company of loose ladies. The Jew pays these ladies to stroke the thighs of these Big Men. To suck the cocks of these Big Men in the bathroom of the Jew's third-floor suite with its sea view. To spit their semen into his sink –

The Jew looks away from the bathroom door. He shouts, 'Neil! Neil!'

Neil Fontaine walks across the suite to the Jew. He bends over to listen –

'Neil,' says the Jew. 'Be a pal and hire the plane for tomorrow again.'

Neil Fontaine nods. He says, 'Certainly, sir.'

'Do you know what tomorrow's slogan on the banner will say, Neil?'

'No, sir,' says Neil Fontaine. 'I'm afraid I don't.'

'Get stuffed Scargill!' giggles the Jew. *'Get stuffed Scargill!'*

The Big Men queuing for the bathroom applaud.

There is a loud knock on the door to the suite.

Neil Fontaine goes to the door. He opens it. He smiles at the man in the corridor –

'Long time, no see,' says the man in his peaked white cap –

Neil Fontaine smiles. Neil Fontaine nods.

The Jew is standing on the bed. He shouts, 'Who the fuck is it now, Neil?'

Neil Fontaine turns to the room. He says, 'It's Mr Maxwell of the *Mirror*, sir.'

Mr Maxwell of the *Mirror* strides into the room. He opens his arms –

'It's been too long, Sweet Stephen,' he bellows. 'Much too long.'

The Jew jumps off the bed and into the arms of Mr Maxwell of the *Mirror* –

'Captain, my Captain,' squeals the Jew. 'How long has it been?'

Welcome to the New Realism –

The Conference Hall of the 1984 Trades Union Congress, shoulder to shoulder. The Easington Scab might have made legal history with an injunction against the Durham NUM; the Dock Strike might look set to crumble; the steel and power unions might have been booed for their views. But the President had the promises of the General Council; the promise of the total support of their ten million members; the promise to heighten the confrontation; the promise to black all coal, coke and oil –

Promises, promises, promises.

Ray Buckton took the platform. He said, 'It is all too easy to ignore someone else's problems. But it is no good in the long run, because solidarity is not something which comes with conditions attached. Solidarity is a simple principle –'

The noise like thunder –

'– this government has destroyed the dreams and ambitions of a generation. Britain is now a country ruled by fear. The fear of being

234

ill. The fear of losing your job. The fear of not being able to keep up at work. The fear of growing old –

'But we must not let fear extinguish the ideas of trade unionism –'

Like a bomb had gone off.

The Old Man was next. The Old Man said, 'This Congress sends a message to this government that it will not let the miners and their families starve –

'It will not let the miners lose –'

The whole hall shook with it –

'We will not let them lose!'

Like an explosion.

The President rose. The President walked to the front of the platform. He said, 'Give that support today and I am confident that in the weeks ahead we shall grow increasingly strong –'

Like thunder. Like a bomb. The whole hall shaking. Exploding –

'And that we will not lose!'

Delegates clapping their hands and stamping their feet –

Standing shoulder to shoulder.

Terry Winters looked round for the New Realists –

For Bill Sirs. For Frank Chapple. For Eric Hammond. For John Lyons –

They were nowhere to be seen. But Terry could still hear them –

Backstage. Offstage. Whispering.

Terry had had enough. Terry stepped out of the Conference Hall –

Into the sunshine and the sea; the shining badges and sea of banners –

Victory to the Miners! Organize the General Strike! Miners Must Win!

The Revolutionary Communist Party and the Socialist Workers' Party; the Young Socialists and the Old Communists; the Denims and the Tweeds; NALGO, NUPE and the All Trades Union Alliance –

Four thousand men and women from every branch of the NUM –

Pride of place for the Cortonwood banner and the miners that bore it.

They were all here, down by the sea –

Their arms outstretched to shake Terry's hand. To pat him on the back –

To have him sign their *Morning Star*, their *News Line* –

To make sure it was shoulder to shoulder –

Shoulder to shoulder to Victory –

'Keep on keeping on,' they shouted as Terry shook the hands, signed the papers –

Shoulder to shoulder in the sun by the sea. But it was a charade –

Like the small plane in the sky said, *Come off it, Arthur!*

It was a sham and they knew it –

The President and the Proprietor. The Old Man and the Fat Man –

The Chairman and his Boss –

A dirty fucking lie –

And everyone saw it. Everyone heard it. Everyone smelt it –

Tasted it. Knew it –

Everyone except the men and women out in the minefields.

Late till eight. It is the busiest shopping night of the week at the Morley branch of Morrison's supermarket. The Mechanic and Adam are in the back of the Ford Cortina. Phil is in the driver's seat. The Mechanic has the shotgun and the stopwatch. Adam has the handgun and the holdall. Phil turns into the car park. It is two minutes past eight o'clock. The place is almost deserted now. The last shoppers leaving. Phil drives slowly through the car park towards the store. He reverses into a parking space. The Cortina faces the exit, their backs to the supermarket. Phil watches through the rearview mirror, the Mechanic through the wing. Adam looks straight ahead. The Mechanic and Phil see the two security guards and the manager wheel the trolley along the row of cash registers. They fill bags with notes and coins from each till. The two security guards and the manager then push the trolley back up the aisles towards the office and the safe. The wages for the week are also in the safe in the office. Phil looks at his watch. The Mechanic looks at his. Phil nods. The Mechanic nods. Adam puts his crash helmet on. The Mechanic puts his on. It is five minutes past eight o'clock. The Mechanic opens the back door on the left side of the car. Adam opens the back door on the driver's side of the car. The Mechanic and Adam get out. The Mechanic and Adam stand in the car park. The Mechanic and Adam put their visors down. Phil starts the car up. The Mechanic starts the stopwatch –

Here. We. Go –

Through the automatic doors. Hit the fire alarm. Chaos –

Up the aisle to the office. Through the door –

'What the –'

Punch to the first security guard. He goes down –

Punch to the second. He goes down –

Kick to the first guard. He stays down –

Kick to the second. Down and out –

The Mechanic drags the manager across his desk by his tie –

Puts the manager's face to the safe and shouts, 'Open it.'

The manager dithers. The Mechanic turns the manager's face to the first guard –

Adam puts the handgun to the guard's temple. He cocks the hammer –

The manager opens the safe.

The Mechanic pushes him away. 'On your knees. Hands behind your back.'

Handcuffs on. The Mechanic kicks him over.

Adam fills the holdall with wage packets and banknotes.

The Mechanic looks at the stopwatch. 'One minute thirty –'

Adam nods. Adam keeps filling the holdall. Adam shouts, 'Done.'

They leave the office. Leave them on the floor –

Down the aisle. Through the automatic doors –

The back doors of the car open –

Jump inside. Phil puts his foot down and they are –

Gone. Just like that –

Eight minutes past eight o'clock –

Just. Like. That.

either. Just music – *Agadoo*. Keith pulls into car park. Pete says, Probably be back to Kiveton tomorrow. Keith nods. Chris nods. I nod. Pete gives us three quid each. I say goodbye. I walk over road to Bottom Club. I get in our car. I drive home. I park in drive. I unlock door. I step inside – There's nothing. No one – *My hands are black. My face blue. The sea is cold. The wind old –* **Day 189.** I wake up at midnight on a pile of clothes on bedroom floor. That's all that's left. Clothes and bits of my gear. Nothing else now. Makes place seem massive. Ironic really, Cath had always wanted a bigger place. Makes it smell, though. I walk from room to room. I open up windows. Room to room. Downstairs. Letter from TSB still on floor in hall. Back up stairs. Then down stairs again. End up stood in kitchen. No cooker now. No fridge. No washing-machine. Nothing. Just spaces where they used be. I just stand there looking out on back garden again – It's black. Pitch black. Pissing it down – Never going to be a patio now. No conservatory here. I light a cigarette – Expensive habit that, she says. I turn round – Nothing. No one – I close my eyes. My heart – *You have stolen my language. You have stolen my land –* Bloody hell, says Pete. Thought you'd have buggered off and left us again by now. I say, You bloody want me to, do you? He shakes his head. He says, You know I don't – Then shut up and open that envelope, will you? He laughs. He opens envelope. He takes out paper. He says, Silverwood. Entire room groans. Keith shouts, Lovely. Pete says, Where were you expecting? Las bloody Vegas? How about Doncaster racecourse? says Tim. John Smiths brewery? Tell you what I'll do, says Pete. I'll have a word with King Arthur next time he pops round, shall I? You do that, says everyone. You do that. Pete smiles. He says, Now that's all sorted, let's have you all up Silverwood then. **Day 192.** About hundred yards from pit, headlights go on full in our faces. *Krk-krk.* Bastards. Hands straight up to shield our eyes. Few stones aimed at lights. Hear horses coming then. Dogs. Vans. Everyone off like a shot. Into woods. Off road.

Through trees. Best plan. Out of lights. Into fog and mist. Hooves still coming. Dogs barking. Headlights shining through trunks and branches. Throwing shadows left and right. Police boots over deadwood. Truncheons banging on their shields. Lads going down. Falling over stumps and fucking roots of trees. Picked up by snatch squads and beaten badly. No arrests today. Just lot of fist. Mainly older blokes getting it and all – Hear them go down but you can't see them. Fog and lights in your eyes – I hear voices above me then. Look up and there are blokes hanging from trees – Just swinging there in fog with lights behind them. Dangling like strange fruit off branches – Police and dogs waiting for them underneath. Truncheons out and teeth bared ready for fruit to fall – For dead to drop. It is Yorkshire, 1984 – *You have buried my family. You have buried my faith –* **Day 195.** I wake on floor again. I get up off floor. I walk over to window. I look out – There's a car on road. Passenger door open. There are men in car. Man at gate – There are shadows over man. He stares up at house. He points up at window. His bones white in night – I step back out of sight. Into my own shadows. I stand against wall. I hold my breath – I listen to gate open. I hear footsteps on path – I hear them whisper. I hear them echo – Hear them moan. Hear them scream – It is dark. I swallow. I spit. I swallow again. I hear knock on door. I listen to letterbox rattle – I listen to it whisper. Listen to it echo – Listen to it moan. Listen to it scream – It is dark. I close my eyes. I open my eyes. I close them again. I listen to him try door. I hear him shake it – I hear him whisper. Hear him echo – Hear him moan. Hear him scream, Martin! Get up, you lazy fucking sod. **Day 201.** Pete comes back from Panel. Pete says, It's provocation. Pete's right. Provocation is only word for it – DHSS now said contractors at Maltby are engaged in secondary strike action. Not laid off like they'd said before. DHSS has stopped their dole – Contractors have gone back. Board have fucking stuck them in their back-to-work figures – It's bloody bollocks.

The Twenty-eighth Week

Monday 10 – Sunday 16 September 1984

Terry Winters was in the bar of the three-star Ellersly Hotel, Murrayfield, Edinburgh. Terry was on the phone home. No one was on the other end. The phone just rang and rang in the empty hall of his empty house in Sheffield. Terry sat at the bar and listened to it ring and watched the ice in his vodka melt. The President was upstairs in a bedroom with the Chairman. Terry didn't know why they bothered. The President didn't want to be here. He was only here because the Chairman was here. The Chairman didn't want to be here, either. He was only here because the power workers were tired of being booed and spat at. The Chairman had even arrived with a bag over his face. The President had said the Chairman needed to seek professional advice. The Chairman had said he was concerned about the effect of the stress on the President's health. The President said the Chairman obviously needed a break. The Chairman stuck his tongue out. The President stuck his out. The Chairman threw his hands up. The President winked. The Chairman wanted the President to drop his trousers and spread his cheeks for Maggie. The President didn't want to play Rita. The President wanted to be Peter. The President wanted the Chairman to get on his knees and suck Little Arthur. The President wanted it to be on the front page of every paper in the land. The top story on the *Nine O'clock News*, the *News at Ten* and *Newsnight* –

'*The Chairman sucks the President's cock.*'

Then everyone could go back to Sheffield, Florida, Moscow or wherever.

Instead back they both went before the TV cameras to call each other names. Before the microphones and tape-recorders to worry about each other's physical and mental well-being.

Terry yawned. Terry played with the last of the ice in his glass –

The phone was still ringing in Sheffield. The barman staring at Terry –

Terry hung up. Terry finished his vodka. Terry went back upstairs.

He knocked on the President's door. Joan opened it. Terry went inside –

The Chairman had retired for the night. The President was on the phone.

Len had a map out on the President's bed. Terry said, 'Where next?'

Len looked up. He looked over at Joan. Joan said, 'Monk Fryston again.'

'Closer to home, I suppose,' said Terry.

Joan nodded. Len looked back down at the map on the bed.

The President had turned his back to the room. He was whispering into the phone.

Paul came into the room with the day's faxes. He didn't knock. He never knocked. He just dumped the faxes on the bed. Every single mention of the dispute for the day –

Every single word from every single media.

Terry picked one out of the pile. He said, 'How about this one?'

Len looked up again. The President turned round –

Terry laughed. Terry said, 'Official – Chairman sucks President's cock.'

The President looked at Terry then returned to his call. Len to the map on the bed. Joan stared out of the window into the night. Paul smiled –

'That's a real gift you've got there, Comrade,' he said. 'You're wasting it on us.'

'It was just a joke,' said Terry.

'No,' said Paul. 'A joke is putting a bag over your head as you enter a hotel.'

'It was a joke,' said Terry again. 'I'm sorry.'

Paul shook his head. Paul said, 'Jokes elicit laughter, not pity.'

Terry Winters blinked. He wished he'd not had that vodka. He said again, 'Sorry.'

The President finished his call. *Click-click.* The President glanced at Terry again.

Len got up off the bed. Len said, 'We should go, Comrade President.'

'Now?' said Terry. 'This very minute?'

Len nodded. Joan nodded –

Paul smiled. Paul said, 'It's later than you think, Comrade.'

Terry ignored him. Terry ran to his room. Terry packed in two minutes flat. Terry went downstairs. Terry checked everyone out. Terry settled the bills –

Terry walked out to the car –

The car was full. Everyone had their eyes on the floor of the car, almost –

'There's a direct train to York,' said Paul. 'Call us when you get in, won't you?'

Terry nodded. Terry blinked. Terry waved goodbye. Terry watched them leave –

The press and the television on their tail –

In hot pursuit.

Terry went back inside the hotel. Terry went to their public toilets –

He sat in a cubicle and he cried. He cried and he cried.

He took a black marker pen from his jacket pocket. He took the top off. He drew a big, hairy cunt in a heart of swastikas on the back of the cubicle door.

Then Terry dried his eyes. He put the top on the pen. The pen in his pocket.

Terry went into the bar. Terry ordered another vodka. Terry picked up the phone –

Terry called Diane. *Click-click.* Diane answered. Terry had some things to say –

Diane listened. Then Diane spoke and Terry listened. Terry hung up –

Terry took a taxi to Waverley. Terry Winters boarded the direct train to York.

Phil and Adam stand around the kitchen table to watch the Mechanic count out the cash. The lolly. Fifty for Phil. Fifty for Adam. Fifty for the Mechanic. Fifty for Jen. The Mechanic glances up at Phil and Adam. Phil and Adam want to say something. The Mechanic stares at Phil and Adam. Phil and Adam smile. Phil and Adam look back down at the money. The loot. Fifty for Phil. Fifty for Adam. Hundred for the Mechanic. Hundred for Jen. The Mechanic looks back up at Phil and Adam. Phil and Adam want to say something now. The Mechanic stares at Phil and Adam. Phil and Adam are still smiling. Phil and Adam look back down at the money again. The lucre. Phil and Adam won't say anything –

The Mechanic knows they won't.

*

The Prime Minister has been at Balmoral. The Jew was not invited. The Jew dreams of the day he will be. The Chairman went to Chequers on her return. The Jew was not invited. The Jew accepts the Prime Minister and the Chairman sometimes need to spend some time alone together. Some time, sometimes. The Chairman has met with the Labour Party too. The Jew was not invited there. The Jew didn't care. It would have been nice to have been asked, though. The Chairman met with the TUC too. The Jew was not invited there, either. The Jew really didn't care. The Jew didn't want that invitation –

The electricians and the engineers want the Board and the Union to talk –

To talk, talk, talk.

The Cabinet and the civil servants are worried too. They are worried about the docks again. They are worried about NACODS. They are worried about the press and the television. They are worried about Mr and Mrs Joe Public –

Cads. Caitiffs. Chickens. Cowards. Craven –

They worry the Prime Minister. Her Cabinet and her public –

'It's always the same in times of war,' says the Jew. 'Everybody wants to win. Everybody wants the victory. The spoils. But never the price –'

Neil Fontaine nods. Neil knows the Jew is right.

'If it wasn't for Norman on the inside and yours truly on the out,' muses the Jew, 'the miners would be singing the *Red* bloody *Flag* at their victory parties tonight.'

Neil Fontaine nods again. Neil knows the Jew is right again.

'But over my dead body,' says the Jew. 'Over my dead body, Neil.'

Neil Fontaine nods once more. Neil tells the Jew he is right once more –

That is what Neil Fontaine is here for. What Neil Fontaine is good for.

The Chairman and the President appear together, side by side, in Yorkshire –

They appeal for peace. For quiet. For their secret talks to be kept secret.

The Jew calls the Chairman. The Jew tells the Chairman, 'Forget it. Fuck him –

'Fuck them all.'

The Jew hangs up. The Jew is disappointed. The Jew is jealous –

The Board and the Union are still on speaking terms –
Still, still, still talking, talking, talking –
The Jew will soon put a stop to that.

The gentlemen from the media had chased them the length and breadth of the country, North to South, East to West. Keystone Kops on the trail of the Chairman's Daimler and the President's Rover –

Edinburgh to Selby –

The Chairman and the President had appeared side by side, shoulder to shoulder, on the steps of the Monk Fryston Hotel to plead with the media to leave them alone –

Then it had been back down the back roads in the dead of night –

Selby down to London; London back up to Doncaster –

The offices of British Ropes in Doncaster –

For more warm bottles of water. More cups of tea. More stale ham sandwiches. More margarine stains. Shirtsleeves and stubble. Sweat and bad breath –

So near –

Terry Winters looked at his watch. Half-past one in the morning –

The hour was late. The paper was on the table. The deal there to be done –

So near and yet so –

Under the bright strip lights, the President and the Chairman rubbed their eyes. The heating hummed, Dick and Tommy from the Board's eyes closed –

Paul and Ted from the Board went out to get more coffees.

'Perhaps we should all sleep on it?' said Terry. 'Meet again on Friday?'

The President and the Chairman looked across the table at each other –

So near and yet so far –

It was agreed to meet again. On Friday. In London.

Terry tapped Dick on the shoulder. Dick wiped the spit from his collar.

Paul and Ted came back with the coffees. Paul said, 'What's going on?'

'It's too late,' the President told him. 'Meeting again on Friday.'

Paul slammed down the coffees. Paul looked at Terry –

So near and yet so far; too near and not far enough for some.

'All that is needed for evil to triumph', announces the Jew for the hundredth time today, 'is that good men do nothing.'

The Jew has raised five hundred thousand pounds to make sure evil does not triumph –

That good men do something. Those good men like the Jew –

From out of the shadows, the Good Jew steps again.

His themes for this week are the deterioration in a number of coal faces and the acceleration in the number of new faces; 177 this week –

The resistance of the cell versus the rule of the mob; the subtext –

There is work for those who want to work. But for how much longer?

From out of the shadows, Neil drives the Jew again –

The Jew has chosen the Social Democratic Party Conference for this moment –

The Jew has had Neil Fontaine bus them in to the Buxton Pavilion, Derbyshire.

'Gentlemen of the Fourth Estate,' says the Jew, 'may I proudly present to you the one and only National Working Miners' Committee –'

The Jew applauds alone as the four public faces of the NWMC emerge –

From out of the shadows –

Nervous in their old boots and new suits, shaved and groomed for the cameras, the NWMC might well be four hired taxi-drivers on wedding or funeral duty.

The Jew puts a hand on Fred's back. The Jew grips Jimmy's shoulder. He says, 'These brave men are but a few of the many brave men who are on the front line, fighting for what they believe in. These men need to know they are not alone –

'These men need to know they have friends. New friends –

'For their president stands before the trade union movement and claims he is striking for the right to work. Ladies and gentlemen, fifty thousand of his own members are *working* for the right to work. Working and fighting against that dictator and his stormtroopers, those thugs and those bullies who would attempt to deny ordinary men and their families the *right* to work through violence and through intimidation –

'For those who want to work, we salute and support you!'

Neil Fontaine watches from the wings as the hacks in their packs lap it all up –

The Jew in full flight. The Jew says, 'Fred?'

Fred Wallace stands up. Fred unfolds his piece of damp paper. He reads from it: 'The National Working Miners' Committee is a genuinely national committee from Wales, Derbyshire, Lancashire, Staffordshire, Warwickshire, Yorkshire and Nottingham. The committee is financed by collections at working pits and by contributions from ordinary members of the public sent in response to advertisements placed in the national press. The committee has shunned offers of help from big business and even from Conservative miners.

'Our legal constitution states that our aims are: a) to ensure that the NUM and its constituent areas are controlled by and for the membership and to protect the democratic processes of the Union; and b) to ensure the legal rights of all members of the Union and their relatives and dependants, and to protect them from or compensate them for any loss arising from the abuse of such rights.'

Fred Wallace folds his piece of damp paper back in two. Fred sits down again.

The Jew back on his feet. The Jew says, 'Jimmy?'

Jimmy Hearn stands up. Jimmy straightens his brand-new tie. He smiles. He says, 'My name is James Hearn. I'm from Lea Hall Colliery. Believe it or not, I voted to strike. However, the majority of men at our pit voted to work and I must respect that decision, because that is their wish. I am here today to defend that democratic decision against the bully-boys and the hit squads, the baseball bats and the jackboots of the Yorkshire Mafia that have terrified our children and our wives on the streets of our villages and our towns. I am here today to say to you, and to say to them, enough is enough.'

Jimmy Hearn loosens his tie. Jimmy sits back down.

The Jew applauds. The Jew says, 'There are thousands of men like Jimmy across this country. There are thousands more desperate to join him. Now they can –

'The National Working Miners' Committee will finance any miner who wishes to enforce his right to work and who is in need of help. Call us today –

'Not tomorrow. Not the day after. Today!'

The Jew puts a hand on Fred again. He grips Jimmy's shoulder again. He says, 'The next President of the NUM could very well emerge from the membership of the National Working Miners'

Committee, and it is most unlikely that he will have to wait for the present holder of that office to retire.'

In the shadows, Neil Fontaine watches –

Neil Fontaine waits –

In the shadows, the bloody shadows.

The Mechanic drives the JCB off the road. Up the side of the garage. Through the yard at the back. There is a lot of spare land behind the wrecks and the parts. It is ideal. The Mechanic starts to dig. To set the metal teeth into the ground. To turn the earth. To scoop it out into the digger's mouth. To pile it up on the side. In mounds. The Mechanic cuts the engine. He jumps down from the seat. He stands at the edge. He looks down into the fresh pit. He smells the dirt. Tastes it. The Mechanic goes back through the yard to the garage. He opens the door of the Cortina. He drives it out of the back of the garage. Through the yard. The Mechanic stops by the pit. He keeps the handbrake off. He gets out. He rolls the car forward with one hand on the steering wheel. The front tyres go over the edge. The car rests on its chassis on the edge. The Mechanic gets back into the digger. He uses the machine to nudge the car into the pit. The car tips over the edge. It lands on the bottom. The Mechanic starts to move the mounds of earth –

To bury the Cortina.

Doncaster back to Sheffield; Sheffield back to London –

From British Ropes to the Rubens Hotel, via the NEC meeting in Sheffield.

This time there was room for Terry Winters. The drive down like a dim dream. Service station to service station, Loyal Len stopping at every single services on the M1. The President and Terry straight to the phones –

The men from NACODS had met in their tiny terrace office in Doncaster. Their Deputies' delegates had voted for a vote. Voted for a vote to strike –

The Day of the Pawns –

The Colliery Overmen, Deputies and Shotfirers were set to deliver.

NACODS would strike. NACODS would settle. The miners would be saved –

Not their President. Not the Yorkshire Galtieri. The Yorkshire Stalin –

Just the miners; that was the plan. One of the many –

'Piggies in fucking middle,' Jimmy had said to Terry. 'That's all we bloody are.'

'Maybe, then,' Terry had said, 'it's time these little piggies went to market.'

'Going to make chops of us,' laughed Jimmy. 'That what you're saying?'

'Or maybe you can bring home the bacon for everyone,' said Terry –

Jimmy had laughed and laughed and then Jimmy had hung up.

The Board stood up in the Rubens. The Board read out the Doncaster agreement:

'– in the case of a colliery where a report of an examination by the respective NCB and NUM qualified mining engineers establishes that there are no further reserves that can be developed to provide the Board, in line with their responsibilities, with a base for continuing operations there will be an agreement between the Board and the unions that such a colliery shall be deemed exhausted –'

The Union said, '– in line with the Plan for Coal –'

The Board said, '– in line with our responsibilities –'

The Union pointed their fingers. They said, '– in line with the Plan for Coal –'

The Board folded their arms. They said, '– in line with our responsibilities –'

The Union shouted, '– in line with the Plan for Coal –'

The Board shouted back, '– in line with our responsibilities –'

The Union said, '– in line with the bloody Plan for Coal –'

The Board said, '– in line with our bloody responsibilities –'

The Union said, '– in line with the fucking Plan for Coal –'

The Board said, '– in line with our fucking responsibilities –'

The Union threw the paper across the table. The Board tore it up –

The Union stood up. The Board waved goodbye –

The Union slammed the door. The Board picked up the red phone –

The time for talking was through.

Pure fucking provocation – This is same DHSS that refused a family a grant to bury their twelve-year-old handicapped son because dead lad's dad was on strike. Same DHSS that let families and their kids freeze and starve in dark. That drive young lads out on to slag heaps to sift through spoil for crumbs of black fucking coal that their dads have fucking brung up out of earth in first place. DHSS that would watch them young lads die picking that coal, crushed under weight of a tip that wouldn't sodding be there in first place if it weren't for fact that some young lad's dad had risked his bloody life every day of that fucking life to keep other folk warm, fed and lit – He was only fourteen, says Keith. Lad from Upton. Fucking fourteen. Everybody shakes their heads. Everybody says, Fourteen. Pete says, Nineteen eighty-bloody-four and a kid dies coal-picking. There'll be a lot more before she's through with us and all, says Chris. Everybody nods. Everybody says, Bastards. That's mood as we set off in dark up to Maltby. **Day 202.** Press say later that we had bottles. Bricks. Catapults. Air-guns. Fired pellets – Liars. Bloody fucking liars – We've got clumps of fucking mud is what we've got. Aye, we take down branches to build barricades to stop scabs. Do that, that's true. Take down some trees from Maltby Wood – But mesh on front of their vans brushes them branches aside like they're not there – Like nothing is. Don't stop, either. Keep right at us – Nowhere for us to go. Nowhere for us to run. Nowhere to hide – Two lots of their riot squad coming out of woods. Each side of road. Trap us in a pincer movement or what-have-you – Banging on their shields. Their dogs bloody barking – Frightening. Fucking frightening – Nowhere to go. Nowhere but down – Just like last week at Silverwood. Same game – No more arrests. Just assaults – Duffel coats. Anoraks. Parkas. Hats and scarves. Wellington boots. Docs. Ordinary boots and shoes. That's all we have – Nothing that can save us. That can save us from them – Lad behind me goes down. Down hard – Perspex shield in back of neck. Truncheon on crown of head. Hear his skull crack – Hear him scream. Hear him moan – Down hard onto ground. Down hard and he stays down – Hear him echo. Hear him whisper, Help me somebody. Help me – Keith and me have got him in our arms. Pick him up between us. Dirt and muck stuck to half his face with his own blood – Blood on our duffel coats. On our anoraks. Our parkas. Over our hats and our scarves. On our Wellington boots. Our Docs. Our ordinary shoes – Keith and me and some other lads knot handkerchiefs together to bandage up his head. I look up. Policemen just standing there, watching us with their shields – He needs an ambulance, I say. They look down at lad on ground in pool of his own blood. They spit on him. They laugh their cocks off at him – Hope cunt fucking dies, they say. Hope he fucking dies – They'll not say that again, I think. Not to Martin Daly. But then they walk away. Just leave us – To reverse. Regroup. Ready for village – They're done with us. They're ready for village now – Done with us. For now. Pete puts lad on backseat of a car with two other blokes – Bloke with a broken arm. Bloke with three broken fingers – Pete says they beat up Kevin Barron and all – He's MP for Rother Valley. Our MP – Pete sends them all to Badsley Moor Hospital. No one speaks on way home in car. Keith puts on radio. Tory fucking cunt comes on. Represents Police Federation. Tells whole world that police should be free to fire plastic bullets at pickets – His name is Eldon Griffiths. He is a Member of Parliament too, as well as a cunt who'll burn in hell – Keith puts his foot down on brake. He stops car. He rips radio out. He gets out – He throws radio on ground. He jumps up and down on it in road – His name is Keith Lewis. He is a miner and a father of two – *The soil is cold. The wounds old* – Telephone wakes me up about two. **Day 205.** Incoming calls only now. Noise it makes in an empty house – Wake bloody dead, it would. Think it might be Cath. Never know – It's Keith. *Click-click.* He says, There's thousands of police at pit. Fucking thousands. *Krk-krk.* Thousands? I say. Joking with us? I wish I were, he says.

The Twenty-ninth Week

Monday 17 – Sunday 23 September 1984

The Jew stands at the foot of his bed in his suite on the fourth floor of Claridge's. The Jew is still in his silk dressing-gown and slippers. The Jew is practising his golf swing again. The Jew and the Chairman have spent the weekend at Sir Hubert's house in Wiltshire. The Prime Minister and her husband came for dinner on Saturday night –

Sir Hubert gave the Jew a cheque for £250,000 –

The Jew thanked him on behalf of the National Working Miners' Committee –

The Chairman thanked him on behalf of the National Coal Board –

The Prime Minister thanked him on behalf of the nation.

The Jew is still excited. He'd draw Neil a picture if he had the time –

'Denis is as dry as tinder,' says the Jew. 'You'd adore him, Neil. Adore him.'

Neil Fontaine smiles. Neil Fontaine nods.

'There we were discussing our friends in South Yorkshire and the Sheffield Stalin when Denis, who had been quietly practising his golf swing by the fireplace, shouts out that we should intern the lot of them,' laughs the Jew. 'Intern the bloody miners!'

Neil Fontaine smiles again. Neil Fontaine nods again.

'And the Chairman,' says the Jew, with tears in his eyes, 'he strokes his chin and looks across the table at the PM and says, "Might not be such a bad idea –"

'"Might not be such a bad idea!"' screams the Jew again. 'Can you imagine it?'

Neil Fontaine doesn't smile. Neil Fontaine just nods –

Rows and rows of Nissen huts. Rolls and rolls of barbed wire –

Factories and chimneys. Badges and banners –

The yellow Coal Not Dole *stickers. The black stench of death.*

The Jew takes another swing with his invisible club. He shouts, 'Fore!'

Brass in pocket. Dogs in the back. The Mechanic has a plan. His master plan –

He makes the calls. The connections. The introductions.

Money. Dogs. Plans packed. The Mechanic drives down to the Cotswolds –

He makes more calls. More connections. Introductions –

Appointments.

The Mechanic parks behind the Avenging Angel in Cirencester. He turns off Jimmy Young and Mrs Thatcher. He goes into the pub –

The Mechanic spots him immediately. In the corner. In a dirty suit and a Paisley waistcoat –

Hand out, the Mechanic asks, 'Tony?'

Tony Davies nods. He shakes the Mechanic's hand. Holds it a moment too long –

The Mechanic pulls away. He points at Tony's drink. 'Another?'

Tony Davies nods. 'Thank you. VAT, please.'

The Mechanic orders a brandy and a double vodka and tonic at the bar. He takes them back over to the table in the corner.

'You're a gentleman,' says Tony Davies. 'Thank you. Cheers.'

The Mechanic smiles. He raises his brandy. 'Cheers.'

Tony Davies drinks quickly. Down in one. Then asks, 'How do you know Julius?'

'The usual places. Faces,' the Mechanic says. 'You know?'

Tony Davies nods. 'Roland said you might know what's happened to him.'

'I might,' the Mechanic says. 'I might.'

Tony Davies leans across the table. 'He was my friend. How much do you want?'

'Not money,' the Mechanic says. 'Information. I'll tell you what I know and you tell me what you know.'

Tony Davies smiles. Tony Davies winks. 'All that I have is yours.'

'Julius Schaub is dead,' the Mechanic tells him.

Tony Davies stops smiling. Tony Davies blinks. 'How can you know that?'

'I did some work with him,' the Mechanic says. 'It got very badly messed up. Julius got blamed.'

Tony Davies sniffs. Nods to himself. Then shrugs. 'I heard. Shrewsbury.'

'Then I won't waste your time any longer,' the Mechanic says and stands up –

Tony Davies grabs the Mechanic's arm. 'I didn't mean it that way.'

'Another drink then?' the Mechanic asks him.

Tony Davies smiles. Tony Davies nods. 'That would be very kind of you.'

The Mechanic orders another brandy and another vodka and tonic. He takes them back over to the table in the corner.

'A true gentleman,' says Tony Davies. 'Thank you.'

'John Parish? James Riley? Pete Lucas? Neil Fontaine?' the Mechanic asks him.

Tony Davies puts his drink down. Tony Davies nods.

The Mechanic smiles. He says, 'When did you last see him?'

Tony Davies sighs. 'Last month in London.'

'To do with Schaub?'

'Yes,' says Tony Davies. 'To do with Julius.'

'What did he say?'

'He didn't say anything. Just assaulted me. Followed me home. Threatened me.'

'You were lucky,' the Mechanic tells him. 'He killed your mate Schaub.'

Tony Davies shakes his head. Tony Davies says, 'How do you know that?'

'Friend of a friend,' the Mechanic says. 'You know?'

Tony Davies looks at the Mechanic. 'Roland told me you had contacts.'

'But not the one I need,' the Mechanic says. 'How did you find Fontaine?'

Tony Davies finishes his vodka. 'You must want him pretty bad, cowboy.'

The Mechanic stares at the man in the dirty suit. The Paisley waistcoat –

The flowers and the stains –

He says, 'Do you want me to show you just how bad?'

Tony Davies shakes his head one last time. He sighs and says, 'The General.'

Neil Fontaine drives the Jew up to Victoria. The Jew watches the crowds flow –

Back to work with Mr Sweet.

The Jew has promised people the Earth. The Jew has promised people results –

The Jew has delivered neither earth nor results. The Jew has delivered only sky –

Big, grey, empty, English sky.

For all his many working committees. His many legal moves. His many adverts –

His very many promises to very many people –

The Earth has refused to move, the results refused to come.

There has been no mass return to work. No cracks in the coalfields.

People are still waiting; still waiting for the Earth; still waiting for the results –

People who don't like to be kept waiting –

Important people. Impatient people.

The Jew walks into Hobart House and the doors in the corridors close before him. The Jew does not care. The Jew has enough to worry about –

'No, no, no,' the Jew scolds Neil. 'The whole thing to the right. To the right.'

Neil Fontaine has a mouthful of pins and a handful of map –

Neil Fontaine holds the map up on the wall opposite the Jew's Hobart House desk. He twists his neck to look back round at the Jew –

The Jew shakes his head again. The Jew says again, 'To the *right*, Neil.'

Neil Fontaine moves the map further to the right. He turns back.

The Jew nods. The Jew says, 'Pin it there, Neil. Pin it there.'

Neil Fontaine takes the pins from his mouth. He puts them in the four corners.

Neil Fontaine steps back –

The huge map of the British coalfields looks crooked. Not straight.

The Jew doesn't care. He is back in his biscuit tins, sorting out his pins –

The red pins. The yellow pins. The blue pins –

The bullets for his battles. The forces for his fields. The battlefields of the North –

The numbers he needs. To win the war –

The Numbers War.

The Jew has been inspired by the work of the North Derbyshire Area Director. The Jew has met Mr Moses. Mr Moses targeted Shirebrook Colliery in July –

There are now almost a thousand men back at Shirebrook –

The Jew sees no reason why this cannot be replicated across his entire wall map.

He has his biscuit tins. He has his new pins. His demands and his secretary –

Chloe crosses her legs. Chloe takes a note –

The Jew wants a copy of the entire payroll for the National Coal Board. The Jew wants every miner's name checked against police and county court records –

The Jew wants weaknesses –

Men who have transferred to their pit. Men who live a distance from their pit –

Men who are married. Men divorced. Men who have children. Men who can't –

Men who have mortgages. Men who have debts –

Men who used to work a lot of overtime. Men who used to have a lot of money –

Men who have weaknesses –

Age. Sex. Drink. Theft. Gambling. Money.

The Jew wants lists –

Area by area. Pit by pit. Shift by shift. Miner by miner –

Picket by picket –

Village by village. Street by street. House by house. Man by man –

Scab by scab.

The Jew wants to see the pins change –

Red to yellow. Yellow to blue –

Back to work with Mr Sweet –

'The canteen cat comes in from the cold,' shouts the Jew. 'It counts.'

Paul stood in the doorway. Paul watched Terry Winters walk down the corridor from his office to the lift. Every time Terry left his desk. There was Paul. In the doorway to his office, watching him walk down the corridor to the lift. Terry had stopped the first time. Terry had said, 'Can I help you?'

'You've done enough already, Comrade,' Paul had said. 'You've done enough.'

The second time, Terry had asked, 'Is something wrong?'

'Just you, Comrade,' Paul had said. 'Just you.'

Terry hadn't stopped the third time. Terry had walked on by –

Paul blamed him. Blamed Terry for everything –

The collapse of the talks. The state of their finances. The fate of the legal actions –

The Derbyshire Three had won their right to work. The Derbyshire NUM was now bound by injunctions guaranteeing no disciplinary hearings against the three men from Bolsover, Markham and Shirebrook –

Paul blamed Terry. Blamed him for everything.

Paul was the least of his worries, though. Terry knew time was running out –

There was a shortage of shotguns and a queue for the President's skull –

Every day another death threat. Today's had been to the Independent News Room –

The President would be shot if he came to Stoke tonight.

The Special Branch had demanded the President accept a detail of their best men. The President had laughed in their faces. The President had said, 'They're already here.'

The President put down the phone. *Click-click.* The President's hands shook –

Terry knew time was running out. Fleeing –

Terry wrote warnings in soap on the mirrors in the bathrooms of St James's House. Terry wiped them off with paper towels that smelt of schools. The Tweeds and the Denims came in. They washed their hands in the basin next to his. They looked at him as if he were from another planet. Terry walked back down the corridor to his desk –

Paul was there. In the doorway to his office. He grabbed Terry's arm as he passed. He held his hand. He sniffed his fingers –

'Someone's been drawing obscene pictures on the toilet doors,' he said.

'I've seen them,' said Terry. 'There are swastikas shaped in a heart around them.'

'Very artistic,' said Paul. 'Now why do you do it, Winters?'

Terry shook his head. He said, 'You've got the wrong man this time, Comrade.'

'I'm watching you, Winters,' said Paul Hargreaves. 'And I'll catch you –'

Paul blamed him. Blamed Terry for everything.

Terry didn't have time to care. Time was running out. Escaping –

Terry needed the President's ear. Terry walked back down the corridor to the lift. Paul watched him. Terry Winters took the lift up to the tenth floor –

There was a queue for the President's ear –

Terry waited in line. Behind the bishops and the Members of Parliament; the men from NACODS and ACAS; ASLEF and the TGWU.

Terry looked at his watch. Time was running out. Telephones were ringing –

But Terry had to be a patient man. Diane had said his turn would come.

Diane was not wrong. Terry whispered three words in the President's ear –

He said, 'Mohammed Abdul Divan.'

Neil Fontaine opens the door. Jennifer pushes straight past him into the hotel room. Jennifer empties her handbag onto the floor. Her pills. Her prescriptions. Her purse. Jennifer kneels among her possessions. She spreads her property out across the carpet. She searches for the newspaper cutting. She holds it up –

'You fucking liar,' screams Jennifer Johnson. 'He's not dead. He's back.'

Know what it fucking means and all, don't you? Means fucking war, that's what it means. I tell him, I'm coming down now – Pick up anyone on way you can, he says. Fucking anyone and everyone – I will, I say. I'm coming now. I hang up. I lock up. I get in car – I drive to Geoff's. Haven't seen him in donkey's ages. Don't matter now – But lights are off when I pull up. Remember he's got kids. Think better of it – Don't know anyone else out our way. But I see Chris. I stop for him. He gets in. He says, You heard, then? Aye, I say. Keith called us. He nods. He says, Rang us and all. I thought it were bit strange before like? What were that, then? I ask. Before, he says. This police van were doing circles all round village. Right up by Terrace and Hall. Then back down. Must have passed us five time while I were walking dog. Keith said some of lads had seen it when they come back from Brook-house picket. It were still there at chucking-out time. Up by Barrel – More than one van by sounds of it now, I say. He nods again. He asks, Know who it is, do you? I shake my head. I say, Do you? He shakes his head. He says, Fucking cunt, whoever he is – Dead cunt and all, I say. Then I see roadblock up ahead, just past Rising Deer. I think, Here we go – I stop car. I wind down window – *Krk-krk*. Met twat in his white shirt sticks in his head. He says, Morning, scum. I can see Chris is nervous. I think, I'm saying nothing here. But Pig says, Come on then, wankers, where you think you going? I work at Thurcroft Colliery, I say. He laughs. He says, No you don't. You're on fucking strike, you lying lazy little cunt – It's my pit, I tell him. I want to picket in. He yawns in my face. He says, Fuck off home. Six pickets, Doris. That's the law – Bugger it then, I say. I'm going back to bed – That's a good Doris, he says. Make sure you take Eddie fucking Large with you. I nod – I wind window back up. I reverse down road – Pig in his white shirt turns to his mates. They laugh at us. They wave bye-bye – Chris says, Which way now? Dump car. Go over fields, I say. Head for Welfare, I reckon. Chris nods. Do just that – Ditches. Hedges. Fields.

Hedges. Ditches. Fields. Ditches. Hedges. Fields – Roadblocks on every road in. Take a few back gardens on our way – Drop over a couple of walls. Down an alley or two – Find ourselves by school. Cut through playground – Keith up ahead. By Welfare – I start across road to meet him. Chris behind us – Then I see them. Hundreds of them. Fucking hundreds of them. Hundreds of bastards – Fucking army of occupation, that's what they are. Lined up across foot of Pit Lane – No way anyone is off up there to Hut. I get to where Keith and about ten others are. I say, What's going on, then? Fuck all, by looks of it, he says. They're fuck-ing everywhere. Chris says, What about back way? Down Steadfolds Lane, that way? Few of lads are nod-ding. Keith says, Better than standing round here like lemons. Everyone starts off down Katherine Street towards junction with Sandy Lane – That's when it starts. For real. Kicks off. Big time – First we know of it these lads are coming down road behind us. Legging it – Pigs! Pigs, they shout. Pigs are coming! I'm up at front. I turn round to see what fuss is – Two police vans are coming full tilt up Katherine Street at us – Fuck! Look, someone says. Fuck – I turn round again to see another vanload coming down Sandy Lane – Shit! Shit, Keith's saying. Shit! – Two of vans have got their back doors open. Pigs are out with their trun-cheons – Split up! Split up, someone else says. Split up! – I jump over a hedge into this garden. First few cop-pers go straight past us – Past us into Keith. Whack – First one's got his tit-helmet in his hand. Belts Keith with it – Keith goes down like a sack of spuds. Face all cut open by nipple of tit – Hands over his face. Blood through his fingers – He looks up. Looks up straight into this other copper's boot – Crack! I see his teeth and shit fly out all over place – That's it for me. Bastards – Fucking bastards. I jump back over hedge and charge them – Four of them laying into him. Keith out cold – I scream, Fucking going to kill him, you bastards. He's had enough – Cunt with his tit in his hand says, It's your turn then, is it? – I say, How about just you

The Thirtieth Week

Monday 24 – Sunday 30 September 1984

He has the introduction. The connection. He makes the call. The appoint-
ment –
The Mechanic drives North. Far North. Into Scotland –
The dogs in the back.
He takes the A66 from Scotch Corner to Penrith. The A74 from Carlisle to
Glasgow. Then the A82 all the way past Glencoe –
Towards the General. In his castle on Loch Linnhe.

The President had met the Leader of the Labour Party. The President
and the Leader had had constructive discussions. The President was
to speak at the Labour Party Conference in Blackpool next week –

The President would speak, and this time they would listen –

The whole country would listen now.

The Dock Strike might be over. There might be other court
actions –

But NACODS had rendered all these things academic.

NACODS were set to strike. Power cuts were but weeks away –

General Winter on the march, and so was his namesake.

Terry picked up the phone on his desk. *Click-click.* Terry dialled
Bath –

'It's almost over, love,' said Terry. 'Please come home.'

Then Terry hung up. *Click-click.* Then Terry picked it up again.
Click-click.

The footsteps in the dark corridor. The knock at the door. The turn of
the handle –

The news he dreaded. The news they all dreaded:

The NACODS men at Sutton have voted for strike action by 90 per cent –

'Ninety per cent!' screams the Jew. 'It's the most moderate pit in the
country!'

The Jew blames the Chairman for this. The Jew hates the Chairman
for this –

It was the Chairman who had threatened these men with the sack –

The Jew wonders sometimes who really pays the Chairman's wages –

Moscow or Margaret?

The telephones start to ring. The faxes start to come –

More footsteps in the corridor. More knocks at the door. Turns of the handle –

There will be no safety cover when NACODS strike. There can be no mining without safety cover. There will be no mining, so there can be no working miners. There will be no working miners, so there can be no coal –

'No fucking coal!' shouts the Jew. 'No fucking coal!'

The Jew throws his biscuit tins across his office –

The blue pins. The yellow pins.

'He will have won!' shrieks the Jew. 'He will have fucking won!'

The Jew falls to the floor beneath the huge, crooked map of the British coalfield –

The map covered only in red pins.

'He will have won and we will have lost!' screams the Jew. 'Lost!'

The Jew sobs. The Jew weeps –

'Everything will be ruined,' whispers the Jew. 'Ruined.'

His men come for the Mechanic at the Ballachulish Hotel. His men march into the bar in uniform. His men march the Mechanic out. His men put the Mechanic in the back of a Land-Rover. His men blindfold the Mechanic. His men drive the Mechanic away from the Ballachulish Hotel. His men stop to open metal gates. His men leave the roads marked on maps. His men speak into radios. His men talk in codes. His men stop to open another metal gate. His men drive uphill. His men slow down. His men come to a dead stop. His men remove the Mechanic's blindfold. His men open the back of the Land-Rover. His men order the Mechanic out. His men lead the Mechanic through a training camp. His men march the Mechanic into a castle. Through the courtyard. Up the stairs. To stand before his door. His men knock. His men leave –

The door opens.

Today is the day –

The day of the decisions. The decisions that will determine the dispute –

The day the Jew is nowhere to be seen.

Neil Fontaine knocks again on the double-doors of the Jew's suite on the fourth floor of Claridge's. Neil Fontaine unlocks the doors and enters the suite. He walks across the deep carpet. He pulls back the heavy curtains –

The Jew's bed is bare. The sheets wrenched. The blankets perverted.

Neil Fontaine walks across the deep carpet to the bathroom door –

The deep, *damp* carpet.

Neil Fontaine stands in the stain outside the bathroom and bangs upon the door –

Neil Fontaine kicks in the door.

The Jew lies naked on the tiles of his bathroom on the fourth floor of Claridge's.

Neil Fontaine wraps his waxen body in the monogrammed towels and holds him –

The Jew opens his eyes. He looks up at Neil. The Jew asks, 'Did we win, Neil?'

'There's good news and there's bad,' says Neil Fontaine.

'The bad news first, please, Neil.'

'It did happen,' says Neil Fontaine. 'NACODS have voted to strike.'

The Jew nods. The Jew wipes the tears from his eyes. The Jew sniffs –

'And the good news?' he asks. 'You did say there was some good news?'

'Don and Derek are outside with Piers and Dominic,' says Neil Fontaine.

The Jew sniffs again. The Jew squeezes his nose between his fingers and nods –

'The show must go on, Neil,' he says. 'The show. Must. Go. On!'

Neil Fontaine goes back out into the corridor. He asks the four men to step inside. Tells them the Jew is feeling a little under the weather.

'Maybe we can cheer him up,' says Derek Williams.

'Let's hope so,' says Neil Fontaine and opens the door for them.

Piers Harris and Dominic Reid lead the way. Don and Derek follow –

The Jew is sitting on the settee in his dressing-gown. The Jew says, 'Welcome.'

Neil Fontaine sits the four men down. Neil Fontaine takes their orders –

Two gin and tonics. Two pints of bitter –

'And a brandy for me,' says the Jew. 'A large one, please, Neil.'

The Jew turns to the men. *His men.* He says, 'What news from the Inns of Court.'

'The strike is unlawful in Derbyshire and unofficial in Yorkshire,' says Piers.

Dominic nods. He says, 'The judge did not order a ballot, though.'

'Did the Union attend?' asks the Jew.

Piers shakes his head. He says, 'Their lawyer said they'd over-looked it.'

The Jew looks at Don and Derek. He asks, 'Will you go to work on Monday?'

Derek looks at Don. Don looks at Derek –

Don and Derek both nod.

The Jew smiles at Don and Derek. The Jew looks at his watch. The Jew says, 'Let's see what Arthur Stalin has to say about that, then. Neil, the television, please.'

Neil Fontaine walks over to the TV. He switches on the *Channel 4 News* –

There he is. Bold as brass. Their president –

The Jew smiles. He picks up the remote control. He presses record on the video –

'– I'm going to say this quite clearly: any miner in this Union and any official in this Union who urges or crosses a picket line in defiance of our Union's instructions runs the risk of being disciplined. There is no High Court judge going to take away the democratic right of our Union to deal with internal affairs –'

The Jew presses stop. The Jew claps. The Jew applauds –

The Union would not accept the court's decision. The Union insisted the strike was official –

Don Colby and Derek Williams would be scabs. Official.

The Jew looks over at Don and Derek again –

Don and Derek sitting on the fourth floor of Claridge's with their two pints of bitter –

The Jew says, 'That's not very nice, is it?'

Don and Derek shake their heads and sip their pints of bitter.

The Jew looks over at Piers and Dominic with their two gin and tonics –

The Jew says, 'That's not strictly legal, either, is it?'

Piers and Dominic shake their heads and sip their gin and tonics.

The Jew looks at the four men and their four drinks –

The Jew says, 'That's contempt, isn't it?'

The four men nod their heads.

The Jew laughs. The Jew claps his hands. The Jew shouts, 'Champagne, Neil.'

Don and Derek smile and drain their two pints of bitter –

Piers and Dominic frown and put down their gin and tonics –

'Might it not be rather tricky to actually serve a writ on them?' asks Dominic.

The Jew shakes his head. The Jew winks. The Jew raises his brandy glass –

'Piers, get me the writ,' he shouts. 'Neil, get me the helicopter.'

The Jew buries his brandy in one. The Jew picks up the telephone –

'Hi-ho. Hi ho,' sings the Jew. 'It's back to work we *all* go.'

Diane picked Terry Winters up after the Executive. Terry watched her legs as she drove. Diane took the A630 to Doncaster. Terry touched her knees as she drove. Diane passed through Rotherham. Terry squeezed her legs as she drove. Diane came to Conisbrough. Terry put his hands up her skirt as she drove. Diane turned left by Warmsworth Primary. Terry put his hands between her legs as she drove. Diane parked in Levitthagg Wood. Terry pulled down her tights and knickers. Diane pulled up her skirt. Terry undid his trousers. Diane undid her blouse. Terry took out his cock. Diane straddled Terry Winters. Terry was going to be late for his meeting with Mohammed Abdul Divan.

The Mechanic had seen him once before. In 1975 –

A recruitment meeting at a Heathrow hotel.

General William Walters doesn't remember the Mechanic. But the Mechanic remembers him –

The Apprehensive Patriot –

The former NATO Commander-in-Chief, Allied Forces, Northern Command. Friend of the late Lord Mountbatten. Templer of Malaya –

The Duke of Edinburgh.

Founder or member of Red Alert/Civil Assistance. Royal Society of St George. The Unison Committee for Action. Great Britain 1975. Aims of Industry. Self-Help. Movement for True Industrial Democracy. National Association for Freedom –

Philip for President.

The General's man pours the malts. His man serves them. His man leaves them.

The General raises his glass. He says, 'One of Frank's boys in Ulster, I hear.'

'Yes, sir,' the Mechanic says. 'I was, sir.'

'Imagine you must have spent some time in the Darklands, then.'

'Yes, sir,' the Mechanic says again. 'Rhodesia, sir.'

'Bloody mess,' says the General. 'Bloody mess. What do you do now?'

'I rob supermarkets and threaten striking miners, sir.'

The General nods. He gets up slowly. He turns to his window and his local view –

Lock Linnhe. Lismore Island. Kingairloch. The Sound of Mull.

'Never really cared for her much,' says the General. 'Problem was she was always Airey's girl. Better than Queen Teddy and all those other sausage jockeys. But still much too fond of the clipped-cock brigade for my liking –

'Poor woman has had bad advice. In love with the sound of her own voice now. Thatcherism. Reaganism. Monetarism. Load of tosh-ism. Forms of Socialism in disguise. End up selling us all down the river for a few votes from the council houses. Not a government, they're a cabal. Bunch of bloody Jews who can't keep their filthy hands to themselves. Plain greedy, the lot of them. That's their problem. Mines should be owned by the government. Gas, water and electricity. Like the army and the police. Privatize this. Privatize that. End up with the whole bloody country owned by foreigners. Crush Communism, trample down trade unionism. By all means. Of course, you do –

'But you don't sell the bloody silver to do it –

'I told her straight, "Lie down with dogs, Hilda, and you'll get up with fleas –"

'But you see, the problem with most people is that they think they're immortal. That life is an inexhaustible well. But, in truth, everything happens only a certain number of times and a very small number really. How many more times will we remember a certain afternoon in our childhood? A former friend we have not seen for many years? How many more times will we watch the full moon rise? Perhaps ten? Maybe not that. Yet it all seems endless. Bloody endless. But not to men like us, David. Not to us –

'Men who have seen slaughter. Felt fear. Tasted terror –'

'Yes, sir.'

'Men like us know some things are simply not for sale.'

'Yes, sir.'

The General watches the Mechanic. The General nods. The General smiles –
The sun sets late and long over Lock Linnhe.

The General pours more malts. The General pats the Mechanic on his back –

The full moon rises before it wanes.

The General says, 'There really is only one solution to this problem.'

and me, then? Go on, just you and me? But they just laugh and charge at me. Four of them – Me thinking, Stay on your feet, Martin. Stay on your fucking feet – But I go straight over with first two bloody punches. Fucking hell, I think. It's hammer time for me – Wham. Bam. Thank you, ma'am – They keep on belting me with fucking truncheons. Battering me, they are. Fucking leathering me – This one saying over and over, Get up and fucking walk, cunt! Get up and fucking walk! Then van must have come and they sling us in back – Keith on one seat. Hands full of teeth and gums – Me on other. Blood everywhere – Pig van sets off, then stops again. Doors open and they only go and sling in Chris – Fucking mess and all. Right proud, they are, all pigs. Chris being big lad he is – Head busted open. They're still hitting him as van sets off again – You're fucked, you three, they tell us. Having you for riot – I didn't bloody do anything, Chris says. I were just stood there – Shut it, Haystacks, they say. Belt him one again – He can't even get up on seat. Just lies there between their boots – I keep it shut. More worried about Keith. He's not right, you can tell. He needs a fucking hospital – I look out back. Looks like Laughton Common. Think maybe they're taking us to Dinnington. But then van turns off. Down a lane onto Common – Fucking hell, I think. No police stations down here. No fucking hospitals, either – Nothing. No one – Begin to think this is it. End of road. Van stops. Doors open – They say, Get out, you fucking scum. Bastards – I get out first. I've got Keith by arm. Chris behind us – Middle of fucking nowhere. Just fields and stuff. Light now – Two coppers grab each of us. By us hair. By us throats – Pin us up by some fence posts. Top of this banking – Then Big Cheese gets out of front of van. He walks over to us – I can tell he's worried about Keith and all. Has a good look in his gob – It's like fucking Nicaragua, this. They'll rape us and shoot us and stick us in this fucking ditch – But then Brass turns to me. He says, Open your mouth. I look him in his eyes. I open my mouth. He looks inside. He says, Right, shut it. He goes over to Chris. He says same. He does same. Chris says, I want to go home now. Brass looks at three of us. Brass shakes his head. He says, Go on Queen's Highway again today and I'll have fucking lot of you. Then he looks at his lads. He smiles. He gives them nod – Fucking bastards kick us down banking into ditch. Fuck off in their van – Bastards. Bastards. Fucking, fucking bastards – I lie there in that ditch and I want to scream at sky, I do – Fuck me. I wish them dead. I wish her dead. Her and every fucking cunt that ever voted for her – I get up off ground. I look round – Keith face down in ditch. Chris caught on some barbed wire – I turn Keith over. I wipe his face with my hand – Keith, Keith, I say. Come on, lad. Let's have you up and home. He shakes his head. He's still got his eyes closed. Come on, I say. We've got to get off – But he just shakes his head again. I try to prop him up against side of ditch – Then I go over to get Chris off wire. He's in a bad way and all – His face and hands all cut. Head split open. Nothing left of his bloody coat – He says, Our Val's going to kill us – She's not, I say. Don't be daft. Takes about five minute to get him free of that barbed wire. Then I say, Give us a hand with Keith, will you? What we going to do? he asks. Where we going to go? Nearer Dinnington now, I say. Go down their Welfare. Use their telephone. Let your Val know where you are. His Margaret. Try to get hold of Pete. Then find someone to give us a lift to a bloody hospital. Chris nods. He walks over to where Keith is. He's got his eyes open now. I say, Back in land of living, are we? Keith shakes his head. He says, That what you call this place, is it? Come on, I say. Shut up and get up – He just looks at me, though. Into my eyes – He says, Know who fucking scab is, don't you? **Day 210.** I still can't believe it's him. I know fucking bloke – I like him. I drink with him – He can be tight. He can be moody. He can be a bit of a slack bastard. Bit of a moaner – But he's not a fucking scab. Not the Geoff Brine I fucking know – Just can't believe it's him. I go over there. I want to see him with my own two eyes. I want to talk to him. To ask

The Thirty-first Week

Monday 1 – Sunday 7 October 1984

The President loved Blackpool. The Illuminations. The trams. The Tower. The rock –

The Winter Gardens. The Conference. The Heroes' Welcome. The full support –

'– we are witnessing not the Fascism of Hitler or Mussolini, nor the military dictatorship of a Pinochet or Franco, but the creation of a sort of controlled democracy, a sort of top-hatted Fascism, a mixture of Thatcher's Victorian values and modernistic techniques. An Orwellian Big Sister-ism where the workers are kept as they believe in their proper place – at the bottom of the heap. This is very much the ugly face of Conservatism which tramples on the more responsible values of the one-nation Macmillanites –'

Most of all the President loved to see their leader suffer. The Welsh Windbag. His face as red as his hair. The man who had described the President as the labour movement's equivalent of a First World War general. The President loved to see him suffer as he listened –

'– this Conference pays tribute to the historic struggle of the miners in 1984. This Conference deplores the total dishonesty of the Conservative government's determination to attack the National Union of Mineworkers and the whole trade union movement by repressive legislation and an unprecedented and wholesale operation involving unlawful actions of the police, organized violence against the miners, their picket lines, and their communities by means of an unconstitutional and nationally controlled police force –'

The Conference applauded and cheered. Their leader writhed and squirmed –

The President was in his element.

Personally, Terry Winters preferred the Pleasure Beach. The Gold Mine –

The roller-coasters and the rides. The circus and the hats –

Kiss me quick. Squeeze me slow –

The element of surprise –

The man came down the aisle during the debate on local Labour Party reforms. Terry opened his eyes and there he was. The man was standing over them with a photographer. The man had papers in his hand. The man leant across Terry. The man dropped the papers into the President's lap. The President looked up. The man told him, 'These are committal proceedings to put you in Pentonville Prison for contempt.'

The Jew bounced back. He always does. That's the Jew for you. Like a bouncing bomb –

And Blackpool had been a big blast. His finest hour –

Mission impossible –

Death or glory.

The High Court had issued the orders for contempt early on the Monday morning. The orders had to be served on Stalin that day. Had to be served or they'd expire –

Neil Fontaine picked up the process server at dawn in Mansfield –

Don Colby and Derek Williams had packed their snap.

Neil drove the server down to Battersea heliport at ninety miles an hour –

Don and Derek had kissed their wives goodbye.

The Jew was waiting with the writ in his flying-jacket and his goggles –

Two thousand pickets waiting for Don and Derek at the Manton gates.

The Jew flew Neil and the server the two hundred miles to the Winter Gardens –

Two thousand pickets waiting to tell Don and Derek the strike was official.

Neil had forged the passes to the floor. Neil had bribed the stewards on the door –

Two thousand pickets waiting to call Don and Derek scab, scab, scabs.

Their President looked down at the papers in his lap –

The strike was not official. Don and Derek were not scabs.

The server had served the writ –

The President was in contempt. Don and Derek were back at work.

It was, without a doubt, the Jew's finest hour to date –

Mission accomplished –

The impetus regained.

*

The dogs bark and bound along the beach at Brighton. They play among the
pebbles. Tails up and tongues out. They tumble through the tide –
   The Earth tilts. The Earth turns.
   There are the things you know. The things you don't.
   Then there are the other things. The things in between –
   The Earth hungry. The Earth hunts.

The Jew is back on the road again. The Jew has an extra-special guest
to guide today –
   The Prime Minister to the North Yorkshire Police Divisional Head-
quarters –
   The very centre of the target of the latest back-to-work drive.
   The Prime Minister is here to thank the troops. Her boys –
   The Prime Minister rallies them on their return. Back from the bat-
tle lines –
   From Brodsworth. From Denby Grange. From Kellingley. From
Rossington –
   The Prime Minister is impressed by the job they've done –
   The length of the land. The breadth of Britain –
   From Harworth to Hunterston. From Kiveton Park to Kent, Wooll-
ey to Wales –
   Everywhere they've been –
   From Ollerton to Orgreave. From the village streets to the picket
lines –
   Everything they've done –
   'Many, many thanks,' she says. 'We are all extremely grateful for
what you have done, and so are the overwhelming majority of the
British public –
   'Many, many thanks for all you have done.'
   The Prime Minister leaves by the rear of the building. Her car is
waiting –
   The black Mercedes, too.
   The Prime Minister sits in the back with the Jew in the car park.
   The Prime Minister is here to thank the Jew. Her boy –
   The Prime Minister is impressed by the job he's done –
   The length of the land. The breadth of Britain –
   From Cortonwood to Claridge's. From Shirebrook to the Strand,
Blackpool to Brighton –
   Everywhere he's been –

From the front lines of the North to the pocket books of the South –

From the coalfields to the courtrooms –

Everything he's done –

'Many, many thanks,' she says again. 'I don't know what I'd do without you.'

The Jew blushes. The Jew gushes. The Jew presents her with his latest works –

The Miners' Dispute: A Catalogue of Violence –

'– the planned attacks and the unplanned violence –'

He details the intimidation of Don Colby and Derek Williams and their families –

'– paint stripper. Heavy wooden staves. Rivet guns. Death threats. Vehicles driven at speed at these men and their families –

'– the raw and naked intimidation –

'– the working miners are in the front line of the fight for freedom. Every working miner, every day, as he leaves his home to go to work, faces the possibility that his wife and his children will be abused, threatened, or even attacked while he is at work. These men are not scabs. These men are lions –'

The Prime Minister agrees. The Prime Minister applauds –

'The best of British.'

The Prime Minister appreciates everything the Jew has done –

Everything he is doing –

But something is wrong. The Jew can sense it –

The Prime Minister looks out of the window. She shakes her head.

The Jew is on the edge of the backseat. The Jew touches the arm of her suit –

He says, 'If there is anything more I can do. Anything at all. Please tell me.'

The Prime Minister nods. She turns to the Jew. Unburdens herself –

The Chairman is the cause of her concern. He no longer has her confidence –

The Prime Minister likes men she can set her watch by –

Serious. Steadfast. Strong. Systematic –

'Men like you,' she says. 'Men like you, Sweet Stephen.'

The Prime Minister worries about NACODS; that the Deputies' day will dawn. The Prime Minister worries the Chairman fails to see the seriousness of the situation –

'The fate of this government is in his hands.'

'I will do anything you ask,' promises the Jew. 'Anything.'

The Prime Minister suggests the Jew actively involve himself in this problem. The Prime Minister suggests the Jew approach the Great Financier for the best solution. The Prime Minister suggests the Jew ask certain people to name their price –

'Everybody has one,' she says. 'Everybody.'

The Prime Minister suggests the Jew pay the price. The Jew agrees.

Neil Fontaine opens the back door for the Prime Minister –

The Prime Minister gets out of the back of the black Mercedes.

Neil Fontaine has an umbrella waiting. He walks her to her Daimler. The Prime Minister rests her hand upon his arm. She says, 'Thank you, Neil.'

Five writs had been served upon five leaders of the National Union of Mineworkers. Five writs served for contempt of court. Five writs served on the floor of the Labour Party Conference. The process photographed for the front page of the *Daily Express* –

There were bound to be recriminations. There were recriminations –

There was also anticipation –

Excitement.

The President went from fringe meeting to meeting. From ovation to ovation –

Branches and palms beneath his feet. Straw and clothes spread upon the floor –

The President rode his donkey up and down the Golden Mile –

Here to banish the money-changers. The dealers in doves –

Here to accept his fate. His imprisonment. His crucifixion. His martyrdom –

'– they have come today for the National Union of Mineworkers. But we are going to resist with all the power we can muster and if that means we have to suffer, either being fined or sent to jail, then that is something we will have to accept. Because I want to make it clear that if the offence I have committed is contempt, I plead guilty. Because the only crime I have committed is to fight for my class and my members –

'I am not someone who wishes to go to Pentonville Prison, but I want to make it absolutely clear that if the choice facing me is to be committed by the High Court to spend a prison term in Pentonville or any other jail for standing by this trade union and our class or, alternatively, having to live with the imprisonment of one's own mind for betraying one's class, then there's no choice as far as I am concerned –

'We have come too far and we have suffered too much for there to be any compromise with either the judiciary or the government –

'I stand by my class and by my union – and if that means prison, so be it.'

The President bowed his head. The President raised his fist –

He was the Resurrection and the Light.

The whole room rose as one. Clapped their hands as one. Stamped their feet –

The President stepped back from the podium. The President left the platform.

The President parted the sea. The President walked on the water –

He worked his way through the crowd –

The shakes of the hand. The pats on the back –

Terry Winters waited by the door for the President. Now was Terry's chance –

He took his hand out of his pocket. He stepped forward out of the crowd –

'President,' said Terry. 'I'd like to introduce Mohammed Abdul Divan.'

The President looked at Terry. The President looked at Mr Divan.

Mohammed Abdul Divan put his hand out. He said, 'I am here to help.'

The President took the outstretched hand. The President shook it.

him what the bloody hell he's playing at. Fat fucking chance of that though – Police have got his whole bloody street sealed off. *Krk-krk*. Two cars at end of his drive. Tit-heads at his door. Boards over all his windows. *Scab* sprayed over all boards – Neighbours say wife and kids have gone into hiding – New names. New addresses – He leaves house on a mor-ning with a hood over his head, they say. I stand there on pavement outside his house. I shake my head. I still can't fucking believe it. You stupid fucking cunt, I think and shake my head again. But I'm raging inside. Raging. I shout at his house, You know what you've fucking started now, don't you? But it just sits there. Boarded up and blind. But fuck it and fuck him – He's fucking dead. Dead to me. Dead to us all – I go home. I open door. I put on light – It doesn't work. They've cut us off again – Notice on mat in hall along with another letter from Board and another from TSB. I kick them out of road and walk in. I shut door. I stand in hall – No furni-ture. No food. No gas. No electricity. No wife. Nothing – Not even a bloody exit. Nothing. No way out. No one – I go up stairs. I lie down on floor. I pull some clothes over us. I close my eyes and I pray. Pray I wake up one day and they're all dead – Banks. Electricity Board. DHSS. Coppers. MacGregor. King. Heseltine. Lawson. Ridley. Hav-ers. Walker. Brittan. Tebbit. Thatcher – Dead, fucking lot of them. Them or me. Dead – *It is dark. There are whispers. There are echoes – Cwithan. Scriccettan. Things fall apart* – **Day 211.** War. That's what it is now – Pete always said it was civil war. But there's nothing fucking civil about it – It's a one-man war. Lads want that one man dead and all. Fuck-ing strung up – Things he's done. Things he's caused. Things he's brought to village. Things pigs have dished out on his behalf – Nippers nicked. Blokes beaten. Folk frightened. Knuckle that Keith, Chris and me got. Boot that others took – Things he's brought to village. Things he's caused. Thing he's done – Shame. Shame. Shame – Every day he works. Shame and fucking siege – Fucking siege. That's what it is. A fucking siege – For

one scab. One bloody fucking scab. No one else. Just him – He's going to have to pay price for what he's done. Price is revenge – Revenge. That's what folk want – Revenge. What everybody wants – Picket. Non-picket. Miner. Non-miner. Man. Woman. Young. Old – Revenge. For what he's done. Every single person in village wants it – Revenge. They're going to fucking get it and all. One way or other – Pete has petitioned Panel for a mass picket. Panel are taking their bloody time. Lads are impatient – Few of them were over at Silverwood and ambushed a few coppers. Pigs will want their pound of flesh for that and all. But it made lads feel better. Less fucking helpless at any rate – They won't wait much longer, though. Pete knows that. Panel do, too – Then yesterday another fucking scab only goes and joins Geoff the Mega Scab. That's it now. Panel will have to give go-ahead for mass picket – There's going to be one any-way. Come what may – I get down to Welfare for half-four in morning. Feel-ings are running high. Folk pat us on back. Folk ask after Keith. Folk ask after Chris. That's why I'm here. That's why most folk are here – Ladies from Action Group. Pensioners. Everybody – Pete's wife is handing out whistles to all lasses. Make some noise, that lot will – Everybody'll know we are here. Know why we're here – Pete has his plan. Pete lays it out. Lads listen – Past two days scabs have come in Brampton way. From by me – Few start on again about how scabs are not even from vil-lage. Outsiders – Foreigners. Just like me – Pete shuts them up. Pete tells us all where to go. Picket is to be all along Woodhouse Green to junction by post office. By police station – Pigs have had sense to shut place up, though. Not that it stops them getting dogs out for us – And that's what we get. Dogs barking and usual chorus of Morning, wankers! Least we're team-handed today – Lads here from Maltby. Din-nington – Thousand of us facing thou-sand of them. Them and their dogs at six in morning – Then lasses with their whistles start up. Hear them for miles – Means only one thing. Kick-off – Bus on its way. Bertie the Scab Bus – Ten cop

The Thirty-second Week

Monday 8 – Sunday 14 October 1984

It is the last night of the Conference. It has been a good conference, too. The Home Secretary has attacked their president. The Minister has had a good go, too –

They all had. Even ministers the Jew did not care for.

The talk was of police that did not buckle. Governments that did not crack –

Governments that would not let the working miners down –

Of heroes and villains. Last battles and lost causes. Winners and losers.

There had been standing ovations for the Widow Tams from Shirebrook –

For Bolsover Bill, Creswell Chris and Warsop Wendy –

For Don Colby and Derek Williams. For Fred Wallace and Jimmy Hearn.

Tomorrow the Prime Minister will close the Conference with her own speech. Business will return to London. Normal service resumed. But there is still tonight –

The last night of the Conference is the night the Jew likes best –

The night to boast. The night to gloat –

The Union was fined two hundred thousand pounds for contempt yesterday. Its president one thousand pounds, personally. Its president who had stood on the steps of his Sheffield redoubt and committed further contempt –

The Jew knows they'll never pay. The Jew knows what this'll mean –

V.I.C.T.O.R.Y.

So this night belongs to him. It is *his* night. His night to prance. His night to preen –

The Jew faces the mirror in his suite at the Grand. He fiddles with his bow-tie –

'Mirror, mirror, on the wall, who is the sweetest of them all?'

Neil Fontaine takes the white tuxedo with the gold epaulettes out

273

of the wardrobe. He walks over to the mirror. He helps the Jew into the jacket.

'How do I look, Neil?' asks the Jew. 'Be honest now.'

'Distinguished, sir,' replies Neil Fontaine. 'Very distinguished.'

The Jew smiles. The Jew is happy. The Jew is in love.

Neil Fontaine holds open the doors of the suite for the Jew and then locks them. Tonight Neil Fontaine will watch over the Jew. But from a safe, discreet distance.

So Neil Fontaine waits as the Jew wades down the stairs into the happy hordes –

The boring backbenchers. The courteous constituents. The jaded journalists –

All waiting on a wink or a word from the well connected or the wealthy.

The Jew is straight to the Minister. The Jew shakes his hand. The Jew slaps his back –

The Jew congratulates the Minister on his speeches and his stance. The Jew leaves –

'I must say the waiters get more forward with each passing year,' says the Minister.

The Jew doesn't hear. The Jew is a busy bee. The Jew is already out the door –

Next door. To the Metropole. The Starlight Room.

The Jew alights on Edward du Cann. Sir Robin. The Chief Whip and his wife. The Chairman of the Conservative Party –

The Jew shares sentences with them all –

Heads back. Mouths open. Teeth shining. Tongues pointing. Eyes dead. Cold.

The Jew spots Denis in his evening dress. Denis points at the Jew's white tuxedo –

'Anyone order a kebab?' shouts Denis to the laughter of the Starlight Room –

And the Jew laughs too, long and loud (well, what else would he do?) –

Denis slaps the Jew on the back. Denis digs the Jew in the ribs –

After all, Denis is only pulling the Jew's leg. Only pulling his leg, you know?

Denis invites the Jew back to the Grand. To drink champers with Lord Mac.

The Jew and Denis leave the Starlight Room arm in arm. Back to the Grand –

The Jew *just* loves the Grand. The Jew *simply* adores the Grand –

Between the two piers, the Great and the Good, the Wicked and the Wise –

Home to Napoleon III and the Duke of Windsor; JFK and Ronald Reagan.

The Prime Minister is upstairs working on her speech for tomorrow –

The Jew would love to help. Denis feels the Jew has done quite enough of that –

Now is the time to drink. Denis steers the Jew into Lord Mac's suite.

Neil Fontaine stands outside the suite on the fifth floor of the Grand Hotel and listens to the corks pop and the glasses chink. More bottles open and more toasts raised. Neil Fontaine stands outside the suite on the fifth floor of the Grand Hotel and waits –

This is what he does. This is what he's always done –

Neil Fontaine watches and Neil Fontaine waits –

He watches the doors open and close. He waits for the people to come and go –

For Room Service to fetch and carry at the beck and call of the high and mighty –

For the Young Conservatives to stagger and stumble up and down the corridor –

Down their trousers and up their skirts. Up and down the darkening corridor –

He watches and he waits for security to sweep through the floor on the hour –

Every hour. Every floor. Every hour. Every floor. But not this hour. Not this floor –

Neil Fontaine looks at his watch. He taps it. He waits. It is half-past two –

The lights in the corridor flicker. The shadows on the wall lengthen.

Neil Fontaine opens the door to the suite. Neil picks the Jew off the floor –

His bow-tie loose, a bottle in his hand, the Jew asks, 'Where next then, Neil?'

'I think a short stroll along the seafront before the sack, sir,' suggests Neil.

The Jew nods. The Jew tries to focus. The Jew falls against the corridor wall –

Neil Fontaine helps the Jew to his feet and back down the stairs to the lobby –

The Jew hails the heavy drinkers still up in the lobby and the lounges and leaves.

Neil Fontaine guides the Jew across the pavements and onto the Promenade.

The night is not cold. The night is not dark –

The moon is bright upon the beach.

The Jew stares out to sea. The Jew sways. The Jew steadies himself upon the rail –

There are tears in his eyes. Tears upon his cheeks. Upon his fingers –

The Jew wipes his face. The Jew sniffs. The Jew sighs. The Jew turns to Neil –

'They hate me, Neil,' says the Jew. 'I know they do. They wish –'

A thunderous noise behind them. A terrible rumble beneath them –

'What the bloody hell was that?' asks the Jew. 'An earthquake?'

Neil Fontaine stares out at the black sea. Neil Fontaine closes his tired eyes –

'No,' he whispers. 'It was a bomb, sir.'

The Mechanic looks at his watch again. He puts the dogs in the back of the Ford. He drives to the phone box. He parks. He gets out of the car. He waits outside the phone box. He looks at his watch again –

The phone rings at 3 a.m.

The Mechanic steps into the phone box. He picks up the phone. He listens –

To Irish voices. Drunk and victorious. Grateful but broke –

Fuck.

Talk. Talk. Talk. Talk. Talk. Talk. Talk. Talk. Talk. Talk. Talk. Nothing but fucking talk. Terry Winters locked the front door. Terry went down the drive with his suitcase in his hand just as Theresa and their three children came up the drive with their suitcases in their hands. Terry Winters stopped. Terry put down his suitcase. He opened his mouth. Theresa Winters didn't stop. Theresa put her key in the lock. She opened the front door –

There were two taxis at the end of their drive.

Christopher, Timothy and Louise stood on the front step and stared at their father. Terry Winters smiled. Terry waved. Christopher, Timothy and Louise waved back. Theresa Winters came back out. Theresa shepherded her children in off the step. She stared at her husband. Terry Winters smiled. Terry waved –

Theresa Winters slammed the front door in his face.

There was only one taxi at the end of the drive now –

The driver put his hand on the horn. The driver held it there.

The Jew opens his mouth. The Jew shits his pants. The Jew runs for his life –

Runs back across the road towards the Grand Hotel –

The front of the hotel collapsing before them in an avalanche –

Floor by floor. Room by room. Brick by brick –

In a slow, hesitant avalanche.

Neil catches the Jew. Neil grabs him. Neil holds him –

'No, sir,' he shouts. 'There is nothing you can do.'

The Jew rages at Neil. The Jew howls at the night. The Jew screams at the hotel –

The sound of a fire alarm ringing and ringing and ringing –

The masonry falling floor by floor. Room by room. Brick by brick –

'Let go of me! Let go of me!' shouts the Jew. 'Bloody let go of me, man!'

'No, sir,' says Neil Fontaine. 'I can't do that, sir.'

'Damn you, Neil!' shrieks the Jew. 'I should be there! I should be in there!'

Neil clutches the Jew. Neil hugs the Jew. Neil cradles the Jew –

He buries the Jew's head in his jacket. He strokes the Jew's hair with his hand –

He kisses the top of the Jew's head as they watch and they wait –

As an ambulance appears. And another. And another. And another ten arrive –

Their sirens and their lights in the dead silence of the night.

The police put a cordon across the remains of the front of the Grand.

People appear in knots. To stand and to stare. To sob in their knots –

Their eyes are red. Their skin is white. Their veins are blue –

The living and the dead, sat in their dressing-gowns and their pyjamas –

In striped and stained deckchairs, under a bright and bloody moon.

The President was back in Paris on business. It was a flying visit to Montreuil in the midst of the NCB–NACODS–NUM negotiations at ACAS. The President thanked the officials from the French and Soviet trade unions for their generous offers of aid. The President had detailed the physical and financial attacks upon his union and its members; the CGT had agreed to send a forty-five-truck convoy of food and the Soviets had smiled favourably on the President's request for a forty-five-truck convoy of Moscow gold –

It was a good, good day.

Terry Winters and the President moved on. Up the stairs. Down the corridor –

Terry Winters knocked on the door. Mohammed Abdul Divan opened it.

The President and Terry shook hands with Mohammed Divan. They went inside. They sat down across the table from another man.

'Comrades,' said Mohammed. 'This is Salem. The man from Libya.'

Pockets empty. Dogs in the back. His plan in shreds. His master plan –
The Mechanic makes another call. And another. And another –
Nobody knows much. Nobody's heard much. Nobody says much –
'But try the next mass picket,' Phil Taylor tells him.
The Mechanic hangs up. He leaves the phone box. He gets back in the car –
Throws the dogs a couple of bones. Scraps.
The Mechanic switches on the Tandy scanner. He listens to the loose talk –
The dogs fighting in the back over the scraps. The crumbs.

Neil Fontaine carries the Jew out of the Metropole next door and along the Promenade. The Jew has been watching the horror show unfold on breakfast TV with everybody else. The pictures of Norman in pain. The pictures of the Grand in ruins –

The pictures of the Prime Minister safe and sound.

Neil Fontaine helps the Jew out of his soiled, white tuxedo with gold epaulettes. The local branch of Marks & Spencer opened early to clothe the refugees. Neil Fontaine has chosen a plain blue blazer and dark grey trousers for the Jew to wear today.

Neil Fontaine puts the blazer over the shoulders of the Jew –

Neil opens the door of the Mercedes. The Jew gets into the back of the car –

He does not speak for hours. He just sits and stares out of the window –

The pier and the Promenade. The sky and the sea –

The day he was not meant to see.

The Jew does not speak until Neil Fontaine says, 'It's time to go, sir.'

'Thank you, Neil,' says the Jew. 'Thank you.'

The Jew walks along the Front. The Jew enters the Conference Hall –

There is no *Land of Hope and Glory* today. There is just the Prime Minister –

Safe and sound. Alive and kicking –

The Prime Minister. *His* Prime Minister –

'The bomb attack on the Grand Hotel was first and foremost an indiscriminate attempt to massacre innocent, unsuspecting men and women staying in Brighton for this Conservative Conference. Our first thoughts must be for those who died and for those who are now in hospital recovering from their injuries. But the bomb attack clearly signified more than this. It was an attempt not only to disrupt and terminate our conference; it was an attempt to cripple Her Majesty's democratically elected government. This is the scale of the outrage in which we have all shared, and the fact that we are gathered here now, shocked but composed and dignified, is a sign that this attack has failed and that all attempts to destroy democracy by terrorism will fail –'

The Jew is on his feet. The Jew applauds. The hall on its feet. The hall applauds –

'Now,' says the Prime Minister, 'it must be business as usual –'

The Prime Minister talks of local government. Defence. Europe. Unemployment –

His Prime Minister speaks of lions and the best of British –

'– the strike is not of the government's seeking. Not of the government's making. The sheer bravery of the men who have kept the mining industry alive is beyond praise. "Scabs", their former workmates call them –

'Scabs? They are *lions* –

'What a tragedy when a striking miner attacks his workmate. Not only are they members of the same Union, but the working miner is saving both their futures. To face the picket line day after day takes a special kind of courage. It takes as much, even more, for the housewife who stays at home –

'These people are the best of British –

'Just as our police – who uphold the law with an independence and restraint, perhaps only to be found in this country – are the admiration of the world.

'This government did all it could to prevent the strike. Some would say it did too much. We gave the miners their best ever pay offer, the highest ever investment and, for the first time, the promise that no miner would lose his job against his will. This was all done despite the fact that the bill for the losses in the industry was bigger than the annual bill for all the doctors and dentists in all the National Health Service hospitals in our United Kingdom.

'But this is a dispute about the right to go to work of those who have been denied the right to go to vote. The overwhelming majority of trade unionists, including many striking miners, deeply regret what has been done in the name of trade unionism. When the strike is over, and one day it will be over, we must do everything we can to encourage moderate and responsible trade unionism, so that it can once again take its respected and valuable place in our industrial life.

'But we face today an executive of the NUM who know that what they are demanding has never been granted, either for miners or workers in any other industry –

'So why then demand it? Why ask for what they know cannot be conceded?

'There can be only one explanation –

'They do not want a settlement. They want a strike – otherwise they would have balloted on the Coal Board's offer. Indeed, one-third of the miners did have a ballot and voted overwhelmingly to accept the offer.

'But what we have seen in this country is the emergence of an organized revolutionary minority who are prepared to exploit industrial disputes, but whose real aim is the breakdown of law and order and the destruction of democratic parliamentary government. We have seen the same sort of thugs and bullies at Grunwick, more recently against Eddie Shah in Stockport, and now we see them organized into flying squads around the country.

'It seems there are some who are out to destroy any properly elect-ed government. To bring down the framework of the law. This is what has been seen in this strike –

'But the law they seek to defy is the common law, upheld by fear-less judges and passed down across the centuries. It is legislation scrutinized and enacted by the Parliament of a free people. It is British justice and it is renowned across the world.

'This nation faces what is probably the most testing crisis of our time –

'The battle between the extremists and the rest.

'But we fight as we have always fought, for the weak as well as the strong –

'For great and good causes –

'To defend against the power and might of those who rise up to challenge them.

'This government will not weaken. This nation will meet that chal-lenge –

'Democracy will prevail!'

It is the speech of her life; the life she almost lost.

The Jew is on his feet with the entire hall. The Jew applauds with the entire hall –

One. Two. Three. Four. Five. Six. Seven. Eight –

For eight minutes the hall applauds.

The Jew has tears running down his face, tears streaming over his skin –

Streaming down mountains. Running in rivers –

Rivers of blood. Mountains of skulls.

cars before it. Ten cop cars after it – Flies past us at eighty mile an hour. Right up Pit Lane and in – That's that then, I think. Think wrong – Turn round to see this police Transit coming towards us with searchlight on. Fuck-ing wedge of riot coppers with full-length shields behind it – Everyone starts to edge back. Backing away – Knowing what's fucking coming for us. Knowing what we're fucking going to get – Few of lasses from Action Group try to send some lads off down ginnels and over gardens. But fucking pigs have them. Either send them back or handcuff them to lamp-posts and gates for later. Then I hear them – Hear hooves. Ten horses behind riot squad and dogs – This other wedge of coppers coming out, too. Foot of lane. I look at my watch – Half-six when whistle goes and horses charge and all bloody hell is let loose on us – Their commander today is a fucking cunt. He says clear as day, Get bastards and do them – Fifty reporters next to him. Fifty camera-men. Not one bastard will report it. Not one bastard will film it. No report of what that cunt said. No fucking film of all chaos that follows – Everybody run-ning. This way. That way – Truncheon for this one. Truncheon for that one. For this one. For that one – Horses and boots pushing us back up towards Barrel and over motorway bridge. Folk running out into traffic and what have you. Then this big cheer goes up. I turn to look back – Lad has chucked a bin lid at that bastard on white horse. Knocked him flying off horse onto ground. Fucking brilliant. To see him lie there in road. That cunt off his white bloody horse. That cunt and his horse that have chased and fucking hit us all over bloody county – Doesn't last long, mind. Next bin lid misses and it's back on with running shoes – Past Barrel and over bridge. Lads down on motor-way among cars – Like fucking Orgreave all over again. Folk doing anything to get out of way – But pigs just keep on coming. Boots up your arse. Truncheon to your hands. Back of their shields into back of your neck. Truncheons to your head – Then, bingo. Fucking bingo – Lads find a pile of bricks and bloody stones. Let fuck-ing fly and all – Pigs have got their shields up but they're only them short, black, round ones. Have to fucking retreat, don't they? – Bricks and stones. That's what it takes to save us. Bricks and bloody stones – I pick up bricks. I pick up bloody stones. I fucking throw them and all – First fucking time. This is what it's come to for me – To make them leave me be. To save myself. To get away. To be fucking free – Not everyone's that lucky, though. Lot of blokes get a lot of fucking hammer. They take twelve lads away just for having dirt on their hands. Least it isn't blood – Not like him. *Him* – Him that brought them here. Him that's caused it all – That went back to work. To work? – To scab. To sit on his arse all day up at pit – To play hands of cards with bastard police. Loses his fucking wages to Met, I hear – That sorry scab and his sorry hand. His sorry wages in their greedy paws – Tears in his eyes, they say. Tears in his wife's eyes. Tears in his kids' eyes – Him under his hood. Her with a new name. New address – Tears in police eyes and all. Tears of laughter – Laugh at fucking lot of us, they do. Met. MacGregor. Thatcher. The lot of them. The whole bloody fucking lot of them – Laughing at us in our little villages with our little pits. Our little accents and our little clothes – Cunts. Bastards. One day – you'll see. You'll see – *In the dark lands, I have a can-dle in my hand. I walk over heaps. Heaps of fragments. The candle in my hand, in the dark lands* – **Day 221.** I open my eyes on floor under my coat and I remember – Talks collapse. Pits collapse. Strikes collapse. Hotels collapse – But she bloody survives. Lives to tell tale – Fucking lot of them: King. Heseltine. Lawson. Ridley. Havers. Walker. Brittan. Even Tebbit – Iron Bitch with-out a bloody scratch. *Fuck me* – If she'd had a shit and not a pee, what a differ-ent place this world would be. And to think there's still them that say there's a god up there – It's going to go on for ever, this is. Fucking for ever now – **Day 223.** It's total now. Relentless. Total and relentless provocation and aggression against – Every pit. Every village. Every day. Every hour – Kell-ingley. Maltby. Kiveton Park. Allerton-

The Thirty-third Week

Monday 15 – Sunday 21 October 1984

These are days the Jew was not meant to see. The Jew says so over and over and over. From breakfast to bedtime. Morning, noon and night –

Times have changed. The Jew sees things more than ever in just black and white –

Night and day. Wet and dry. Bad and good –

Them and us –

'You are either one of them,' says the Jew again. 'Or one of us.'

The Jew is back in business. Back behind his desk.

There are flowers from the National Working Miners' Committee –

Telephone calls to be returned. Telegrams to be answered.

The talks between the Board and the Union at the Advisory Conciliation and Arbitration Service collapsed again last night. The sides had met for less than two hours. The Jew is happy the talks failed. The Jew hates ACAS and all it stands for –

Appeasement. Compromise. And. Surrender –

The old days.

It had been created by a Labour government. Designed for a Labour government –

To interfere. To negotiate. To barter and to abdicate.

It stank of Labour. It stank of defeat. It stank of the past –

The bad old days.

The Jew is happy to watch it fail. Happy to watch them all fail –

Their president and the Union have stated their defiance of the High Court fines. The Jew is very happy about that, too. This time the Jew can admit he is happy –

'The times have changed,' the Jew tells Neil again. 'The times have changed.'

Neil Fontaine waits in the corridor outside the Chairman's office in Hobart House. The men in suits pace up and down. Up and down. Letters of resignation in their hands.

Neil Fontaine looks at his watch again. He taps his watch. It starts again –

Places to be. People to meet. Things he must know.

Neil Fontaine and the men in suits listen to the Jew ranting on the inside –

'This strike is a political strike, make no mistake. Its outcome is not just the concern of the Board, and it never has been. The very future of this country depends on a total defeat of that man and all that he stands for. So there can be no settlement. There can be no agreement. There can be no compromise. Therefore, there must be no further negotiations. There must be no further promises of no more compulsory redundancies. There must be no amnesty and no jobs for any miners convicted of criminal offences.

'The times have changed and I can tell you when they did –

'The times changed at exactly six minutes to three last Friday morning.'

Terry Winters had a lot of airport time to kill. Terry read Conrad. Terry read Greene. Terry read Fleming. Terry couldn't concentrate. Terry picked through the newspapers. *Bombs. Terrorists. Failed talks. Court fines. The President's forfeit paid anonymously.* Terry was needed there. There. There. There. Not here –

Frankfurt, fucking Germany.

Terry Winters made more calls to Sheffield. *Click-click* –

To Diane. *Click-click.* To Theresa –

But no one answered the phone. No one returned his calls. Told him anything. Mohammed brought Terry another cup of coffee. Mohammed sat down next to him. Mohammed talked about Al-Zulfikar. Politics in Pakistan. Vengeance. Doncaster Rovers. The price of bread. Corner shops –

Terry Winters wished he'd fucking shut up.

Salem returned. Salem shook his head. Salem said, 'Twenty-four hours.'

Terry rolled his eyes. Terry went back to the airport hotel. Terry checked in again. He lay down on the single bed in his single room. He tried to sleep. He couldn't sleep. He cut up *The Secret Agent* to make new codes. He used *England Made Me* as a football. He threw *The Spy Who Loved Me* at the wall –

He shouldn't be here. He should be there. There. There. There –

Terry made calls to Sheffield. *Click-click.* To Diane. *Click-click* –

But no one answered the phone. No one returned his calls. Told him anything. Mohammed knocked on Terry's door. Mohammed asked if Terry was hungry for dinner. Terry told Mohammed he was busy. Terry said he had things to do –

Terry washed his underpants in the small sink in the corner of his room –

He dried them with a hairdryer he had borrowed from reception –

Terry's hands were red raw. Terry wondered what the fuck he was doing.

Neil Fontaine serves two large brandies in the suite on the fourth floor of Claridge's.

The Great Financier nods. The Great One is always willing to help –

'You know that, Stephen,' he says. 'Especially in times such as these.'

The Great Financier lost his Carlton tie in the bomb. It has yet to be replaced.

'Yes, and I appreciate that,' says the Jew. 'She knows it, too. She appreciates it.'

'But, but, but,' smiles the Great One, 'does the Chairman?'

The Jew smiles back. The Jew says, 'He is beginning to see the light.'

'The City worries about our American friend,' says the Great Financier.

'I read my balance sheets,' says the Jew. 'I know how the City worries.'

'Seven billion lost in just one day yesterday,' shouts the Great One. 'One day!'

'I know,' says the Jew. 'I know.'

'I'm losing money hand over fist here, Stephen,' he says. 'Hand over fist.'

'We all are,' says the Jew. 'We all are.'

'Is that supposed to make me feel better?' asks the Great Financier. 'Is it?'

The Jew closes his eyes. The Jew shakes his head.

'I know bankruptcy would be nothing new to you and yours,' says the Great One. 'But it would be to the rest of us. Remember that –'

'So you're pulling up the drawbridge, then?' asks the Jew. 'Circling the wagons?'

'Stephen, Stephen, Stephen,' says the Good and Great One. 'Did I say that?'

'Don't seem awfully keen, though,' says the Jew. 'Not your usual helpful self.'

'I *will* help,' says the Great Financier. 'But there will have to be stipulations.'

'There is always a catch,' says the Jew. 'The strings that must be attached.'

'I do have reservations about these legal proceedings,' says the Great One.

'What kind of reservations?'

'I worry you'll make a martyr of the man,' he whispers. 'A Marxist martyr.'

'He's Aryan,' says the Jew. 'He has his own myths. His models. His messiahs.'

'So let's not add to them, shall we, Stephen?' smiles the Great Financier.

'The wheels have been set in motion,' says the Jew. 'It is out of our hands –'

'Pay the man's fine for him,' says the Wise One. 'Anonymously.'

'What?' squeals the Jew. 'I will do no such thing.'

'Bloody will, Stephen,' he says. 'Or he'll go to jail and you'll lose. We all will.'

The Jew slumps back in his chair. The Jew waves his brandy glass at Neil.

'Do this, Stephen,' says the Great Financier, 'and I will do the rest.'

'Everything?' asks the Jew. 'Everything?'

The Great and Benevolent One takes out his chequebook. He says, 'Everything.'

The Mechanic comes down the A1 *towards Doncaster. He turns off onto the Barnsley Road. He drives into the centre of the city. He joins the Bawtry Road by the racecourse –*

He follows it down to Rossington.

There are police all over the place. Everywhere. Not even four in the morning yet. There's one police car already lying on its roof by the police station. Its wheels in the air.

This is a mistake. The Mechanic knows that. But there are things the Mechanic doesn't know –

Things he needs to know. Has to know –

Personal *things.*

He parks away from the pit behind a school. He leaves the dogs in the back of the car. He makes his way to where the action is. He has got his hat down and his collar up. His yellow stickers on and his hands in his pockets.

It's all happening here today. The pickets have trapped the police in the pit yard. The police have called for reinforcements. The convoy of reinforcements is coming –

Two abreast down the road at ninety miles an hour.

The pickets along the road let fly with the stones from the first vehicle to the last –

Thud. Thud. Thud. Thud –

Rock after rock. Brick after brick. Stone after stone –

For each one of the sixty police vehicles.

This one horsebox mounts the pavement. Hits this one lad full on. Bang –

Leaves him for dead in his donkey jacket –

The police laugh. The police cheer. The police beat their shields.

The Mechanic stands outside a pub. He stares into the faces –

Men running in every direction. Police charging about after them.

There are ambulances now. Barricades burning –

Police vans fitted with mesh and grilles driving into the barricades –

The air filled with smoke and screams. The dawn keeping its distance –

Violence. Injuries. Arrests –

This is not what the Mechanic is looking for. Not why he is here.

The Mechanic turns and walks away –

Jen is not here. Jen. His Jen –

The rumours all wrong. The whispers well wide –

Thank. Fucking. Christ.

The Mechanic walks back to the car. The dogs are barking. The Mechanic puts the key in the door –

'Hello. Hello. Hello,' says the voice behind him. 'And what have we here?'

The Mechanic doesn't turn round. There's no point. He knows who it is.

'Didn't realize armed robbers had a union,' says the voice. 'TUC affiliated, are you?'

The Mechanic doesn't move. No point. He keeps his eyes on the dogs in the back.

'Put your hands on your head,' says the voice. 'Do it slowly.'

The Mechanic puts his hands on the top of his hat. He does it slowly.

Handcuffs go on his wrists and the voice says, 'Now turn around. Slowly.'

The Mechanic puts his hands down. He turns around. Slowly.

'Hello, Dave,' says Paul Dixon of the Special Branch. 'Miss me, did you?'

Neil Fontaine helps the Jew dress for the dinner. Neil Fontaine drives him to the dinner –

The AIMS of Industry's 1984 National Free Enterprise Awards.

The winners are Mr Eddie Shah, Mr Walter Goldsmith and the Prime Minister –

Her speech is also a winner. The theme of her speech –

No Surrender.

It is perfectly timed. *Perfectly.* For the times have truly changed –

NACODS have called a national strike from Thursday 25 October.

The Cabinet is nervous. The City is nervous. The country is nervous –

The Jew is not. The Jew knows the times have changed –

It is a dangerous game. Expensive, too. But the Jew will win –

The Jew will not drop the ball. The Jew will not sell the pass.

The Jew whispers in the Prime Minister's ear. The Jew squeezes her arm. The Jew kisses the Prime Minister on both cheeks. The Jew congratulates her –

He congratulates her many, many times on her many, many victories –

Past, present and future.

Bywater. Yorkshire Main. Woolley. Brodsworth. Denby Grange. Rossington – But it works against them. Works in our favour – Folk can see them for what they are now. Folk can see through media lies – *Smile* – Makes many more folk support us now. Older blokes. Pensioners – Lot of them that hadn't had a good word to say about King Arthur and Red Guard two week back. They've all changed their bloody minds sharp enough now – Now they've seen what police and government are like with their own eyes. Now it's in front of their faces. Here on their own bloody doorstep – People want to picket now. Pete sets up a roster. Twenty-four-hour cover in six shifts. Both gates. Front and back – Least half of village turn out for afternoon pickets. People like that picket – Scabs can see us all stood there. See our faces proud and plain as day. Theirs hidden in their hoods – Let them see us see them. Let them know we know them – Like it says on wall, *We will not always be poor, but they will always be scabs* – **Day 232.** This is worst day yet. By a fucking mile. Everyone just stood there in front of TV. Fucking shell-shocked. Whole of bloody Welfare. It started out bad enough this week. First so-called power-men had voted against supporting us. Them that could even be arsed to bloody vote. Exact fucking opposite of what was said at TUC. Rest of week we've stood out as usual in all bloody weathers, at all bloody hours. Here and at Brodsworth. Kiveton Park. Rossington. Yorkshire Main. News is full of them two fucking scabs from Manton again. Back at bloody court after our brass. Our fucking brass from our fucking pockets which we've given to our bloody Union. Not to two fucking narks like them and some High Court fucking puppet of a judge. Lot of lads don't think much of it – It's only brass, let them have it. Render unto Caesar. No bloody strike pay anyway. That's attitude – But I saw look in Pete's eye when it first come on news. Told me it was more serious than most folk thought. Pete's got a good head on him. Knows what's what. He warned us not to get our hopes up about NACODS. He was fucking right and

all. Thing is, no one honestly believed they'd come out for us – Not in their heart of hearts. Not that lot – But you can't stop yourself bloody dreaming, can you? Hoping against hope – Knowing it would have helped us all. Both them and us – But in end they just want brass without any hassle. Like a fucking holiday for them, this is – Just show your face every morning. Tell manager you've been intimidated. Then fuck off back to bed or whatever – They had a golden opportunity to do something fucking decent. But they took their thirty pieces of bloody silver. Left us worse off than before – Mick McGahey spoke for everyone on news. Mick said, I regret very much the attitude taken by NACODS. First in compromising themselves before the NCB. Second in making things much more difficult for the NUM, who are seeking a principled solution to this dispute – Arthur was next. He just said, There'll be no compromise. It will be a long, hard, bitter battle – Then this morning, just when you think it can get no fucking worse, Board make their big bribe – Four weeks' holiday money if you're back in before 19 November – *Fuck me.* Bribing us back with our own brass now – Know there'll be some daft enough to take it and all. Been eight month of this now – Eight month. Thirty-four week. Two hundred and thirty-odd fucking days – Pete opens another envelope. Pete reads it. Pete says, Kiveton again. Here we bloody go, someone says – Here we go, I shout back. Here we go – Then whole bloody room joins in, Here we go, here we go, here we go – Here we go, here we go, here we go – Here! We! Go! **Day 236.** I got no bloody choice. Way I see it – I have to survive. To survive I need brass. To get brass I pick coal. Pick coal to sell – Either that or go back down to Southampton or somewhere. Find another labouring job. Then I'd not be able to picket. Not be able to do anything for strike. Not pull me weight. Don't fancy that again. Fucking lonely enough as it is – Hate bloody Saturday and Sundays. Hate them. Worst days of week – Least when they came for furniture they left shed alone. Left my barrow and my shovel. Thing I need

The Thirty-fourth Week
Monday 22 – Sunday 28 October 1984

Salem said, 'Your visas are ready.'

Terry Winters and Mohammed Divan went to the Libyan People's Bureau in Frankfurt. Terry and Mohammed presented their passports. The Libyan diplomats of the People's Bureau gave them their visas. There was no Libyan People's Bureau in London. Not since the death of WPC Yvonne Fletcher in April. Not since she was shot outside the Libyan People's Bureau in St James's Square by Libyan diplomats. Next door to ACAS. Salem had worked at the People's Bureau in London. Until he'd been deported.

Salem said, 'Your flights are booked.'

Salem gave Terry Winters and Mohammed Divan their tickets to Tripoli. Terry and Mohammed flew Lufthansa from Frankfurt to Tripoli. The plane left in the evening. The flight took four hours. There was no alcohol on the flight. There was no Coca-Cola. There were no direct flights from London. Not since the death of WPC Fletcher in April. Not since she was shot by Libyan diplomats.

Salem had said, 'You will be met at the airport.'

Terry Winters and Mohammed Divan landed at Tripoli International Airport at midnight. The head of the Libyan General Producers' Union and three other officials were there to meet them. Arabic kisses and European handshakes were exchanged. Introductions made. Two taxis were waiting to take Terry and Mohammed the twenty miles from the airport into Tripoli. Terry was escorted to his taxi. One member of the welcoming committee sat in the front seat. Terry sat alone in the back as the taxi sped off through the night. Black prayer beads swung from the rearview mirror. Loud Arabic music blared from the radio. The taxi-driver smoked heavily and flashed his headlights. The member of the welcoming committee turned around occasionally to grin at Terry. Terry Winters stared out of the window at Libya. It was pitch black beyond the lights of the motorway.

Salem had said, 'Rooms have been reserved for you at the Al-Kabir Hotel.'

The taxi came out of the dark into the city. It sped through the deserted streets; the narrow alleys and the wide boulevards; the Arabic and the European. The driver sounded his horn as he crossed junctions and passed through red lights. Terry bounced up and down on the back seat. The driver held down his horn and kept his foot on the pedal. The member of the welcoming committee turned around to grin at Terry again. Terry thought of Theresa. Terry Winters thought of another taxi in another city on another street on another day in another life –

This taxi pulled up in front of an illuminated hotel.

Salem had said, 'You will have guides.'

Mohammed Divan was waiting outside the Al-Kabir with three Libyan men. Mohammed introduced Terry to their guides in the empty lobby of the Al-Kabir. Their guides ordered tea for Terry and Mohammed from a boy behind a bar that sold only tea. The boy brought Terry and Mohammed warm Arabic tea in small Pyrex glasses. The three Libyans held their prayer beads in one hand and filterless cigarettes in the other. Terry wanted to go to bed. First Terry was shown his schedule. Terry and Mohammed were to relax for a few days –

To see the sights and the sounds of Tarabulus al-Gharb.

'For a few days?' said Terry. 'I can't stay here for a few days. I'm needed –'

Mohammed spoke in Arabic with the three Libyans. Mohammed turned to Terry –

Mohammed shrugged his shoulders. The three Libyans nodded –

'Everything is arranged,' they said. 'Salem has arranged everything.'

Dixon stops the car opposite Rotherham police station. He hands the Mechanic his hood. Dixon leaves.

The Mechanic stands outside the police station. He stamps his feet in the last of the night.

There are men parked across the road. Men with notebooks. Men with cameras.

The bus arrives. The doors open.

The Mechanic puts on the hood. He climbs up inside. He doesn't pay the driver –

He walks down the aisle. He takes a seat halfway up.

The bus is off again. The bus is cold and dark. The bus is damp and stinks –

It stinks of cigarettes and sweat. It stinks of fear. Dread –
Guilt.
The Mechanic stares through the slits in the hood –
There are eight policemen. Two other men in hoods.
The Mechanic stares through the windows and the mesh –
There are now police cars in front and back of them.
The men in hoods bow their heads. The police lower the visors on their helmets –
'Here we go,' *one of police shouts.*
Sixty. Seventy. Eighty. Ninety miles an hour –
The bus picks up speed. The bricks hit the bus –
Sixty. Seventy. Eighty. Ninety –
Bang. Bang. Bang. Bang –
Blue lights and burning barricades:
Welcome to Kiveton Park.
The bus stops inside. The mob bays. The gates close. The mob barks –
The smell of blood. The stink of shit –
The men in hoods run from the bus to the office. The men in hoods hide inside.
There are boards across the office windows. Heaters on. Kettles boiling. Cigarettes lit –
The three men keep their hoods on. Heads bowed.
Police come in and out off the fire escape. Tell them how the battle's going –
'They're letting horses out for a gallop,' *police laugh.* 'Bit of exercise for them.'
'Who's that then?' *other police ask.* 'Fucking horses or pickets?'
The three men keep their mouths shut under their hoods. Police don't like that –
'Take them hoods off,' *police say.* 'No one can see you in here, can they?'
'It's better this way,' *the Mechanic says from under his.* 'Leave us be.'
'Anyone would think you were fucking ashamed of yourselves,' *police laugh.*
'Afraid of us, are you?' *police ask.* 'Afraid we'll grass you up to that mob?'
'Imagine if we did,' *police say.* 'They'd have you swinging from pit head.'
'There's no need for that,' *the Mechanic tells them.* 'Pack it in.'
'Or what?' *police ask.* 'You'll go home, will you?'
'Like to fucking see you try that,' *police laugh.*
'Not last ten seconds out there without us,' *police say.* 'So be fucking nice.'
The other two men in their hoods are shaking. Their legs are trembling.

The Mechanic hates the police. Pigs. Fucking hates them. Cunts –

'You know why they won't take their hoods off?' pigs ask each other.

'They're afraid one of them will go back on strike and grass other two up.'

'I'd have stayed out with scum,' pigs say. 'Least scum can hold their heads up.'

'Just long enough for us to give them a crack,' pigs laugh.

'I've heard enough,' the Mechanic tells them. 'Shut up.'

'Or what, scab?' pigs say. 'What you going to fucking do?'

The Mechanic stands up. He takes off his hood. He stares at the pigs in their white shirts. He says, 'I'll walk out that door and out them pit gates, that's what I'll fucking do.'

Eldest pig walks over to the door. He opens it. He says, 'Be my fucking guest.'

The Mechanic stares at the four pigs. The two hooded scabs. The open door –

The noise of the battle outside filling the office. The shouts. The sirens.

'Fucking got cold feet, have you, hard man?' another pig says –

The Mechanic stares back at him. He shakes his head. He smiles.

'Fucking funny, is it?' pig asks. 'Thought you were going to walk out that door?'

'Think I will,' the Mechanic says. 'And think I'll show lads on picket line this –'

He takes out a wad of cash from the pocket of his jeans. He holds it up. Counts –

Sixty. Seventy. Eighty. Ninety quid –

'Fuck is that?' pigs ask him. 'Your wages for a year?'

'No,' the Mechanic says. 'It's what you lot paid me to act as a scab for day. That's what it is.'

Boss pig slams the door shut. He says, 'Fuck off. Fuck off.'

The Mechanic shakes his head. 'No. You fuck off and make your call.'

The two scabs stare up at the Mechanic through the slits in their hoods –

The tears in their eyes.

'Tell you this,' the Mechanic says to them. 'I'd rather be a scab than a pig any day of fucking week.'

The scabs bow their heads in their hoods. Their hoods heavy –

Their tears on the floor.

Terry Winters opened his eyes. He blinked at the ceiling. He remembered where he was. Terry got out of bed. He opened the window on to the balcony. He stepped outside –

It was warm. It was beautiful.

The balcony opened out on to the Green Square. Terry could see the Red Castle. The mosques and their minarets. The Medina and the markets –

Terry could smell the Mediterranean. Terry was amazed. Terry was excited.

Terry went back inside. Terry took his underpants off the window ledge. Terry dressed. Terry opened his door –

His guide was sitting on a chair in the corridor. His guide smiled. His guide said, 'Sabah alkheer.'

Terry smiled back. Terry asked, 'Good morning?'

His guide nodded. His guide smiled again. His guide said again, 'Sabah alkheer.'

'Sabah alkheer,' repeated Terry.

His guide laughed. His guide shook Terry's hand. His guide said, 'Breakfast?'

'Please,' said Terry. 'Lead on.'

'This way,' said his guide. 'Mister Mohammed is waiting.'

Terry followed his guide down the corridor and stairs to an elegant dining room. Mohammed was sitting on the terrace with coffee and an Arabic newspaper.

Terry sat down. Terry said, 'Sabah alkheer.'

Mohammed laughed. Mohammed said, 'Sabah alkheer.'

Terry looked up at the blue sky. The white buildings. The flowers on the terrace. The guides at the next table. Terry said, 'This is not what I had imagined.'

The waiter brought over fresh coffee. He served Terry orange juice and croissants.

Mohammed smiled. Mohammed said, 'What had you imagined, Comrade?'

'I don't know,' said Terry. 'But not this. Not paradise on Earth.'

Mohammed laughed again. Mohammed spoke to the guides on the next table –

The guides laughed. They raised their Pyrex glasses. They said, 'To paradise.'

'You have seen nothing yet, my friend,' said Mohammed. 'Just wait.'

Terry Winters couldn't wait. Terry sensed he had found something special here. He wolfed down his orange juice and croissants. He asked for guidebooks and for maps –

Terry Winters wanted to know everything there was to know about Libya.

Mohammed smiled. He called Salem. Salem joined them for their tour –

The Jamahiriya Museum. The Red Castle. The Marcus Aurelius Arch –

The Al-Nagha Mosque. The Ahmed Pash Mosque. The Medina –

'If people back home could see me now,' said Terry every five minutes –

'Terry Winters – our man in Tripoli,' he laughed. 'They'd never believe it.'

Mohammed and Salem nodded. Mohammed and Salem smiled.

They took Terry for lunch near Green Square. The restaurant served spaghetti –

Terry wasn't interested. Terry wanted what the locals wanted.

Mohammed and Salem took Terry for a local lunch near the Medina. Terry ate fasoulia. Terry ate kouskesy. Terry ate lahm mashouy.

'Delicious,' declared Terry Winters. 'The best meal I've ever eaten.'

Mohammed and Salem laughed. Mohammed and Salem put their thumbs up.

Terry pointed at the big portrait of Muammar al-Gadhafi on the restaurant wall. Terry said to Salem, 'I'd like to shake your leader by his hand. Congratulate him.'

Salem stopped smiling. Salem shook his head –

Mohammed didn't. Mohammed nodded. Mohammed put his thumb up –

Mohammed said, 'Why ever not?'

Salem shrugged. Salem dropped Terry and Mohammed back at the Al-Kabir.

Terry went upstairs for a rest. Terry lay on his bed. Terry closed his eyes.

NACODS have called off their strike in return for modifications to the colliery review procedure and an agreement to pay deputies. The High Court has ordered the sequestration of NUM assets after their failure to pay the £200,000 contempt fine –

These are fine days for the Jew; these days he was never meant to see.

Neil Fontaine has been picking up Northern men with Southern tastes at pre-arranged times in pre-arranged places. He has driven these Northern men to West London hotels. He has stood guard outside the locked doors of their hotel rooms as the Jew has opened his briefcase and chequebook for these Northern men with their Southern tastes –

'Everybody has their price,' the Jew has repeated all week. 'Everybody.'

The Jew has held long meetings with the Great Financier and some of his friends. He has met with Piers and Tom Ball. Don Colby and his mate Derek. Even Fred Wallace. Their finances are secure. Their strategies remain solid. Their legal actions will continue. There are even new moves afoot. Fresh friendships to form –

'Everybody needs a friend,' the Jew has said more than once. 'Even me.'

These are very good days for the Jew; good days in a bad and ungrateful place –

The knives still out in Hobart House. Knives as dull as the stains on their suits. The suits in which they whine and scheme against the Jew. The suits in which they plot. The suits in which they run and tell their tales to the Minister of the bad things the Jew has said and done. The Jew is not worried. The Jew does not care –

The Jew is immortal –

The events of the past few weeks have taught the Jew that, if nothing else –

'– in the boardrooms and the lounges. The executive suites and dining rooms. These are where our battles are now, Neil. These are where the dragons must be slain. Upstairs as well as downstairs –'

Neil switches off. He stares at the silent TV screens. Just the teletext on –

'– these talking-shop tacticians are as dangerous as any flying Red Guard –'

The telephone rings on the Jew's desk.

'– no more talks. An end to talks. The time for talking –'

Neil Fontaine picks up the phone. 'Mr Sweet's office. How may we help you?'

Neil Fontaine listens. Neil says, 'One moment, sir.'

Neil Fontaine puts the call on hold. Neil says, 'The Minister for you, sir.'

The Jew rolls his eyes. The Jew hates the Minister. Loathes the man –

The Jew knows the Prime Minister does too. Hates him. Loathes him –

But one never knows when one might need a goat in the case of an escape –

The Jew picks up the phone. The Jew says, 'Peter? What a pleasant surprise –'

Neil Fontaine switches back off. He stares at the silent TV screens again.

The Jew stands up. The Jew opens his mouth. The Jew shrieks, 'Tripoli?'

The Jew looks across the desk at Neil. He shouts, 'Get me *The Times*, Neil!'

Neil Fontaine picks up the other phone. *The Hot Line*. Neil Fontaine dials –

These good days, these days the Jew was never meant to see, have just got better.

Terry Winters dreamed Arabian dreams of sword swallowers and the hand of Fatima. Veiled brides for seven brothers. Black and hairy cunts in hearts of bleeding swastikas. Mint tea and Persian tulips. Minarets and muezzins –

Mohammed was calling him. Mohammed was banging on his door.

Terry opened his eyes. The room was dark. Terry got up and opened the door.

Mohammed said, 'Are you ready, Comrade?'

'Ready for what?' asked Terry.

'The dinner with the Libyan trade unions,' said Mohammed. 'Why you're here.'

Terry nodded. Terry remembered. Terry washed. Terry dressed.

Mohammed and Terry took a taxi to a large hotel on the seafront.

Terry Winters was the guest of honour. Mohammed Divan was his translator.

Terry and Mohammed were shown into the Banqueting Hall. Terry was welcomed with a white spotlight and loud applause. Terry blinked. Terry bowed. Terry waved. Terry was led through the tables. Terry was seated in the top chair on the top table –

Under the painted eyes of an elevated portrait of the Colonel.

Terry was served grilled seafood and olive salads. Terry asked for extra kouskesy.

The various members of various unions made various speeches as

Terry dined. The speeches had been translated into English and typed out for Terry to follow as he feasted. The speeches spoke of solidarity. Shoulder to shoulder. Arab and European. Then it was Terry's turn. Terry stood up. Terry spoke without notes –

Terry spoke of the strike. The eighteen months since the overtime ban had begun. He spoke of their reasons. The threat to their jobs, their pits and their communities. He spoke of the government. The use of the police and the law. He spoke of the brutality. The arrests. The beatings. The kidnap. The torture. The sieges. He spoke of the suffering. The poverty of his people. The hunger of their children. He asked the trade unions of Libya to support their struggle by any means necessary; by banning the recently increased exports of oil to Britain for use in oil-fired power stations; by boycotting the renewed attempts by a hypocritical British government to better trade links with Libya; by blacking all trade and training with the National Coal Board; by giving the National Union of Mineworkers as much money as they could spare –

'– so that the Fascism of the present governments of the United States and the United Kingdom may soon be replaced by revolutionary Socialism. That Internationalism may replace Imperialism. That the paradise you have built here may one day be the paradise that all nations may build and hold as dear as you hold this –

'Friends. Comrades. Brother Arabs. I salute you,' said Terry. 'And I thank you.'

There was loud applause again. There was the white spotlight. Terry blinked. Terry bowed. Terry waved goodbye as he was led through the tables to the front door.

Terry and Mohammed stepped out of the hotel. Terry and Mohammed stopped –

Dozens of military vehicles had encircled the front grounds of the seafront hotel. Soldiers stared at Terry and Mohammed. Helicopters flew overhead in the night sky –

Salem jumped down from a jeep. Salem said, 'You wanted to meet the Leader?'

Terry looked at the jeeps. The personnel carriers. The guns. Terry nodded.

'Well, the Leader of the Revolution wants to meet you too,' said Salem. 'Get in.'

*

Dixon pulls up opposite the pig shop. He opens the passenger door –

The Mechanic crosses the road. He gets into the Montego.

'Not very fucking smart that, David,' says Paul Dixon. 'Not very smart at all.'

'Put a fucking leash on them, then,' the Mechanic says. 'What I do with my dogs.'

'You're supposed to do me a favour,' says Dixon. 'Then I do you one.'

'Exactly,' the Mechanic tells him. 'So you owe me a favour.'

Dixon turns. He grabs the Mechanic's face. He pushes it against the side window and says, 'Fuck you, Johnson. Fuck you. I could nick you like that –'

Dixon clicks his fingers in the Mechanic's face –

'Waltz you through the fucking courts. Watch them throw away the key.'

The Mechanic closes his eyes. He nods –

Dixon lets go of him. He sits back behind the wheel and says, 'Now fuck off.'

'You what?' the Mechanic says. 'You said –'

'Them shotguns made you fucking deaf, have they?' says Dixon. 'Fuck off.'

'You've got a name and address,' the Mechanic says. 'I want it. I need it.'

'Fuck off,' repeats Dixon. 'We're through. You're a fucking liability, you are.'

'You promised me her name and address,' the Mechanic says.

Dixon turns to the Mechanic. He points a .38 up at him. 'I've changed my mind.'

The Mechanic stares down at the gun. The Mechanic nods –

He hates the police. Pigs. Fucking hates them. Cunts –

The Mechanic opens the passenger door. The Mechanic gets out –

The Mechanic slams the door on Paul Dixon, Special Branch.

Terry and Mohammed flew through the Libyan night in the back of Salem's military jeep. The convoy of vehicles had long left behind the narrow alleys and the wide boulevards of Tripoli for the desert and the dark. Terry had watched Tripoli disappear in the dust and noise of the caravan. Now Terry stared up at the bright stars in the black sky. Terry Winters had never seen so many stars in his whole life. It was incredible. He had never seen any stars in the sky above Sheffield –

'If people back home saw me here now,' said Terry. 'They'd never believe it.'

Mohammed leant forward and spoke first with Salem, then he sat back. Mohammed said, 'Comrade, Libyan TV would like to film your meeting with the Leader, but Salem thinks it might cause embarrassment for your Union and yourself, if for any reason it was to be shown in the West.'

Terry shook his head. Terry said, 'Embarrassment? I don't see why.'

'Then they can film the meeting?' asked Mohammed. 'You're sure?'

'I am not ashamed to be here,' exclaimed Terry Winters. 'I am honoured.'

Mohammed smiled. Mohammed leant forward and spoke with Salem again. Salem turned round to speak to Terry. Salem said, 'If that is what you wish, Comrade.'

'One thing,' said Terry. 'Please teach me the correct way to greet the Leader.'

Salem looked at Mohammed. Mohammed grabbed Terry by each shoulder. Mohammed whirled Terry round to face him –

Mohammed kissed Terry once on each cheek. Hard –

'Now you try,' said Mohammed.

Terry held Mohammed by his shoulders. Terry kissed Mohammed hard.

Salem clapped. Salem pointed out of the windscreen. Salem said, 'Almost there.'

Terry strained to see ahead. Terry could see nothing. Nothing but desert and dark. Then the escort of jeeps and personnel carriers swept out of the desert and the dark and through the gates of a hidden fortress cloaked in walls of shadow –

Through the gates past rows of black tents and through another set of gates in another wall of shadows past more rows of black tents and through another set of gates in yet another wall of shadows to the biggest, blackest of the Bedouin tents –

The jeep stopped in the sand.

Salem opened the doors. Terry and Mohammed got out –

Salem went to speak with soldiers dressed in black fatigues.

It was cold out here and Terry wished he had brought his coat.

Salem came back over to the jeep. Salem said, 'Follow me.'

Terry and Mohammed followed Salem inside the big, black Bedouin tent. Through dim doorways in black walls past bright rooms through more dim doorways in other black walls to a bigger, brighter room –

Salem stopped here. Salem turned to them and said, 'Please wait.'

Terry and Mohammed waited among the cushions and the carpets. Terry stared at the walls and the floor. The shadows and the light. Terry waited for Salem –

For Salem and Colonel Muammar al-Gadhafi –

The Leader of the Revolution.

Salem came back inside. Men with guns followed him. Men with cameras –

The men stood to either side of the doorway with their guns and cameras –

Their guns and cameras trained on Terry. Pointed at Terry. Rolling –

Three. Two. One and, Action –

Colonel Muammar al-Gadhafi entered the room. He went over to Terry Winters. The Colonel put out his hand. Terry Winters shook the Colonel's hand –

Terry Winters embraced the Colonel. Terry Winters kissed the Colonel –

The Colonel gestured to the cushions. The Colonel called for mint tea.

Terry sat down beside the Colonel. Terry drank mint tea with the Colonel.

The Colonel smiled at Terry Winters. The Colonel spoke to Terry Winters –

Salem translated. Terry listened. The cameras rolled again –

The Colonel had agreed to meet Terry. The Colonel was pleased to meet Terry. The Colonel was always pleased to meet fellow trade unionists. The Colonel had agreed to listen to Terry. The Colonel was pleased to listen to Terry. The Colonel was always pleased to listen to fellow trade unionists –

The Colonel stopped speaking. Salem stopped translating. Terry started speaking –

Salem started translating again. The Colonel listened –

Terry spoke of the strike. The threat to their jobs. Their pits. Their communities. The use of the police and the law. The brutality. The arrests. The beatings. The kidnap. The torture. The sieges. The suffering. The poverty. The hunger. The struggle –

Terry spoke of the hopes for his visit. That the trade unions of Libya support their struggle by any means necessary. That exports of oil to Britain for use in oil-fired power stations be banned. That attempts to improve British trade links with Libya be boycotted. That all trade and training with the National Coal Board be blacked. That the people of Libya and the Leader of their Revolution support the members of the National Union of Mineworkers and its president in their revolutionary struggle to defeat the Fascism of the Thatcher government. By any means necessary –

Terry Winters stopped speaking. Salem stopped translating.

The Colonel stood up. Terry stood up.

The Colonel gave Terry Winters three copies of his *Little Green Book*.

Terry thanked the Colonel many times. Terry shook his hand again. Many times.

The Colonel left the room. Terry and Mohammed left the fort with Salem.

The jeep took them back to Tripoli. Through the desert and the end of the night –

The dawn rising out of the desert with the city. Like a mirage, thought Terry –

'– I fly for refuge unto the Lord of the Daybreak,' quoted Salem from the Koran. 'That he may deliver me from those things of mischief which he hath created –'

Terry nodded. He had never seen a dawn like it in his life. It was extraordinary –

The dawn. The stars. The food. The people. Their leader. The whole country –

'People back home could have seen me with the Colonel,' said Terry –

'Terry Winters and Colonel Gadhafi,' he laughed. 'They'd never believe it.'

Mohammed and Salem laughed. Mohammed and Salem put their thumbs up.

The jeep came through Green Square. The jeep stopped outside the Al-Kabir.

Terry and Mohammed got out. Salem had places to go. Salem said goodbye –

'And thank you,' said Terry Winters. 'That was the best night of my life.'

now is a riddle. Lady Luck smiles for once. Next door's rabbit died and bloke lets me have hutch. Ideal that. Like a bloody riddle kit. Mesh and wood off hutch. Use hacksaw on it. Bang four pieces into a square. Tack mesh onto bottom – That's my riddle. I'm set – Both good and bad time to start up, though. It's getting cold so there's a demand – There's a demand because there's no free coal. No concessionary coal – Means there are more folk at it, though. Lot have been doing it since start. That means all best stuff's gone from yard. No easy pickings – Board are having clampdown on security and all. Because of all vandalism – Big riot in Grimethorpe week before when all South Yorkshire coppers pulled a load of lads who were at it. Pigs are all over place anyway because of Geoff the Scab and his mates – It's bloody dangerous, too. Not forget that – Lad already died at Upton. Fourteen-year-old – But what you going to do? Live off a quid a picket and hope for a bit from petrol money? – I've been going in car with Tim and Gary again this past week or so. I asked them if they fancy coming with me – Make a proper job of it on weekend. Bit of brass for themselves – Jump at chance. Tim says a mate of his was nicked in yard by this copper from Met. Didn't charge him or anything. But bastard made him tip out what he'd got. Night's work down drain. Gary says they've got Alsatians up there, too. Set them on you – Three of us decide it's best to stick to spoil. Right up on top of heap is best place, too. Dig a fucking hole up there. Bottom of that is where your bloody nuggets are – Hard fucking work, spoil is. But least with three of us we can rotate jobs a bit, though. First thing is to get to bloody stuff. Have to dig through all dust that's been pressed and packed down on top. There's always a good foot or so of that. Then comes softer muck. Load of that. Maybe four foot or more. Best stuff is under that. Then you get riddle out and go to work with sieving. Take it in turns to shovel and sieve. One with shovel and two with riddles. Fucking back-breaking, it is. Not alone up here, either. Like bloody Gold Rush on top of

here, it is. First day here we realized we needed a bigger riddle. Did well enough, but knew we could do a lot fucking better. Flogged what we had. Brass we made we bought some more wood, more mesh and more bags. Made this six-foot bloody riddle. Huge it is. Today we're doing a bag every quarter of an hour. Six big shovel loads of stuff on riddle at a time. Fill a bag every fifteen minutes. Do sixty bags over weekend. Eight-hour days, like. Hard fucking days, too. Flog each bag for two quid a pop – That's forty quid each. Forty fucking quid – Take orders for next week and all. Like a proper fucking business – Daft thing is, I've got this forty quid in my pocket. I don't know what to do with it – I buy twenty Park Drive and a pint. Have a bag of chips on way home – That's it. Lie down on floor under my coat and I'm straight out – That bloody knackered, hands that bloody raw. Like a light – *Fragments come away under my tread. Fragments fall* – I wake up under blanket on bedroom floor. Middle of night. I get up. I go down Welfare – **Day 239.** I get my orders from envelope. I go and do my picket. Kiveton Park again today. I take Tim and Gary and this other young lad. I drive down back roads and side-streets. I park car a good two mile or so from pit gates. I fall in and walk with rest of lads. I take abuse from police on way to front with rest of lads. *Krk-krk.* I get stopped and searched for fireworks with rest of lads. I get to front with rest of lads. I stand in dark and cold with rest of lads. I squint into their searchlights with rest of lads. I blink with rest of lads. I tell television crews to fuck off home with rest of lads. I hear scab bus coming up lane with rest of lads. I push with rest of lads. I shove with rest of lads. I shout with rest of lads. I call them what they are with rest of lads. I call them scabs with rest of lads. I watch their bus go in with rest of lads. I listen to coppers laugh and chant and bang their shields with rest of lads. I turn and walk away with rest of lads. I take abuse from police on way back to car with rest of lads. I drive Tim and Gary back to Thurcroft with that other young lad. I go in Welfare with most of lads. I get

The Thirty-fifth Week

Monday 29 October – Sunday 4 November 1984

The Board dropped the ball. The President's man caught *in flagrante* on film in the arms of the Tyrant of Tripoli. The Union's begging bowl outstretched to the Terrorist's Friend. The sponsors of the Irish Republican Army. The assassins of WPC Yvonne Fletcher. Their president with his pants down. His monstrous political agenda finally exposed. National news. International news. Hold-the-front-page fucking news –

But the Suits of the Board had dropped the ball.

The Chairman had been back in Boston for a weekend with his grandchildren. The Jew left here to hold the fort. The Jew issued instructions in the Chairman's name. The Suits ignored his instructions. The Suits squabbled –

Say this. Don't say that. Push this agenda. Not that –

The Suits had dropped the ball between them. Dropped it for the last time –

Heads would now roll. Heads for tall poles.

These are the nights of the long knives, and the Jew has the sharpest blade of all –

No more distraction. No more conciliation. No more negotiation –

Much more litigation. Much more retaliation. Much, much more determination –

To win, win, win, win, win, win, win, win, win, win, win and win again.

But the Jew knows they need a better public face. No more plastic bags on heads –

Neil Fontaine carries videotape after videotape up from the office to the Boardroom. The Jew and Tom Ball watch videotape after videotape. The Jew and Tom Ball are searching for Mr Right. A public face. A Mr Fixit to make things right. The Jew and Tom Ball finally find their Mr Fixit –

The parrot who blinked the least. The parrot who smiled the most –

The Jew will dispatch Neil to the North. To fetch their Mr Fixit –

Neil Fontaine jumps at the chance. The chance of a ghost.

Terry Winters and Mohammed Divan had changed planes in Frankfurt. Terry and Mohammed had sat in the lounge. The British papers full of reports on the sequestration. The collapse of the latest talks. The intransigence of the President. The persistence of the Chairman. Terry Winters and Mohammed Divan had both agreed the strike was set to run and run. That the Union would need all the cash they could get. Terry Winters and Mohammed Divan had congratulated each other on a job well done. They had boarded their flight to Manchester and home. Shared a taxi from the airport to Victoria Station. Then Mohammed Divan had gone one way and Terry Winters the other. Terry had sat on the train to Sheffield and studied Libyan. Terry would surprise them all with his stories and secrets from Tarabulus al-Gharb. Terry had even thought of going straight to the office. But Terry wanted to see Theresa and the children. Terry had missed Theresa and the children. Terry had wished they had been there with him. Had seen what he had seen. Done what he had done. Terry had taken a taxi direct to his three-bedroom home in the suburbs of Sheffield, South Yorkshire. The house had been dark. The curtains not drawn. Terry had paid the driver. Terry had walked up the drive. Had put his key into the lock. His foot in the door, when the two men had stepped out of the shadows of South Yorkshire and said, 'Care to comment on reports that you have just returned from a meeting with Colonel Gadhafi himself in Libya? That you were sent there on behalf of the President of the National Union of Mineworkers? That you were there to obtain money and guns for your war against the government? Care to comment on such reports, would you, Mr Winters? Care to comment, Mr Winters? Care to comment, Comrade?'

Neil Fontaine sits in the pew. He bows his head. He says a prayer –
  Just the one –
  Bring her back. But back to stay.
  Neil Fontaine leaves St Pancras. He drives into the North again –
  Unscheduled diversions in the long, dark Northern night –
  But no one speaks since the bomb. No one answers their phone.
  Now Neil Fontaine must hunt alone in the long, dark Northern night –

The usual haunts. The usual ghosts.

Neil Fontaine listens to them play on Police Radio 1, these orchestras of ghosts –

Waltzes for the wounded. Laments for lost loves. Sad songs of sin.

Neil Fontaine comes off the M18. Neil Fontaine joins the A630 to Armthorpe –

This is where the strike is today. This is where they'll be today –

Markham Main Colliery. All Saints Day, 1984.

Neil Fontaine parks the Mercedes in the shadows, out of the lights of the strike –

Five hundred pickets. Possibly less. Three hundred police. Possibly more.

Neil Fontaine watches the paperboy ride his bicycle in and out of them –

The milkman make his rounds. The local people walk their dogs.

Neil Fontaine watches the police clear the road of the paperboy and milkman –

Neil Fontaine hears the convoy approach. The shouting and the shoving start.

Neil Fontaine spies the man he wants. *His prey for the day.* Neil Fontaine smiles –

He moves away from the front line with the milk float as his shield.

He spots the Montego up a side-street. He hides near by. He stakes out the street –

His prey watches pickets disperse. His prey walks backwards up the pavement –

Neil Fontaine pounces. Neil Fontaine pulls his prey over the privet hedge –

Neil Fontaine punches his prey. Punches him twice. Punches his prey hard.

He drags him down the side of the house. He puts Paul Dixon up against the wall.

'Talk to me,' says Neil Fontaine. 'Tell me the things I don't know.'

'What the fuck were you doing kissing Colonel bloody Gadhafi on TV?' shouted Paul.

The Conference Room table was covered with newspapers and their headlines –

Outrageous! Obscene! Odious! Own Goal!

Newspapers and their headlines. Headlines and their photographs –

Terry and Mohammed talking. Terry and Salem eating. Terry and the Colonel –

The Colonel and the Judas. The Judas Kiss. The Kiss of Death.

Terry Winters had his hand up the sleeve of his shirt. Terry scratched his arm. Terry screwed up his face. Terry bit his tongue. Terry closed his eyes –

'You fucking knew about all this, did you?' Paul asked the President.

Terry opened his eyes. Terry looked at the President. Terry smiled –

The President stared at Terry. The President shook his head.

Terry dug his fingers into the tops of his legs. Terry tried not to screeeeeeeeeeeam –

Paul looked at Terry. Paul shook his head. Dick shook his. They all did –

'You're either Special Branch', said Paul, 'or the stupidest bloke I've ever met.'

Terry had his hands under his thighs now. Terry scratched the backs of his legs.

'Or both,' said the President.

Terry put his hands over his face. Terry scratched at his neck and his scalp.

'I can't trust him,' said Paul. 'I don't even want to be in the same room as him.'

Paul stood up. Dick stood up. They all stood up –

They all walked out.

Terry Winters looked around the room again. Everything was in cardboard boxes. Boxes of files to go. Boxes of food to stay. The building ringed by miners from Durham. The doors on the eighth floor locked and guarded by the Denims and the Tweeds –

The monastery was under siege. The monks afraid. The abbot –

Terry Winters smiled at the President again. The President looked away –

'Get out of bloody sight,' said the President. 'And stay there.'

Phil Taylor calls. Phil has the flu. Phil can't make it. Fuck Phil.

The Mechanic calls Adam Young. He tells him, 'There's been a change of plan.'

The Mechanic picks Adam up. He drives them into Leeds. To Millgarth –
It's morning. It's a market day –
There are two of them.
They pull into the car park between Kirkgate Market and the bus station –
They watch a man lock his yellow M-reg. Cortina. The man walks towards them. The man passes their car and heads up Kirkgate. He has two empty shopping bags –
'Here we go,' says Adam.
Drum roll –
The Mechanic gets out of the Fiesta. He walks over to the yellow Cortina. He puts the key in the door. He turns the key. The lock gives. He opens the door –
'Hello, hello, hello,' *whispers the voice behind him –*
The Mechanic has the .38 out. He has it in his hand. He spins round –
The Mechanic pulls the trigger –
He goes down. This uniformed piece of shit goes down –
It's not who the Mechanic thought it was. Fuck. *Not who he thought it was at all –*
The Mechanic looks up. He sees Adam running –
The Mechanic looks down. Fuck, he sees another copper on the deck on his radio.
The Mechanic walks over to him. He stands over him. He stares down at him –
The Mechanic shoots him once and then he runs –
Runs and runs and runs –
Out onto New York Street. Down Kirkgate. Through the graveyard –
There are policemen chasing him. Members of the fucking public –
Guilty feet. Got no rhythm. Guilty feet. Got no rhythm. Guilty feet –
Back out onto Duke Street. Down Brussels Street. Up Marsh Lane –
The Mechanic turns right into the Woodpecker car park –
Jumps the fence onto Shannon Street.
The Mechanic stops a Transit. He shows the driver the gun. 'Get out! Get out!'
The driver opens the door. The Mechanic pulls him out. Leaves him on the road –
The Mechanic drives off –
Fuck, fuck, fuck, fuck, fuck, there's a helicopter overhead. Sirens –
Up the York Road. Turns right. He takes the hard hat off the passenger seat –

The Mechanic dumps the van. He walks across the York Road. Hard hat on –

Up Nickleby Road. Torre Road. Nippet Lane. Beckett Street. To the hospital –

The Mechanic finds another Ford. He puts the key in another lock. He turns the key. He opens another door. He gets in –

Drum roll –

He is a dead man. Maybe not today. Maybe tomorrow –

Maybe not tomorrow. Maybe next week –

Maybe not next week. But the Mechanic is a dead man –

He knows that now. Now it's too late –

Too late to turn back. Turn back the clock –

The clock ticking. Tick-tock –

It's November 1984 and England will tear him apart –

Leave him for dead. Tick-tock. Dead –

Just. Like. That.

my dinner with some of lads. I have a pint in Hotel with a few of lads. I crack jokes about Gadhafi with a couple of lads. I give a lift up Hardwick Farm to this one lad. Then I go back to my blanket on bedroom floor in middle of afternoon and I lie there and I think, Fuck this for a game of soldiers. I get back up from blanket on bedroom floor. I go down stairs and out to shed. I get my barrow and get my shovel. I get my riddle and get some bags. I stick them in back of car and drive down to village. I go back on spoil and back to work. I dig and I sieve. I dig and I sieve. I watch my hands turn red and night come down – I watch pit and pit watches me – I work near kids and I work near mothers. I see folk I know and folk I don't. I count blokes on their tod and blokes in teams. I fill one big bag and I fill another. I put first bag in barrow and push barrow to boot. I put bag in boot and push barrow back for second. I put second bag in barrow and push barrow back towards where car is – *Fuck*. Bloody security man is stood there, waiting for us – He says, Bloody going with that? Taking it home, I say. You're bloody not, he says. That's theft, that is – How's it theft? I ask him. I dug it. It's fucking mine – Is it fuck, he says. You want to dig coal, go back to work, you lazy bastard – I look at him. I look at bag. Took me four fucking hour, I say. That did – Fucking waste of time, then, he says. Takes this Stanley knife out of his little uniform – I'll give you half of what I get for it, I say. I swear to you – Fuck off, he says. That hard up, I'd just fucking take it off you, wouldn't I? You might fucking try, I tell him. But that'd be all you'd fucking do – He steps towards us. Listen twat, he says. I could have thee for theft and trespass – I look at him. I nod. You could do, I say. Aye – But I'm not fucking going to, am I? he says. Tell you why, shall I? Go on, I say. Let's hear you, then – Because I work twelve hour a day out here for a quid-fifty an hour, that's why – I nod again. Say nothing this time. Just listen – So tip that bag out that barrow, he says. And we'll say no more about one in boot – **Day 245.** Pete opens envelope. Pete looks at paper. Pete says, Back to Brodsworth. Everybody nods again.

Everybody goes out into rain again. I'm down to drive. Not many cars left. Takes mine a few turns to start. No sign of Gary or Tim this week – Except on top of spoil. Don't blame them – Miss them, though. Their company – Least Keith's back. Back with his new teeth – Police State took them out, he laughs. Welfare State put them back in – Fucking country, says other lad in with us. Bloody brilliant – Park down in Adwick village. March up to pit. Find rest of Thurcroft lads. Look out for bus – Push and shove. Shove and shout. Shout and hurl abuse at scabs. Do my fucking picket – Feel like a bloody robot sometimes, though. I walk back ahead of Keith. Jacket over my head. Pissing it down it is now so I start to run – Not looking where I'm going, am I? Run straight into this copper – *Bang!* Nearly knock him for six. He says something to us. I don't hear what it is. I just keep going. I get back to car. I get in. I shut door. I look up. I see him coming over to car. That copper. I see his gob opening and shutting like a fucking fish, but I can't hear him – Next news he's got his fucking truncheon out. He shatters my bloody windscreen. His mates starting on every other car. Every other fucking car – Bang. Bang. Bang. Smash. Smash. Smash – Every fucking windscreen. Just sat here covered in glass, me – Shards in my hair. Cuts all over my face – Feels like I've been stung by a load of fucking bees. I don't want to bloody cry, like – Not in front of all lads. But I don't know what else to fucking do – **Day 246.** I miss her. Miss her all time – **Day 247.** Letter on hall floor's not from her. Never is – It's from him again. Personal touch this time – *Dear Mr Daly, How much would you like for your soul? That's only thing you have left, we have heard. No wife. No wage. Nothing left now. We want to help you avoid aggro and intimidation. So here is a little tear-off slip and a first-class freepost return envelope. Please enclose your fucking soul. Remember, no stamp needed* – Bribes, blackmail and browbeating. That's what our leader said – Good King Arthur. He was fucking right and all, our Arthur – Right as bloody usual. Love him or hate him, he's always

The Thirty-sixth Week

Monday 5 – Sunday 11 November 1984

Terry Winters raged. Terry Winters roared –

'That bastard has betrayed me for the last time,' he ranted. 'The very last time.'

Diane ran a bath for Terry. Diane dabbed warm water on Terry's arms and legs. His neck and face. She soothed his skin and bones. His brow. His conscience –

'Think about the money,' said Diane.

'They'd be bankrupt already without me,' said Terry again. 'They need me.'

'They need you,' agreed Diane. 'But they don't deserve you.'

The Mechanic stands in the phone box. He takes a breath. He dials her number –

It rings once. She picks it up. She says, 'David?'

'Mum,' says the Mechanic. 'It's me.'

'Oh, love, where are you? Where have you been? Been worried sick –'

'I can't tell you,' says the Mechanic. 'I can't stay on here long, either –'

'Picture's on front of every paper. Every news. Every time I switch it on –'

'I know, I know –'

'But they've not said your name,' she says. 'Haven't been here, either. I –'

'They won't.'

'I don't understand,' she says. 'Why won't they?'

'Because they want me dead, Mum. That's why.'

Poor woman doesn't speak for a moment. Then she asks him straight. She says, 'Did you do it, love? Did you kill that policeman, David?'

'Yes,' says the Mechanic. 'I did.'

'Then you'd best be off then,' she says and hangs up.

Terry Winters stayed under the sheets until the children had left for school. Theresa for work. No risk of silences on the stairs. Coldness over the cornflakes. Hysterics in the hall. Terry Winters would have stayed in bed all day –

But there was always a chance that Diane might phone.

Terry went down the stairs. Terry ate his cornflakes. Terry stood in the hall –

There was always a chance.

The Jew is the boss now. Mr Fixit his face. The newest face among the many new faces. The Suits did not go gracefully. The Suits kicked. The Suits screamed. But the Suits went. The Jew is the boss now. The Jew calls the shots. The tunes. The Jew gives the orders. The area directors meet every Monday, Wednesday and Friday. The directors sit on the phones in the Conference Room. They need the numbers of new faces from their areas. Mr Fixit writes the figures up on the wall. The Jew totals them up –

Eight hundred and two today; two thousand two hundred this week.

Neil opens the biscuit tins. Neil changes the colour of the pins –

From red to yellow. From yellow to blue –

Twenty-eight point five per cent now blue; some blue in all twelve areas –

Nottinghamshire leads the way as ever. But Derbyshire has made the most gains. Yorkshire, the North East, Scotland and South Wales remain very, very red.

The area directors sit around the conference table. Mr Fixit chairs the meeting. Mr Fixit wants to know what works and what doesn't. The Jew takes the minutes –

'There is a sense of isolation,' says Scotland. 'After NACODS.'

The North East disagrees. The North East says, 'The business in Libya.'

'The bonus,' say the other areas. 'That's the only reason they're returning.'

The Jew shakes his head and sighs. The Jew puts down his pen and says, 'Gentlemen, gentlemen. The only reason they are returning is because there is no hope upon their horizon. No hope whatsoever. The strike stretches out before them like an endless sea of suffering. A desert of debt, poverty and pain. And their president can give them nothing to take away their pain. Nothing to ease their suffering –

'No support from other unions. No money. No prospect of talks –

'No talks means no hope and no hope means they'll return and continue to return.'

Mr Fixit nods. The directors nod. The Jew nods –

The Chairman sits in the corner and plays patience with himself.

The directors go back to the areas. To fight the good fight. To win the just war –

Mr Fixit takes the numbers downstairs to show the press they are winning.

Neil Fontaine drives the Jew to Downing Street to tell her they are winning –

The Minister comes out. The Jew goes in.

Neil looks at his watch. He taps it. It starts again. But Neil hasn't time –

The Jew comes back out. The Minister goes back in.

Neil opens the door for the Jew. The Jew says, 'Dublin, please, Neil.'

'Certainly, sir,' says Neil. He starts the car. He switches on the radio –

Ronnie's on the radio. Cowboy Number One. Ronnie's won a second term –

'This is the start of everything,' says Ronnie. 'The start of everything.'

Terry Winters drove into Sheffield. Terry parked his car. Terry went back to work. Terry didn't show his pass. The miners from Durham standing sentry knew Terry Winters –

Everybody knew Terry Winters now –

'Gadhafi rules OK, eh, Tel?' they shouted. 'Ayatollah phoned back, has he?'

Terry Winters smiled. Terry tried to laugh, but their slaps on his back were hard. The digs in his ribs hurt. The hands in his hair rough –

But there was always a chance that Diane might phone again.

Terry went inside the building. Terry got in the lift with the Denims and the Tweeds. Terry pressed the button for his floor. The Denims and the Tweeds stared at him. The Denims whispered to the Tweeds. The Tweeds giggled behind their hands. The Denims sniggered. Terry got out of the lift. Terry walked down the corridor –

No Paul today; Paul was making speeches about comrades who broke ranks –

'– I can tell you they will be treated like lepers –'

Terry Winters unlocked his office door. Terry went inside. Terry took an aspirin. He sat down under the portrait of the President. His desk was covered in paperwork. There was two weeks' work piled up. The sequestration. The very many ramifications. The fears over the finances. The trouble with the overseas transfers. The concerns about the currencies. The urgent messages from Luxembourg to read. From Geneva. Dublin. The problems over the properties. The complications with the cars. The worries about the wages. The legal actions for and against. North Derbyshire now. South Wales again. The moves to make the national and area leaders personally liable for the fines and the costs. The injunctions against the use of Union finances to fund illegal picketing in an unlawful strike. The renewed requests for rallies. The requests for resources. For remuneration. The urgent calls from Samantha Green, six times, to return. From Clive Cook, four times. Bill Reed, twice. No urgent calls to return from the President. From Theresa. Diane. Terry Winters took another aspirin. Terry sank down under the portrait of the President and waited for the phone to ring –

There was always a chance.

The Earth tilts. In for a penny –

The Mechanic steals a white Ford Fiesta. He drives out to the lock-up at Pickering. He parks near the lock-up. He sits in the Fiesta. He watches the lock-up. He waits. He sees no one around. He approaches the lock-up. He takes out the keys and opens the doors. He looks around. He leaves the Fiesta in the lock-up. He takes the bus to Scarborough. He catches a coach down to Hull. He walks to Hull Royal Infirmary. He sits in Casualty. He waits for visiting to begin. He steals a grey Ford Escort from the car park. He drives back to Pickering. He parks. He sits in the Escort. He watches the lock-up. He waits. He sees no one around. He takes out the keys and opens the doors. He looks around. He waits. He goes to work on the cars. He sprays the Escort black. The Fiesta red. He puts the Fiesta plates on the Escort. The Escort plates on the Fiesta. He waits until it's dark. He drives to the Dalby Forest in the Escort. He parks. He waits. He walks through the Dalby Forest to the place. He stops. He waits. He digs up the guns. He unwraps them. He takes out the Browning automatic. The twelve bore. He wraps up the .38. He puts the .38 back in the hole. He buries it. He puts the pistol and the shotgun in the bag. He walks back through the forest to the car. He drives back to the lock-up. He parks near the lock-up. He sits in the Escort. He watches the lock-up. He waits. He sees no one around. He

unlocks and opens the doors. He looks around. He waits. He makes certain.
Bloody certain –

In for a pound. The Earth turns again.

'There can be no forgiveness,' the President had said. 'No forgiveness.'

The President had been electric. The President had brought the whole place down. He had stood alone on the platform. No trade union support. No Labour Party support. Just the President. But everyone who had heard him had been convinced by him. Everyone would leave Sheffield City Hall more determined than ever. Terry Winters too. The President had shaken his hand as he had left the platform –

The President had even smiled at Terry.

It was late now. Terry didn't want to go home. Terry didn't want to go back to work. Terry made his way through the crowd to the exits. Terry saw Bill Reed –

Bill Reed saw Terry.

Terry looked away. Terry pushed through the crowd towards the exits –

Bill Reed was calling his name.

Terry got to the door. Terry went down the steps. Terry broke into a run –

There can be no forgiveness.

Terry escaped. Terry sat in his car with the heater on. Terry was hungry –

Terry drove to a Chinese restaurant in Swinton. Terry sat on his own in a corner. He made notes on his napkin. He put it in his pocket. He asked for the menu. He ordered a pint and prawn crackers. Chop suey and chips. Ice-cream for after.

Terry sat in the corner of the Chinese restaurant and thought about bad things. Debts. Divorce. Death. Then he forgot the bad things and thought about other things. Promises. Promotion. Paradise. But the bad things never forgot Terry. The bad things followed him. Tailed him and taunted him. Hunted him and haunted him –

To recognize and remember them. To love, honour and obey them.

Terry picked up his chopsticks. Terry put them back down again –

'Not losing your appetite, are we, Comrade?' asked Bill Reed.

Terry looked up at Bill. Bill winked. Terry looked back down at his plate.

The waiter pulled a chair out for Bill. The waiter handed Bill a menu.

'What do you recommend, Comrade?' asked Bill.

'Suicide,' said Terry.

'Now, would that be for me or for you?' asked Bill again.

'Both of us,' said Terry. 'It could be a pact.'

'But that would mean you'd have to keep your word, Comrade,' said Bill Reed. 'And there's a few folk out there who might bet against you on that one.'

'What do you want?' asked Terry.

Bill Reed put down the menu. He stood up. He said, 'Let's go for a drive.'

Terry Winters pushed his food away. He asked for the bill. He paid by credit card. He followed Bill Reed out into the car park.

Bill opened the door of his brand-new Granada. He said, 'Take mine, shall we?'

'Where are we going?' asked Terry.

Bill Reed smiled. He winked again. He said, 'You'll see, Comrade.'

Terry got into the Granada. Terry had no choice –

He never did.

The backseat was already covered in papers and briefcases. Files on the floor –

'Excuse the mess,' said Bill and started the car. He pulled out fast into the road –

Foot down, he laughed and sang, 'Here we go, here we go, here we go.'

Thick fog blanketed the county, the land lost under cumbrous cloud –

The roads dark, the roads dead. No sound, no light –

Just Bill and Terry hurtling through the night in a brand-new Ford Granada –

'Here we go, here we go, here we go –'

Bill taking every corner blind –

'Here we go, here we go, here we go –'

Every bend faster than the last –

'This the kind of suicide you wanted, Comrade?' he shouted.

Terry shook his head. His whole body –

'Here! We! Go!' shouted Bill –

Terry screamed, 'Let me out! Let me out!'

Bill slammed his feet onto the brakes and the Granada screamed to a stop –

Terry flew forward. Hit his head. Down into the dashboard. Up into his seat again.

There was no light. There was no sound. The road dark. The road dead –

Terry turned to Bill. Bill was staring straight ahead. Terry said, 'Where are we?'

Bill put a finger to his lips, then his ear. Then his eye. Then the windscreen –

Terry Winters peered out through the glass into the fog. Terry listened –

He could hear a deep, low rumble approaching. He wound down his window –

The rumble was getting louder. Terry got out of the car into the night and the fog –

He stood on the wet road. Between the wet hedges. Under the wet trees –

He turned to look behind him. Lights hit him full in the face. Blinded him –

He put his hands over his eyes. But he wanted to see. To see what it was. To see –

Transit after police Transit tear through the fog in a massive metal motorcade –

One, two, three, four, five, ten, fifteen, twenty, twenty-five, thirty, forty –

Fifty police Transits, one straight after another. Eighty, ninety miles an hour –

Then gone again. No light. No sound. The road dark. The road dead again –

Just the smell of exhaust. Between the hedges. Under the trees.

Terry got back in the car. Bill had his eyes closed. Terry grabbed his arm –

'Where are we?' said Terry again. 'What's going on?'

Bill put a finger to his lips again. His ear and then his eye. 'Patience, Comrade.'

Terry sat back in the passenger seat and Terry waited. He watched. He listened –

319

He switched on the radio. Switched it off again. On again. Off again. He listened –

'There can be no forgiveness.'

He listened and he heard whispers. He heard echoes –

'No forgiveness.'

He sat forward again. Whispers and echoes. Echoes and shouts –

He stared out through the windscreen into the dark. Shouts and screams. Swords –

Swords and shields. Sticks and stones. Horses and dogs. Blood and bones –

The armies of the dead awoken, arisen for one last battle –

The windscreen of the Granada lit by a massive explosion –

The road. The hedges. The trees –

Fire illuminating the night. The fog now smoke. Blue lights and red –

Terry shook Bill's arm. Shook it and shook it. Bill opened his eyes –

'Where are we?' shouted Terry. 'Where is this place?'

'The start and the end of it all,' said Bill. 'Brampton Bierlow. Cortonwood.'

'But what's going on?' screamed Terry Winters. 'What's happening? What is it?'

'It's the end of the world,' laughed Bill Reed. 'The end of all our worlds.'

bloody right – I remember when we first come here. Folk had stories about him even then – That Union were building him a mansion with a big electric fence. Pack of dogs to guard him – That he got all his cars as rewards from Czechs or Soviets. For his spying and agitation – Load of lies even then. Even then – Thing I remember most, though, is what they used to call tenners round here: *Arthur Scargills* – That's what miners called ten-quid notes in South Yorkshire. Because no bugger had ever bloody seen one till Good King Arthur came along – **Day 251.** I can't sleep. I can't close my eyes – Petrol bombs. Burnt-out cars and buses. Huts and Portakabins on fire. Blazing barricades. Houses evacuated. Transit vans with armour fitted special to them. Horses and dogs out – Like something you saw on news from Northern Ireland. From Bogside – Never thought I'd live to see anything like it here. Not here in England. Not in South Yorkshire. Not at fucking Cortonwood, of all bloody places – I just can't believe some of things I saw. Here in my own country, with my own eyes – Lads trapped in playground of Brampton Infants, raining bricks down on coppers as coppers leather anyone they could get their fucking shields and bloody truncheons on. Mothers and their little kiddies trying to make their way inside school for assembly time. Kiddies crying and shitting themselves. Head-teacher out there in playground appealing to both pickets and police to pack it in. No one listening to her – Broke your heart, it did. To see it happen here – Happening everywhere else, though. Happened to us, like – Bloody shock, though, when Pete had opened up envelope and said it was Cortonwood. Someone told him to fuck off. Not to joke about thing like that. Pete said it wasn't a joke. He wished it bloody were. But it isn't. It isn't a joke – It's war. Fucking war this time. For real – World War bloody Three, that's what it looked like – Thick fog. Pitch black. Fires and barricades up everywhere – Never seen so many bottles and bricks thrown. Bus shelter going. Lamp-posts going. Methodist chapel wall. Road running with milk from milk float lads have hijacked –

Battle of Brampton Bierlow, in shadow of Cortonwood Colliery. That's what it was – Three thousand of us. Least two thousand of them, easy – All this for just one bloody scab. Just one bloody scab and he's a fucking foreigner – Transferred him in special, like. Cortonwood lads have hung a stuffed dummy from a gallows above Alamo – *This is for scabs*, sign said round its neck. That was all last Friday. That was bad enough – Today's Monday. This is worse – Six of them now. Six fucking scabs back at Cortonwood. Unbelievable – Keith reckons half of them are pigs – Hope they are. But in my heart, I know they're not. Know they're fucking scabs. Makes me rage inside. Makes me boil. Does same for everybody – Tension's immense. Immense – Real fucking fury there is now. But it's hopeless. Thousands of police. Thousands of them – Horses. Dogs. Vans. Shields – Beat all that lot and there'd still be another thousand more waiting up side-roads. Parked up in a lay-by with their radios on. Thousand more just waiting for bloody word, champing at bit. Just once I'd like us to turn up and it be only us and scabs – Us and ours. Not so we could give them any hammer – Just so we could talk to them. Talk sense back into them – Tell them how they've kicked us all in teeth. Stabbed us all in back. Broke our fucking hearts – But it's hopeless. Fucking hopeless – This is worse than Orgreave. Like a last, final war really has been declared on both sides – No more prisoners. Just us and them – Folk nothing but a number now. Just another bloody body. Fucking cannon fodder. Fight to finish, they keep saying – But there's no finish. Because it just goes on and on and on – Last man standing job. To victor spoils, winner take all – Right across South Yorkshire: Bentley. Dinnington. Dodworth. Frickley. Hickleton. Maltby – Right across whole area. Breaks your heart, it does – Trampled and truncheoned. Bitten and beaten. Bricked and stoned – Your trampled, truncheoned, bitten, beaten, bricked and stoned bloody heart. **Day 255.** Two young brothers died coal picking at Goldthorpe. Names were Paul and Darren. Paul was fifteen,

The Thirty-seventh Week

Monday 12 – Sunday 18 November 1984

The Jew and Neil Fontaine are spending a dirty weekend away. The Jew flies first class. Neil Fontaine back in economy. Heathrow to Dublin for the Union's not-so-secret stash. The money has been traced. Sheffield to the Isle of Man. The money has been tracked. From the Isle of Man to Dublin. The money has been found. The money has been frozen. Three million pounds of the Union's money. But the Union has appealed to have it freed. The Jew worries about the Irish High Court. The Jew worries the Union might even win. The money escape. The money evaporate. So the Jew flies in to wine the Irish solicitors. To dine the English sequestrators. The Jew has large amounts of donated cash to flash. Neil Fontaine leaves the Jew up to his tricks. Neil Fontaine goes out to make movies. Dirty home movies. He visits the judge at his nice family home in a nice part of town. The judge grants the injunctions against the NUM. The judge swears not to lift them. Neil Fontaine drives back to the Jew's Dublin hotel. The Jew has retired early upstairs. Downstairs Neil Fontaine doesn't sleep. He locks the door. Puts a chair against the door, TV and radio on loud. Neil Fontaine dislikes Dublin. Dislikes Ireland. Dislikes the Irish. Both the South and the North. Catholic and Protestant. Two states only. Drunk or hungry. The Taigs in the North the worst. Drunk *and* hungry. The worst three years of a bad life. These are some of the things he tells himself to stay awake in Ireland. To stop sleep fall. The dirty dreams descend. Neil Fontaine doesn't sleep in Ireland. Doesn't close his eyes. He sits up in his chair and watches the coalfields burn on TV.

Everyone sat in silence while Terry Winters swept the Conference Room for bugs again. Terry had bought the bug detector out of his own money from a mail-order surveillance catalogue. It had arrived today. Terry planned to sweep the entire building. Every office. He also wanted to do Huddersfield Road. The President was impressed. Not Paul –

'Had a duster and brush with you,' he said. 'Kill two birds with one stone.'

Terry turned round. He tapped his headphones. He put a finger to his lips.

'Ridiculous,' said Paul. 'If there are any bugs, he's the one who's planted them.'

Terry switched off the machine. He took off his headphones. He put his thumb up.

'Thank you, Comrade Chief Executive,' said the President. 'The place is clean?'

'As a whistle,' said Terry.

'Then it's safe for you to make your report now, is it, Comrade?' asked Paul.

Terry nodded. He put his thumb up again. He handed out photocopies.

'As you can see,' he said, 'the first phase of the operation has been a success.'

Everybody stared down at the photocopied columns of figures.

'As you can see,' started Terry again, 'only eight thousand one hundred and seventy-four pounds has been seized to date.'

'I can't read any of this,' said Paul. 'Where was it seized from?'

'From the Midland Bank here,' said Terry. 'And the Power Group.'

'What about Dublin?' asked Samantha Green. 'That money?'

Terry nodded. Terry said, 'It remains subject to the injunction. Frozen.'

Paul squinted at Terry's sums again. Paul asked, 'How much exactly?'

'Two million seven hundred and eighty-five thousand four hundred and ninety-nine pounds,' said Terry.

'And the rest?' asked Paul. 'The ones that got away?'

'I cannot reveal the exact location,' said Terry. 'Or locations.'

'Has he told you?' Paul asked the President. 'Please tell me he's told you.'

'The Chief Executive is the only person who needs to know,' said the President.

Paul shook his head. Paul said to Terry, 'Have you any idea what you're doing?'

Terry Winters smiled at Paul. Terry Winters stuck his thumb up again.

Samantha Green stared at Terry Winters and his thumb. She shook her head now. She said, 'I do hope the majority of assets are back in Britain, as we discussed.'

Terry lowered his thumb. Terry tapped the side of his nose with his finger.

'President,' said Samantha Green, 'if the sequestrators prove that the Union transferred assets abroad, then they can make a strong case for a breach-of-trust action. The sequestrators could then ask that a receiver be appointed to run the Union.'

The President looked at Terry Winters. He said, 'Comrade Chief Executive?'

'They have to find the money first,' said Terry. 'And they won't.'

Paul groaned. Paul shouted, 'You said same fucking thing about South Wales!'

'South Wales didn't follow my instructions,' said Terry. 'I warned them.'

'Well, Comrade, I'm warning you here and now,' said Paul. 'Don't fuck this up.'

Terry Winters smiled. Terry said, 'Thank you for your advice, Comrade.'

Paul smiled back. Paul stuck his thumb up. Paul ran it across his throat.

Terry turned to the President, then to the room. He said, 'Thank you, Comrades.'

Everybody nodded. Everybody waited for Terry to leave –

Terry picked up his bug detector and headphones. Terry left the room backwards –

Everybody sat and watched him go in silence –

Terry shut the door. Terry went back downstairs. Terry unlocked his office door. Terry collapsed in his chair under the portrait of the President. Terry took four aspirins –

The men at Abervan had dangled a noose over the Fat Man –

The red light on his phone was flashing.

There was a noose and gallows at Cortonwood –

Terry picked it up. *Click-click.* Terry said, 'Chief Executive speaking.'

It was the hour of the lynch mob. The year of the noose –

'Guess who?' she said.

Terry swallowed the aspirins. Terry said, 'Where have you been?'

'Doesn't matter,' she said. 'Guess what?'

Terry stood up. Terry said, 'What?'

'I've got a present waiting for you,' she said. 'When do you want it?'

Terry blinked. Terry stuck out his chest. Terry said, 'All night.'

'Not that kind, silly,' she said. 'This is a different kind of present.'

Terry sat back down under the portrait of the President. Terry said, 'What kind?'

'The kind you get from corner shops in Bentley,' she whispered.

Home sweet home for Stephen sweet Stephen in his fourth-floor suite at Claridge's.

Neil Fontaine helps the Jew dress for the banquet. The Lord Mayor's Banquet.

Neil Fontaine drives the Jew to the Guildhall. The Jew is excited –

'These are days we were not meant to see,' he says. 'Rare days indeed, Neil.'

Neil Fontaine watches the Jew enter the Guildhall. Neil Fontaine starts the car –

He drives to the river. In the dark. He parks by Traitor's Gate –

He searches the stations. The signals. He seeks the signs. The symbols. But there is nothing here. Here no one. No one who cares –

Neil Fontaine tries to pull himself together. Put the pieces back his way. He switches on the radio. He listens to the Lady –

'– we are drawing to the end of a year in which our people have seen violence and intimidation in our midst: the cruelty of the terrorists, the violence of the picket line, the deliberate flouting of the laws of this land. These challenges shall not succeed –

'We shall weather the tempests of our times.'

He sits by the river. In the dark. Down by Traitor's Gate –

He whispers her name. He calls her name. He screams her name –

The cruelty. The violence. The laws of this land –

By the river. In the dark. By the gate –

The tempests of our times.

The Earth hungry. The Earth hunts again –

Eyes wide. Mouth open. Nose bloody –

'The keys,' the Mechanic says again through the balaclava.

The manager blinks at the Browning. He opens a drawer. Holds up the keys.

'You do it,' the Mechanic tells him.

The manager nods. He walks backwards to the safe. Turns and bends down.

'Faster,' the Mechanic shouts.

The manager fumbles with the keys. He drops them. Looks up at the Browning.

The Mechanic cocks the gun. He says, 'Last chance.'

The manager picks up the keys. He opens the safe. Waits.

The Mechanic throws the bag down on the floor. He says, 'Fill that.'

The manager reaches into the safe. He takes out cash and cheques. Fills the bag.

'Just the cash,' the Mechanic says. 'Just the cash.'

The manager throws cheques to one side. He takes only cash. Puts it in the bag.

'That's enough,' the Mechanic shouts. 'Pass it here.'

The manager hands him the bag. He looks up the barrel of the gun. Waits again.

'On your knees,' the Mechanic tells him.

The manager kneels down. Head bowed. Hands together. He prays –

He prays and the Mechanic runs –

Her eyes wide. Her mouth open. Her nose bloody –

The Mechanic runs from the hungry Earth. The Earth that hunts him.

Neil Fontaine picks the Jew up at Claridge's. Neil Fontaine drives the Jew to the Carlton Club. The Jew meets the Great Financier at the Club. The Great Financier gives one hundred thousand pounds in cash to the Jew. Neil Fontaine drives the Jew to Hobart House. The Jew meets the National Working Miners' Committee in their new office. The Jew gives eighty thousand pounds in cash to the National Working Miners' Committee. Neil Fontaine drives the National Working Miners' Committee to the Inns of Court. The National Working Miners' Committee meet their legal representatives. The National Working Miners' Committee give seventy thousand pounds in cash to their legal representatives. The legal representatives give writs against the twenty-two members of the National Executive Committee of the National Union of Mineworkers and the five trustees of the Yorkshire Area to the National Working Miners' Committee. The writs make the twenty-two members of the National Executive personally liable for the two-hundred-thousand-pound fine for contempt of court and forbid the use of Union money to fund picketing or strike-related activities in the Yorkshire Area. Neil Fontaine drives the National Working Miners' Committee back to Hobart House. The National Working Miners' Committee meet the Jew. The National Working Miners' Committee give the writs to the Jew. The Jew posts the writs to the twenty-two members of the National Executive Committee of the National Union of Mineworkers and the five trustees of the Yorkshire Area –

This is the way the world works. This small, small world –

The way it tilts and the way it turns –

The way it tilts and turns again.

Darren fourteen. They were digging to get some pocket money for Christmas presents. Digging it out with their bare hands for two quid a bag. Two pound notes. That was all. Spoil heap fell on them. Crushed them. Buried them. Suffocated them. Killed them. There were no television cameras there to see it happen. No reporters. Just two little lads lying dead under a mountain of muck. Two little lads who wanted to buy their mam and dad a Christmas present – Their father doesn't have a job. Father doesn't have any brass – He doesn't have his lads now. Nothing now – They are fifth and sixth to die coal-picking in Yorkshire. This year. Nineteen eighty-four. Three of dead weren't even old enough to smoke. Let alone vote – There's silence in Welfare today. All day. Even in kitchen. No one speaks. No one – *The fragments tumble down. The fragments clatter below – They whisper and they echo –* I wake up. I get bus into Sheffield. **Day 261.** They're putting up Christmas lights. Christmas tree. I can't remember last time I was here. It must have been with our Cath, I suppose. Used to go in twice a month without fail when we first moved here. Window shopping. Looking at all things money could buy – Three-piece suites. Fitted bedrooms. Fridge-freezers. Video-recorders – Cath didn't like to just look, though. Had to have something. I encouraged her and all. Made her feel better. That would last a day or so. Then catalogues would come back out. Tape measure. Like a drug with her, it was. Buying stuff. Filling up all empty spaces. Needed her fix or there was no talking to her. It was like an addiction. Even had a stone façade stuck on front of house. How much had that cost us? Fuck me, it looked daft. But that's why I'm here, though. To see if I can see her. But deep down in my heart I know I won't – I just wander about looking at all them things I can't have. Then things I'll never ever have again – Three-piece suites. Fitted bedrooms. Fridge-freezers. Video-recorders – Things I don't even want again. Things I never wanted – They don't have one thing I want. You can't buy thing I want. Not round here. Not any more.

Not in Britain today – Thing I want is to go back. Back to my place of work – Not on a bus with mesh over windows. Not in a hood with slits for eyes – I want to drive back up there. Park my car up with all other cars. Go into locker room and have a laugh with lads. Take cage down. Do my shift and have my snap. Do some graft and come back up. Wash up and clock off. Drive straight back home – Back home. Home to wife. My wife. My Cath – That's what I want. That's all I want – My wife back. My job back – My life. Life I had – That's all I want. But I don't see it. Not here. Not today – **Day 264.** Sunday again. Fucking Sunday. I can't stay in house. I go down Hotel. I've got just enough for half a pint. Walk there and back will take up most of day. Fresh air helps me sleep. I don't know how much more of this I can take. I really don't. I know there were them that thought it was best thing that ever happened to them. First few months. Especially some of them with kids – Time in house with them. Helping them with their homework. Doing different stuff. Stuff they'd never had time for before – Swimming. Football. Fishing. Hunting – I wonder how they feel about it all now. After nine months. Nine bloody months – Nine months of toast for their breakfast. Nine months of soup for their dinner. Nine months of spaghetti for their tea. Nine months of their kids without any new gear. Nine months of their kids on hand-outs and other folk's cast-offs. Nine months of their wives trying to make ends meet. Nine months of their wives trying to hold them together. Nine months of them slowly falling apart. Nine months of them watching every single news programme there was. Nine months of them talking about nothing else. Nine months of them arguing and arguing and arguing and arguing and arguing. Nine months of them going up to the bedroom. Nine months of them lying on their backs. Nine months of them staring up at ceiling. Nine months of them wishing they were fucking dead – **Day 267.** *I stop to rest on the heap. I watch fires light up ahead. This place is old. This stede is niht. This place is cold.*

The Thirty-eighth Week

Monday 19 – Sunday 25 November 1984

Terry Winters waited until the children had left for school. Theresa for work. Terry went out onto the landing. He pulled down the ladder to the loft. He climbed up the ladder. Terry looked into the loft. He saw the two suitcases standing in the shadows –

Kiss me.

Terry got up into the loft. He walked across the chipboard. He took down the two suitcases. Terry went down the stairs with them. He left them on the kitchen floor. Terry went out to the garage. He opened the boot of the car. He took out two more suitcases. He carried them back inside. He put them down on the kitchen floor, next to the two suitcases from the loft –

Kiss me in the shadows.

Terry Winters went over to the cupboard under the sink. Terry took out a black dustbin-liner from under the sink. He took the bin-liner into the pantry. Terry emptied cream crackers and digestive biscuits out of their tins. He threw away cakes. Terry filled the bin-liner. He took it outside. He put it in the dustbin. Terry went back inside –

Kiss me, Diane.

Terry laid the four suitcases out on the kitchen floor. Terry opened the suitcases. He stared at the money. The money in the suitcases. Terry put his hands in the suitcases. The suitcases full of money. Terry sat at his kitchen table and counted out the money. The money into piles. Terry put some of the money into the empty biscuit tins. He put some of the money into the cake tins. He put the tins back on the shelves in the pantry. Terry split the rest of the money between the four suitcases. He left two of the suitcases up in the loft again. He put the other two suitcases back in the boot of his car –

Kiss me in the shadows.

Terry sat at the wheel of his car. He had followed Diane's instructions to the letter. The instructions she had written out. The instructions he was to destroy –

Kiss me in the shadows of my heart.

331

Terry Winters turned the key. Terry Winters was on his way to work –

Revenge. November 1984.

The nightmare is persistent. Neil Fontaine dreams of her skull. Her beautiful, white skull. Her skull and his candle. Her skull on the table and his candle in the window. He wakes in his room at the County. The light is still on. He sits on the edge of the bed. The notebook in shreds. He picks apart their lives and puts the pieces back together his way. He stands up. He pulls back the dawn curtains. The bed is unused. The sheets cold –

His prayer unanswered.

Neil Fontaine stands at the window. The real light and the electric –

Jennifer scowls and sticks out her tongue.

There are always, always, memories like these –

'You want a fucking picture, do you?'

These scars across your country. These scars across your heart.

The Mechanic stands in the phone box. He dials the number –

Phil Taylor's wife picks up the phone. Click-click. *She says, 'Hello?'*

'Is Phil there?' the Mechanic asks her.

'He's at work,' she says. 'Who's this?'

'He feeling better then, is he?'

'Who is this?' she says again.

'Just tell him Dave called,' the Mechanic says and hangs up, then picks up again –

Click-click, *what a beautiful noise that is; the sound of surveillance; of –*

Predictability –

There's nothing special about Special Branch. They follow people. They watch people. They go through people's dustbins. They blackmail people. They bully people. They like to dress up and pretend they're not themselves. Pretend they are other people. Not what they seem. But they're just perverts –

Dirty old men.

They go through the files. They find someone they like the look of. They study that person. They follow them. They watch them. They wait until that person does something bad. Something illegal. Like an armed robbery or the theft of a car. Then they blackmail that bad person. They bully them –

Intimidate and cajole them.

They make that bad person their slave. They make them do anything they ask. They make them do more bad things. Much worse things. Dirty things. Like burglaries. The theft of documents. Then they blackmail that bad person all over again. Bully them. Groom them for other men. Then they pass them on up the chain –

Like a parcel of meat.

Terry Winters sat under the portrait of the President. Terry took another two aspirins. There were now thirty individual legal actions. Thirty separate requests to examine the books and accounts of the national and individual areas. There was no end in sight now. The President said the strike was solid. The Board said the strike was crumbling. The President said there were one hundred and forty thousand men on strike. The Board said there were sixty thousand men breaking the strike. Terry knew the figures didn't add up. It didn't matter either way. The Board said there was nothing to talk about. That there could be no more negotiations. The door now closed. No more secret talks about talks. The door locked. No more words about words. The key upstairs. The ball in their court. Terry picked up the telephone on his desk –

Click-click. He dialled Huddersfield Road. *Click-click.* He asked for Clive Cook –

But no one had seen Clive. Not this week. They could put him through to Jack.

'It's OK,' said Terry. 'I'll call back.'

Terry Winters hung up. Terry took another aspirin. He put his head in his hands.

The telephone buzzed. The light flashed –

Terry picked it up again. *Click-click.* Terry said, 'Chief Executive speaking.'

'It's Joan,' said Joan. 'The President would like you to step upstairs, Comrade.'

'This very minute?' asked Terry. 'I was just –'

'This very minute,' said Joan. 'It's urgent, Comrade.'

Terry started to speak, but Joan had already hung up. Terry put down the phone. He swallowed another two aspirins. He stood up. He left his office. He locked his door. He walked down the corridor. He didn't take the lift. He took the stairs, one at a time –

There were no index cards in the right-hand pocket of his jacket.

Terry knocked on the President's door. Len opened it. Terry stepped inside –

Joan was standing at the President's shoulder. The President sat behind his desk.

Len closed the door. Len locked it. Len leant against it. Len folded his arms.

'You wanted to see me, President?' asked Terry. 'I was told it was urgent.'

The President put his finger to his lips. The President nodded. Joan nodded too. The President scribbled something on a piece of paper. He handed it to Terry –

Terry read, *The Soviets have delivered. We are expected at the Embassy.*

Terry looked up. The President put his finger to his lips again. Terry nodded –

Terry pointed to himself. The President nodded again. His finger to his lips.

Len took the piece of paper out of Terry's hands. Len held it to his lighter. Len burnt the piece of paper in the glass ashtray on the President's desk.

The President and Joan put on their coats –

Len went with Terry for his.

Phil the Grass lives with his wife and two children in a nice private house on a nice private estate in Selby. Phil has a haulage company that used to be on the brink of bankruptcy. But, thanks to the miners' strike, Phil will soon be able to afford to live in an even nicer private house on an even nicer private estate –

If Phil lives that long (which he probably will).

The Mechanic knows they intimidated and cajoled Phil Taylor to grass. He knows they bullied him. He knows they blackmailed him. He knows they waited until Phil had done something bad. Something illegal. Like an armed robbery. He knows they were watching him –

Just as the Mechanic knows they are watching Phil Taylor now. In his nice private house on its nice private estate in Selby. Knows they are sat watching Phil in their six-month-old Montego. In their sweater and their jeans. Their polished size tens –

Desperate for a piss behind a nice private tree (if they live that long) –

He has his cock in his hands. Piss on the bark. Piss on his boots.

The Mechanic puts the nose of the gun against the back of his skull and says, 'Hello. Hello. Hello.'

He doesn't try to turn round. There's no point. He knows who it is.

'Put your hands on your head,' the Mechanic says. 'Do it slowly.'

He puts his hands on the top of his head. He does it slowly.

The Mechanic puts handcuffs on his wrists. He says, 'Now turn round.'

He turns round. Handcuffed hands over his open fly. His dripping cock.

'Hello, Paul,' the Mechanic says. 'Did you miss me?'

Paul Dixon, Special Branch, shakes his head savagely from side to side –

He sees his widowed wife. His fatherless daughter –

'It was Fontaine,' sobs Paul Dixon. 'Neil Fontaine.'

The Jew dances across the rugs and carpet of his suite on the fourth floor of Claridge's. The Jew is still in his tails, a late cocktail in his right hand, tomorrow's *Times* in the left. The Jew asks Neil Fontaine to turn up the radio –

'– you could drag me to hell and back, just as long as we're together –'

Neil Fontaine turns up the radio. Neil Fontaine mixes the Jew one last cocktail. Neil Fontaine hands the Jew the latest photographs with a screwdriver.

The Jew sits down on the sofa. The Jew examines the photographs one by one –

The President speaking in Cardiff. Birmingham. Edinburgh and New-castle.

The President in his car. His office. His street and his home.

The President meeting the TUC. The Labour Party. The French and the Soviets.

The President talking. Whispering. Grimacing and glowering.

The Jew puts down the photographs. The Jew says, 'His war is lost.'

Neil Fontaine nods. Neil Fontaine hands the Jew a fresh cocktail to celebrate.

The Jew smiles. The Jew laughs. The Jew thanks Neil and raises his glass.

The Jew's insistence on intransigence has been vindicated –

No one mentions power cuts any more; no one talks of general strikes –

Man by man. House by house. Street by street. Village by village. Pit by pit –

The Jew is winning his war –

4484 back last week; 4982 this week.

The Jew downs his drink in one and picks up yet more reports from the pile –

The Jew never rests. The Jew loves to dwell here among the details and analyses; to speak of the deterioration of the coal faces and the need for compulsory redundancies; the prospects for privatization, the rebirth of the industry and the creation of wealth –

Remarks here and remarks there; words in this ear and words in that –

Words in *her* ear; words that win wars.

For the Prime Minister is winning her war; her many, many wars –

The IRA. British Leyland. GCHQ. Cammell Laird. CND. The Belgrano. *The GLC.*

She never rests. *Ever.* But she prefers to live among the larger print and syntheses; to talk of the dangers to democracy from the ruthless few; the terrorist gangs at one end of the spectrum and the Hard Left at the other; inside our system, conspiring to use union power and the apparatus of local government to break, defy and subvert the laws –

These are her *words; her words that win wars; her many, many wars.*

The Prime Minister and the Jew; together they are winning the war, all her wars. But the Jew knows there is still work to be done. Much more to come. Much worse –

The sight of strikers in the snow. Their children in the cold –

Northern funerals and famine; local poverty and pain.

The Jew knows there will be those without the stomach, the guts or the balls –

Neither the courage nor the conviction. Not the will to triumph.

The Jew puts down his papers. The Jew raises a last glass before bed –

'Now is the time to steel ourselves,' declares the Jew. 'The final hours are here. The endgame approaches, Neil.

'That one last battle nigh.'

The four of them caught the five o'clock early evening train from Sheffield to London. The four of them got a table in second class. The other passengers in the coach stared. One man threw a meat pie at the President. An old woman chucked a cup of scalding tea. Loyal Len and the guard tried to calm things down. Joan wiped pie and tea from the President's suit and tie –

'This wouldn't happen if we were sat in first class,' said Terry.

The President picked pieces of hot pie from his hair. He shook his head. He said, 'This wouldn't happen if we abolished first class, Comrade.'

Terry Winters nodded. Terry sponged his newspaper dry with his handkerchief. He looked at his watch –

The train was fifteen minutes late into London. Len went off to get them a cab –

The President, Joan, Terry and Len took the taxi direct to the Embassy.

The President borrowed Terry's calculator. The President punched numbers. The President wanted cash commensurable to the Soviet support of 1926.

The taxi stopped at the back door to the Embassy. Terry Winters paid the driver.

The Soviet Labour Attaché and diplomatic staff were waiting to welcome them. To take them inside. To offer them tea and biscuits in large and under-heated chambers. To make small talk about composers and goalkeepers –

The living and the dying. The dying and the dead.

Then the Labour Attaché asked to speak with the President in private.

Joan, Terry and Len went outside to wait in the large and under-heated corridor. To sit and stare at the social-realist paintings of the Soviet state. To shiver and snooze.

The President came out fifty minutes later with a smile and a spring to his stride –

The President had got his way. The President had got what he wanted.

The President, Joan, Terry and Len stepped out of the Soviet Embassy –

The flashbulbs exploded. The cameras rolled. The microphones pointed.

Len hailed them a cab to the Barbican. They sat in silence in the back of the taxi. The taxi stopped outside the President's block of flats. Terry paid the cab driver again. The President and Joan walked on ahead. Len waited for a word with Terry Winters. Terry put away his wallet. Terry smiled at Len. Len punched Terry in the stomach –

'That was the fucking last time,' said Len Glover. 'Last time you betray us.'

Terry knelt on the pavement. Terry held his stomach. Terry coughed.

'There was just us four that knew about that meeting,' said Len. 'Just us four.'

Terry coughed again. Terry clutched his stomach. Terry shook his head.

'It had to be you that tipped off the press,' said Len. 'It had to be you, Winters.'

Terry shook his head again. Terry rubbed his stomach. Terry tried to stand up.

Len pushed him back over. Len kicked him in the stomach. Len spat on him.

Terry tried to stand up again. Terry gripped his stomach. Terry shook his head.

Len pushed him back over onto the ground again. Len walked away. Len shouted, 'You're fucking finished, Winters. Fucking finished.'

Terry shook his head again. Terry touched his stomach. Terry tried to stand –

But Terry was laughing. Terry's sides splitting. Terry howling –

'Look in the mirror, Len,' shouted Terry. 'Look in the mirror, Comrade Len!'

Martin

This stede is dimm. I watch fires die up ahead. I pick up a fragment in my hand – Don't fly as much as before. Can't. Problems enough on our own doorstep. Half of cars are knackered and all. Mine's still out front with black bin-bags for a windscreen. Pete's asked Barnsley for some brass for it. He's heard nothing back. They've got a van for this morning. Lot of usual lads – Keith. Tom. Chris – No sign of Gary or Tim again. They told me they were going on spoil seven days a week now. I've not been for a bit. There are no more blind eyes and back handers on top now – They catch you, they sack you – That was message from pit. Likes of Tim and Gary don't give shit, though. No choice, way they see it – They catch them, they catch them. They sack them, they sack them – Makes no odds to them. Fucking DHSS are withholding another bloody quid from folk. Them that even fucking get anything in first place – Talk about nails and bloody coffins. Turns of fucking screw. Fuck me – This morning it's Frickley. More to show willing than anything else – Down Welfare for half-four. Bacon sandwich and a cup of tea and we're on road for five. Usual arguments about best way versus this way and that way. Head up through Thurnscoe and Clayton. Back way into Frickley and another front line. Keith parks up and out we get. It's cold and damp. *Krk-krk.* There are about sixty police. Two hundred pickets, maybe. Scab bus comes up and there's a big push – Line breaks for a moment. But only for a moment – Bus goes in and that's that again. People start to walk off. Back to their cars and their vans. Police giving out their usual wit – I catch eye of one of them. Always a fucking mistake – He steps out into road in front of all his mates. He gives us a right boot up my arse. He says, Come on, Doris, pick your fucking feet up. He kicks me again couple of times. I just keep walking – Keeping my head down. Feel fucking daft, though. Two foot tall. Everyone watching him kick us like that – Two foot tall, that's how I feel. Every fucking day. Two foot fucking tall – **Day**

269. Keith drops us off. Has a laugh with us about state of our car, then he goes back home. He's his wife and his kids. Has it hard but he has them – Police can spit on him. Make their comments. Push him about. Kick him up arse. Chase him. Beat fuck out of him. Take out his teeth even – But he's got his wife and his kids. He's one of lucky ones – I open door. Nothing. No one – Just another fucking copy of *Coal News* waiting for us on floor with another fucking letter from Mr Moore at Colliery. That and a letter from TSB in Rotherham and another one from solicitors – They never give up, those kind. Never – Nails and coffins. Turns of screw – Bloody lot of them. Like an army, they are – I shut door. I stand in hall – I look up at my watch. It isn't even twelve o'clock yet – Not even halfway there. Not even close – I walk through into kitchen. Place where kitchen used to be – I look out on back garden. I light a cigarette – Expensive habit that, she says. I turn round – I fly off handle. Shut up! Shut up, I shout. Shut up! I go back into hall – I pick up that letter from Mr Moore. I stand there in hall with it in my hand – *I put the fragment to my face – I open it – It is cold and it is old –* I read bloody thing this time – *I hold the fragment to firelight –* I read his offer – *I see it for the first time –* To meet me any time I want – *I see it and I stare –* To meet me any place I want – *I step back –* To discuss my future – *I look around me at this place –* My welfare and my happiness – *This place is old. This stede is niht –* My safety and my security – *This place is cold. This stede is dimm –* My change of heart and my piece of mind – *I see this place for what it is. I see this fragment for what it is –* To arrange my return. My return to work – *I hold the fragment of a skull in my hand, stood upon a mountain of skulls –* I drop letter on pile. Pile of statements and bills. Bills and final demands – *The skulls sat in monstrous and measureless heaps. The empty nests of dreams and desires –* Demands and threats – *Delusions and deceptions –* I close my eyes – *I whisper. I echo. I moan. I scream –* I open my eyes. I stand in my hall – *Under the ground –* I moan and I scream.

The Thirty-ninth Week

Monday 26 November – Sunday 2 December 1984

The Mechanic drives to his mother's house at Wetherby. He has come to say goodbye. Not see you later. He gets out –

Drum roll –

Here come the dogs. Down the drive. Tongues out and tails up. Fuck, he missed them. Missed his dogs. Dog might not stab you in the back. But dog could still break your heart. He knows that now. The dog loves you, and you love the dog –

Breaks your bloody heart –

The Mechanic knows that now. Now it's too late.

He looks up from the dogs. He sees his mother in the doorway. He stands up –

She shuts the door. She turns the key. She draws the curtains –

It is midday. Noon. November 1984.

The Mechanic puts the dogs in the back of the Fiesta. He drives up to the Dalby Forest with them. They get out. They walk through the forest to the place –

The Mechanic kisses the dogs. The Mechanic shoots the dogs.

He digs two pits near an old badger sett and buries them next to Dixon –

Their scents confused. Their bones mixed.

Stay. Fucking. Free –

Free of everything and everyone. Their scent and their bones.

Terry Winters had his head against the window. Terry stared down at the streets below. He didn't know if it was dusk or dawn any more. He'd not been to bed in over two days. He ate only aspirins. He drank only coffee. High Court orders had been served on Paul and Dick as they left Congress House in London last night. The bailiff had thrown the orders into their car. Dick had thrown them back out. Left the papers to scatter into the night. But the orders had been served. The orders effected. Paul and Dick phoned Terry from London. *Click-click.* Paul and Dick told Terry exactly what they thought of him. Told him again and again. The orders meant their funds had been found in

Switzerland and Luxembourg. The orders meant their funds would be frozen –

Five million in Luxembourg. Five hundred thousand in Switzerland –

Everything undone.

Terry had to get to the money. Terry had to get to it as fast as he could. Terry knew he could engineer the release of the money in the Luxembourg courts; that the orders were not valid outside the UK. Terry knew then he could move it –

If he could get there and get there in time.

Terry picked up the phone. *Click-click.* Terry phoned round airlines and airports. *Click-click.* Terry phoned the local owners of private aircraft and airstrips. *Click-click.* Terry chartered a plane. The plane would cost twelve thousand pounds. Terry said yes, he'd pay cash.

Terry phoned Mike Sullivan. *Click-click.* Terry told him to pack his bags –

To meet him at Leeds–Bradford airport.

Terry drove home fast. Terry had to pack quick. Terry had to pack cash –

The President was on the radio. The President talked of their debts to the dead.

Terry went up his drive. Terry went into his house. Terry went into his pantry. The tins were still there. The tins full of money. Terry emptied all the tins into one big black bin-liner. Terry thought that was enough. Terry left the suitcases alone in the loft. Terry looked at the clock on the wall. Terry piled the empty tins back up in the pantry. Terry walked out of the front door of his house with the big black bin-liner in his hand –

Terry stopped dead in the drive. Terry dropped the bin-liner onto the ground.

The President was standing at the end of the drive with Len.

Terry Winters said, 'I can explain.'

The President shook his head. The President nodded to Len –

Len walked up the drive. Len picked up the bin-liner. Len opened the bin-liner.

Terry said again, 'I can explain.'

The President shook his head again. Len took hold of Terry by his arm –

They took Terry with them. They took Terry in –

They tied Terry to a table. Told Terry to take his time. Take this time to think.

Terry sat in his vest and underpants on the tenth floor of the Union Headquarters. The President would talk to Terry only in his vest and pants. He didn't trust Terry –

Not after what Len had told him. The things Len had told him.

Len leant against the door. Len with his arms folded. Len with his eyes on Terry.

The President had counted out the packets of twenty-pound notes into three piles. Each pile contained one hundred packets. Each packet contained two hundred pounds –

There was sixty thousand pounds in used twenty-pound notes on the table.

The President looked down at the cash. The President looked back up at Terry –

'It's from the CGT in Paris,' said Terry again. 'I swear.'

'I don't care where it's from,' said the President. 'But I care where it was going.'

'I was bringing it here,' said Terry. 'To pay for the plane and the mortgages.'

'I'd like to believe you,' said the President. 'I want to believe you, Comrade.'

'Mike Sullivan is waiting for me at the airport,' said Terry. 'Just ask him.'

The President looked at Terry Winters. Terry Winters in his vest and underpants.

'I swear,' said Terry again. 'What else would I be doing with it?'

There was a knock at the door. *Silence.* There was another knock at the door –

Len looked at the President. The President nodded. Len opened the door –

'It's urgent,' said Joan. 'The High Court have appointed a receiver.'

The Earth tilts, the Earth turns. The Earth hungry, the Earth hunts –

The Mechanic drives. He steals another Ford and drives South. He ditches that car and steals another. And drives. He burns this one and steals another, then another –

Her eyes wide. Her mouth open. Her nose bloody –

And drives and drives. He pushes one into the River Avon and sells

another one for scrap. He steals the next one from a supermarket car park –
  The Earth hunts you, you run. You run, you hide. Hide in the last place –
  Bypasses Worcester and Shrewsbury. Takes the A49 to Hereford then
Leominster. Ludlow to Wistanstow. Joins the A489 to Church Stoke. The
A490 straight to Welshpool. Follows the A483 North to Llanymynech and –
  The very last place.

Neil Fontaine drives the Jew and the Chairman North to Castleford. Hooded pickets armed with baseball bats attacked and badly beat a working miner in his own home at dawn yesterday morning. The man had returned to work at Fryston Colliery only four days before. He had done so because he had two young children. He had done so because he had a pregnant wife. He had done so because he had debts. He had done so because he had no way to repay his debts. He left his house at half-past four yesterday morning for a pre-arranged rendezvous with a Coal Board van. Twenty pickets were waiting for him outside his home. The pickets warned him not to go to work. The pickets made threats against his pregnant wife and two young children. The man walked back towards his house to telephone the police. The pickets called him a scab. The pickets chased him into his garden. The man ran inside his house. The pickets kicked open his door. The pickets wore combat jackets and balaclavas. The pickets carried baseball bats and pick-axe handles. The man told his pregnant wife and two young children to hide upstairs. The pickets caught the man in his own front room. The pickets set about him with their bats and steel-toe-capped boots. His wife and children listened from inside a bedroom wardrobe to their husband and their father screaming down below. The pickets broke his ankle. The pickets broke his shoulder. The pickets dislocated his elbow. The pickets dislocated his other shoulder. The pickets broke two ribs and bruised the rest. The pickets blackened his eyes. The pickets broke his nose. The Jew had been appalled when Neil had told him this tale. The Jew told Neil they must visit this Richard Clarke in his hospital bed. This lion of a man. The Chairman had been equally appalled when the Jew had told him. The Chairman told the Jew they must visit this hero in his hospital bed –

This lion of a man in his hospital bed –

'I'll not let them stop me,' Richard Clarke tries to tell the Chairman and the Jew. 'This has just made me more determined.'

The Chairman gives him autographed books about mining, and comforts his wife.

'When he comes out of hospital he'll go back to work,' says pretty, pregnant Mrs Clarke. 'We are not going to be beaten by these thugs.'

Neil Fontaine shows in Stanley Smith. Stanley also recently returned to work. Last week someone set fire to his £40,000 home in Pontefract.

The Jew steps outside. The Jew shows in the press.

The press take out their pens. The press take their photos –

'Everyone should get back to work to change Union rules,' says Richard Clarke. 'NUM President should have to be re-elected every three years.'

The Jew smiles. The Jew nods. The press write. The press nod.

'They emphasized that they would kill my two-year-old daughter,' says Stanley. 'And the main target in this blaze was her bedroom. That about sums it all up for me. They openly told me they would kill my daughter, and they have tried to do just that.'

The Jew dabs his eyes. The Jew nods. The press write. The press nod.

The Jew picks up a *Get Well Soon* card from Richard Clarke's bed-side table. The Jew shows it to the press. The Jew reads it aloud:

'"All the best to a very brave man who deserves a medal and all the miners' thanks. The rest of us are too scared, but you have shown the way –

'"From another miner on strike, but not half as brave as you."'

The Chairman lets go of pretty, pregnant Mrs Clarke. The Chairman has things to say –

'This was a horrific and brutal attack on an innocent working man in his own home, while his beautiful wife and two children cowered upstairs, petrified and terrified. This is the visible proof of what we have been saying for months now that, but for these IRA tactics of violence and intimidation in the pit villages, many thousands more men would have gone back to work by now and this strike have soon been over.'

The Chairman puts away his piece of paper. The Chairman looks at the Jew –

The Jew looks at Richard Clarke. Richard Clarke nods. Richard Clarke says, 'This visit was a wonderful surprise and the Chairman has given me lots of reassurance, which I needed. He told me that if I needed to move away from the area, I could do so. But I don't think I will need to do that. He wished me a speedy recovery and asked after my wife and children. He gave me two signed books on mining, which not many folk can have. I will keep them for ever to pass on to my children, for their children, and their children's children.'

The Jew claps. The Jew nods. The press write. The press nod –

The Jew reminds the press of the Prime Minister's *ruthless few*. The Jew says –

'They blind police horses. They spike potatoes with nails. Uproot lamp-posts and loot local shops. They use petrol bombs and ball-bearings. Bottles and bricks. Air-guns and catapults. They run wires across roads to maim and decapitate police and former friends. But I would like to reassure all working miners, and the many striking miners who wish to return to their jobs, that the Board has begun a comprehensive review of security for all working miners and their families. We are well aware of the Union's tactic of visiting and intim-idating the sick and elderly parents of working miners. We condemn out of hand these attacks against the sick, the old and the lonely. These are the very members of society that the Union is supposedly pledged to defend. Measures are being taken as I speak to ensure that no working miner, or member of his family, is ever again subject to the horrific assault suffered by Mr Clarke in his own home. Thank you.'

Richard Clarke nods. The Chairman nods. The press nod. Every-one nods.

The nurses come to clear the room of the guests and the press.

The Jew steps outside to talk to the police about the progress they're making.

Neil Fontaine makes calls on hospital phones. Neil Fontaine makes calls to arms –

Neil has drawn up a list of potential recruits for the Jew's private plan –

The Jew's private army for Pit Land Security.

Neil spies Grey Fox in the corridor. Grey Fox has things to say to the Jew –

How his wife has left him. Taken his kids. How he's too sick with worry to work.

Neil Fontaine shakes his head. Neil Fontaine says he's sorry. Really very sorry.

346

The former Grey Fox sits in the hospital corridor with his head in his hands.

Neil Fontaine goes out to find the Jew. The Jew is standing alone in the car park –

The light is fading. Night forming. The light failing. Night falling –

The Jew asks aloud, 'How long will it be before these thugs murder someone?'

The Mechanic parks well away. He waits until it's dark. Night. He goes to the boot. The trunk. He takes out the rucksack. The spade. He walks through the fields. The streams. He comes to the trees. The branches. He hides in the hedgerow. The bushes. He covers his face in mud. Dirt. He digs a hole. A pit. He gathers branches. Leaves. He gets into the hole. The ground. He pulls the branches over the top of him. In his hide –

The Mechanic watches. The Mechanic waits –

For the headlights to come and the Rover to stop. The car door to open and close. For the feet to carry the shopping up the path. The cottage door to open and not close.

The Mechanic pushes away the branches. The leaves. He gets out of the hole. The pit. He walks down to the cottage –

Up the path. To the open door of the very last place you'd think to look.

The Mechanic steps inside. He says, 'Penny for your thoughts, Jen.'

Jennifer drops her shopping. Jennifer whispers Neil's name –

She calls out Neil's name. Shouts out Neil's name. Screams out Neil's name for –

The very last time.

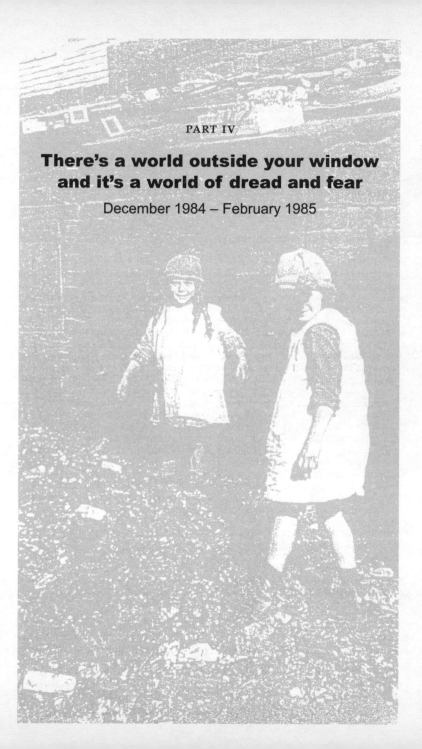

PART IV

There's a world outside your window and it's a world of dread and fear

December 1984 – February 1985

Total darkness again – Had its own rhythms, did strike. Life of its own. Peaks and troughs. There'd be storms and there'd be quiet. Quiet and then storms again. Now it was quiet again. Quietest it had ever been. Tense, though. Now some had gone back from **village**. Rumour. Lot of rumour. Folk would stop us in street to tell us Alan from their road hadn't picked up his parcel in over two week. That them in 16 had just come back from Canaries and how could they do that if he were still out, like? It was building. I could feel it – Christmas coming. General Winter on horizon. Power cuts not far behind him. Due a harsh winter and all – One last storm. Then home straight – That's what I told myself. That's what I said, Home straight – *Touch my nose with my finger. Not see my finger* – Mary had taken extra shifts up at factory, so I'd make breakfast and wash up before I went down Welfare. First her and our Jackie thought it was a bit of a laugh, me in **kitchen**. It wasn't that funny now. Not that I couldn't fry a couple of eggs. Bit of bacon. But it was just another of them signs. Signs that things weren't right. Least with them both working I had something to cook – Lot that didn't. Bloody lot – I put breakfast onto plates and took it through. Mary had scissors and glue out, cutting up bloody paper fore anyone had had a chance to read thing. For her scrapbook. *True History of Great Strike for Jobs*, that was what she called it. Filled three books now. Most of it were lies, said so herself. Bloody lies, she'd say as she cut stuff out. Tory bloody lies. But what she'd do was, under all lies she cut out, she'd then write truth of matter. Even had two of books signed by King Arthur himself – Just another way to pass time, I suppose. Between news – That was all we seemed to do these days, wait for bloody news to come on. Then it was all about money – Fines, sequestration. Receiver – Like that was only thing that mattered. It was only thing that fucking mattered to them on other side. Money – There were blokes down **Welfare** who read three papers a day. Then there were them that sat at home, glued to teletext. Not much else to do. Not now – Flying had dropped off since Dinnington last month. Branches just didn't have brass to keep sending lads out – Only got about five hundred turning out for a mass picket now. Police had that contained, no bother. Didn't even let lads shout. Heard tales of some blokes being done for glaring at scabs, police making lads stand with their eyes on floor – Nick you for sneezing, some of them. Just to get two days' paid leave and expenses when you went to court – If they couldn't charge you, they'd take you for a drive. Throw you out back of their van – Parachuting tests, they called it. Bastards got away with bloody murder – Had our own pit to picket anyway. Everyone did – That and coal picking. That was what most lads did – Picked coal. Picketed pit. Read papers and watched news – That was all there was now. That and worry. That was it – I was down Welfare most of time now. I was writing a lot of letters and making visits – I felt bad about some of them that had gone in. Felt we could have prevented it, like. Not all of them. Because some of them were just like that – Whatever you'd have done, it wouldn't have been enough. Folk were just born like that. Or their wives – But couple of them had been on their own. There'd been a death in family or wife had left them. Board had taken advantage of their weakness and got them back in. Now we'd set up a sort of monitoring system. Regulars at Welfare would let us know if anything had happened to anyone. Ears to ground. If anyone were having any problems, either with money or family worries. Then I'd go up and see them. Try to help them out if we could. Tell them about loans we could arrange for them through Union. That sort of thing. I'd send a letter first, then follow it up with a visit. Take a parcel out to them. Especially if they weren't in village and were somewhere further away. I kept writing to them that had already gone back and all. I didn't advertise it because there were them that wouldn't have had them back anyway – *Once a scab, always a scab* – That lot. That was what scabs thought themselves, though – They'd crossed line. No turning back – I'd talk to some of them on telephone.

The Fortieth Week

They had lost control. Lost control of their money. Lost control of their membership –

Two of their members in South Wales had dropped a concrete block from a bridge onto a taxi taking a working miner to Merthyr Vale Colliery. The block had gone through the windscreen. The taxi-driver had been killed. He had two children, his wife expecting their third at Christmas. Two young miners from the Oakdale and Taff Merthyr collieries had been arrested and charged with murder –

They were thugs and bullies. Hooligans. Terrorists and now murderers –

They were all lepers now –

Their offices were their hospitals. Their villages, their colonies.

There was silence in every office on every floor of every one of their buildings. There was silence in the street, their buckets empty now –

Just buckets of rain. Buckets of pain –

Bomb scares and death threats came by the hour. Letter bombs in the hate mail.

The President was frightened. Frightened of the outside. Frightened of the inside. The President didn't trust anyone but Len and Joan –

The crows circling the monastery. The wolves at the gates –

The Moderates were meeting. Meeting with the TUC and with the Labour Party. Meeting in corridors. Meeting in motorway hotels. The backrooms of pubs –

Meeting and talking –

Talking of breakaways. Talking of returns without settlement or returns with a settlement. Hands over their mouths. Behind their backs –

Talking and planning –

Planning to sell out. Planning to cave in and compromise. Planning their coup –

Scheming and plotting –

Plotting his downfall. His descent and demise. Conspiring and dreaming. Dreaming of the President's defeat –

His destruction and death –

The President caught between the rocks of the Right and the hard places of the Left. Cornered and trapped, he lived behind locked doors. He spoke in secret and talked on to tape. Taped all transmissions, recorded all reports. Joan cooked his food. Len tested it. The President ate only small amounts, staggered in stages. He drank only boiled water. The President left the locked doors of his office only for rallies. He travelled only in the Rover. Driven only by Len –

Len paid miners to watch the Rover twenty-four hours a day. Len paid men to watch the miners watching the Rover twenty-four hours a day –

From Friday 30 November 1984.

Today was Monday and tonight the President was to appear at a rally in Stoke. There had been bomb scares and death threats all day. Men with muffled voices had phoned local radio stations and whispered their warnings.

The President took Terry Winters and Paul with him. The President never let Terry out of his sight. The President had Terry and Paul stand before him on the stage. The President shared the platform with the Labour Leader. Terry Winters stared out into the spotlights –

He watched for the nooses. He waited for the snipers.

The Leader spoke first. The Leader said the violence had to stop –

The violence *must* stop and the violence must stop *now*.

Hecklers called him a traitor. Judas. Scab! Scab! Scab!

The hecklers were ejected. The Leader given a standing ovation.

The President stood up behind Terry and Paul –

The Town Hall fell silent –

The President's voice was uncertain here. The President's words were unsure now. The President admitted his deep shock at the tragic death of the taxi-driver –

He was given a standing ovation. The Town Hall sang the *Red Flag* –

Then the Town Hall fell silent again.

Len went for the car. Terry and Paul shielded the President as he left the building. The President sat in the back of the Rover between them, drenched in sweat and shaking. Len stayed in the fast lane all the way back to Yorkshire. Len dropped Terry off first. There was a police car parked outside his house –

There was a police car parked outside all their houses now.

These have been most fortuitous days for the Jew –

The murder of this taxi-driver in South Wales. The appointment of the receiver. The resignations of a few more Suits –

'I could not have planned it better had I tried, Neil,' muses the Jew.

The Jew is sitting pretty behind his desk and a huge new advertisement –

It'll pay every miner who's not at work to read this.

The Jew reorganizes his desk into two simple halves –

To the right are the reports on the progress of the receiver and the sequestrators. To the left are the reports on the progress of the National Working Miners' Committee.

The Jew tracks the information from both left and right on his graphs and maps. The Jew walks round to the front of his desk. The Jew touches his graphs and maps –

The rising blue lines and the many blue pins –

The Jew runs a finger up and down North Derbyshire –

'Is it not a beautiful thing, Neil?' asks the Jew. 'To win?'

Neil Fontaine picks red pins from out of the carpet. Neil Fontaine nods.

'There were but three hundred and forty-three local lions in May,' says the Jew. 'To think there are now four thousand and forty-three in North Derbyshire alone, Neil.'

Neil Fontaine nods again. Neil Fontaine puts the red pins in the bin –

'Four thousand and forty-three of them!'

But there is a price (there is always a price) –

The Jew has asked Neil to provide security for the homes of every working miner; every single working miner; every single home –

Neil jumps at the chance. The chance of a ghost. The ghost of a chance –

He leaves the Jew to sit pretty at Hobart House. He makes the usual calls –

Jerry Witherspoon. Roger Vaughan. The General –

No one answers the phone. No one takes a message. No one returns his calls.

He makes the usual rounds. He knocks on the usual doors –

The Special Services Club. The Institute of Professional Investigators. The TA –

But no one answers the door. No one knows his face. Remembers his name –

This is how it feels to be out in the cold.

He rents two post-office boxes and he places two adverts in the right magazines. He reserves a room in a hotel out by Heathrow. He pays cash money for all these things –

He uses the name Mr Farrant.

Fuck them. Fuck them all, thinks Neil Fontaine –

Promises Neil Fontaine.

The President was staying in Sheffield until the very last minute. Paul and Terry Winters travelled down to London separately. Paul in second class. Terry in first. Paul and Terry checked in to the County separately. Paul got a single room with a sink. Terry got a double with a private bath. Paul and Terry had both registered under assumed names –

Paul chose the name Smith. Terry chose Verloc –

Terry had been rehabilitated. But not by Paul. He had had a choice –

The President had had no choice.

Terry and Paul took separate taxis to the High Court.

The lawyers representing the working miners had claimed the Union trustees, including the President, were not fit and proper persons to be in charge of other people's money. Not fit and proper persons –

Including the President.

The High Court had agreed. The High Court had removed the five trustees. Including the President. The High Court had appointed a receiver to take control of the Union's funds and assets.

The receiver was a Mr Booker. Mr Booker planned to leave for Luxembourg. Mr Booker intended to seek the release of the Union's five million pounds held in a small private bank account there –

Immediately.

Terry and Paul had come to the High Court to appeal. To swear not to move the money. To assure the court they would abide by its jurisdiction.

The lawyers for the working miners said such words were worthless. The lawyers said the Union had embarked on a concerted course of action to hide its funds –

From Sheffield to the Isle of Man. From the Isle of Man to Dublin –

From Dublin to New York. From New York to Zurich –

From Zurich to Luxembourg.

The lawyers said the Union did not recognize the court. The Union had not purged its contempt. The Union continued to be in serious and deliberate contempt of orders, which placed the funds they held on behalf of their members in jeopardy.

The lawyers said the Union, including the President, were not to be trusted –

Especially the President.

The High Court agreed. The High Court asked for the word of the President.

The President was not in court.

Terry and Paul asked for a ten-minute adjournment. Terry and Paul rushed out to the phones. Terry and Paul called Sheffield. Terry and Paul asked for the President –

The President was not in Sheffield. The President was travelling to London –

The President could not be reached.

Terry and Paul went back before the High Court. Terry and Paul told the judge that the President was on his way to the court. Terry and Paul asked for an adjournment until tomorrow. Terry and Paul said that then the President would appear.

The High Court did not agree. The High Court rejected their appeal –

The appointment of Mr Booker as receiver stood –

Mr Booker held the purse strings now. Mr Booker was the boss.

Mr Booker left for Luxembourg –

Immediately.

Paul took a taxi to Congress House to wait for the President and brief the TUC. Terry took a taxi to sit at a table in the bar at the County and pray –

Pray for miracles. Pray for resurrection. Pray for redemption –

Terry closed his eyes. Terry bowed his head. Terry said his prayers.

'Your lips are moving again, Comrade.'

Terry opened his eyes. Terry looked up. Terry crossed himself.

Bill Reed sat down. Bill Reed put an envelope on the table.

Terry looked at the envelope. Terry looked at Bill. Terry said another prayer.

Bill tapped the envelope. Bill winked. Bill said, 'Gotcha.'

Terry picked up the envelope. Terry opened it. Terry took out the contents –

'Hubert Harold Booker, come on down,' laughed Bill Reed. 'Because, tonight, this is your life.'

Terry read the contents. Terry was amazed. Terry looked at Bill –

Bill looked at his watch. Bill said, 'The President's train is just arriving.'

'This is dynamite,' said Terry. 'You must take it to the President, Comrade.'

Bill shook his head. Bill said, 'The Fourth Estate have copies. That's enough.'

'But the President should know what you have done for him,' said Terry.

Bill shook his head again. Bill said, 'The President doesn't need to know.'

'But you would be forgiven,' said Terry. 'Your friendship restored.'

Bill stood up. Bill said, 'Secret loves are best kept secret, don't you think?'

Terry looked down at the table. The marks and the scars in the wood.

Bill Reed put his hand on Terry's shoulder. Bill Reed said, 'You go to him.'

And Terry went to him. Terry ran to him. Terry met with him –

The President, Terry and all the President's men met with the TUC for six hours. The President asked the TUC to take out leases on all the Union's property. The President asked the TUC to pay the wages of all the Union's employees –

The TUC said they would need legal advice. The TUC were worried they would be held in contempt for assisting the National Union of Mineworkers –

The President shook his head. The President rolled his eyes.

The President and all the President's men met the National Executive Committee. The NEC voted eleven to six to recommend that the Union's cash be brought back to Britain, bringing the Union back into compliance with the law –

The President had supported the recommendation –

Terry was amazed. Terry was anxious –

The NEC were recommending to the Special Delegate Conference that the Union pay the £200,000 fine for contempt and obey all future court actions –

That there could be no disciplinary measures against scabs –

That they would have to hold a national ballot, if the court so decreed –

That the strike was unofficial –

Terry was appalled. Terry was afraid.

The meeting broke up in the small hours. Len drove the President and the ladies back to the Barbican. Terry and Paul walked back up to the County –

They took different routes.

Mr Verloc had messages waiting. Mr Verloc asked for an early morning alarm call and for *The Times*, the *Telegraph*, the *Guardian*, the *Mirror* and the *Morning Star*.

Mr Verloc did not sleep. Mr Verloc did not need his alarm call –

Mr Verloc read the headlines. Mr Verloc read the stories –

Hubert Harold Booker was vice-president of a Derbyshire Conservative Association. Hubert Harold Booker was an ex-Tory councillor. Hubert Harold Booker was a member of the Institute of Directors –

Hubert Harold Booker was also in for a shock and the sack.

Mr Verloc ate breakfast alone with half a smile and a slice of toast.

Terry Winters walked up to Congress House for the Special Delegate Conference. The President had called the delegates to discuss the legal assault upon the NUM –

To debate the three options. To decide on the best course to take.

'Comrades, we will win this strike because the issue is right,' said the President. 'No matter what actions are taken against the NUM or its officers, it will not deter people in this Union who fight for what they know to be right: the right to work.'

The two hundred and twenty delegates applauded their president.

The President sat down. Paul then stood up and outlined the options –

'The Union could ignore the courts. The Union could take no action whatsoever. The Union could recognize the supremacy of the High Court and thus purge its contempt; pay its fine, but gain the release of its funds.'

The two hundred and twenty delegates argued. The delegates squabbled and spat. The two hundred and twenty delegates fought. They bickered and they brawled –

Terry got a message from Mike in Luxembourg. Terry went to the phone –

'Comrade, the bank have refused Booker admittance,' Mike Sullivan told Terry. 'The bank won't hand over any money to any third party without a local court order. Booker is going to have to go to court here in Luxembourg to establish the validity of their claim. The plan's worked!'

'Of course,' said Terry. 'Didn't I say it would?'

Terry hung up. Terry went back inside the conference to break the good news –

'Good news, Comrades,' shouted Terry. 'The receiver has been defeated.'

There was applause for Terry Winters. There were accolades for Terry Winters –

The two hundred and twenty special delegates voted 139 to 80 to reject the moderate recommendation of the National Executive to bring their bacon back home to Britain. The money was to stay right where it was –

In the more than capable hands of their Comrade Chief Executive –

Terry Winters was absolved. Terry Winters was astonished.

The Kalamares in Inverness Mews, the Capannina on Romilly Street, the Scandia Room in the Piccadilly Hotel, the Icelandic Steakhouse on Haymarket –

In 1969. In 1972. In 1974. In 1979 –

These were the times and the places where Malcolm Morris had sat and stared into the silences and the spaces –

The loving wife he'd never met and the whore he had. The lovely children they'd never had and the abortions they had.

The waiters did not bring him the menu. The waiters did not take his order –

Malcolm Morris was nothing but a ghost now. Nothing but a shadow –

A shadow in the back where the light did not reach.

Mr Verloc woke up in his double room at the County. He was naked in his private bath. The water was cold, the shower still running. Mr Verloc dried and dressed himself for the day ahead. Mr Verloc ate breakfast alone with a sore cock and extra toast –

Terry had known it was risky. Diane had known it too. But they just didn't care. Diane wanted to fuck Mr Verloc in his double room at the County. In his private bath. And Mr Verloc wanted to fuck Diane to thank her for all the things she'd done. So Terry and Diane had waited until the President was back at the Barbican; Paul and Dick in the Crown & Anchor with everyone else. Then Terry had gone to King's Cross for Diane –

And no one saw them. Not even the moon.

Diane had fucked Mr Verloc in his double room at the County. In his private bath. Then Mr Verloc had fucked Diane to thank her for all the things she had done –

And no one heard them. Not even the man pacing about in the room upstairs.

Mr Verloc finished his breakfast. Mr Verloc went back up to his room to pack. Mr Verloc checked out before Mr Smith.

Terry spent the morning back at Congress House on the phone to Luxembourg –

'The bank won't let us move the money until after the court has made its decision as to the validity of the receiver's claim against us,' said Mike in Luxembourg.

'Find out all you can about the judges,' Terry told him. 'And fax it to Bill Reed.'

Terry hung up. Terry went upstairs to the President and the TUC Seven –

The President wasn't asking for sympathy. Just sympathy strikes –

But the Seven said they would need legal advice. The Seven were still worried they would be held in contempt for assisting the National Union of Mineworkers –

The President shook his head again. The President rolled his eyes again –

The President went back to Sheffield.

Terry and Paul went back to court. Terry and Paul took separate taxis.

Hubert Harold Booker had asked to be allowed to resign.

Terry and Paul agreed. They argued he was not a fit and proper person.

The court did not agree. But the court accepted Mr Booker's resignation.

Terry and Paul asked that the Union be taken out of receivership. Terry and Paul argued that the trustees of the Union were fit and proper persons –

Including the President.

Terry and Paul argued that the trustees were only following the orders of the Union's National Executive when the money was transferred from British to foreign banks. Terry and Paul argued that the trustees, including the President, were therefore very fit and proper persons to be in charge of other people's money –

Fit and proper persons. Including the President –

Especially the President.

The High Court did not agree. The High Court appointed a new receiver to take control of the Union's funds and assets.

The receiver was a Matthew Ruskin. Mr Ruskin planned to leave for Dublin. Mr Ruskin intended to seek the release of the Union's two and a half million pounds held in a secret bank account there –

Immediately.

Terry and Paul asked for an adjournment. Time to appeal.

The High Court did not agree. The High Court rejected their appeal –

The appointment of Mr Ruskin as receiver stood –

Mr Ruskin held the purse strings now. Mr Ruskin was the boss.

Mr Ruskin left for Dublin –

Immediately.

Terry and Paul travelled back to Sheffield separately. First and second class –

There was still silence on every floor of their building. Still silence in the street –

Just the buckets of rain. The buckets of pain –

The bomb scares and death threats still coming. The letter bombs in the hate mail.

Terry Winters drove back to his three-bedroom home in the suburbs of Sheffield. There were no lights on, the police car still parked outside –

They were all still lepers. Second class, the lot of them –
Forever lepers now.

Tell them it weren't like that. That if they stopped scabbing they'd be welcomed back – They didn't believe me. They saw graffiti all over village – *We won't forget scabs* – Drawings of gallows and nooses. Wall of shame up by gates. Signs in pubs and shop windows telling them their business wasn't wanted – They weren't daft. Not that daft, anyway – They heard words on picket line as bus sped them inside. They saw faces filled with hate – They'd gone too far. They knew it – They were lost to most folk. Dead – *Hammering in distance. Maybe here. Near* – I went over to Silverwood on Monday for **Panel** – Just Mondays at moment. Unless something sudden came up – No more new faces going in. Big back-to-work push had finished. Time to take advantage of their bribes had passed. Our own brass drying up, what with sequestrators and receiver. More bloody cars packing up and all. Packing up or smashed up. Johnny reckoned that had been bloody plan all along – Police had waited until High Court had begun to bite. Then they'd gone in with their truncheons into cars – Not just what had happened to our lads at Brodsworth. Happened everywhere and all on same day – Tyres had been slashed. Windscreens smashed – Knew it meant we wouldn't be able to fly as much and that saved them brass, I suppose. Main thing now was taking care of business at your own pit – It was twenty-four hour a day now. Front and back – Broke it down into six shifts. Each shift were four hour. Long enough now winter were here. Lads had used this old horse-box to put a little hut up there on front gate. They'd stuck a stove and couple of car seats from scrap inside. Them on back gate just used old snap cabin that was already there. Folk had their preferences, both for time and for folk they'd be stood with. There were family commitments and what-have-you to take into consideration, too. I was in **Welfare** doing that up when Barry came in to tell me latest – Fucking hell, I said. You're joking? Barry shook his head. I got my coat and we walked up to Pit. Under-manager was waiting for us by hut. Morning, Pete, he said. I said, There's

floor lift, is there? That what you saying, is it? Under-manager had a big drawing of flood. He said, Just take a look, Pete. Barry and under-manager held corners of paper so I could have a good look. We all got your letter, I said. But what do you expect us to do? Pete, there has to be some safety work done or – Not by my men, I told him. They cross a picket line for any reason, they're scabs – They came in before in summer, he said. You all helped us then – Aye, I said. There was no picket line then, though, was there? No picket line then because there were no bloody scabs. That's why we helped you. And what thanks did we get? You took bloody scabs back. That's what thanks we got. Get them to bloody help you – We didn't want scabs back, he said. Board made us take them. We had to – That's as-may-be, I said. But there's a picket line now and no one will cross it – So what do we do? he said. Just let waters keep rising? Let all them bloody scabs you got in there deal with it, I told him. There's not enough of them and them we have are useless and you know it. I said, You shouldn't have took them back then, should you? He shook his head. He said, Pit will flood and then there'll be no bloody work for anyone. That what you want? Look, I said. I'll phone Barnsley and get Union engineer in. See what he says – Thank you, Pete, said under-manager. Thank you very much – *Smell of wood. Mice* – Tommy Robb came out minute I phoned. *Click-click.* Tommy was Union's mining engineer for this area. He met Barry and me and manager and under-manager. Picket had been taken off for duration of our visit. Tommy wanted to go down straight away. This was a problem because only folk doing winding were members of management union who shouldn't have been anywhere near bloody winding gear in first place. There was no way Tommy and me and Barry were off down if they were doing winding. That meant I had to get in touch with Winders' delegate. *Click-click.* I called him up and he came out to wind us down. That was what I was dreading. Fucking dreading it, I was – Been best part of a year since I was down there. Reason more

The Forty-first Week

Monday 10 – Sunday 16 December 1984

The Jew has spent the weekend in retreat at Colditz. He has gathered his majors and generals. He has had them pack their black suits and ties. He puts on his leather flying-jacket. Neil Fontaine performs the safety checks on the helicopter. They eat hearty breakfasts in the Jew's enormous kitchen. Then the Jew flies the leaders of the National Working Miners' Committee down to Cardiff –

The cloud is heavy. The visibility poor. The journey rough. The passengers green.

Neil Fontaine has hired a limousine for them. He drives them from the airport to the crematorium. The National Working Miners' Committee smell of cigarettes and last night's ale. They argue among themselves about money. Two of them vomit into carrier bags at the side of the road. The Jew sits in the back among his majors and generals and looks at his watch. They are late for the funeral of Derek Atkins.

Neil Fontaine takes two wreaths out of the boot of the limousine –

'You have paid the supreme price for democracy.'

He hands the two wreaths to the National Working Miners' Committee –

'In glory may you rest in peace.'

The National Working Miners' Committee go into the crematorium.

The Jew waits in the car with Neil Fontaine. The Jew does not speak.

Rain sweeps down from the Brecon Beacons and the Black Mountains –

Down and out into the mouth of the Severn.

Half an hour later, the family of the murdered taxi-driver leave the crematorium.

Neil Fontaine opens the back door of the limousine. He holds an umbrella over the Jew. The Jew walks up to the family. The Jew embraces the dead taxi-driver's common-law wife under their dif-

ferent umbrellas. He puts an envelope full of cash into her wet
hands –

'Your common-law husband did not die in vain,' the Jew tells the
young widow. 'We shall fight on and we shall win.'

Malcolm Morris asked for his key to Room 707. Malcolm took the lift. He
walked down the corridor past the bathrooms –

The rooms were all empty. The rooms were all quiet.

Malcolm unlocked the door. He stepped inside. He hung the Do Not
Disturb *sign on the outside handle of the door. He closed the door. Locked it.*
He took off his shoes. Placed them on the double bed. He drew the curtains.
He took off his trousers. Placed them on the bed. He took off his jacket. Placed
it on the bed. He stood before the mirror. He unwrapped the bandages. Took
the cotton wool out of his ears. He looked into the mirror –

A new face in an old place.

The army had taught him how to live. How to survive. To stay alive for
'85. The army had taught him to expect the knock on the door in the middle
of the night. The drive out into the woods. The nozzle of the gun at the back
of the skull. The spade and the hole. But then they would never know –

Never know the truth from the lies. The lies from the truth –

Never know the secrets sold. The secrets saved –

The things he'd kept up his sleeve.

The army had taught him how to live. How to survive. Ulster honed those
habits, whetted the ways –

To live among death.

Then the service had brought him back. Brought him home. To live alone
in a house with a car and a pension plan. Brought him back to listen. To lis-
ten for the knock on the door in the middle of the night. The drive out into
the woods. The gun at the back of the skull. The spades and the holes –

The truths and the lies. The secrets saved and the secrets sold –

The things up his sleeve.

The service had brought him back. Back home –

To die among life.

Malcolm Morris picked up the phone. He dialled the number. Made the
call.

The Jew is livid again. Fucking furious this time. Yesterday was the
first day coal had come up from the Yorkshire seams since the strike
began. It was a victory, a famous victory in the long campaign –

Miners mining at Manton.

It should have been front-page news. Headlines for them. Death knells for Stalin –

But no.

The Minister has hijacked the Jew's agenda. The Minister has been holding secret meetings with the TUC. The TUC have gone over the heads of the NUM. The Minister has gone over the head of the Chairman. The Chairman and the Jew –

'No fucking wonder the numbers have dried up, Neil,' shouts the Jew –

The Jew must guard against weakness. Inside and out. Outside and in –

The Jew cannot rest. The Jew must not rest.

Neil Fontaine rights the hotel furniture. He picks up the morning papers. He nods. Neil Fontaine drives the Jew to Hobart House. He waits outside the Chairman's office –

The Chairman is already livid. Already fucking furious –

'That damned junkie hands out one hundred grand to them,' shouts the Chairman. 'Hundred fucking grand to the bloody Red Guard for Christmas. Just like that!'

'I think,' says the Jew, 'we should pay the altruistic Noble Lord a visit.'

Neil Fontaine drives the Chairman and the Jew to a private Harley Street clinic. Neil Fontaine accompanies the Chairman and the Jew to a private upstairs room –

The Jew knows Lord John of old. Lord John wakes up to greet him long and lost –

'Stephen, sweet Stephen!' he shrills. 'Where have you been all my life?'

The Jew sits down on the edge of the bed. He has Lord John's hand in his own.

'How frail you look, dear Johnny,' says the Jew. 'Are they treating you well?'

'The nurses are harridans, Stephen,' pouts the Lord. 'Harridans!'

'Johnny,' says the Jew. 'I'd like you to meet the Chairman of the Coal Board.'

The Chairman steps forward. The Chairman nods, but does not offer his hand.

The Lord giggles. He whispers in the Jew's ear. He hides his face in his pillows. He peeps out from behind his fingers. He asks, 'Did he bring me grapes, Sweet Stevie?'

'Johnny,' says the Jew, 'did you give money to the miners?'

The Lord sits upright in his bed. He tidies himself and says, 'And what if I did?'

The Jew slaps Lord John across his face. The Jew shouts, 'Idiot! Fool!'

The Lord collapses in tears into his sheets. He pulls his pillow to him. He hugs it.

'Do you want your dear mummy to work in Woolworth's, Johnny?' asks the Jew. 'In a uniform? With her name on a tag?'

The Noble Lord shakes his head.

'That's what their president has in store for our Queen,' says the Jew.

The Noble Lord sobs.

'Just imagine what he has in mind for you, Junkie Johnny,' says the Jew.

The Noble Lord looks out from behind his pillow. He asks, 'What, Stevie? What?'

The Jew turns to Neil Fontaine. Neil Fontaine hands the big envelope to the Jew. The Jew opens the envelope. He lays out the photographs on the Lord's bed –

Ten photographs of beaten faces; of broken bones and burnt-out homes.

Lord John stares. He swallows. He says, 'To me? They plan to do this to me?'

'Much worse,' says the Chairman. 'Much, much worse.'

Lord John pales. He puts his hand to his mouth. He says, 'What have I done?'

The Jew goes to the Lord's bedside drawer. He takes out the Lord's chequebook. 'How much did you give them, Johnny?' he asks. 'How much?'

'I feel such a fool,' says the Lord. 'Fool! Fool! Fool that I am!'

'How much, Johnny?'

'Ten thousand? One hundred thousand?' he says. 'I can't remember now.'

The Jew opens the Lord's chequebook. The Jew writes out a cheque –

'This is one for two hundred and fifty thousand pounds,' he says. 'Just sign it.'

'Then everything will be all right?' asks the Lord.

The Jew nods. The Chairman nods. The Jew hands the Lord his pen.

'The Queen won't have to work in Woolworth's any more, will she?'

'No, Johnny,' says the Jew. 'The Queen will be fine, if you just sign that.'

The Lord smiles. The Lord signs the cheque. The Lord hands it to the Jew.

'Thank you very much,' says the Jew. 'You've turned a bad day into a good one.'

The President had appeared before Rotherham Magistrates over charges of obstructing the Queen's Highway at Orgreave on May 30 1984. The magistrates had found him guilty. The magistrates had fined him two hundred and fifty pounds, plus seven hundred and fifty pounds costs. Meanwhile, the government had agreed to meet the entire costs incurred by the receiver and the sequestrators, and more High Court actions had been brought to make the national and area officials of the Union personally liable for monies spent on the strike. The Nottinghamshire Area had also voted heavily in favour of a new constitution to give them greater autonomy from the National Union of Lepers –

The President was back locked behind his door. Not touching his food.

Len Glover came into Terry Winter's office. Len didn't knock –

Terry was sat under the portrait of the President. Terry looked up at Len –

Loyal Len had a bandage across his nose and two black eyes. Someone had thrown a tin of cat food and a can of extra-hold hairspray at the President –

They had missed the President.

Len said, 'The President wants you to come to Goldthorpe with him.'

Terry shrugged. Terry nodded. Terry put his coat back on.

Loyal Len drove. Terry Winters sat in the back of the Rover with the President. The President talked about moving the families of Union employees into the St James's building. For protection –

Insurance –

Terry tried not to listen to the President. Terry didn't want to think about Theresa. Think about Christopher, Timothy or Louise. Terry had enough to think about.

Len parked outside the Goldthorpe Miners' Welfare Club. Len paid four local lads to watch the Rover. Len and Terry rushed the President out of the back of the car –

Up the steps. Into the hall. Through the crowd –

The rapturous welcome. The thunderous applause –

To the stage and onto the podium.

The President stood on the stage. The President poised at the podium –

The branch banner hanging behind him on the wall.

The President turned to see the branch banner. The President stared at the banner. The President turned back to the hall. The hall packed to capacity. Eager and expectant. The President closed his eyes. The President bowed his head –

The hall silent.

The President opened his eyes. The President raised his head. The President said –

'You are not saying: "Here we go." You are saying: "Here we are" –

'We are here and have found ourselves!

'And with that spirit, this government and their courts can put their receivers in; they can put their sequestrators in; they can smear us and they can attack us –

'But there's one thing for certain: provided we stand firmly together, your Union –

'Not *my* union, not any *receiver's* union –

'*Your* Union is on its way to the greatest victory in history!'

There was rapture. There was thunder –

The President bowed his head. The banner hanging behind him –

Rapture and thunder –

Terry looked at his watch. The clock ticking. The storm soon upon them all.

The Chairman goes home to the States for Christmas. The Jew moves down the hall into the Chairman's office. He cannot go home. He must stay to guard against weakness. Guard against defeat –

Inside and out. Outside and in –

There are still Suits about. There are still Suits out to settle –

Informal talks. Preliminary discussions –

The papers full of Christmas cheer. Hints of hope. Peace in the coalfields.

The Jew shows some Suits the front door and the street. The Jew sends others on compulsory leave. The Chairman has given him permission. Permission to use his name. The Jew uses it. Uses it to guard against weakness –

Defeat.

There are still new battles to win. New campaigns to run –

Here's something for every miner to think about in the New Year.

The Jew already knows his New Year's resolution. It's the one he always makes –

For the worldwide defeat of Marxism, Communism and all forms of Socialism.

The Jew has good reason to believe his wish might finally arrive in '85.

The Prime Minister has invited the Jew to dinner with Mikhail Gorbachev. Mr Gorbachev is from the Politburo. Mr Gorbachev is tipped for the top. The Prime Minister says Mr Gorbachev is a man they can do business with.

The Jew hopes the PM is right. The Jew will put Mr Gorbachev to the test. The Jew will ask Mr Gorbachev to stop all Soviet support for the NUM –

For the worldwide defeat of Marxism, Communism and all forms of Socialism.

The Jew can't wait to meet Mikhail Sergeyevich Gorbachev –

For the New Year to begin. For this Christmas to end –

Foul feast of the pagan and the Roman.

The Jew hates Christmas. Neil, too.

than any other I got involved with doing Union – *Hammering stops. Mice gone* – I didn't want to be down there any more. I hated it. But I wasn't going to show it today. Not in front of management. Not in front of scabs – They'd actually had sense to lock scabs up when we went through yard. Must have stuck them in offices or somewhere. Thing was, I was that worried about going back down that I didn't think about scabs. I got into **cage** with Tommy and Barry and manager and we went down – *Different noise now* – No one spoke until we got **down there** and Tommy started to have a look about. Took him for ever, it did – Fucking for ever. I thought I was going to collapse. That bloody nervous – Slightest sound set us off and there's always strange fucking noises down there. Especially with water. I don't think I spoke once whole time I was down there – Three and a half fucking hours. It was worst when we were going back up – Thing was out of practice and it was stopping and starting like an old fucking woman. Longest fucking ride up I'd ever had – It were worth it, though, I suppose. Tommy said it wasn't that bad. There was no need for lads to go in. There was enough of management there to deal with it. Thing now was to get message out to all lads. Fucking rumours flying about – Pit was falling to bits. Pit was going to be lost. Be no pit to go back to – Must have been coming from scabs, most of it. Had to be. Even after we'd been down, there were still them that said we hadn't – That it was a lie and we'd never gone down. That pit was too flooded even to check on it. That it'd be shut before Christmas if lads didn't go back in and start on safety work – Pack of lies. Bloody lies – But fucking hell, did folk go on about it. They'd come up to you in street and call you a liar to your face – I couldn't be doing with it. Not now – I just gave them Tommy's number at Huddersfield Road. Told them to phone him themselves. Did my head in, to be honest. These fucking rumours – No end to them. To any of it – *Sound of hooves. Horses' hooves again* – Latest police trick was to take photos of folk up at **picket**

line. *Smile*. Lot of rumours again about why they were doing that. Folk reckoned it was because they were going through all film they had of mass pickets. Using photos to identify anyone who they'd caught on tape throwing. That way police could nick them and Board could sack them. Then there'd be no need for mass redundancies. Half of workforce would have already been sacked. That was rumour anyway. That and talk about privatization of pits, too. That was another big one doing rounds. This was reason why so many had got so agitated about flooding and general state of pit – No one was going to buy a broken pit, were they? Top of all that, you had business with Nottingham changing their rulebook. Moving closer to UDI – It was going to happen. That was obvious – Good riddance to bad rubbish, said most blokes. They'd come crawling back like last time – But then brave talk stopped and rumours started up about future of NUM. About what would happen if there were two unions and so on – Rumours. Tension – It was all scabs' doing. They had no shame these days – There was one older bloke who had been on bloody committee at one time. Had always claimed he was right Militant. Even been to Soviet Union with King Arthur once. Liked to tell you how it was paradise on Earth. Two of others had been two of hardest we'd had on picket lines. Dead keen, they'd been. Liked nothing better than a scrap with coppers. Had called first scab all names under sun. Now they were sat on scab bus, laughing and waving at all their old mates on picket line. It were these three who were behind all rumours – Rumours that filled emptiness. That was thing that made it worse – Never any bloody news to give lads. Rumours were all they had – Dark days now. Days when I'd walk round village and it was like walking round **village of dead** – Like one of them old photos or something. Little figures all thin and drawn – Their clothes hanging off them. Pushing their babies down to Welfare – Ladies going through bundles of other folk's clothes. Cast-offs and hand-me-downs – Putting tins and packets into boxes. Making three meals

The Forty-second Week

Monday 17 – Sunday 23 December 1984

The Right Honourable Member of Parliament met Malcolm Morris in the
underground car park –
  In the shadows at the back, where the lights did not quite reach –
  His mouth moved. His fingers pointed. He asked Malcolm questions –
  Malcolm could not answer. Malcolm could not hear –
  But Malcolm had the tapes.
  In the shadows at the back, where the lights did not reach –
  They would find the answers here. They would hear the tapes –
  These field recordings of the Dead.

Terry stuck two bitten fingers in his ears. They were playing carols in
the corridors again. For morale, said the Denims. Even the Tweeds
agreed. Terry took another three aspirins –
  Christmas. Christmas. Christmas –
  It was all anybody ever talked about. Phoned about. *Click-click –*
  Lorryloads of toys from France. From Poland. From Australia –
  Santa suits and plastic trees. Party hats and pantomimes –
  Turkeys and all the fucking trimmings –
  It was all anyone thought about. Cared about. Almost –
  Terry picked up his files. Just his files. He didn't need his calculator
these days.
  Terry locked the office. Terry took the stairs up to the Conference
Room –
  The lift was out of order.
  Terry tapped on the door. Terry went inside. Terry took his seat by
the exit –
  The Fat Man and his seven Fat Friends had just made their report –
  The report which said that efforts to block the supply of oil had had
little discernible effect; that there was no likelihood of crucial fuel
shortages at the generating stations; that prospects for an early settle-
ment of the dispute were remote –
  Remote.

So the Fat Man and his seven Fat Friends had been to see the Minister –

Again.

The President looked up with tired eyes at the Fat Man and his seven Fat Friends. The President wasn't sleeping. Dick wasn't. Paul. Len. Joan. Alice. Mike –

None of them were –

Always light, never dark.

'We don't want the TUC or anybody else to go along and argue a case that effectively undermines the NUM,' said the President again.

The Fat Man did not blink. Did not bat an eyelid. He said, 'What *do* you want?'

'Do you remember all the promises you gave in September?' asked the President. 'The decisions the TUC conference made? The financial support? The physical support? The practical support? The total support?'

The Fat Man did not flinch. Did not move a muscle. He said, 'I remember.'

'Good,' said the President. 'Because *that's* what we bloody want.'

The Fat Man flinched. That Fat Man said, 'It's too late now.'

'It's late, I'll give you that,' said the President. 'But not *too* late. *Never* too late.'

The Fat Man blinked. The Fat Man said, 'The entire TUC could be bankrupted. The entire movement in the hands of receivers and sequestrators –'

'Aye,' shouted the President. 'And there'd be battles and there'd be bloodshed. And the working class would as one rise like lions after slumber –

'In unvanquishable number. For we are many and they are few –'

Terry Winters started to cough. Terry Winters couldn't stop –

Terry made his excuses. His exit. His way back down the stairs.

Terry took more aspirins. His head against the glass. Terry watched the city –

The Christmas lights. The street lights. The shop lights. The office lights –

Always light, never dark.

Terry looked at the calendar. He looked at his watch. Terry was going to be late –

He locked the office. He ran down the stairs. He went for his car –

The remains of Roche Abbey had been chosen for the rendezvous –

Terry drove out through Rotherham, across the M18 and South at Maltby.

The dark Sirocco was already parked, waiting for Terry.

Terry pulled off the A634. Terry parked and Terry waited –

There was a tap on his window. There was a torch in his face –

Terry put one hand up to shield his eyes and released the car boot with his other.

Then the torch was gone. The boot full.

Malcolm Morris pressed play. Malcolm played it all back. All of it –

The voices from the shadows at the back, where the silences did not quite reach –

'– first heard in a room with bright lights and no windows and a locked door, screaming I came into this place. It was Easter Sunday and I was on my back on the bed in her blood, kicking and screaming. The woman in the blue apron took me in her arms and scrubbed me clean of the blood and wrapped me in soft white sheets and a yellow woollen blanket, smiling and kicking, I shat everywhere and she scolded me –

'I hate you –'

These promises from the shadows, where their threats did not reach –

'– three houses in three years, these memories from these years. The man in his shop with his loose teeth that fell on the stone floor and broke at my feet. The woman in the lane with the dog that jumped up and barked into my pram. The trees in the park with the words in their bark that must have hurt –

'I love you. I love. I love you –'

These voices from the shadows at the back, where the silences did not reach –

'– heard my name called in a classroom with long lights and high windows and locked doors, screaming I'd come into this place. It was Monday morning and I was on my back in the gym in my own blood, kicking and screaming. The man in the black gown took me by my ear and scrubbed me clean of the blood and dressed me in harsh white shorts and a soft cricket sweater, smiling and kicking, I shat everywhere the first time –'

These curses from the shadows, where his prayers did not reach –

'– more houses in more years, more memories from more years. The man in the uniform who said he was my father and shook me by my hand. My mother in tears who called him a liar and slapped his face raw. The doctor in the white coat who said he would help us and gave us all pills –'

These voices from the shadows, where the silences did not reach –

'– new town, new school; the same frown, the same fool in class-rooms less bright and windows less high but with doors still locked, sniffing I came into these places. It was Friday teatime and I was on my back on the playing field in my own blood, aching and sweating. The captain of the house took me by my hand and showered me clean of the blood and watched me dress in my clean cotton pants and blue school shirt, giggling and kicking, he shat everywhere the first time –

'I love you –'

This was a truth from the shadows at the back, where their lies did not reach –

'– that last house from that last, final year, these last memories from that last, final year. The man in the uniform who said he was my father and carried me out to his car, kicking and screaming. My mother in tears who cried and chased the car to the end of the lane. The doctor in the white coat who ran behind her with his help and his pills –

'I hate you. I hate you. I hate you –'

These lies that drove the truth from the light. Into the shadows –

The voices that followed. Into the silence.

Neil Fontaine drives out to the hotel by Heathrow. Neil Fontaine checks into the hotel. Neil Fontaine uses the name Anthony Farrant. Mr Farrant goes up to his double room. Mr Farrant has their letters in his hand. Mr Farrant waits for the applicants to arrive –

The light fades. The light fails –

There is a call from the front desk. There is a knock on the door.

Mr Farrant opens the door, Neil Fontaine opens his mouth –

Jerry Witherspoon and Roger Vaughan are stood in the corridor –

There are carols playing –

Jerry has a handkerchief over his mouth. Roger has a black bin-liner in his hands.

Neil Fontaine steps back into the room. Jerry and Roger follow him inside –

Jerry shuts the door. Roger puts the bin-liner on the bed –

'This came to the Jupiter offices for you,' says Roger. 'Merry Christmas, Neil.'

Neil Fontaine stares at the bin-liner. He says, 'What is it?'

'I would hate to spoil the surprise,' says Roger.

Neil Fontaine shrugs. He goes over to the bed. He opens the bin-liner –

There is the box for a portable TV inside. It has been opened and resealed.

Neil Fontaine takes the cardboard box out of the bin-liner. He opens the box –

There is something tied up inside a supermarket carrier bag.

Neil Fontaine takes the carrier bag out of the box. He undoes the carrier bag –

There is a parcel wrapped in old newspapers.

Neil Fontaine takes out the parcel. He unwraps the newspapers –

The severed head of Jennifer Johnson stares up at him –

The former Mrs Fontaine.

The Kalamares in Inverness Mews, the Capannina on Romilly Street, the Scandia Room in the Piccadilly Hotel, the Icelandic Steakhouse on Haymarket –

The quiet times and empty places where Malcolm conducted the orchestra –
In their silences. In their spaces.

The waiters did not bring them menus. The waiters did not take their orders –

They were shadows. They were ghosts –

The orchestra of ghosts –

Back from the Dead to the Land of the Living.

a day for soup kitchen – Lads just doing our own pit and coal-picking. Pushing their barrows up to spoil – Looked like ants, they did, up there on top of heap. Pushing their barrows back down lane – Minds just set on Christmas now. Raffles and parties. Presents and dinner. That's all folk talked about – Christmas. Christmas. Christmas – Talked about it more than bloody strike itself. Especially after last picket on twenty-first – Been a bigger push than usual. Bit of a drink – Not even got that now for a while. So I didn't blame them – Thinking about Christmas. It was just when it was all over and done with – That was what worried me. Them first few days of January – longest month of bloody year. Bad enough when you weren't on strike – I went into back of **Welfare**. Put on my Santa suit ready for party – Hardly move in there for all presents. Food that had been collected – Presents from SOGAT. From CGT in France. Loads of food and drink from NALGO people in Sheffield. Housing Department of local council had held a raffle – Four hundred kids going mental. Never seen such a mountain of presents and stuff – Crackers. Chocolates. Trifles. Sweets. Sandwiches – Our Mary said it took them five hours just to butter all bread for potted meat sandwiches – Ham. Pork. Salmon. Cucumber – You name it, it was there. Kids were in heaven and, I tell you, all grown-ups had tears in their eyes. This one little lad comes up to me. He tugs on hem of my Santa suit and he says, I hope my dad's on strike next year, Santa. And that was just young ones – There was a disco for older lot and a gift voucher each. Trip to pantomime in Sheffield and all – Busy time. Not all glad tidings, mind – Rumours were still there. Tension – People **out and about**. Few drinks in them – Drink got to folk more and all. Now they didn't have it as often as and as much as they'd like – Few pints and things would get said. Things would get heard. Things would get done – If there was going to be trouble, it was going to be this week. This one scab – One of them younger ones who'd been an active picket before. This one had had

his fair share of bother before strike. Big mouth on him. Quick with his fists. Not sort to keep his head down. Even if he was scabbing – He'd been out and about in village. Told a few of younger lads that him and other scabs had got a hit list of all pickets that had called him – Told folk he would have his revenge. It was all talk. Never came near Welfare with it, either – But it got to younger lads. Lads who he'd been out picketing with not a month ago. Lads who'd looked up to him – This one bloke, Steve, he hated this scab. Had had bother with him since they were in same class at school – Friday night before New Year, they crossed each other's path again in village. Steve had a go – Told him he should be ashamed of himself. Scab said Steve was on hit list and he'd have him – Steve went back to pub. Kept drinking. Then he goes up to **scab's house** and chucks a milk bottle at it. Bottle goes through window – Minutes later scab has put Steve's windows through with an airrifle. Steve goes back up to scab's house – Scab comes out with a hatchet in his hands. Police come – Krk-krk. Police don't touch scab. Just cart Steve off to **Maltby** – Don't let him see a solicitor. Don't let him see his wife. Don't let him have his phone call – Police want Steve to grass up folk for vandalism to pit and NCB gear. Police want this so Board can sack them – Steve tells them nothing. Keeps it shut – Police took him to **Rotherham police station**. Police charged him with threatening behaviour and criminal damage. Bring him straight up. Judge fines him four hundred and ten quid – For one window. No charges for scab. Nothing – I didn't say anything to Steve but I knew Board would sack him. That was policy now. *Fuck* – New Year's Eve we put on a token picket up at pit. I spent night on picket line up by **hut**. Our Alamo – Decked out in a bit of tinsel. Trees tied up – There was a good atmosphere. Folk came out from houses near by and gave us food and drink. Lots of other people stopped by for a song and a chat. Just a couple of police on. Local bobbies keen to be mates tonight. Had a drink with them at midnight. Bite to eat – Like they did with Hun. No man's

The Forty-third Week

Monday 24 – Sunday 30 December 1984

Terry put down the phone. Terry sighed. Terry smiled. Terry clapped his hands –

The Union had regained partial control of the Dublin money. The seques-trators had admitted in court that they were having great problems getting to the miners' money.

Terry stopped clapping. Terry stopped smiling –

Terry tried to remember what he had been doing before the phone rang –

Terry saw all the boxes stacked up in his office. The papers piled up on his desk. The empty cups on the windowsill. The aspirin bottles in the bin. The Denims outside. The Tweeds upstairs. The Red Guard downstairs –

Terry walked over to his jacket. Terry went to the right-hand pocket of his jacket. Terry needed an index card –

The phone rang again on his desk.

Terry walked back over. Terry picked it up. *Click-click* –

'It's Christmas time,' sang the voice on the end. 'There's no need to be afraid –'

Terry sat down. Terry said, 'What do you want, Clive?'

'Let me guess,' laughed Clive. 'You're Scrooge in the Union pantomime?'

Terry said, 'I haven't the time for this –'

'Really?' asked Clive. 'But I'm the ghost of all our Christmases-yet-to-come –'

'Fuck off,' shouted Terry. 'I'm going to hang up right –'

'I'm sorry,' said Clive. 'I just wanted to say thank you. That's all.'

'For what?' asked Terry.

'For not saying anything,' whispered Clive. 'For being a pal. I owe you one.'

'You owe me nothing,' spat Terry. 'Nothing. Now fuck off –'

'Don't be like that,' said Clive. 'We're on the same side. Both want the same –'

Terry hung up. Terry stood up. Terry went back over to the pocket of his jacket –

The index cards were gone.

Terry closed his eyes. He saw the cards on the kitchen table. He opened his eyes. He saw the boxes and the papers. The cups and the bottles. Terry looked at his watch –

It was home time. Christmas time –

Terry locked up the office. Terry went down the stairs. Terry drove to his house –

On the radio. Again and again. Over and over, *Do They Know It's Christmas?*

He opened the front door of his three-bedroom home in the suburbs of Sheffield. The lights were not on, his family not home –

Terry Winters couldn't remember when he'd last seen Theresa and the children. They must have all gone down to Bath to stay with Theresa's parents for the holidays. Terry had put all their presents under the Christmas tree ready for them, but they'd left them there under a coat of fallen pine needles and cold, dark lights.

Terry closed the front door. He stood his briefcase and the suitcases in the hall. He went into the front room. He walked over to the socket in the wall. He switched on the lights on the tree. He sat down on his sofa in the shadows of South Yorkshire, in the suburbs of Sheffield –

In the house with the lights flashing on and off, off and on, and nobody home –

It was Christmas Eve, 1984.

Neil Fontaine has made mistakes. Neil Fontaine has paid the price –

Now is the time to make things right. Now is the time to pay it all back.

Neil Fontaine makes calls. Neil Fontaine pays visits –

Pockets full of change and his little black book. Telephones and doorbells.

No one answers their phone. No one answers their door –

He kicks in doors. He tips up tables. He cracks heads. He breaks bones.

Nazi bones. Nazi heads. Nazi tables. Nazi doors –

East End pubs and West End bars. South London skins and North London toffs.

Neil Fontaine drives through the old years and the new. The sleet and the rain –

Now is the time. To make things right. Now is the time. To pay it all back –

Sick of the lies. Sick of the life. Sick of the death –

The severed head of his ex-wife in the boot of his car.

The President had been voted Man of the Year. The Prime Minister, Woman of the Year. But the Man of the Year was locked away in his office at the top of the monastery –

There were wolves at the gate, there were carrion circling overhead –

Now there were rats within the precinct walls –

The Militants were mutinying. The Militants were muttering about the President. The Militants moaning about his navigation. The very direction and course of the dispute. The lack of vision and initiative –

The Militants and the Moderates. The shots from both sides now.

So the Man of the Year stayed locked in his office during the hours of daylight. The television tuned to Ceefax and Oracle. The Shostakovich on loud, twenty-four hours. He wrote letters to the families of jailed miners. He told them how proud they should be of their fathers and sons. Their husbands and brothers. How he had nothing but admiration for these magnificent men who had fought to save their jobs, their pits and their communities –

Nothing but admiration.

Len carried in the cardboard boxes. Len put them on Terry's desk. Len went back down for more. Terry opened the boxes. Terry stacked up the bundles on the desk. Terry counted out the cash. Len brought in another box. Len left it on the floor. Terry put the bundles back in the boxes. Terry noted down the names of the donors and the amounts donated. Len came back with another box. Len said, 'That's the last one for now.'

Terry nodded. He asked, 'There will be people outside all night?'

'It'll be safe enough in the safe,' said Len. 'Just bring it up when you're done.'

Terry shrugged his shoulders. Terry got on with it –

Len left him to it. Left him alone among the boxes –

It was Boxing Day, 1984.

Terry went back to work. He wrote down the names of the unions and local authorities. He pencilled in the amounts. He banged away on the calculator. He put the money back in the boxes. He taped up the boxes. He wrote words and numbers on the cardboard in black felt-tip pen. He sat back down in his chair under the portrait of the President. He took off his glasses. He rubbed the bridge of his nose. He swallowed another two aspirins. He drank another cup of cold coffee. He blinked and put his glasses back on –

The red light on his phone was flashing on and off, on and off, on and –

There was always a chance.

Terry picked it up. *Click-click.* Terry said, 'Chief Executive speaking.'

'Merry Christmas, Comrade Chief Executive,' she said.

Terry's stomach tightened. Turned and flipped. He said, 'Merry Christmas.'

'I've got a present for you,' she giggled. 'Your Christmas present.'

'A Christmas present for me?' asked Terry. 'Really?'

'Sorry it's a day late,' she said. 'When would you like it, Comrade?'

Terry looked at his watch. It had stopped. He said, 'Where are you?'

'Where do you think?' she laughed.

Terry wound up his watch. He said, 'Just give me an hour to sort things out here.'

'I'll be waiting,' she said and hung up.

Terry put the phone down. He picked it back up. *Click-click.* He dialled home –

He listened to it ring and ring, echo in the empty hall of their empty home.

Terry hung up. He picked up a box to take up the stairs to the President's office. He put it back down. He opened it back up. He took out four big bundles of cash. He put them in his briefcase. He taped up the box again. He changed a three into a two on the top of the box. He altered the figures in the book. He carried the first two boxes down the corridor to the stairs. He took them up to the President's office. He put the boxes down in the corridor. He knocked on the door –

The music symphonic, deafening.

'Who is it?' shouted Len from the inside.

'It's me,' replied Terry, 'the Chief Executive.'

The music stopped and Len unlocked the door. He said, 'All done?'

'Nearly,' said Terry. 'Just the last four.'

Len picked up the ones at Terry's feet. Terry glanced inside at the President –

He had his glasses on, writing at his desk. He didn't look up at Terry Winters.

Terry went back down for the rest of the money. Len followed him.

They picked up the last four boxes. They carried them out to the stairwell.

Len asked, 'What you doing tonight, Comrade?'

'Why?' said Terry. 'Why do you ask that?'

Len said, 'Just asking, that's all.'

'Sorry,' said Terry. 'Been a long day.'

Len followed Terry up the stairs. Len said, 'Been a long bloody year, Comrade.'

'You're right there, Comrade,' said Terry. 'You're right there.'

Terry kept open the door for Len with his back. The boxes in both arms –

Len stopped in the door. He stared at Terry. He said, 'So what are you doing?'

'Think I'll just go home to the family,' said Terry. 'Yourself?'

Len nodded. Len said, 'Planning to picket a power station.'

'With the President?' asked Terry.

Len nodded again. Len walked down the corridor. Len said, 'Join us, Comrade.'

'I'd love to,' said Terry, 'but I have neglected the wife and kids this Christmas.'

Len stopped outside the President's office. Len turned to Terry Winters. Len said, 'Just put the boxes down there then, Comrade. I'll take them from here.'

'Are you sure?' said Terry. 'I can bring them in for you.'

'Thank you,' said Len. 'But you've done enough, Comrade.'

'Merry Christmas and happy New Year then,' said Terry. 'And to the President.'

'And to you and your family, Comrade,' said Len. 'Theresa and the kids.'

Terry Winters walked back down the corridor. Terry took the stairs two at a time. He went back into his office. He picked up his brief-case. He locked the door behind him. He switched off the lights as he went. He took the lift down to the ground floor –

There were no Tweeds. No Denims –

Just the Red Guards on the door.

Terry gave them a tenner for a drink and wished them season's greetings.

Terry clutched the briefcase. Terry walked quickly to the car.

Terry drove to Hallam Towers. Terry went straight up to Room 308 –

Terry had an erection and a briefcase full of cash.

Terry Winters knocked on the door. Terry said, 'Room service.'

Malcolm caught red buses. Malcolm took black taxis –

The streets quiet, the city dead. The trains empty, the ghosts overground –

From station to station. Place to place –

The lights blew in the wind. The lights fell in the rain –

His shoes full of holes on pavements full of holes. His dirty raincoat in a dirty doorway –

Hobart House and Congress House. Claridge's and the County Hotel –

The buildings quiet. The buildings empty.

Malcolm had his key. Malcolm took the lift –

An old black man pushed an industrial vacuum cleaner down the seventh-floor corridor. There were rope marks around his neck. There were scars across both his wrists. The light flickered on and off, on and off. The lift door opened and then closed –

Deserted silences. Deserted spaces –

From place to place. Room to room –

The bodies hiding in the fixtures. The bodies hanging from the fittings.

A young Asian woman washed industrial-strength bleach down a seventh-floor wall. There were whip marks across her backside. There were wounds around her vagina –

She was naked from the waist down. Bleeding from the waist up.

The television in the corner switched itself off and on, off and on –

The Prime Minister talked of resolution. The Prime Minister talked of exorcism.

'Everybody's saying it'll soon be over,' said Diane. 'You know that, don't you?'

'I know,' said Terry.

'Two months, maybe even less,' she said. 'That's what they're saying.'

'I know,' said Terry again.

'The finances won't recover,' she said. 'The Union will split in two.'

Terry's stomach tightened. Turned and emptied. Terry nodded.

'They'll look for scapegoats,' she said. 'They'll look to you.'

Terry nodded again. Empty and turning. Terry felt sick.

'You need an escape plan,' said Diane. 'Funds.'

Terry got out of bed. Terry opened his briefcase. Terry put the money on the bed –

'Will you help me?' said Terry. 'Help me escape? Disappear? The two of us?'

'If that's what you want,' she said. 'If that's what you really want.'

land in World War One – In end there were quite a few at hut for countdown. Everyone was upbeat and positive. Difficult to tell how they really felt, though. Lot of us stopped on right through until sun came up. Took it in turns to get warm in hut or go across road to one of houses. They kept an open door for us, did some of pensioners who lived up there. Not just on New Year's Eve. There were two who'd been in last big one. Back in '26. They'd soon get going. Tell you who'd scabbed and who'd stayed out. Folk had long bloody memories and when sun did come up there was a bit of emotion. I know I felt it. I got off home pretty sharp after that. Mary and our Jackie were asleep. I sat on **settee downstairs** for a bit. Just me and tree and all cards. I'd be glad when tree came down and it got put away for another year. Just didn't seem same this year. Ironic really, because I'd never been to so many bloody Christmas parties in my life. I didn't usually bother about it much. I couldn't remember what I'd done last New Year. I went up to **bed**. Tried not to wake Mary. But it was too light to sleep now and she'd be up to make dinner soon – *I start running. Running and running* – I pushed chicken round my plate. Every family had been given a free chicken – That's all I'd done this bloody Christmas, give out free fucking chickens. Make sure no one got two and someone got none. I shouldn't have taken off that Father Christmas hat – Mary had made a big effort today, though. Made us put on paper party hats – I wanted to enjoy it. But one look at this bloody **room** said it all – Lights were all on in kitchen and dining room. Bloody tree in corner flashing away. Heating on full. Cooker on all morning. Radio. TV – It were all bloody on. Everything that could be and there still wasn't so much as a flicker – Not a single fucking flicker after ten bloody months. Not one power cut – Just more fucking bills we couldn't pay. *Fuck* – How much was it fucking costing them to do this to us? How bloody much? They'd sit on their fucking hands and watch this country crash before they'd break and give us even an inch. *Fuck me*. I pushed that

chicken round through gravy and knew I should have been more grateful. Tried to smile for Mary and our Jackie. Brave face and all that bollocks – There were them that would have no special dinner this New Year, I knew that. Not just them in fucking Ethiopia or Sudan, either – Here in South bloody Yorkshire. Then there were them lads starting five-year prison sentences down in Kent – It was then that it dawned on me. Hit me for first time – That it was over. All over now. Finished. Bar shouting – Just a matter of time. Be like waiting for end of bloody world – I looked up from chicken. From trimmings – Mary and Jackie were watching me. Our Jackie holding a cracker out for me – I didn't want to let her see what I was thinking. I closed my eyes – *Deeper and deeper* – I lay on **bed** after lunch. Listened to match on Radio Sheffield. Wednesday bloody beat Man United two–one. Two-fucking-one! Put us up to fifth. Final scores were coming in, Mary sticks her head round bedroom door. Big smile on her face, scrapbook in her hand. Never know, she said. Might be an omen. I laughed. I gave her a big kiss as I went down stairs. I loved her. I *really* loved her. Her and our Jackie. Didn't know what I'd have done without them – Not this. I couldn't do this without them, I knew that – I was a lucky man. I knew that – *Faster and faster. I turn corner* – There were six **front gate** pickets up by hut on Pit Lane. There were also a fair few out today down road and all. Police had got hundred lads surrounded at junction by post office. *Krk-krk*. Not as many police as usual, either. Bit of snowballing going on, which was pissing them off. They got on their radios for cavalry. *Krk-krk* – Transits appeared full of riot squad. Then scab bus came up road at usual eighty mile an hour and into yard – Got welcome it deserved and all. I had a good look to see how many they had this morning – It didn't look any more than before. Just usual wankers – Big two-fingered salute from two of them. One lad drawing his finger across his neck – I had a meeting with Panel over in Silverwood, so I walked back down to Welfare with some of lads. Most of

The Forty-fourth Week

Monday 31 December 1984 – Sunday 6 January 1985

The Jew hates even New Year. The Jew hates holidays. Full stop. The Jew hates all rest. Neil Fontaine hates New Year too. Holidays and all the rest now. But Neil needs time –

Time to make things right. Time to pay it all back.

The Jew asks Neil to drive him to Nottingham for New Year's Eve. The Jew has organized a countdown party for the Board and his new toy, his embryonic new union. The Jew asks Neil to take this time to review the home security of the working miners. The Jew fears there might yet be one last wave of attacks and retribution to come –

For the Jew understands that scores are there to be settled –

Crimes punished. Justice exacted. Vengeance wrought –

Neil Fontaine jumps at the chance. The chances and the ghosts.

Neil leaves the Jew to his plots and his plans. His speeches and schemes.

Neil drives further North. There are speed restrictions on the M1 –

Snow and sleet. Fog and frost. Rain and ruin.

Neil Fontaine visits Wood Street police station, Wakefield, and Millgarth, Leeds. There are people who know him here. There are people who owe him here –

People consumed by this bloody strike. People consumed by this fucking war.

He chooses his questions carefully. He asks his questions ambiguously.

He hears horror stories about dead coppers. Hears rumours about missing men –

Philip Taylor. Adam Young. Detective Sergeant Paul Dixon –

David Johnson, a.k.a. the Mechanic.

Neil Fontaine drives further North again. He parks, watches and he waits again –

Parks, watches and he waits outside the home of Paul Dixon, Special Branch.

But Paul Dixon's not coming home for New Year's Eve. Not this New Year's Eve. His daughter stands on her tiptoes at the window and looks out over the tops of the Christmas cards at the man in the Mercedes who is not her daddy –

Her mother pulls her away from the glass by her sleeve and she shouts and scolds.

Paul Dixon is not coming home.

There was no one on the desk when Malcolm walked out of the County. He rang the bell but no one came. He left his key with the long wooden handle on the register. He cut through Endsleigh Square onto Gower Street. He took a taxi to the station and the train to Birmingham New Street. No one on the gate when he came out of the station.

He walked down to the Rotunda. He looked for the pubs he had known –

The Mulberry Bush. The Tavern in the Town –

They were gone.

He called a private hire cab from a card in a phone box. The cab drove him out to Handsworth. It dropped him off and left him on the street. He walked among the blacks and the whites, the yellows and the browns, and he remembered different times in different colours –

'You want business, do you, love?' she asked –

She was not so young. Not so black –

Malcolm nodded. Malcolm said, 'Yes.'

'Hand, French or full?' she asked. 'Five, ten or thirty?'

Malcolm nodded again. Malcolm said, 'Full.'

'You got a car, have you, love?' she asked.

Malcolm shook his head. Malcolm said, 'No.'

'Not to worry,' she said. 'Back to mine it is, then.'

Malcolm nodded. Malcolm said, 'Thank you.'

'Just round the corner,' she said. 'This way –'

Malcolm followed her round the back to the steps above a launderette.

'Give us the thirty quid, then,' she said by the door.

Malcolm gave her the money and she opened the door –

'Age before beauty,' she said.

The flat was dark. The electricity off.

'Go through to the front,' she said. 'There's light from the street.'

Malcolm went through to the front. To the light from the street –

Day and light. Light and shadow. Shadow and night –

'Put this on,' she said and handed him a condom.

Malcolm unbuttoned his coat and trousers. Pulled down his pants. Put it on.

'Which way do you want it?' she asked. 'Religious or heathen?'

Malcolm nodded. Malcolm said, 'Heathen.'

'Thought you would,' she said and took down her panties. Bent right over –

The wounds still weeping.

Malcolm walked with the dawn out to the old coke depot at Saltley Gate –

The Winter Palace, 1972.

Malcolm climbed up onto the roof of the municipal lavatory –

Close the Gates! Close the Gates! Close the Gates!

He listened as he looked to the horizon. The lost and empty horizon –

It was cold and almost time.

Malcolm climbed down from the roof. He stepped inside the toilets –

He removed his bandages. His dressings. He made the call.

Neil Fontaine makes his excuses. He leaves the Jew hungover in his Nottingham hotel. Neil Fontaine drives North again. First to Leeds. Then onto the York Road. Neil Fontaine turns off before Tadcaster. Neil Fontaine comes to the village of Towton –

Neil Fontaine knows this might be a set-up –

That is what they do. Set things up. This is what he does –

He parks at the end of the road. He watches the unlit bungalow –

He waits in a Yorkshire cul-de-sac. This is what Neil Fontaine does –

In the middle of the night he parks in the dark at the end of all roads –

The noises in his head. The holes in his heart. The pits in his belly –

This is what he has always done. Park, watch and wait –

But tonight the traps are empty. Tonight the bait just rotting on their teeth.

Neil Fontaine gets out of the car. Neil Fontaine makes his way over the fields. Neil Fontaine watches the back of the bungalow. Neil Fontaine waits for night again –

For the bungalow to fall dark. The bungalow to fall silent.

He climbs the fence. He drops into the garden. He watches and he waits –

The two dead crows lie upon the lawn, untouched –

The bungalow dark. The bungalow silent.

He crosses the lawn. He works on the French windows. He opens them –

Neil Fontaine enters the bungalow –

The place dark. The place silent.

He goes from room to room. Empty room to empty room –

The place stripped bare but for curtains and carpets, a sofa and a table.

David Johnson is not coming home either –

The trail cold. Dark and silent. The end dead –

Here in a Yorkshire cul-de-sac.

Neil Fontaine sits in the dark and the silence on David Johnson's sofa –

He lights a cigarette. He inhales. He exhales –

Two steel knives on the glass table –

The severed head of their former wife between them.

The President had come out from behind his desk. The President had come out fighting. The President had spent his New Year on the picket lines. The President had spent New Year's Day itself on the picket line outside Thorpe Marsh power station, near Doncaster. The President had smiled for the solitary camera crew from Germany –

'The only difference between now and March 1984', the President had told them, 'is that we are more convinced and more confident of winning now than we were then.'

Then the Germans had gone home and left the President and Len alone –

Just the President and Len with their flasks and their mugs out in the cold.

No massed guard of pickets beside them. No halting the power supply –

No champagne breakfast in bed in Room 308 of the Hallam Towers Hotel.

Terry made Diane keep the TV off; there was always something or someone on. The Leader or the Fat Man. A Militant or a Moderate. A Denim or a Tweed. A Minister or a Suit from the Board. From studio to studio, they went. From TV-AM to *Newsnight* –

In circles, they went. In circles, they talked.

It was distracting and Terry Winters needed to stay focused on the job at hand –

There were meetings planned for all this week, in preparation for next week; everyone knew next Monday would bring the end of the Christmas truce –

Hostilities would be resumed.

Terry left Diane in bed. For now. Terry got dressed. For now –

Terry travelled down to Birmingham. Terry took his seat at the table –

The Knights of the Hard-Left Table.

'This coming Monday will mark the beginning of a new phase,' declared Paul. 'The Board will concentrate all their energies on stepping up the back-to-work movement. Upon gaining their magical *fifty per cent –*'

Fifty per cent. Fifty per cent. Fifty per cent –

The mantra for the remaining months, maybe weeks or possibly only days ahead –

Fifty per cent spelt death for the Union and glory for the Board.

'These scabs and their NWMC have succeeded in cutting off our arms and legs,' continued Paul. 'Their legal actions together with our own –'

'Incompetence?' suggested Dick.

Paul looked over at Terry. Paul shook his head. Paul said, 'Or intrigue –'

'That's a very serious accusation, Comrade,' shouted Bill Reed. 'Very serious.'

Paul nodded. Paul said, 'These are very serious times –'

'Depressing times, too,' said Terry. 'Our members and their families are starving. Our members and their families are freezing. Our members and their families are crying out for new initiatives and leadership. But here we all sit, with our toasted sandwiches and our central heating, and squabble among ourselves, debating rule changes to a rulebook that won't have a bloody union to rule over, if we don't all face up to the reality of the situation, and fast –'

'The reality of the situation?' laughed Paul. 'You'd know about reality then, would you, Comrade?'

'I know this strike has cost over two and a half billion pounds,' shouted Terry. 'That this government will spend however many billions it takes in order to beat us –

'That's reality,' said Terry. 'I know that.'

Paul shook his head. Paul sighed. Paul held up his palms. Paul sat down.

Bill Reed squeezed the end of his nose between two of his fingers and said, 'WE. ARE. ALL. BEING. MANIPULATED. AND. DESTROYED –

'DESTROY –
'DESTROY!'
'But by whom?' asked the President. 'That's the question.'

It has just gone midnight. Neil Fontaine washes his hands again in the sink of the private bathroom of the Jew's office at Hobart House. He washes them again and again. He dries them and goes back into the office.

The Jew is standing by the phones with his tins full of pins. The Jew is waiting for the word from the area directors. The Jew and the directors have high hopes for high numbers today. There have been adverts in all the newspapers. New bribes on the table. Under the table, too. Tax-free incentives. Interest-free loans. Cash advances –

Safety in numbers. High numbers. High hopes.

The Chairman has even called from Palm Beach to wish them luck –

They will need it. In his heart of hearts, the Jew knows they will.

The Jew stands by the phone with his tins of pins and waits for the word –

But in his heart of hearts, the Jew knows it won't come. Not this morning. Not yet.

The directors will blame the weather. They'll say next Monday will be better –

The Jew will be disappointed. But in his heart of hearts, the Jew won't care.

The Jew stares at the remaining clusters of red pins on his map. The Jew smiles. The Jew likes symmetry. Precision. In his heart of hearts. The six points of a star –

'March the sixth,' the Jew tells Neil. 'That will be the last day of this dispute.'

them popping into soup kitchen for their breakfasts on their way home. There was snow on ground and sun out now. Mood still seemed positive and I felt guilty about way I'd been over New Year. Maybe it'd be all right. But then I opened my eyes and I looked about us – Folk waiting for a word down **Welfare**. Folk queuing out door for electricity payments – Lads pushing their barrows through village to riddle through snow on top of spoil. Police on every corner. Either spitting or smiling at women with their babies – Place looked like a late fucking Christmas card from hell. A bloody, fucking hell – I got in car. I switched on engine. Let it turn a bit. Got it going – Went down **Panel**. People had something to look forward to before Christmas, said Derek. There was a sense of purpose and a sense of community. Knowledge that people were there to help. There were supporters coming up from London. From down South. From abroad. Now people just see strike with no end in sight. Except defeat – Heathfield coming out like that and saying there'd be no power cuts, said Tom. That were a disaster, that. Like saying we'll have to be out another year, that is – If that's what it takes, said Johnny. That's what it takes – Johnny, I said, with best will in world, folk can't do it – Not another year. Derek nodded. This kind of talk's premature, said David Rainer. Talking like we've lost – Talking realistically, said Tom. That's what we're doing. Derek nodded again. He said, If there are no power cuts, our whole strategy's buggered – Buggered anyway, I said. There's been no support whatsoever. Just talk. Not one single leaflet. Not one fucking march. After all that was said at Congress in September – No brass. No support. Nothing – That's trade union movement for you. History repeating itself, said Johnny. That's what it is. David Rainer shook his head. He said, Been out longer than in 1926 now – Result will be same though, said Tom. Beaten and divided – Beaten and divided, said Derek. That's what it'll be. Mark my words – There was this portable television we had in **Welfare**. Little black-and-white one, on its last

legs, it was. It was in good company and all. Folk would just sit there all bloody day and watch it. Just waiting for some news. I dreaded it when I came back from Panel and I had nothing for them. Half of them knew more than me anyway. They all had a different paper and would sit there and compare notes. There was not much else to do. Just wait for news and talk – Talk, talk, talk. That's all I'd bloody done for past ten months – Talk and listen. But folk had enough of it all now, I could tell. Local folk – Lot of their goodwill was fading now we were into January. Police presence wasn't as heavy in village itself. Like folk had forgotten what had happened. I'd hear people moaning about amount of stuff miners' kids had got for Christmas. Like it were kids' fault – Hear them moaning about miners and their families having too much to eat and drink. To smoke – How they weren't as bad off as they made out. How they liked being on strike – It got our Mary right mad. Nearly got her sacked from factory – This supervisor was going on about how she'd seen all Christmas parties on telly for kiddies with all raffles and stuff. How miners had never had it so good and why was it only miners that folk ever felt sorry for? – No one had done anything for her and her family. Not when her husband was out during steel strike – Mary had had a right go. Told her she knew nothing. That she had no idea how hard up folk were. That it was the kindness and generosity of others that had given them kiddies a Christmas. People from down South and people from abroad. Not round here. How miners had supported the steelworkers. How they had made sacrifices for them. But where were steelworkers now? That was what Mary wanted to know – Woman had backed off when she saw how worked up Mary was – But it wasn't just her. There was moaning all over now – Feeling it had gone on too long. People wanted to get back to normal – Pensioners. Shopkeepers. Local businesses – Painters and decorators. Builders and garages – Each one of them had been undercut by miners looking for a bit of cash in hand. Folk

The Forty-fifth Week

Monday 7 – Sunday 13 January 1985

The Right Honourable Member of Parliament had come back for more in the underground car park. In the shadows at the back, where the lights did not quite reach –

His mouth moved again. His fingers pointed. He asked Malcolm more questions –

Malcolm still could not answer. Malcolm still could not hear –

But Malcolm had more tapes –

From the shadows at the back, where the lights did not reach –

They would find more answers here. They would hear more tapes –

More recordings of the Dead.

Today was the day. Yet another of the days. These endless fucking end days –

Another NEC meeting. Another showdown between the Militants and Moderates. There would be an attempt to expel Nottingham. There would be a move to restructure and reorganize the remaining areas. The Militants would then command the majority on the Executive. The Militants would then have the initiative. The Militants would then control the course of the dispute –

Then the witch hunts could begin. The witch hunts and the inquisition –

The torture and confessions. The trials and executions. Burnings and beheadings.

Today was the day and Terry wasn't invited. Terry wouldn't be missed.

Terry Winters had the house to himself. Terry got out of bed and went to work. Into the loft and the suitcases. Into the pantry and the biscuit tins.

Terry called the office. He told them he was going to Bath to pick up his family. He said he'd be back in the office tomorrow or the morning after. The weather willing –

This fucking weather.

He would have to change routes. He didn't want to cross the Moors on an A road. He'd have to go up to the M62. He rechecked her plans and reset his watch –

He could still do it, but he'd have to get his skates on.

Terry locked up. Terry put the suitcases in the boot. Terry set off –

Sheffield up to Junction 42. The M62 to Manchester –

Snow. Sleet. Rain. Sleet. Snow. Sleet. Rain. Sleet. Snow –

Through Manchester into Liverpool. Terry Winters boarded the fast ferry –

The last fast ferry to Dublin until the weather improved.

Terry hated boats. Terry hated the sea. The currents and the depths –

Terry knew this would be a nightmare.

But Diane had said the airports were being watched. Terry's face too well known.

Terry knew she was right. Terry knew he was a national hero to some people –

The enemy within to others. Terry knew she was right. It was the price of fame.

Terry left the suitcases locked in the boot. Terry sat in the bar and drank –

Puked and puked –

The crossing rough. The crossing slow. The crossing taking forever.

Terry had another drink and tried to read the papers –

The papers full of the Big Freeze. Record demands for power. But no power cuts.

Terry puked again. Terry drank again. Terry took out his own papers –

Their own Big Freeze. The eight million pounds still frozen overseas.

Terry looked at his watch. He was going to arrive too late for the banks –

For the regular banking hours. But Diane had phoned ahead. Made arrangements.

Terry disembarked in Dublin and went straight to the bank.

The bank was waiting for Terry –

Mr Winters and his suitcases were expected.

Terry Winters opened the account in the name of Pine Tree Investments –

It was a name that had come to him when he'd been putting out the kids' presents –

Diane liked the name too.

The President, Paul and Dick were listed as joint trustees with Joan and Mike. However, only Terry could authorize deposits and withdrawals from the account, transactions that could be completed only by the appropriate password –

The password known only to Terry and Diane. The account known only to them –

The account containing £250,000 and counting.

Hats off to Diane. It truly was a master plan –

If the account was discovered, then Terry was only protecting the Union's assets. If they tried to make a scapegoat out of Terry, then he had his exit. They both did –

Terry would divorce his wife. Diane would divorce her husband.

Terry and Diane would catch the first fast ferry to Dublin –

Terry and Diane would go to the bank. Terry and Diane would say the word –

The money would be theirs. The future would be theirs –

A £250,000 future and counting.

Malcolm Morris pressed play again. Malcolm played it all back again –

Again and again. All of it. Over and over –

More voices from the shadows, where the silences did not quite reach yet –

'– my father took me from my mother. Not to raise me, but to train and cure me. He failed me and I failed him. He took his own life as I took mine. Lincoln College, Oxford, offered me a place out of respect for him and pity for me. I took up their offer of Medieval and Military History, out of pity for him, and paid my last respects with three last little words –

'I hate you –'

More lies from the light, from which the truth ran and hid. In the shadows –

'– in a dull room in Great Marlborough Street they asked me dull questions and I gave them dull answers. Then they offered me tea laced with whisky and a dull job, which I took with a handshake and a peppermint for the train back to Oxford –'

This one promise from those shadows, where their threats would not follow –

'– Diane was morbid even then. Drawn to secrets, suicides and sex. She pretended to like my poetry. She pretended to like my personality. She pretended to like the inside of my pants, and I pretended too. It was all good practice. It was all good fun. Then it all went wrong when I said those three last little words –

'I love you –'

This one truth from the shadows inside, the lies upstairs and down –

'– I got off the tube at Hyde Park Corner and walked up Park Lane and onto Curzon Street and on a grim September day I stepped inside Leconfield House and they put me to work behind a grim desk in a grim, windowless room for the rest of my grim days, laced with whisky and peppermints they all said would help pass the grim time –'

These whispers from the shadows, where their spirits had all fled and hid –

'– they gave me the Yorkshire branches of the Communist Party of Great Britain. *The British Road to Socialism* and *The Theory and Practice of Communism* to read on all those long lunch breaks from which they never returned –'

Those slim truths from those dark pages, where their fat lies had not yet reached –

'– and I got off the tube at Hyde Park Corner and walked up Park Lane and onto Curzon Street and on a dead August day in 1969 I stepped inside Leconfield House and they gave me a dead letter with Diane's name crossed out and mine pencilled in, marked *Urgent* and stamped *Ulster* –'

That voice from the shadows at the back. The silence at the gates –

The scissors in her hands. Hungry.

Neil Fontaine pours the drinks in the Jew's Hobart House office. He pours large ones. Stiff ones all round. One thousand two hundred new faces went back in yesterday. Thirty-eight per cent of all miners now working –

But it's not enough. Not yet. It's never enough. Not now.

The bloody Bank of England has been forced to step in to save the Midland Bank. Two billion pounds pumped into the system overnight. Interest rates going up, up, up –

The total cost of the strike ballooning –

A huge red balloon and still rising.

There have been calls from the Great Financier. There have been angry calls. Threatening calls –

For restitution and remuneration. For retribution and retaliation.

The Jew has made promises and pleas. Supplications and solicitations –

But it's not enough. It's never enough –

The Jew knows it and the Jew knows why –

Christmas was finished. New Year was finished. Everything was finished –

It was time for each miner to make up his own mind.

But there is talk of talks about talks again. Third parties on the television –

Pressure mounts for peace. Prospects of fresh pit peace talks.

The Jew curses. The Jew fumes. The Jew rages. The Jew roars –

'They have stayed out for ten whole months,' the Jew shouts down the telephone. 'Ten whole fucking months! They're not going to surrender all that sacrifice and scab if there's a chance of a settlement, are they? Tell the Minister to call me –'

The Jew slams down the phone. He slumps in his chair. He stares at his guests –

Piers Harris and Dominic Reid look at their nails and their notes –

Don Colby and Derek Williams look at each other and raise their eyebrows.

'I'm calling off the dogs,' says the Jew. 'There's no sense in any further legal attacks upon the Union, not now it is under the control of the receiver.'

Piers and Dominic nod. Don and Derek scratch themselves.

'Of course, we'll continue to pursue personal actions against individual members of their National Executive,' promises the Jew. 'And the restraints on mass pickets.'

'The other actions should be suspended, then?' asks Piers. 'Indefinitely?'

The Jew strokes his moustache. The Jew nods. The Jew walks over to his map. 'The focus now will be upon the return to work and upon our friends in Nottingham.'

'Nottingham?' asks Derek. 'They're practically all at work anyway.'

'The men might be at work,' says the Jew. 'But their union remains on strike.'

Don and Derek are frowning. Piers and Dominic nodding now.

'Those men need a new union,' says the Jew. 'That will be our next victory.'

The tape had stopped turning. The orchestra had stopped playing –

The restaurant was quiet. Empty now –

The Right Honourable Member of Parliament sat at a table among the shadows at the back, where the lights did not quite reach and the waiters never brought the menu and never took his order –

Malcolm Morris watched him. Malcolm Morris waited for him –

In the silences. In the spaces –

The Right Honourable Member pressed the eject button. He picked up his pen. He turned the pages of the transcript. He underlined. He circled. He scored –

These transcripts of the Dead –

Their comminations.

eager to help them by putting work their way. Didn't seem as much like charity. Local shops and all – These folk had all given. But there was never any end to it. Never anything to receive in return. Now they'd nothing more to give. They just wanted it to end. We all did – And it got to you. It really bloody did – The moaning and the grumbling. The rumours and the whispers. The ups and the downs – Felt like progress. Then next news momentum had just disappeared – No talks at national level. Nothing – Then talks were back on again. Then they weren't – Frustrating and it began to take its bloody toll. You'd see it in people's eyes – The way they sat. The way they approached you over things – Electricity bills. Car repairs. Shoes for the young ones. Anything – People were more agitated. Jumpy. Quick to anger. To blame Union more and more – But it were these peaks and troughs that did it. False dawns. These ups and downs – Lads would see six o'clock news and hear they were still talking. Lads would go to bed thinking they'd be back at work next Monday – Brass would be coming in again. Debts going back down – Wake up to find out talks had failed again. And that were that then for next few weeks or months – Back to picketing or coal-picking. Just waiting – *I go down. Down* – To break things up a bit we started sending a few cars out to power stations. Relieve boredom – I went over in **car** to Ferrybridge with Keith and Chris. Martin had done another of his disappearing acts – It was just good to get away from village. Keith stuck radio on – *Last Christmas*. Least it wasn't that fucking Band Aid record. Billy in Hotel had been telling us how that was all a government plot to distract public sympathy away from miners. Make miners look greedy next to little brown babies dying of starvation in Africa. That was how BBC had come to film it. How they'd sent those pop stars over there. He went on a bit, did Billy – Rattle off Ridley Plan to you. Tell you how he'd seen his brother's lad on picket line. His brother's lad who was in the British Army on the Rhine. His brother's lad dressed as a copper – Thing is, said

Keith, he might be right about that bloody record. People giving to them, they won't be giving to us. Chris nodded, See his logic – I switched radio off. Wished I'd never opened my mouth now – Got to **Ferrybridge** and they gave us a gate and some leaflets. There were a couple of blokes there from SWP. Keith had a laugh with them. Taking piss like always. Fucking freezing though, stood before that thing – That power station. Big clouds of white smoke against that heavy grey Yorkshire sky. Ticking over without a care in world, it was. Like we weren't even here – Made your eyes smart. Two cars from Frickley came up to relieve us at lunchtime. Bloody glad to see them. Keith dropped us back at **Welfare** and him and Chris went up to Soup Kitchen for their lunch. Bet you it's casserole again, said Keith. Don't care what it is, said Chris. Long as it's bloody hot. I did without. I didn't have time. Knew queue would be there and it was. Hardest hit were them that had had babies on way when strike started. Didn't plan on having a baby and no brass at same time. Emotional period in people's lives at best of times. Took its toll, you could see. Husbands would be out picketing for their quid or doing a bit of cash in hand and wife was left inhouse with new baby and worry of bills and food and mortgage and what-have-you. These lasses going without meals to make sure baby got what it needed – Lot of these were the ones that were splitting up. Blokes who should have been on top of world looked like bottom had dropped out of it – I could hear babies crying before I even set foot in place. Screaming place down – Where's my fifteen quid, Pete? shouted Adrian Booker. You got my fifteen quid yet, have you? He said it every fucking week. He wasn't only one and all. Sixteen quid now government were taking off benefits in lieu of strike pay. Blokes like Adrian Booker would go down DHSS and argue with them. DHSS would send him back here to argue with me. It was their wives that had started it. How Union should give their men strike pay. Thing was, I agreed with them. But what could you do? There wasn't even enough brass to

The Forty-sixth Week

Monday 14 – Sunday 20 January 1985

There were never any standing ovations now. There were never autographs for the kids. Never songs in his name. There was just the
silence –

The silence of the strike rolling towards the edge of the cliffs –

The petrol gone. The engine off. The brakes broken and the doors
locked –

Eighty thousand faces pressed against the windows –

The cold seas breaking on the rocks below, waiting.

The Jew has Neil doing this. The Jew has Neil doing that. This for him
and that for them. This for the Chairman and that for Tom Ball. This
for Piers and that for Dominic. This for Don and Derek and that for
Fred and Jimmy –

Morning, noon and bloody night –

The Jew has him running here. The Jew has him running there.
Here for the Jew and there for them. This article over to *The Times* and
that paper over to the High Court. These reports up to the Chairman
and those rulebooks up to Mansfield –

Mr High and bloody Mighty. His beck and fucking call –

Neil Fontaine needs to be out on the pavements. To be stood in the
doorways –

Station to station. Place to place –

Knightsbridge flats and Mayfair clubs. Empty bars and rented
rooms –

Room to room. Service to service –

To watch their windows and their doors. Their gardens and their
car parks –

Their comings and their goings –

But Jerry and Roger never come. Jerry and Roger nowhere to be
seen –

Jerry and Roger have gone –

To ground.

*

'The dead hand of Number 10,' the President had said and the President had been right –

The President and the Chairman had been set to meet at one of the coal industry's many social and benevolent gatherings. Then the Board abruptly cancelled the gathering –

'Her dirty fingerprints,' the President had said and bowed his head.

They were handing out more three- and five-year jail sentences to the Kent miners. They were cutting the Pit Police Force by a third. Restarting production at Kellingley. There were now seventy-three thousand men back at work –

They were saying it was all but finished –

All over bar the shouting –

'Why on earth do they think we are fighting to defend these stinking jobs in the pitch black? There are no lavatories or lunchbreaks, no lights or scenery –

'We are fighting because our culture and our community depends –'

Terry switched off the radio. He didn't want to wake them. Terry had work to do –

Back among the cake and biscuit tins. The cereal boxes and the Tupperware.

Dublin had been a success. Diane had been pleased –

Pine Tree Investments was up and running –

Her schemes and his dreams –

Hand in hand.

The corridors were long, the carpets old and wrong. The lights flickered off and on –

The lift door opened and closed and opened again and out they fell –

Diane Morris and Terry Winters were young and drunk.

She had her hands up his neck and in his hair. His up her legs and at her hairs. They fumbled with their clothes. They fumbled with their key –

The door opened and closed and opened again and in they fell –

The room was small, the carpet crawled. The light flickered on and off –

The bed creaked. The headboard banged. The wall shook –

They were not as young as they used to be. Not as drunk as they used to be.

She had her nails in his arse, then his back. His cock in her mouth, then her cunt –

Malcolm Morris sat in the corner with bloody fingers in his bleeding ears,
watching his wife fucking Terry Winters –
Off and on, on and off. On and off, off and on –
'I hate you. I hate you. I hate you.'
For the next ten bloody, bleeding, fucking years. Her scissors in his hands.

The war in heaven raged on. The Militants and the Moderates tearing their wings off. Nottinghamshire were stripping their president and their secretary of their positions. Exiling them to Sheffield. Determined to declare independence. South Derbyshire set to join them. This was all they talked about in the corridors and the canteen. The pubs and the bars around the Headquarters. Not the strike. Not their members stood out in the snow. Not their families –

They could swing in the wind now.

Just like Terry. They had left Terry on his own to handle the sequestrators and the receiver now. The legal actions. The day-to-day finances. The requests for this and the requests for that. The President had asked only that nothing further be written down. That all their existing files and records be shredded –

The paper trail burnt.

Terry liked that idea. He had actually been the one who'd suggested it –

Or had it been Diane?

But the cash kept on coming in. In briefcases and boxes, in suitcases and sacks. From home and abroad, from near and far. And the cash kept on going out. In briefcases and boxes, in suitcases and sacks. Home and abroad, near and far –

Terry sat in his office under the portrait of the President, surrounded by mountains of money. Len and the Denims brought it up from the cars and the taxis, from the trains and the planes. Terry wrote out receipts in pencil for the donors to burn –

Terry doled out the funds –

Forty-five thousand pounds for Yorkshire. Thirty-five thousand for South Wales. Twenty-five thousand for Durham. For Scotland and for Kent –

For wages. For rent. For food. For kids. For bills. For transport. For picketing –

Twenty thousand. Fifteen thousand. Ten thousand. Five thousand –

The money-go-round never stopped. Len and the Denims brought it up –

The Tweeds took it back down in twos; others came up from the areas personally.

Terry's fingers smelt of money. Terry's hands smelt of money –

Diane liked that. The smell of money. The scent of cash –

'The world is our oyster,' she liked to say and sniff him like a dog –

Like a dog.

Terry checked the phone was working. *Click-click.* Terry had an erection again –

Terry locked the door. Terry went back to his desk. Terry opened a box –

Money. Money. Money. Always funny –

Terry filled his briefcase. Terry shut and locked it. Terry erased this figure here. That figure there. Terry went back to the door. Terry listened. Terry unlocked his door. Terry checked the corridor. Terry got his coat. Terry put his briefcase under his arm. Terry took it down to his car. Terry put it in the boot with the suitcases. Terry –

'That where you keep the bodies then, is it, Comrade?'

Terry shut the boot. Terry turned round. Terry dropped his keys –

Bill Reed picked them up off the floor of the car park. Bill said, 'Butter fingers.'

'What do you want?' asked Terry. 'Sneaking up like that.'

'I'm sorry,' said Bill. 'I know how jumpy you must be in your position.'

'What do you mean?' asked Terry. 'My position?'

'Just the responsibility of it all,' said Bill. 'The family. The fame –'

'What do you want?' asked Terry again.

'I want to know what you keep locked in the boot of your car, Comrade.'

'It's none of your business,' said Terry.

Bill smiled. Bill nodded. Bill stepped forward. Bill kneed Terry in his balls –

Terry collapsed.

Bill opened the boot. Bill said, 'Planning a few days away with the wife, were we, Comrade?'

Terry lay on the floor of the car park. Terry held his balls. Terry blinked.

Bill opened up the suitcases. Bill whistled.

Terry stood up. Terry pushed Bill away from the boot. Terry said, 'Fuck off.'

Bill pushed Terry back. Bill followed him. Bill poked him in the chest and said, 'You'd better start talking now, Comrade. Tell me what all that fucking money's for.'

Terry stared at him. Terry took a deep breath. Terry said, 'It's for the President.'

'Fuck off, Winters,' said Bill. 'What's it doing in the boot of your car, then?'

'The Union is buying the President's house,' said Terry. 'That's the money.'

Bill Reed shook his head. Bill said again, 'So what's it doing in there?'

'Both the Union and our President are under legal attack, or hadn't you noticed?'

Bill Reed grabbed Terry again. Bill said, 'Fuck off, Winters. You're a liar.'

'It's Union money for the President,' said Terry. 'I'm putting it in a trust. OK?'

Bill Reed stared at Terry Winters. Bill Reed let him go. Bill Reed shook his head.

'What?' said Terry. 'You still don't believe me? Ask him yourself –'

Bill shook his head again. Bill turned round to look behind him –

The President, Paul and Len were walking across the car park.

The President nodded at Terry and Bill. The President said, 'Evening, Comrades.'

Terry and Bill nodded back. Terry and Bill said, 'Evening, President.'

'You two coming to the rally, are you, then?' asked Paul.

'Of course,' said Terry. 'We were just waiting to follow you.'

Bill Reed nodded. Bill Reed said, 'Looking forward to it.'

'Take the motorway to Leeds,' said Len. 'Then the A1. If you can keep up.'

Terry Winters and Bill Reed smiled and watched the Jaguar pull out.

Bill turned to Terry. Bill chucked him his keys. Bill said, 'Do give my apologies.'

Terry closed the boot of the car. Terry locked it. Terry opened the car door.

'And remember,' Bill shouted back, 'all property is theft, Comrade.'

Terry got into the car. Terry slammed the door. Terry drove up to Durham –

He stopped once at Scotch Corner to call Diane, but she had already checked out.

Terry stood at the side of the stage with Len. The President took deep breaths. Then the President said, 'I believe we are in crunch times. I believe we have now entered into a phase that will be the final and decisive stage, if our members remain solid –

'For if we retain our solidarity, we can bring the Coal Board and the government to the realization that there has to be a negotiated settlement.'

There was no talk of victory. There was no standing ovation –

There was no applause.

go picketing any more. Be fucked if government did start moving coal from pit heads to power stations. Not be able to do a thing about it – Not properly. These parcels are supposed to have sausage, some chops, some liver and bacon in them, said Mrs Kershaw. Past three parcels all I've had is bloody mince. But Mrs Wilcox, she's had sausage. She's had chops. She's had liver. She's had bacon – I'm sorry, I said. I'll talk to ladies who are par-celling it all up – Don't bother, she said. They just look out for their mates. I know that sort – I nodded. I wrote it all down – I said, I promise I'll see what I can do – Bloody nothing, she said. That's all *you* can do. This Union is a disgrace. Bloody disgrace. Eggs. Beans. Bread. Spaghetti. That's all we ever bloody eat. For nigh on a year now. But I've seen them and I've seen you too, Peter Cox. Not losing any weight, are you? Not losing any sleep either, I bet – *I wait for horses. Hooves. Batons* – Bad day this one. In a bad week. Hundred and fifty walked back in at Kiveton on Monday. Hundred and fifty in one day. Lot of faces down **Welfare** said it all. Said, That's it then. That's us – Grim sight it was, on news. In snow and slush, frozen and starved back – That was truth of it. Frozen and starved back – Hurt it did, to see them walk up that lane in snow and sludge. Their plastic bags for bits of coal and thin old coats against the cold – Pickets didn't say much to them. This was different now – These weren't your pit idiots. Your shirkers and your arse-lickers. Your head-cases and big mouths – These were honest, decent, hard-working miners who you lived and worked beside. These were your mates with their plastic bags and thin coats in snow and sludge. Frozen and starved – It was a terrible sight. Heartbreaking – Board and government on same news telling us there'd be no more talks. No more concessions – Been three bloody months now since last negotiations. Lot of rumours again – Board said there were now hundred and fifty in at our pit. That they'd had sixty in last two weeks – It was horrible. You didn't know who was scabbing and who was-n't – Blokes would stand there and lie

to your face. People were accusing each other at drop of a hat – Thing was, once someone was branded a scab they'd just think, Fuck it then, and in they went. Board and scabs were behind this – Picking on a whole street at a time. Getting majority back in. Isolating families who were still out. Pressuring them. Putting it about that they'd gone in when they hadn't – Whole teams and all. Face teams. Headings teams – Phoning each other up. All-for-one-and-one-for-all type thing. Didn't care what rest of folk thought as long as all team were agreed. I could see that – Had to work together. To trust each other – Few of scabs were even going about trying to organize returns. There was talk of Silver Birch and National Working Miners' Committee coming up to speak to them. I went to **Panel** and it was same story at all other pits – Talk now of expulsion for Nottingham. An amnesty for miners sacked during dis-pute – I didn't say anything. I just drove **home** – Mary was out at a meet-ing with Action Group. Our Jackie round at her mate's house – Just me. I stuck kettle and news on. I sat down – Ministers were telling media that they ould let the strike run on until it col-lapsed – Telling us. Telling Peter Heathfield. Mick McGahey. Arthur Scargill – No more talks. No more negotiations. No more concessions. No more chances – I got up. I switched it off. I picked up paper. I put it down. I stood up again. I sat back down. I got up. I paced room – I felt like I had a bloody knife in me. I felt cold. Horrid inside. Bloody horrible – I paced and I paced. There were Mary's scrapbooks on side. *True History of Great Strike for Jobs.* I picked them up. Early ones – *Here we go. Here we go. Here we go* – I turned pages. Those first few days in Sheffield – *We will win. We will win. We will win* – Mansfield rally. The Wake-field Gala. Orgreave – I put them down. I paced and I paced. I didn't know what to do. I felt sick inside – Like I couldn't get clean. Like I couldn't get warm – I'd never felt anything like this in my life. I thought, You're crack-ing up here. Be loony-bin for you now, old son – Mary and Jackie will come

The Forty-seventh Week

Monday 21 – Sunday 27 January 1985

'More to the point,' says the Jew, 'how are *you* sleeping, Neil?'

Neil Fontaine sets down the breakfast tray. Neil Fontaine says, 'Like a baby, sir.'

'So we're waking four times a night and screaming blue murder for a suck on a tit and clean pair of jim-jams, are we, Neil?'

Neil Fontaine pours the Darjeeling. Neil Fontaine says, 'Exactly, sir.'

'*Exactly?*' laughs the Jew. 'Very droll, Neil. Very droll indeed.'

Neil Fontaine hands the Jew his morning tea and the day's *Times*.

The Jew is still in his dressing-gown. His slippers up on the sofa of his suite –

He sips his tea and skims the paper and the telephone rings. Three times.

Neil Fontaine picks it up. *Click-click*. Neil Fontaine says, 'Mr Sweet's suite?'

He listens. He hands the phone to the Jew. He says, 'The Minister, sir.'

The Jew takes the phone with a smile and a wink. He says, 'Good morning, sir.'

The Jew listens. The Jew stops smiling. The Jew shouts, 'Did fucking what?'

There were only three days to a week. There were only candles for lights –

'– the CIA believe that the present spate of strikes in Britain has far more sinister motives than the mere winning of extra wages –'

There were rings of tanks around all the major airports –

'– we believe that the aim is to bring about a situation in which it would be impossible for democratic government to continue –'

It was the State of Britain, 1974. It was a State of Emergency –

'– you are restricted and squeamish on your own territory about doing the type of things that have to be done to track down and eliminate terrorists and subversives –'

They prised Malcolm from the six-fingered fist. Put him back inside the belly –

'– the CIA has agents operating on the insides of all the British labour unions. These are British nationals recruited by CIA case officers –'

Back to work. Back to look. Back to listen –

'– and for some time now we have been trying to convince successive British governments of the power of subversives within your trade union movement –'

Back to learn –

'– the present state of Britain makes it a troublemaker's paradise –'

To learn about adultery. Betrayal. Falsity. Infidelity. Perfidy. Treachery.

This was killing Neil. These death throes. This last, final rattle –

The Suits from the Board and the Moderates from the Union have been talking –

Talking. Talking. Talking –

Mines have always closed on the grounds of exhaustion. Mines have always closed on the grounds of geology. Mines have also always closed on the grounds of –

Many, many other things –

Things the Suits and the Moderates have been talking about –

Third-category things.

The Suits and the Moderates have been talking so much they actually think they are making progress –

The Board willing to compromise on the five threatened collieries, specifically. The Union ready to compromise on *uneconomic* collieries, generally –

That's what they're saying. That's what they're telling everyone –

Everyone who's listening –

The government and the TUC. The rest of the Board and the rest of the Union. The working miners and the striking miners. The press and the public –

Telling everyone that *negotiations* were still *possible –*

'Still *possible,*' screams the Jew. 'Over my dead fucking body!'

The Jew will soon see about this –

Two and a half billion pounds have been either spent or lost on the strike to date. Thousands of police and reserves have been mobilized. Thousands of miners arrested. Thousands and thousands of miners and their families have been forever branded scabs. Thousands of miners have chosen to break from the National Union of Mineworkers –

One thousand eight hundred and forty abandoned the strike only yesterday –

'And all for what?' shouts the Jew. 'All for fucking what, Neil?'

The Jew picks up the telephone. *Click-click.* The Jew calls Downing Street –

The Jew talks to the Prime Minister's Chief Press Secretary –

BB will put a spin on all this talking. BB will put a stop to all this talking –

'So the government and the Board are just going to turn their backs on the very people who have kept the lights on this winter?' the Jew asks BB –

'Leave them to the lynch mobs of the Left? Is that their thanks? Their reward?'

The Jew listens. The Jew laughs. The Jew says, 'Thank you, BB, thank you.'

The Jew puts down the telephone. The Jew applauds. The Jew looks up at Neil. 'Looking very pensive there, Neil,' says the Jew. 'Not keeping you, am I?'

The Fat Man and his seven Fat Friends were saying it would all be over in a matter of days now. There was talk of conciliation. *Light on the horizon.* Talk of concessions. *Historic compromises.* The rumour up and down the coalfields. *The end in sight –*

The much-whispered-of Yorkshire revolt dead in the bar of a Normanton WMC –

Now was not the time to start scabbing. Not now, after all these months –

All this pain –

The Fat Man and his Fat Friends had come to put them all out of their misery. And the President knew now was the time. Now, after all these months –

All these false dawns –

The TUC put the twelve-point tentative draft agreement on the table before him.

'This Union is perfectly willing to have negotiations,' the President told them. 'This Union is not arguing that there should be preconditions or a set agenda –'

The President knew this was not the time to start scrapping again. Not now –

The light in the dark marked *Exit*. The light over Terry Winters.

Terry looked at his watch. *Clocks ticking*. Terry said, 'It's time, gentlemen.'

The Fat Man and his seven Fat Friends, the President and his last skinny mates, everyone put down the draft agreement. Everyone turned to look at Terry –

Everyone nodded –

Terry switched on the television in the corner of the room –

TV Eye.

'A lot of heavily loss-making pits will have to be shut down,' she was saying. 'Let's not argue about the definition. Let's just get it written down –

'I want it dead straight. Honest and no fudging –'

The President stood up. He walked slowly over to the television and turned it off. He took the twelve-point tentative draft agreement out of Terry's hands –

The President tore it into a thousand pieces. The President let them fall –

The lights had finally gone out.

'Nothing short of total victory,' shouts the Jew from the back of the Mercedes –

The Jew has been asked to report for duty at Chequers this weekend. *Tout suite*. To report on his union within the Union. The mind games and the endgames –

But there have been harsh words between the Chairman and the Minister –

The one blaming the other. The other blaming the one –

Their different agendas. Their different approaches. Their different games.

The Jew has his own agenda. The Jew his own game to play. To play to win –

'Negotiations now would represent a defeat for the Board and for the nation. For, inevitably, there would be further concessions, in whatever words they were disguised. The time for negotiated settlement has passed. The President of the NUM must accept, in advance of any talks and in writing, that the Board has the right to manage the industry and the right to close pits –

'There must be no equivocation. No prevarication.

'There are those among us, however, who call for bridges to be built over which their president can beat an elegant retreat. Those voices misunderstand the temper of the nation. That man challenged the authority of the state. That man boasted that he would do to this government what the miners had done to the Heath government. That man presided over unprecedented violence and intimidation, corruption and conspiracy –

'The nation wants to see that man defeated and the nation will not easily forgive those who would be held responsible if defeat, whether by compromise or by fudge –

'If defeat were snatched from the jaws of victory –

'For nothing short of total victory is acceptable now,' says the Jew.

Neil Fontaine winds down his window. Neil Fontaine says, 'Mr Stephen Sweet.'

The officer steps back from the car. He gestures at the gates. The gates open –

'So let us set our course for total victory and *only* total victory,' shouts the Jew –

The dead hand of Number 10 at the wheel.

Neil Fontaine drives up the long drive. Neil Fontaine parks before the front door –

There are corpses in the trees. There are heads upon the posts.

They are all stood on the gravel, waiting. Their mouths all open, laughing –

King. Heseltine. Lawson. Ridley. Havers. Walker. Brittan. Tebbit.

'You want a fucking picture?' hisses the Help. 'Round the fucking back.'

Neil Fontaine starts the car again. He parks in the empty garage. He sits in the car. He stares through the windscreen. He sees the Prime Minister at the kitchen window –

She is eating frozen shepherd's pie. She is drinking cheap white wine –

The corpses in the trees. The heads upon the posts –

He smells the fumes. The rivers. The mountains.

He hears the screams –

Her blood and her skull.

413

home and find us in me socks. Drawing little faces on cornflakes like my Uncle Les – This one a copper. This one a picket. This one a copper. This one a picket – Little faces. Re-enacting Battle of Orgreave on kitchen table – That would be me. Mad Pete – I picked up phone. *Click-click* – I was going to call Derek. Tom. Johnny. David Rainer. Keith – I put it down again. I went upstairs – I laid down on **bed**. I closed my eyes – *I look back. Wall of fucking water bearing down again* – I opened my eyes again. I was thinking about my father – How he lived. How he died – He never had a prayer. I closed my eyes again – *Water. Water* – I opened them again. Straight off – Heart beating ten to dozen. Never had a fucking chance – I could hear Mary and Jackie downstairs. Hear kettle go on. Telly again. News again – I wanted to get up. I wanted to go down and see them – To say hello. To have a chat and a nice cup of tea – But I couldn't get up. I couldn't go down – Not let Mary and our Jackie see us like this. Not let them see me with tears down my face – *This wall of fucking water bearing down again. I run* – Difference a bloody day makes. A new day – Talks about talks were back on. Meeting set for Tuesday. Negotiations between our full Executive and Board. Even possibility that they'd talk about pay and overtime ban. Get it all sorted. Once and for all – Delegate Conference had been called to vote on whatever outcome of talks was. Lot of feeling both down at Welfare and up at **Panel** that it'd all be over by weekend – War of nerves, said Johnny. Tom laughed. He said, Well, mine can't talk much bloody more, lad – Mine neither, I said. Dave Rainer nodded. He said, All be glad to hear then that we're going ahead with Cortonwood tomorrow – Nice one, said Johnny. It's a good time to show solidarity and strength, said Derek. With talks and everything. Let them know that there's life in old dog yet – Not bothering with envelopes, said Dave. Just get as many as you can afford to send up there – Everyone nodded. Even me – I hadn't been for it when it was suggested last week. Now, though, it felt good – Good to be doing something. Take your mind off talks

and get you away from TV – I drove back down to **Welfare** and started to phone around. *Click-click*. Put teams together for cars. Had a feeling this would be last one. Lot of us did – There were them who weren't that happy. Few that weren't that keen on going back, you could see it in their eyes – Not because of any political motive or anything like that. Just didn't want to go back underground – I knew how they felt. That time down with engineers, I'd shit myself – They'd had a taste of something else and they'd liked it. Liked it a lot – Blokes who'd worked down pit since they left school. Never known anything else – They'd had a taste of sun and air. Taste of a different life – They were coming up to me, asking us what I thought chances were of going back. Then they'd ask us about redundancy – Especially older ones. Blokes who were only months off retiring – I didn't know what to say to them. Had a feeling there'd be a massive clampdown – Just depended what was said in London. How talks went – I went **home**. Mary and Jackie were still up. Had a crisp sandwich and a chat with them. *Newsnight* came on. Hopes still high of a settlement to end strike by 11 February. Lot of talk now about amnesties for sacked miners. Board saying no way. That wasn't helping. We all went up to **bed** none the wiser – I didn't bother getting into my pyjamas. Had to be up again in three hour – I didn't want to go to sleep, either. Didn't want to close my eyes – *I run. I run and run. I run again* – I woke up. Heart going again. Sweating buckets. Shitting bricks – Mary looking at us. She said, You want a cup of tea, do you? I looked at clock by bed – I best be on my way, I said. I got up. Pulled my trousers over my long-johns. Extra jumper – I leant back over bed and give her a kiss goodbye. I said, I'll see you later, love – Make sure you do, she said. I nodded – I knew she didn't want me going to Cortonwood. But she knew why I was going. I kissed her again. I drove down to **Welfare** – Village dark. Village quiet – But I knew there were eyes watching in dark. Ears listening in quiet – Keith was already down there – I don't want to miss this

The Forty-eighth Week

Monday 28 January – Sunday 3 February 1985

The Right Honourable Member just could not keep away. Just couldn't keep out –
   Of these shadows at the back, where the lights did not reach.
   His mouth moved faster and faster. Finger pointed harder and harder –
   He asked more and more questions.
   There was blood in Malcolm's mouth. Blood in Malcolm's ears –
   But Malcolm had more tapes. Many, many more tapes –
   From the shadows, where the lights did not.
   They would find more and more answers. Hear more and more tapes –
   And they would drown here –
   Here in the answers and the tapes. The shadows and the blood –
   These messages from the Dead. These tocsins for the Living.

They had been pounding on its chest. *Tick-tock.* Banging on its bones –
   Mouth to mouth –
The Labour Party. The TUC. Elements of the government and the Board –
   The kiss of life –
The Union were to meet the Board for substantive negotiations. The Union and the Board would agree on an agenda to end the dispute by February 11. The Union would call a Special Delegate Conference. The weekend would bring resolution –
   But there were fresh wounds upon the headless torso that lay before them here –
The Union insistent upon an amnesty for miners sacked during the dispute; the Prime Minister still insistent on written guarantees from the Union before talks –
   Mortal wounds –
'It has become a purely political strike,' Paul Hargreaves was telling them all. 'And it is clear now that she is very involved in the running of the Coal Board's business, countermanding an arrangement between a senior director and myself –

'She has total involvement and is out to destroy this Union.'

Terry watched Paul. Terry shook his head. Terry hated Paul –

His secret deals with his secret contacts. His secret talks in secret locations –

He hated his naivety. He hated his self-importance. He hated his suspicions –

Paul had finished his speech. Paul had sat down. Paul was staring at Terry –

Terry started to cough. Terry started to scratch his arms. Terry made his excuses. Terry left them to their increasing talk of a return without settlement –

Living to fight another day –

Terry walked down the corridor. He went down the stairs. Terry left the building. He found a phone box. Terry picked up the receiver. *Click-click.* He dialled the number –

They could pound and pound. Bang on and on –

Terry said, 'Clive Cook, please.'

'I'm afraid Mr Cook is on a temporary leave of absence,' said a woman's voice. 'Perhaps I may be of assistance? To whom am I speaking?'

Terry hung up. He stood in the phone box. Terry closed his eyes. He prayed –

It had run and run but now it had collapsed, lying here before him –

Flat out upon the floor. This body upon the shore. The beach soaked in blood. The blue waves stained red –

But Terry Winters knew, *dead was dead.*

From the corner of the Euston Road and Warren Street. From Grosvenor Street and on to the Joint Services Intelligence Centre outside Ashford in Kent –

They had sent Malcolm to Lisburn, Ulster –

To the six-fingered fist that held and gripped. That squeezed and crushed until –

Everything blurred. Everything merged. Distorted and faded –

In the shadows at the back, where the truths and the lies, the promises and the threats, the voices and the silences, the prayers and the curses, became one –

In Lisburn, Ulster –

From there everything whispered. Everything echoed. Everything moaned –

These voices from these shadows, these silences and spaces, these truths and lies, their promises and threats, Malcolm's prayers and his curses –

A deafening, deafening wall of horrible, horrible sounds –

MI5. MI6. Special Branch. The RUC. The army and the SAS –

Until everything became one long, long scream –

One long, long scream of places and names, terror and treachery –

Derry. The Bogside. Belfast. The Lower Falls. The Shankill Road. Chichester-Clark. Faulkner. Stormont. McGurk's Bar. Bloody Sunday. Widgery. Bloody Friday. Direct Rule. Operation Motorman. Sunningdale. The Ulster Workers' Council. Dublin. Monaghan. Guildford. Birmingham. The Miami Showband. Tullyvallen Orange Hall. Whitecross. Kingsmills. Mrs Marie Drumm. Captain Robert Nairac. The Ulster Unionist Action Council. La Mon Hotel. The Irish National Liberation Army –

Directed or undirected, formal or casual, acknowledged or not –

Sources and agencies; agents and informants; information and disinformation –

Codes changed. Numbers changed. Names changed. Places changed –

Tapes changed, but the job stayed the same –

Home or away. Near or far. England or Rhodesia. Yorkshire or Ulster –

The job stayed the same. Always the same –

In the shadows. In the silences.

These are the most dangerous of days. The financial markets are in crisis and turmoil; seven billion pounds have been wiped off the value of shares; base rates have risen between 12 and 14 per cent. There have been calls for a national government. For a government of reconciliation to heal the divisions in the nation. Echoes from the dark days. The Prime Minister and her Cabinet have launched a television offensive –

TV Eye. Weekend World. This Week, Next Week. A Week in Politics –

The message is loud. The message is clear –

No fudge. No forgiveness. No fudge. No forgiveness –

Unmistakable. Unambiguous. Unequivocal –

Explicit.

The Jew stares at the TV. The Jew smiles at her face. But the Jew cannot focus –

'– I do not want another round of talks to fail. I want them to succeed. I

know there are many, many striking miners who want them to succeed too, so they can get back to work and who, I believe, would accept past procedures and would like to get back on that basis –'

'The play's the thing,' mumbles the Jew. 'The play within a play –'

'*– and I want them to go back. But I do not wish their hopes to be dashed by another round of talks, which are doomed to failure. It is because I want the talks to succeed that I do not want these talks to go ahead on a false basis –'*

'A Revenger's Tale,' mutters the Jew to himself. 'A Revenger's Tale.'

Neil Fontaine could not agree more. But Neil can wait no more –

He tucks up the Jew in his bed. He switches off the lights at the wall –

'Sweet dreams, sir,' he calls from the door of the fourth-floor suite –

'He always does,' whispers the Jew in the dark, to no one. 'He always does.'

Neil Fontaine takes the back way down the back stairs to leave by the back door. Neil had a message waiting for him this lunchtime. Three words –

Trident Marine Limited –

Neil let his fingers do the walking. Neil found it in the *Yellow Pages* – Queen Street Place, EC4 –

Right under his fucking nose.

Neil Fontaine changes his clothes. Neil Fontaine changes his car –

He parks again. He watches again. He waits again.

Neil Fontaine breaks into the third-floor offices of Trident Marine Limited.

Neil Fontaine switches on his torch. Neil Fontaine shines a light –

On their offices and their desks. On their letterheads and their directors –

The offices and desks that they share. The letterheads and the directors –

The senior civil servants. The Cabinet secretaries. The City bankers –

The commanding officers of the British armed forces –

Past. Present. And future –

Friendships planted in foreign places –

Malaya. Cyprus. Rhodesia. Ulster. Sheffield. Sizewell –

Jupiter Securities runs Trident Marine. Trident dumps nuclear waste at sea –

For the government. For them. For her.

The restaurant was quiet. Empty again. The chairs on the table. The orchestra gone –

Malcolm put down his evening paper. He shook his head and smiled –

The Right Honourable Member had referred the business to the Prime Minister.

Malcolm traced circles. Loops. Rings with his finger –

There was an ancient, enduring majesty to the annular –

Like the fylfot.

one, he said. Might be last one – You just behave yourself, I told him. He laughed. He said, Be telling that to tit-heads and all, will you? That's what I mean, I said. Just watch yourself. They'll be thinking it might be last one and all. He nodded and we went inside. Lads started to arrive. Big Chris. Kev. Tim. Gary. John from Top. Fair few faces I hadn't seen for a while – Little Mick. Paul Thompson. His Daniel. Graham from Crescent – Last bloody man still out on that street. Best way to let folk know I'm not a fucking scab, he said – Lads all wanting to know what was going on down in London with talks. Not much news in first papers or on radio – Did a quick count of heads. Made sure cars were all full. Brass sorted out. Rang round for them that had overlaid. *Click-click* – Then off we set. Damp and dark as usual. Radio on as we drove. Bit of music to cheer us up – *Nellie the Elephant*. Russ bleeding Abbot – Big Chris telling us all jokes he could remember from time he'd seen Black Abbots at Filey. Least it got us to **Cortonwood** with a smile on our faces. Coppers must have thought we were on happy pills – Lot of them waiting. *Krk-krk.* Transits and Land-Rovers. Mesh across their windows. Line of police with long shields out across road – Knew we were coming, of course. Knew how many by looks of things, too – Lot of us, though. Three thousand – Three thousand men. One bloody message – *No Surrender.* Made our point and all – In every face. In every stare. In every shove. In every shout – *The Miners. United – Will never be defeated. Maggie, Maggie, Maggie – Out! Out! Out!* – Fuck. Keith called round **ours** on Thursday night. He said, They're restarting production at Kiveton tomorrow – I know, I said. It's all over telly – What's going on, Pete? I don't know, I said. I'd no idea – No idea what to tell him. Tell anyone – Talks had collapsed. Thatcher had asked for all kinds of written pre-conditions. Board telling miners to vote with their feet. Looked to be no way out of this for us. Not now – My stomach knotted each time I went down **Welfare**. I dreaded it – Faces. Questions. Looks. Comments – Kev Shaw

sat down. Pete, he said. I've got something to say – I know what you're going to say, I told him. It's all round village – He nodded. He said, It's right and all – I shook my head. I said, So don't waste your breath and my time – Look, he said, you've always been right with me and I want to be right with you – Then don't start scabbing, I said. Not now – He looked at me. He said, I'm going back Monday. Nothing will make me change my mind. I've had enough abuse before I've even set foot in place. But I've seen my kids go without for too long. Wife trying to feed us all on a fiver a week and I've had it up to here, Pete. You've been decent and you've helped us with bills and what-have-you and I've no complaints about you and branch. But I'm off back to work on Monday. Come-what-may – Kev, I said. What do you want me to say? You want some kind of bloody dispensation – I've done my time, he said. I've been on more pickets than most. I nodded. That you have, I said. And now you're going to piss it all down drain and be known for rest of your life as a scab. He looked away then – First time since he sat down. His eyes didn't meet mine – This is going to end, I told him. Not going to go on much longer. Might even be over by Tuesday and you'd have scabbed for just twenty-four hour out of eleven month. He looked up. I shook my head. I said, Twenty-four hour, that might be all you'd have scabbed. But for rest of your life you'd be known as Kev the Scab and your kids as the children of Kev the Scab. He looked away again. Down at floor again. I said, You want to be like one of them old blokes that can only have a pint in Sheffield? Places where no one knows he was a scab sixty year ago. You've seen that one up at top end. Out by bus stop in all weathers? Kev nodded. You know he was a scab? Kev nodded again. You know how many days he scabbed back then? Kev shook his head. He looked at me. I said, Me neither. That's my point – it doesn't matter whether he scabbed through whole strike or just last bloody day – He was a scab then and he's a scab now – Kev had his eyes closed. He nodded – I leant forward. I put my

Much of the country was flooded. The pound had slipped further. There were unreported power cuts. People swinging in the wind. But the Fat Man was back again –

Fresh from tea at the Savoy with the Minister; dinner at the Ritz with the Board –

Here to save the day –

But not Terry's day –

The receiver had five million of their pounds. He was on to the Dublin money too. He had paid all their fines. He wanted to end sequestration. He wanted sole control –

Terry's days were numbered. The clock ticking down. The President's too –

'We are not begging and crawling for a resumption of negotiations,' he shouted. 'And there appears to be a very real determination to make us accept the principle that pits should close on economic grounds even before getting to the negotiating table –'

But the Fat Man just nodded his fat head. The Fat Man was not going to give up. The Fat Man persuaded the NEC to stay in the capital another twenty-four hours –

For a third fucking day.

'I am not walking away from the search for negotiations,' declared the Fat Man. 'The problem is too big to leave alone.'

Fuck. Fuck. Fuck –

Terry had to get out. Had to get away. Had to get home. He had to find a phone –

Terry made the call. Terry went back inside TUC Headquarters –

'There is no possibility at all of this Union ever accepting conditions of that kind,' the President was saying again. 'No union leaders worth their salt would ever be a party to such measures. *Never.* Not in a month of bloody Sundays would –'

There was a knock at the door. There was a note passed to the President –

The President read the note. The President looked up at Terry –

Terry blinked. Terry smiled. Terry said, 'What is it, Comrade President?'

'It's your wife,' said the President. 'I'm afraid there's been an accident.'

The Jew attends the unveiling of a memorial to Yvonne Fletcher in St James's Square. The Jew is in a sombre suit and coat, under an umbrella held by Neil –

'– without the police,' the Prime Minister is reminding the assembled people, 'there would be no law and there would be no liberty –'

The Jew nods in his sombre suit and coat, under an umbrella held by Neil –

His eyes never leave her face; hope never leaves his heart –

But she leaves without a word. Not even a goodbye. Without a second glance –

'Because of her courage, her resilience,' the Jew is quick to tell Neil in the car, 'it's all too easy to forget that behind the Iron Lady mask is a mother and a woman.'

Neil Fontaine nods. Neil Fontaine drives the Jew back to Hobart House –

The National Working Miners' Committee will be waiting for them.

'There is still so much to be done, Neil,' says the Jew. 'In public and in private.'

Neil Fontaine nods again. Neil Fontaine could not agree more –

He is paying men from the small ads ten quid an hour to stand in doorways.

Neil Fontaine parks the car. Neil Fontaine follows the Jew upstairs to his office –

Chloe shows in Fred and Jimmy. Chloe hands the Jew new reports and a coffee –

'Did you arrange a time for the meeting with the Chairman?' asks the Jew.

Chloe bites her bottom lip. Chloe says, 'I'm afraid he's unavailable today, sir.'

'Unavailable? Unavailable to whom?' laughs the Jew. 'Unavailable to me?'

Fred Wallace brushes the top of his trouser leg. Jimmy Hearn fiddles with his ear.

Chloe goes over to the phone. Chloe picks it up –

The Jew strides across the room. The Jew slaps the phone out of her hand –

'Don't you dare humiliate me again,' shouts the Jew. 'Go! You are dismissed!'

Chloe looks at Neil. Neil nods at Chloe. Chloe looks at the door. Neil nods again.

'What are you waiting for?' laughs the Jew. 'A reference? A kiss? A banana?'

Chloe stares at the Jew. Chloe smiles. Chloe leaves the door open on her way out.

The Jew turns to Fred and Jimmy. The Jew says, 'Now, where were we?'

But Fred and Jimmy are staring at the door. Fred and Jimmy staring at Chloe –

Chloe still standing in the doorway. Chloe smiling and pointing at them all –

'There will be a reckoning,' she says. 'There will be a figuring.'

Terry took the stairs two at time. Terry banged on the door –

There was no answer –

Terry banged and banged on it. Doors opened up and down the corridor –

All the wrong doors –

Terry put his head against the door. Terry whispered, 'Please –'

The door opened. Terry fell forward. Into the room. Onto Diane –

'How long have you been stood out there?' asked Diane

'I thought you'd gone,' said Terry. 'I thought you'd left me.'

'I was in the bathroom with the hairdryer on,' she laughed. 'Sorry.'

Terry put his arms inside her dressing-gown. Terry held her by her skin –

'You're hurting me,' she laughed again.

'I want to see you bleed,' said Terry. 'I want to see you're real.'

Malcolm got off at Hyde Park Corner and walked up Park Lane onto Curzon Street –

The streets were quiet, the streets empty. The rain was cold, the wind warm.

He walked past Leconfield House to the building next to the Lansdowne Club –

Curzon Street House, a.k.a. the Bunker.

Malcolm went inside the building. Down the stairs and along the corridors –

The stairs quiet, the corridors empty. The air old, the smell worse.

The lights flickered on and off, off and on. The office doors opened and closed –

Deserted silences. Deserted spaces.

Malcolm reached his room. Malcolm took out his key –

They had changed the lock. They had changed the number –

But it opened all the same (it remembered his name).

Malcolm sat down behind his wooden desk in his windowless room –

He reached for his glasses. He took out his files –

The Campaign for Nuclear Disarmament. The Trade Unions. The *Morning Star*. The Socialist Workers' Party. The Militant Tendency. Local governments and councils. The Workers' Revolutionary Party. The National Front. The British National Party. *Bulldog*. British Movement. Combat 18 –

Counter-subversion. Left and Right. Right and wrong.

They wanted some things to succeed. They wanted some things to fail –

Discrimination and integration. Racism and Socialism –

The nuclear industry and the coal industry.

The lights flickered on and off, off and on. The office doors opened and closed –

Things succeeded. Things failed. Things came together. Things fell apart –

Societies. Governments. Unions. Marriages. Families. People –

Their hearts and their minds.

This was the way the world turned. This was the way the world ended –

A cigarette. A kiss. A wrong number. A look and then silence –

Not with a bang, but with a knock on the door.

'Vote with your feet,' the Board's Mr Fixit was urging strikers. 'Vote with your feet.'

Terry turned into the cul-de-sac. Terry parked the car in front of the house –

There had been pre-executive meetings all last night; there had been fights; accusation and counter-accusation; honourable settlements versus no settlement at all –

Fights to the finish or organized returns with heads held high.

But it will never be enough for them just to lose; they must be seen to have lost –

Her ministers and her Board on television, boasting about not boasting –

Bragging about not bragging. Gloating about not gloating –

Terry switched off the radio. Terry got out of the car. Terry locked the door –

Terry opened the gate. Terry walked up the drive. Terry rang the doorbell –

No answer.

Terry knocked on the door –

No answer.

Terry went down the side of the house. Terry went round the back –

No one.

Terry looked in through the windows. Terry saw –

Nothing.

Terry went back to the front door. Terry banged on it. Terry hammered on it –

'You fucking cunt,' shouted Terry through the letterbox. 'You fucking cunt!'

People came to their curtains. People watched from their windows. People stood on their steps –

Terry punched the door. Terry screamed. Terry kicked the door. Terry howled –

'Bastard!' he shouted again. 'You thieving fucking bastard!'

Terry stormed back down the drive. Terry saw the sign in the garden –

For sale –

The people at their windows. The people on their doorsteps –

Terry raised two fingers to the former friends and neighbours of Clive Cook –

'Fuck off back to your televisions,' shouted Terry Winters. 'Back to your teas.'

Terry got in his car. Terry turned the key. Terry switched on the car radio –

'Figures don't lie,' the President was admitting. 'But liars can certainly figure.'

There were 43 per cent of all miners at work now –

Just 7 per cent to go –

There would be humiliations. There would be recriminations –

Heads on plates, goats outside the gates.

hand on his shoulder. I said, It's not worth it. He nodded again. He opened his eyes. He sighed. He said, Will you have a word with wife for us? I nodded. He said, She's going to go fucking mental. I nodded again. Be in good company then, I said – *Deeper and deeper. Faster and faster – I look back up corridor. Water roaring down* – I couldn't get up. I lay there in **bed** as depressed and fucking down as I'd ever been in my whole life – There were over three hundred back at pit now. They had them washing coal. Yesterday morning these big lorries had come and picked up supplies for power stations in Trent Valley. Had a mass picket waiting for them. But they got in and out no bother. Just showed how low stocks must be for them, though. To have to be moving stuff from here – Fifteen big giant lorries. They were going to move whole fucking lot. All seven thousand tonnes of it – Oh aye, we'd stand there for rest of week. However long it was going to take them – We'd shout and we'd shove. We'd shove and we'd swear – But, fucking hell, I'd have liked to have seen them try to wash and move that stuff if we'd stayed solid – I knew then we could have won. Knew we could have beaten that bitch and all her fucking boot-boys. Her bullies in DHSS and media. Knew we could have beaten them and won because they would have run out of fucking coal – It was that bloody simple. It was that bloody depressing – I had nightmares every time I closed my eyes. Had nightmares every time I switched on TV. Every time I opened fridge. Every time I set foot in village. Every time I went into Welfare or up to Panel – Least bed was warm. Long as I didn't let my eyes close. There was a tap on door. It was our Jackie with a cup of tea. It's gone half-nine, she said. I nodded. I said, I know – What's wrong with you? she asked. You on strike or something? – Get out of here, you cheeky cow, I said. I'll get up when I'm good and bloody ready and not a moment before. She came over to bed and she give us a kiss on top of my head. Happy Valentine's Day, she said. I'm a lucky man, I told her. I

don't deserve you and your mother – You don't, she said. So you best get up before we kick you out. I went up **Panel** – High Court injunction against Yorkshire Area NUM now. Forbade picketing at eleven pits and limited all pickets to six men from pit itself – Last bloody straw, said Tom. Last bloody nail in coffin, said Johnny. That's what it is and branches won't abide by it – They have to, said David Rainer. They have to. I said, You know what this one lad said to me last week? He said, Pete – I used to hate them fucking scabs in Nottingham with all my heart. But you know what? If it hadn't been for picketing them, I'd have had no brass. I'd have starved – No picket. No pay. No scabs. No scoff – Fucking starved without them. Listen to us all, said Dave. Like last bloody days of Third fucking Reich. It's not over yet – But no one said anything. We just got up and went back to our branches to tell them they couldn't even picket their own pit if there were more than six of them – *I see a bloke behind us. Water almost on top of him* – He was sat on our **doorstep**. Soaked through – Like a drowned rat. Shiv-ering, he was – I wanted to punch his fucking lights out. The fucking hell you been? I shouted. Been bloody worried sick about you – I'm sorry, he said. Cath went. House went. I couldn't face it. I couldn't face anyone – Bastard, I said. I had you dead at bottom of reservoir. Topped yourself – I'm sorry, he said again. I've got nowhere else to go – I opened front door. I stuck hall light on. He looked in a right state. I said, Where you bloody been? Doing bricklaying down in London. Bit in Southampton – Why didn't you say something? I said again. Folk been worried sick about you – I'm sorry, he said. I didn't want to say anything because I didn't want pity – Not pity when it's mates, is it? I put fire on in **front room** and sat him down. I put kettle on and fetched him some clean clothes. Thank you, he said. Best stay here, I told him. Until you get yourself sorted out – Mary mind, will she? Probably, I said. But she won't see you on street, will she? I left him to get changed. I made him a cup of tea and

The Fiftieth Week

Monday 11 – Sunday 17 February 1985

Neil Fontaine dreams of her skull. The nightmare interminable. *Her skull and his candle*. He screams in his room at the County. The light always on. He kneels down by the bed. The notebooks all gone. He picks apart the hours. The days. The months and the years. Their lives and their deaths. He throws the pieces against the wall. He pulls down the curtains. He throws them on the bed. The bed empty. The sheets old and stained –

They want some things to fail. They want some things to succeed.

Neil Fontaine stands at the window. The dead light and the electric –

They let some things succeed. They let some things fail.

There are always moments like this. Only ever moments like this –

But for how much longer?

Click-click –

He had called from out of the shadows (where there was only night) –

'Malcolm,' he had said, 'you busy, are you?'

'Why?'

'I'd like to temporarily borrow your auricles, if they're available.'

'Anywhere nice?'

'Shrewsbury,' he had said. 'If you fancy it.'

'If the price is right.'

'Two and a half, plus expenses.'

'You know where I am.'

'Yes,' Neil Fontaine had said. 'I know where you are.'

In the shadows (where there was only night, only endless fucking night).

Click –

It had been a Friday; Friday 9 March 1984.

The Jew is at sea again. Down at Bournemouth with the Young Conservatives to celebrate her first ten, glorious years. Her Great Leap Forward. The Jew bought a card specially –

'Valentine,' he'd sung. His hand on his heart. 'Won't you be my valentine?'

The Jew has a place in his heart for Neil too. And the Jew's left him with lots to do –

'Idle hands,' he'd said. 'Know what they say about idle hands, don't you, Neil?'

Neil Fontaine had nodded. Neil Fontaine had taken out his pen –

'So much to be done,' the Jew had said. 'Minds to be moulded. Hearts to be won.'

To monitor the returns. To assist Piers & co. To chauffeur the Chairman –

Non-stop Neil, that's Neil now. From A to B and back again –

Hobart House to Eaton Square. Eaton Square to Congress House. Congress House to Eaton Square. Eaton Square to Thames House. Thames House to Eaton Square. Eaton Square to the Ritz. The Ritz to Congress House. Congress House to Eaton Square –

Non-stop Neil with the bodies and the bottles. The people and the papers –

The Minister and the drafts. The TUC and the whisky. The Board and –

The eight points thrashed out between the Chairman and the General Secretary.

Neil fetches and he carries. He takes and he leaves. He waits and he watches –

The tensions. The mistrust. The deceits. The misgivings. The lies. The mistakes –

These plays within plays within plays within plays –

The games and the hunts. The traps and the baits –

The meat rotten. The prey starved. The flies fat –

'We'll be watching developments very closely,' Piers is telling the Chairman in the back of the Jew's Mercedes. 'If we find evidence that these orders are not being complied with, if coach firms are still carrying mass pickets to the pits in clear breach of the injunction, then we shall take legal action against them.'

'And what of Yorkshire?' asks the Chairman. 'The Heartland?'

'Tomorrow,' says Piers. 'After tomorrow there will be no more mass pickets.'

Neil drops the Chairman and Piers at Hobart House. Neil checks the Jew's office –

The office empty. The lights and the heating off. The windows open to winter –

His maps and his pins. His charts and his tins. In boxes by the door.

'I need to know everything,' the Jew had told him. 'Absolutely everything, Neil.'

Neil switches on the lights. Neil closes the windows. Neil calls the Jew –

Neil tells the Jew one thousand one hundred and ten men returned this week –

'That's less than last week,' screams the Jew. 'It's just not good enough, Neil!'

Neil tells him about the bad weather. Neil doesn't tell him about the talks –

'The eve of a historic breakthrough,' the Union were saying –

'Uncork a bottle of my finest,' says the Jew. 'I'll be back for dinner, Neil.'

'And not a moment too soon, sir,' replies Neil Fontaine before he hangs up –

Neil is driving the General Secretary of the TUC back to Congress House.

They asked after his wife. They didn't wait for his reply. They didn't really care –

Nothing mattered now, but Terry knew that (Terry has known that for a time).

'It has to be an honourable settlement,' Dick was telling the rest of the Executive. 'The men will not sell their souls now. Not at this stage –'

Everybody nodded. Everybody knew that –

Phrases had become empty. Faces become blank. Words empty. Looks blank –

The Fat Man stood up. The Fat Man distributed photocopies of the agreement –

'This is an honourable settlement,' said the Fat Man. 'Honourable –'

The National Executive flicked through the eight points of the document –

Reconciliation. The right of the Board to manage, the right of the Union to represent. A return to work and a return to a new Plan for Coal. The mod-ification of the Colliery Review Procedure. The incorporation of an independent reference body into the CRP. The future of all pits to be dealt with by this new CRP, including those collieries with no satisfactory basis for continuing operations. The CRP to provide a further review where agreement could not be reached. But, point eight –

At the end of this procedure the Board will make its final decision –

The President put down his photocopy. The President looked up at the Fat Man –

No more talks. No more alterations. No more discussions. No more negotiations –

'This is the best possible deal,' said the Fat Man. 'The best possible deal.'

'So she says,' smiles the President. 'And so he says. And now so you say.'

'But what do you say?' asked the Fat Man. 'You and your Executive?'

'It's unacceptable,' said the President of the NUM. 'That's what I say.'

'So what can I do now?' asked the Fat Man. 'What more can I do?'

'You can pull out the entire trade union movement in industrial action in support of the National Union of Mineworkers –

'That's what more you can bloody do!'

The Fat Man looked up at the President. The Fat Man shook his head –

'It's too late,' he said. 'It's too late and you know it.'

The President looked down at the Fat Man, and the President shook his head –

His fingers squeezed his nose. His eyes filled with tears –

The President looked round the table at the National Executive Committee –

They shifted in their seats. They picked their pants out of their arses and sighed. The will is there, they said. The wording is not, they argued –

Is it hell, they shouted. The wording is there, they said. It's the will that's not –

They lit their cigarettes. They drank their teas. They looked to the President –

The President picked up the points. The President read them through again –

The President put them down again. The President said again, 'Unacceptable.'

No man's land –

The President caught again here. The President trapped again –

Piggy-in-the-middle –

The TUC and the government. *Hand in hand.* The government and the Board. The Board and the TUC. The TUC and his own fucking Union. The Left and the Right. The Militants and the Moderates. The Hardcore and the Soft. The Left within the Left. The Right within the Right. The Tweeds and the Denims. The Traditionalists and the Modernists. The Europeans and the Soviets. The wet and the dry –

The black and the white. The right and the wrong. The good and the bad –

United we stand. Divided we fall –

Factions and fractions. Fictions and frictions –

Never. Fucking. Ending.

The President shook his head. The Executive did not. The Fat Man nodded –

Nodded and nodded and nodded and nodded and nodded and nodded –

'The Minister will help,' he promised. 'The Minister wants to end the strike and, where there's a will, there is always a way.'

The Fat Man picked up his papers. The Fat Man left for Thames House –

Left them to their bitter pills. Their factions and their frictions –

To accept this or reject it. To strike on or return . . .

Terry made his excuses. Told them he had to go. They didn't listen. Didn't care –

To return without an agreement or return with an agreement . . .

Terry took the train back up to Sheffield. Terry sat in first class –

An agreement that had no amnesty or an agreement that did . . .

The receiver had ended the sequestration. The receiver had sole control –

An amnesty that included all sacked miners or that only included some . . .

Terry had to move fast. Terry had to move by night. Terry had lots to move –

The suitcases and the biscuit tins. The cardboard boxes and the padded envelopes. The cash and the columns. The additions and the subtractions. The sums and the cost –

His fractions and his fictions –

The price –

Every. Fucking. Thing.

'Be careful,' said the voice from the doorway to his office. 'Makes you go blind.'

Terry looked up from his desk. *Fuck.* Terry said, 'What does?'

Bill Reed switched on the lights. He said, 'Playing with yourself in the dark.'

'What do you want now?' asked Terry.

'Just wanted to know how your wife was doing.'

'Thank you,' said Terry. 'Recovering very well.'

Bill smiled. 'Reassuring to know such things are still possible.'

'Isn't it just,' said Terry. 'Now was there anything else, Comrade?'

Bill Reed stopped smiling. Bill Reed stared at Terry Winters –

Terry Winters smiled back. Terry Winters didn't care –

Nothing. Fucking. Mattered. Now –

The clock was ticking down. *Tick-tock.* The final countdown had commenced –

These were the last few days.

The Jew is back from the beach. Fresh from the festivities –

'They're holding fucking what?' he is screaming at Neil. 'When? Where? Who?'

The Jew has Neil take him straight to Hobart House –

'Monday! Downing Street!' he shouts into the car phone. 'The Prime Minister!'

The Jew thunders up the stairs. The Jew storms into the Chairman's office –

The Chairman is at his desk. Pen in hand. The Chairman is at his tether's end –

'They are politicians,' he sobs. 'I am just an industrialist.'

'But this is *1985*,' rants the Jew. 'What the fuck is going on?'

The Chairman nods. The Chairman stiffens his upper lip –

'Have they stormed the barricades?' raves the Jew. 'Have they killed the King?'

The Chairman tears up his letter of resignation –

'What time shall I expect the knock upon my door?' laughs the Jew –

The Chairman laughs now. The Chairman reaches out to embrace the Jew –

'Remember,' whispers the Jew. 'There's no politics without industry.'

a slice of toast – So you didn't get much work, then? I asked him. He shook his head. He said, there must be tenthousand miners down there doing same – I wish they'd stayed bloody put, I said. I wish you had – There were no brass, Pete. And I won't beg. Never. That's not me – Least you're back now, I said. You know there are some that had you down as a scab – I know, he said. I saw what they did to house – I'm sorry, I said. He laughed. He said, Not my house now, is it? I stood up. I said, You still be here in morning, will you? He nodded. He said again, I'm sorry, Pete – *Just one bloke. But it's not Martin* – Final push now. Last few days – Board wanted their 50 per cent. Board wanted us beat – Decision was made to go up to **Wath**. This was against wishes of Area. But no one gave two shits what anyone else said or thought now – It was a very personal matter now and if you were still out it was because of you – Not because someone told you to stay out. Not because you were *intimidated* – There were still some rallies in offing. But this looked like last away-day, if you like. Right set-to and all – Had police outnumbered at start. They brought in back-up. *Krk-krk*. Piled out of vans and straight into us. They were local – South bloody fucking Yorkshire. Force we fucking paid for out of our fucking rates – Here to settle scores, I could see that. Bad as anything in whole strike – But I was numb. Fucking numb to it all now – I watched them grab this one lad. I watched them beat him to ground. I watched them jump up and down on him. Big black boots on his chest. Up and down. Up and down. They were animals – Let loose by government. Free to do what the fuck they wanted – They had got away with every single thing they'd tried. There'd be no going back now – No rights for ordinary folk. Not now – Minute we could, we went straight back to car. Legged it – Keith. Martin. Chris. And me. Most folk did – Made our way back from Wath to **Welfare**. More rumours and trouble waiting to welcome us there – Lot of talk that they'd got four hundred back in at work now. That they

didn't need any more – Be younger scabs who had started it again. Big gobs on them – Last two hundred in would be sacked. Hundred would be finished – Two hundred laid off. Anyone who was on strike for more than a year faced automatic dismissal – No-strike contracts being prepared. Redundancy rights would be denied to strikers – Every man who stayed out over twelve months would have to undergo a medical. That was one that had really put wind up folk – I'm going to lose my job, said Billy. I've spent my whole fucking life down there and I know I'd not pass a medical. Not with my chest problems. Problems they gave me. I didn't stay out all this time to let her and all her cronies take away my job on health grounds. Health they bloody took from me – It's not right, I told him. It's just a rumour – That's what you say, said Billy. But you know as much as we do and I'm sorry, but you'll be no good to us when we get back in. Not position Union are in now – He was right. There was nothing I could say to him – Nothing to make it all better. Nothing to make it like it had been – This rate, scabs would be in majority. They'd already taken over Unity Club. Put it about that this Hit Squad of theirs would sort out last of strikers – I knew for a fact that they'd bullied a couple of younger lads into going back. Threatening kiddies of other folk – Kind of blokes they were. But they still had to get a mesh bus into work. One time they did try to walk in, they did it with their eyes on floor – Billy, I said, this morning I saw two scabs walking up our street. You know how I know they were scabs? Because one was walking forwards while other walked backwards. That you, is it, Billy? Walking backwards up a dark street because you're that ashamed of what you've done. That frightened of what folk would say or do to you because of what you had done to them – To their pit. Their village – That you, is it, Billy? Or would you join this Hit Squad and go about picking on young lads? Threatening them. Intimidating them. Waving your pay cheque and your scab brass

The Fifty-first Week

Monday 18 – Sunday 24 February 1985

The cigarette. The kiss. The wrong number. The look and then silence –
  Until the knock on the door, and things fell apart –
  Hearts. Minds. People. Marriages. Families. Unions. Governments and societies –
  They always did. They always have. They always would –
  These fragile things. Burdened. These frail things. Broken –
  Promises and plans. Fidelities. Arrangements and agreements. Allegiances –
  Faiths turned rotten. Faiths gone bad –
Bad Faith, 1969 to 1984 –
  The sounds of the animal kingdom filled the room. The knock on the door again.
  Malcolm walked over to the door. Malcolm touched the Emergency Procedures –
  Malcolm asked, 'Who is it?'
  'Room Service.'

The Fat Man and his seven Fat Friends had met the Prime Minister –
  Little boys on their bellies bare –
Met her one year to the day since she had rejected the no-strike deal at GCHQ –
  She had picked them up off the floor. She had kissed their bleeding bellies better –
No beer and sandwiches. Just lots of coffee and biscuits to pass the time –
  Tea and sympathy, and wasn't it such a shame it had come to this?
Then the Prime Minister had shown the Fat Man and his Fat Friends the door –
  'We have done a good day's work,' the Fat Man told the waiting street –
  'But for fucking who?' the President spat at Terry and the TV. 'For who?'

The Fat Man went from Downing Street first to the Goring Hotel –

The National Executive of the Union were kept waiting; waiting and tired –

From the Goring Hotel back to Congress House –

The National Executive were kept tired; tired and hungry –

For the Fat Man and the Chairman to rewrite the eight points as requested –

The Executive were kept hungry; hungry and desperate –

To the satisfaction of the government. To the satisfaction of the Board –

The Executive were kept desperate; desperate to settle –

To the satisfaction of the TU-fucking-C –

To settle and return to work.

The Executive had been sent home. Then the Executive had been recalled –

Tempers were frayed. Nerves were frayed. Carpets were frayed –

The fifth floor of Congress House. The General Council Meeting-Room –

Around the horseshoe table, the National Executive Committee sat and waited –

Tired, hungry, desperate men gathered in the cold below.

The Fat Man got to his feet. The Fat Man had another document in his hand –

'When we last met,' he told the table, 'the position was fixed. Since then, changes have been made. But the members of the Executive should be aware that it is the clear judgement of the Liaison Committee that no further changes are achievable –

'That is the judgement of us all and we have been told that in writing by the NCB. The changes that have been made have been wrung out of those concerned, after the TUC had made the case at the very highest level –

'There is no higher to go.'

There was silence around the table. There was anger around the table –

'So the TUC is telling this Union that it can make no changes whatsoever to a document that it has had no hand in negotiating?' asked Yorkshire. 'Is that correct?'

'There can be clarification,' said the Fat Man, 'but no negotiation.'

'And if we don't like the clarification?' asked Wales. 'It's take it or leave it?'

'This is their final wording,' said the Fat Man. 'They are clear on that.'

'So what about the amnesty for sacked miners?' asked Kent. 'What about them?'

'There will be no amnesty,' said the Fat Man. 'That also was made clear.'

The table looked at the President. The President looked at the Fat Man –

'I'll give you gentlemen some time alone,' said the Fat Man, as he rose to his feet.

The table waited for the door to close. The table turned back to the President –

The President pushed the paper away. He said, 'It is one hundred per cent worse!'

The table nodded. The table agreed. The table was united –

'A boy sent to do a man's job,' said Northumberland. 'A bloody boy –'

The table nodded. The table shook. The table was furious –

'The Delegate Conference will bloody tear this up,' said Paul. 'Page by page –'

The President nodded. The President shook. The President stood –

'This dispute goes on,' the President told them all. 'This dispute goes on!'

There was no day. There was no light. There was only shadow. There was only night –

The dog no longer a pet, black and starved –

Its master gone, its teeth exposed.

Here came the men. Here came the hour. Here came revenge.

They tied Malcolm's hands and feet to an upturned bed –

In an upstairs room, they put phones on his head –

The tapes he'd made on loud in his ears.

They stripped his clothes, they shaved his hair –

They scoured him with wires and rubbed him rare.

They injected him with amphetamines, industrial bleach.

In the park, they soaked his skin –

Among the trees, with a petrol tin –

Lighter to his face, they illuminated tears.

They blamed his flesh, they cursed his bones –

They watched him blister, burn and moan.
In an upstairs room, with the curtains drawn.
This was the month when the oracles went dumb –
The unhappy eve, the voice, and the hum.
Here came the men. Here came the hour. Here came revenge.
The skulls sat and stared, with their Soviet dreams –
In the shadows at the back, the woman schemes –
Her nipples hard, her milk all gone.
These things they brought, they made him buy –
They told him stories, they sold him a lie.
The room was bare, the curtains torn.
These were her men by the side of the road –
Among the living with their language and code –
Their winter dresses in the summer cried.
They followed his car, photographed his home –
They recorded him on reels and tapped his phone.
The cigarette. The kiss. The wrong number. The look and then silence –
Half deaf in these rooms he hates –
In half light, the rebel angel waits.
Here came the man. Here came the hour. Here came revenge.
In the small hours, the thieves' hours, with their knives of Sheffield steel –
Among the bodies of the animals, the Circle of the Tyrants kneel –
To hear her beat her bloody wings, in her new and lonely Reich –
Herr Lucifer! Herr Thatcher!
Beware! Beware! She will eat you like air –
Beware! Beware! The pits of despair.
There is a man who bought his council house and drives an Austin
Princess –
He has a dark room and a very good stereo –
His wife does knitting jobs. His son is a garage apprentice. Karen still at
school –
The winds will leave seven dead. He is not who he seems –
Beware! Beware! She will eat you like air –
Beware! Beware! The pits of despair –
The temples of doom. The worst weather in weeks –
These are the terms of endearment. This is the knock on the door –
This is their man. This is their hour. This their revenge –
Beware! Beware! The children of a hasty marriage.

*

Neil Fontaine picks up the Jew from the Goring and drives him into Soho for the lunch. The Jew is in a great mood. The Jew is sanguine. The Jew believes again –

The NUM delegates have rejected the TUC agreement. The final hours nigh –

'Make an enemy of Doubt,' the Jew reminds Neil. 'And a friend of Fear.'

The gang's all here. The deeds all done –

Their hatchets buried, the corks pop. The knives sheaved, their glasses raised –

The end nigh –

There is a message waiting for Neil at the County Hotel.

There was a car and its doors were open. There were men and their arms were open –

There was a passenger and her legs were open, waiting –

The German car in the black. The drive out to the forest –

The songs on the radio. The silence in the back –

The unmarked road. The quiet brakes. The exhaust fumes. The open boot –

The spade in the dirt. The hole in the ground –

The soil and the stones over Malcolm's bones.

through grilles on window of a Coal Board bus. That you, is it, Billy? He looked at us. He said, You know it's not, Pete. You know I'll live in shame for rest of my days. Hate myself. But who's going to look after our lass when I'm gone. I know I'm sick and I know I'll not pass their medical. I'm going back to work to pick up them redundancy forms so I can give something back to our lass after all she's given me this past year. Every bloody year of our lives. I'm not going to die of their fucking dust and leave her with nothing. See her out on streets. I'm all she has and this fucking job is all I have. Lose it and we've nothing – There was nothing more to say. I left him be – I went back **home**. I went straight **upstairs** – Put **blankets** over my head. Fingers in my ears – I didn't want to see anyone. I didn't want to hear anyone – *Not Martin. Not my father, either* – This was worst week. Fucking strangest I'd ever lived – There were meetings and there were rallies. I went to the **meetings** and I went to the **rallies** – But it felt like it was all happening to someone else. Not me – The SDC rejecting that final, worthless, fucking document. Last big rally in Trafalgar Square. Nottingham ending OT ban – Then Monday almost four thousand went in. Yorkshire voted to strike on. News that there were over 50 per cent now at work – The endless talk about returns with a settlement. Organized returns without. Returns with an amnesty. Returns without – The **Branch** meeting. Packed – Us all listening to Arthur. Looking to Arthur – I want to make it clear, he said, that there is no way this Executive Committee will ever be a party to signing a document that would result in the closure of pits. The axing of jobs. The destruction of communities – Felt that it was all happening to someone else. That Arthur was talking about something that was happening to other people. In another place – Not to me. Not to my family. Not to my friends. Not to my pit. Not to my village. Not to my county. My bloody country – That I was just a shell. That this wasn't me – Not after all these months. After all these weeks.

These days – Just a shell. An empty shell – *Not this time. Not now* – There were so many **meetings**. There was so much talk – Them that mattered went down to London. Left us here to wait – To wait and watch TV. To watch and wait – It was Sunday again. Day of rest – I was sat there on **settee** with Mary and our Jackie. Martin had gone off to help Chris try to sell some furniture somewhere – TV was on. Not fire – We'd spent afternoon at Pinderfields Hospital in Wakefield because Mary's mother had had a fall and burnt herself with a pan of milk. Had all that and then we'd driven back here in rain – Throwing it down, it was. Bloody miserable day – I was sat there. Cup of tea with no milk again – Middle of *Dad's Army*. Newsflash – *Miners' Strike is over* – That was it. Just like that – I thought I was going to pass out. Right there and then – I could tell Mary and our Jackie didn't want to look at me. Didn't know what to say, did they? But what was there to say? – It was over. Finished. We'd lost. The end – I stood up. Jaw clamped shut. I walked across room. Knocked half a dozen things over as I went – Blinking. Fighting back bloody tears – I walked up **stairs** and ran into **bedroom**. I laid down on **bed**. Face down in **pillow** and I sobbed. Then onto **floor**. I bloody sobbed and sobbed. I could hear phone ringing downstairs. I could hear Mary pick it up. Hear her calling my name. Hear her tell them I must have just popped out. Yes, she said. He saw news. He does know. Thank you. Heard her hang up and come up stairs. Heard her open door and come over to bed – She put her arms round me. Her head on my back – I love you, she said. I'm proud of you. Things you've done. Things you've said these past months. This past year. Just remember that – I wiped my face. I dried my eyes. I turned and I kissed my wife – Kissed her ears. Kissed her eyes. Kissed her mouth. Kissed her hair – I held her and felt her heart beating – Hard. Steady. Strong. True – I felt her heart beating and I closed my eyes – *This time it's me. Here – In the darkness. Under the ground – There's no light. There's no exit – Just me. Here –* **Here** on the **floor**.

The Fifty-second Week

Terry Winters sat at the kitchen table of his three-bedroom home in the suburbs of Sheffield, South Yorkshire. His three children were squabbling again. His wife worrying. Terry ignored them. Breakfast television was showing pictures from the rally in Trafalgar Square yesterday. The final rallies in the final hours. The police put the numbers at less than fifteen thousand. One hundred arrested. Hundreds more batoned. The Union said there were between eighty and one hundred thousand. *Numbers. Numbers. Numbers.* Terry ignored it all. He took an index card from the right-hand pocket of his jacket. He read it. He closed his eyes –

It was blank –

Terry Winters opened his eyes. His children had gone to school. His wife to work. Terry looked down at the index card again. He put his hand into his right pocket again. He took out another card, and another, and another –

They were all blank.

Terry went back to work. Terry sat at his desk. Terry watched Ceefax all day:

Four thousand had returned to work today. Highest ever figure for a Monday. Two thousand more returnees and the Board would then have their magical 50 per cent. Meanwhile, the Nottinghamshire Area Council had called off the overtime ban –

Ten thousand more tonnes a week to the government stockpiles.

Terry changed channels. Terry waited for the next news:

The President and Dick on the steps of Congress House, long coats and faces. 'When history examines this dispute,' railed the President, 'there will be a glaring omission – the fact that the trade union movement has been standing on the sidelines while this Union has been battered.'

Terry switched off the television. Terry waited for the telephone to ring.

Neil Fontaine leaves the Jew among the popped corks and the empty bottles. The party hats and the streamers. The trophies and the spoils. The winners and the victors –

Just six hundred bodies short now.

Neil Fontaine takes a cab to the Special Services Club.

Jerry finishes his cigar. Jerry pushes away the ashtray. Jerry leans forward –

'There is a price,' says Jerry.

Neil Fontaine nods just once. Neil Fontaine says, 'I know.'

Jerry lifts up his napkin. Jerry pushes an envelope across the table-cloth –

Just the one thin, brown envelope.

Neil Fontaine picks it up. Neil Fontaine stands up –

'Love will always let you down,' says Jerry. 'Always has and it always will.'

Neil Fontaine takes a taxi back to Bloomsbury. He walks down towards Euston. He goes into St Pancras. He sits in the pew. He bows his head. He says a prayer –

Just one last and final prayer.

Mardy Colliery, the very last of the Rhondda pits and forever known as Little Moscow, had voted for an orderly return to work –

The Last Waltz had begun –

'My concern now is with holding the line,' said Paul. 'This is not the time to bow our heads. Not the time to go back to work defeated. This is the time to close ranks –

'And urge our members to stand firm, to sustain us through this difficult period. Help us over this last hurdle –'

Nobody nodded. Nobody was listening –

'There's no prospect of victory now,' warned Gareth Thomas from South Wales. 'Not the kind of victory we were all so sure we could achieve a year ago in March 1984. What we must make sure of now is that we do not abuse the loyalty that has been shown to us by the thousands of miners throughout this country, and that loyalty demands –

'Leadership. Leadership. Leadership! Or there'll be no Union to lead!'

The leadership met. *Again.* For seven hours the Executive met. *Again –*

The Executive leadership prepared now to sign the NACODS agreement –

The leadership desperate to sign the NACODS agreement –

To sign it here. To sign it today. To sign it now –

The Executive called Hobart House. *Click-click.* The Executive called again –

Again and again and again and again, the leadership called Hobart House –

Click-click. But no one was answering the telephones down at Hobart House –

Click-click. No need to answer them. *Click-click.* Nothing more to say –

This morning 1114 had gone back. This morning 50.74 per cent of all miners were back.

The majority of the men were gone. The majority of the money was gone –

It was all over. Here. Today. Now –

But Kent and Yorkshire still wanted to stay out to reach a negotiated settlement –

South Wales, with still the fewest scabs, had other ideas –

'We came out as one,' they said again. 'We will go in as one.'

'It is unreasonable on humanitarian grounds', agreed Durham, 'to call upon the membership to endure still further pain and still further sacrifice, to themselves and their families, in loyalty to this Union –'

But there would be further pain and there would be further sacrifice –

For the men. For their families. For their Union –

For weeks. For months. For years and years to come –

'For there can be no reconciliation,' said Scotland, 'until there is an amnesty.'

'The Coal Board, at the insistence of the government,' reiterated the President, 'is not prepared to negotiate. It is a complete war of attrition –

'And we shall have to take a decision in the best interests of our members.'

Four decisions before them. Four last choices –

To stay out, or to accept the National Coal Board's offer –

To return without an amnesty, or to return with one.

The Executive called a Special Delegate Conference for Sunday 3 March.

The Executive left the Conference Room one by one –

Back to their local areas. Their panels and their branches. Their local TV studios –

The President sat alone at the table. The President dried his eyes –

He looked up at the empty chairs. The empty table. The empty room –

The heavy curtains. The chipped cups. The two-way mirrors. The hidden bugs –

'Are you hardcore?' he asked Terry. 'Are you hardcore, Comrade?'

Terry picked up his files. His notes and his sums. Terry picked up his calculator –

'If I flinch from the flames,' said the President. 'Believe not a word I have said.'

Terry left the table. The room and the building. Terry left the President alone –

To his dreams of victory in his night of defeat –

'We are but halfway between Dunkirk and D-Day,' he shouted after them all. 'But halfway, Comrades. On the greatest march this world has ever seen –'

Even in winter the days were too long, the nights old and wrong –

They sat in overheated huts. They stood around unlit braziers –

They clapped their hands. They stamped their feet. They woke the Dead.

They had swapped their badges for cigarettes. Their banners for beer –

There were two teenage brothers. Their bodies black, their faces blue –

Spoil fell from their mouths when they said, 'You don't remember us, do you?'

Malcolm shook his head. Blood dripped from his holes. From her scissors –

In the shadows. The ghosts without. In the silence. The ghost within –

And then Malcolm nodded. For then Malcolm knew –

This was how it felt to be dead. To be buried –

Under the ground.

Terry changed class as the train approached King's Cross. It would end here, in London –

Not in Sheffield. Not in Mansfield. Not in Scotland. Not in Wales –

Terry pushed two suitcases and his briefcase along the platform to the lockers –

Here in London. Today or tomorrow. Saturday night. Sunday morning –

Terry put Suitcase 36 into Locker 27. Terry put the key into an envelope –

There was a meeting of the Left to make decisions for the Executive Committee –

Terry put the envelope in the concourse letterbox. Terry went out to the taxi rank –

The Executive meeting to make decisions for Sunday's Delegate Conference –

Terry got out. Terry paid the driver. Terry checked in to his room at the County –

The Special Delegate Conference to make decisions for their members –

Terry spat blood in his handkerchief. Terry took another handful of aspirins –

Their members standing in the rain. Their members swinging in the wind.

Terry washed his hands. *Again and again.* Terry looked at his watch. *Tick-tock –*

Days to go now. Hours to go. Minutes to go –

Terry picked up the phone. *Click-click.* Terry called Diane as planned –

They spoke of signals. *Tickets and times.* They conversed in code –

Terry hung up. Terry went down the stairs and along to the North Sea Fisheries. Dick and Paul and Len on one table. Joan and Alice and the President on the next –

They had all finished eating. *Tick-tock.* They were waiting for Terry to pay –

Terry paid for the six specials. Terry followed them along to the policy session. Terry kept to his chair in the corner. His mouth shut. His eye on the ball –

Days to go. Hours to go. Minutes to go –

They argued and they argued. *Back and forth.* They argued and they argued –

Broken words. Broken promises. Broken backs. Broken hearts –

The President threw tantrums. *Broken cups.* The President threw fits –

The Left achieved nothing. *Nothing. Ever.* The Left never met again –

Terry paid for twenty breakfasts and followed them to the Executive Committee. Terry kept his chair by the door. Mouth shut. Eye on the ball –

Hours to go now. Minutes to go –

They argued and they argued. *Back and forth.* They argued and they argued –

The Executive had the choices before them. Decisions to make, courses to take. But the Executive could make no recommendations to the delegates –

Hours to go. Minutes to go –

They voted 11–11 not to recommend the South Wales motion for a return to work. They voted 11–11 not to recommend the Yorkshire motion to strike on for an amnesty –

The President had the casting vote. The President would not cast it –

It was deadlock. It was stalemate. It was cowardice. It was abdication –

In the rain, the delegates came to Great Russell Street. In the rain, the hundreds came. In their hundreds to stand outside Congress House. In their hundreds to shout in the rain –

No surrender! No surrender! No surrender!

The main event started on the floor of the conference. The Last Fight –

Minutes to go now. Seconds out –

The fight between Yorkshire in the red corner –

'Out until there's an amnesty and the five named pits reprieved.'

South Wales in the blue –

'A dignified and honourable return.'

Outside the rain fell on the men for six hours as the delegates argued inside –

We've given you our hearts –

'You should have the guts to make a recommendation,' they argued –

We've given you our souls –

'Or you will have ratted out on this strike,' they argued –

We've given you our blood –

'Give them leadership and repay the loyalty they have given you,' they argued –

We've given you everything we had –

'Or sit back with blindfolds on, as the strike collapses around you,' they argued –

And then you sell us out –

'We have to live in the world as it is,' they argued, 'not as we would like it –'

Tarred and feathered with the rest of the scabby bastards –

The Welsh proposal was carried 98 to 91 –

Total. Fucking. Knock. Out; Total. Fucking. Sell. Out –

'Don't anyone in this conference lower their eyes,' the President shouted at them. 'Don't be ashamed of what we have done. We have put up the greatest fight in history –'

It was all over –

'We have not sold our birthrights. We have not prostituted our principles –'

Here –

'The greatest achievement is the struggle itself –'

Today –

'We have changed the course of history and inspired the workers of the world –'

Now –

'Comrades, it is upon such struggles that democracy itself depends!'

Total. Fucking. Silence.

The President walked out of the conference and out of Congress House –

Into the ruin. Into their tears. Into the pain. Into their fears –

Into the media and into the police. Into the miners and into their families –

Into the guilt and the shame. Into the anger and the sorrow –

'This dispute goes on,' shouted the President above the traffic and the weather –

'We're not going back,' chanted the men. 'We're not going back!'

'We will continue to fight against pit closures or job losses!'

'You've been betrayed!' the men screamed back at him. 'You've been betrayed!'

'Make no mistake – do not underestimate this Union's ability to resist!'

'Scum! Scum! Scum!' they wailed. 'Scab! Scab! Scab!'

PART V

Terminal, or the Triumph of the Will

March 1985 –

THIS COLLIERY IS NOW
MANAGED BY THE
ATIONAL
AL BOARD
N BEHALF OF THE PEOPLE
JANUARY 1 1947

Awake! There are screams all over Pete's walls. Awake! Blood running into their carpet – It takes a minute to remember. Lifetime to forget – I lie there on his sofa. I watch them crawl away – I was walking back from my Sunday half. Long way round – Rain had stopped. Tim pulls over – Big smile on his face. His chops – He said to us, Great news, isn't it? What is? I asked him. Strike's over, he said. Haven't you heard? I shook my head. Fucking joking, I said. How's that good news, then? Tim could see I was fucked off. He said, Just be good to get back to work. That's all I meant – I shook my head again. I turned back. **Day 363** – Not over yet. There's still some picket duty today – Lot more here than usual. Feeling there are scores to settle – Lot of hot talk. But in end it comes to nothing – Harder shove. Louder shout – No one wants to get fucking arrested today. No, thanks – Be like one of them blokes got themselves shot on Armistice Day. Nicked today, sacked tomorrow – No, thank you. Not after twelve fucking months – There's another meeting in morning. Third or fourth in a week – Lot of bitterness and anger about events at NEC yesterday. News just sinking in – Mixed emotions. Charged emotions – Yorkshire Area want everyone to march back into their pit together. United – Banners and heads high. Brass bands and what-have-you – But what about them that have been sacked? asks Keith. They going to march back in, are they? – Meeting and whole place descends into bedlam. Pandemonium – Lads are shitting themselves now. Don't know if they'll get taken back or not – Lads being told one thing. Then being told another – Terrible to see. Horrible – Looks of fear on all these faces. Looks of defeat and despair – Faces you've seen on picket line. Faces that have looked into eyes of their horses and their dogs – Their visors. Their shields – Faces that have taken their truncheons and their boots. Battered and beaten – Faces that watched their wives and kids go without. Faces that suffered for twelve fucking months – Faces now lost and frightened. Frightened of what future holds –

Future none of us can afford. Lot of us stay supping today – Night on tiles. Hurts your face – Blow little we have left. Pray they pay us again – Awake! In my coat on Pete's sofa. Awake! Mouth tastes of earth and shit – Least I didn't bloody dream. Them nights over with now – **Day 364**. Mary's made a breakfast for us. Packed us some snap and all – Like first day of spring today. Beautiful – I follow Pete down Welfare for half-eight. Nearly whole of village is out – Lot of emotion. Lads that have been sacked are going to push banner – In front of them, Pete and other three branch officials. Rest of us will fall in behind – I'm stood there thinking, Don't cry and don't look for Cath. Don't cry and don't – But I look about and see Big Chris with his handkerchief out. Soft bastard – Then we're off and I turn round. I can't believe how many there are – More than 50 per cent still out. Easy – Makes me feel proud. Makes me feel sad – To see us all here now. Together – Shoulder to shoulder. United – Marching as one. Now it's too fucking late – Pete and them lot reach gates and call for a minute's silence for those who have died during dispute. That's when I see them – Not just the eight hundred stood with me here on our Pit Lane. The support groups and all those that helped us – Not just them. But all the others – From far below. Beneath my feet – They whisper. They echo – They moan. They scream – From beneath the fields. Below the hills – The roads. The motorways – The empty villages. The dirty cities – The abandoned mills. The silent factories – The dead trees. The broken fences – The stinking rivers. The dirty sky – The dirty blue March sky that spits down upon us now – The Dead. The Union of the Dead – From Hartley to Harworth. From Senghenydd to Saltley – From Oaks to Or-greave. From Lofthouse to London – The Dead that carried us from far to near. Through the Villages of the Damned, to stand beside us here – Together. Shoulder to shoulder. United. Marching as one – Under their banners and their badges. In their branches and their bands – Their muffled drums.

The Last Week

Monday 4 – Sunday 10 March 1985

The Jew had hoped to spend the weekend down at Chequers. The Jew was not invited. The Jew has taken to his bed instead. Blankets up to his neck, hands beneath the sheets, he watches her perform –

'We had to make certain that violence and intimidation and impossible demands could not win. There would have been neither freedom nor order in Great Britain in 1985 if we had given in to violence and intimidation –'

Again and again on the videos he's made. In the scrapbooks he's kept –

'What's the difference between an egg', asks the Jew, 'and our Prime Minister?'

'You certainly can't beat our Prime Minister, sir,' replies Neil Fontaine. Again –

'Very good, Neil,' howls the Jew. 'Very, very good indeed.'

The Chairman is not returning the Jew's calls. Again. Nor is the Minister –

The Jew's only friends are working miners and their greedy wives.

The Jew gives Neil the rest of the week off. The Jew needs to be alone. Again –

With his videos and his scrapbooks. Beneath the blankets and the sheets.

Neil Fontaine needs to be alone, too. Neil Fontaine needs to make things right –

Neil Fontaine heads North. Again.

The General comes into the barracks. Everyone stands by their bunk –

The General marches towards the Mechanic. The General puts him at his ease. The General hands him the note.

The Mechanic takes it. The Mechanic opens it. The Mechanic reads it –

The time and the place. The job and the price –

'There really is only one solution,' says the General. 'Will you do it, David?'

The Mechanic looks up at the General. The Mechanic salutes. 'Yes, sir, I will.'

The funeral marches. In vassal thrall. The pipes and the drums –

'*There will be no recriminations. There will be no talk of victory or defeat.*'

The last procession. In villein bonds. The banners and the bands –

'*But make no mistake, victory it is.*'

Neil Fontaine starts the black car. He drives on to another village –

'*I don't want any gloating.*'

And another and another, until he's seen enough (has seen too much) –

'*No amnesty. No forgiveness.*'

The door is open. The ashtray full. The telephone ringing by his hotel bed.

The Union was sunk. The President spoke on empty decks as the rats stole the lifeboats –

He spoke of the Bolsheviks in 1905. Mao's Long March. Castro in his hills.

But the real pain. The real trouble. It all started here. Today –

The morning after the strike before, Terry knew that (he'd always known that).

The safety-nets. The *cause juste*. The material and practical support –

Just smoke up the chimney now, Terry could see that (he'd always seen that).

They had lost the money. They had lost the men. They had lost the strike –

The witch hunts had begun. The whispers. The fingers. The trials. The burnings –

Diane had said they would and Diane had been right (she was always right).

Terry took the stairs two at a time. Terry banged on the hotel door –

There was no answer –

Terry banged and banged on it. Doors opened up and down the corridor –

The wrong doors.

Terry put his head against the door. Terry prayed. Terry said, 'Please –'

The door opened. Terry stepped forward. Into the room –

Terry looked up. Terry said, 'What –'

Bill Reed was stood in the middle of their hotel room with Len Glover.

Terry said, 'What's happened? Where's Diane?'

'Who's Diane?' asked Len. 'Who are you talking about?'

Terry looked at Bill. Terry said, 'She –'

'Not in them suitcases, is she?' laughed Bill Reed. 'In bits and pieces?'

Terry shook his head. Terry said, 'I –'

Len took the two cases from him. Len opened them on the double bed –

Thousands and thousands of used English banknotes.

'More mortgage payments for the President?' asked Bill. 'That what this is?'

Terry shook his head again. Terry said, 'I can explain. Let me show you –'

Len took one arm and Bill took the other. Down the corridor. Into the lift –

Through the lobby of Hallam Towers. Down the steps. To their car –

Bill sat in the back with Terry. Bill said, 'So where we going, Comrade?'

Terry took them from Sheffield into Doncaster. From Doncaster into Bentley –

'Here,' Terry told them. 'Pull up here.'

Len, Bill and Terry got out of Len's car on the row of old terraced houses.

Terry led them down the street to the little shop on the corner –

Terry opened the door. Len and Bill followed him inside. Terry shook his head.

'Is Mr Divan about?' Terry asked the fat white man behind the counter –

'Who?' replied the fat white man behind the counter. 'Who do you want?'

'Mohammed Abdul Divan,' said Terry. 'He owns this shop.'

'No, he doesn't,' said the fat white man. 'Michael Andrew Damson does.'

'May I speak with him, then?' asked Terry.

'You are doing,' smiled Michael Andrew Damson.

'You're the owner of this shop?' Terry asked Michael Damson. 'Since when?'

'Since my father died in 1970,' he said. 'Now what the bloody hell is going on?'

Len and Bill shook their heads. Len and Bill took Terry by his arms again –

'But I came here last year and I met Mohammed Abdul Divan and his family,' shouted Terry. 'Right where you're standing, behind that counter –'

Michael Damson shook his head. He said, 'You've got the wrong shop.'

'They were from Pakistan,' protested Terry. 'They owned *this* shop.'

'You're confused,' said Michael Damson. 'There's that bloody many of them.'

Terry shook his head. Terry closed his eyes. Terry began to cry –

Len and Bill apologized to Mr Damson. Len and Bill took Terry away.

Bill sat in the back of the car with Terry. Bill said, 'So what now, Comrade?'

Terry took them back to his house in the suburbs of Sheffield, South Yorkshire –

Len, Bill and Terry got out of Len's car in front of Terry's three-bedroom home.

'Please don't say anything to Theresa,' begged Terry. 'Not in front of the kids.'

Bill looked at Len. Len looked at Bill –

'The statements concerning all the money are inside,' said Terry. 'Don't worry.'

'We're not worried,' said Bill. 'Are we, Leonard?'

Len opened the boot of his car. Len took out a large bouquet of dead flowers –

'They look a bit past it,' laughed Terry. 'Who on earth are they for?'

'They were for your wife,' said Bill. 'But the hospital returned them to me.'

'That was thoughtful of you, Comrade,' said Terry, his key in the lock. 'Thank you.'

Bill and Len followed Terry inside. Through his front door. Into his hall –

Terry switched on the lights. Terry said, 'Looks like there's nobody home.'

Len looked at Bill. Bill looked at Len –

They left Terry in front of his hall mirror. They went through his house –

The dead Christmas tree in the front room. The dust-covered presents –

Up the stairs with no carpet. Past the walls with no paint –

The bathtub full of blank sheets of paper. The sink full of brand-new clothes –

Into two empty back bedrooms. The windows broken or open –

The sleeping bags and mucky mags on the floorboards of the front bedroom –

The suitcases full of newspapers. The obscenities on the walls –

Back down the stairs to the kitchen. The radio in the sink. The food on the floor –

The open biscuit tins full of rainwater or piss. The cracked mirror in the hall –

The blank Christmas cards. The empty photo frames in their hands –

Terry stared at Bill and Len in the mirror. Terry opened and closed his mouth –

'There never was any wife, was there?' said Len. 'No kids. Nothing.'

In the shadows of South Yorkshire, in the suburbs of Sheffield –

'Nothing but bloody lies,' said Bill. 'Lies and fucking fantasies.'

In the house with the lights on but nobody home –

Terry Winters had forgotten his lines.

Power –

Harsh service station light. Friday 8 March, 1985 –

Diane Morris puts a cigarette to her lips, a lighter to her cigarette.

Her dog dead at her gate –

Neil Fontaine waits.

Diane inhales, her eyes closed. Diane exhales, her eyes open.

Neil sits and he waits in his car, his soiled black car.

Diane looks at her watch. Diane glances out of the window.

Neil sees her in his mirror, his mud-splattered mirror.

Diane stubs out the cigarette. Diane picks an envelope off the table.

Neil squeezes the steering wheel between his dirty fingers and bloody palms –

Ruin'd and damn'd is her state.

Diane looks at her watch again. Diane stands up.

457

Neil shuts his eyes until she's almost gone. The stink still here. Everywhere –

Loss.

The Mechanic turns into the car park. He is early. The place packed with Saturday lunchtime shoppers. He drives slowly through the car park. Turns into a space next to one of the trolley parks. The Capri faces the supermarket –

A mohican rattling a bucket by the automatic doors –

The Mechanic watches for the car through the rearview mirror and the wing –

Fuck –

A panda car turns into the car park. Makes a circle and pulls up at the back of him. A policewoman gets out of the passenger door. Puts on her hat and walks down the side of him. Off to have a word with the mohican and his last of the plastic buckets –

The Mechanic glances over at the passenger seat. Looks up into the rearview –

Fuck –

A policeman is getting out of the driver's side. The Mechanic boxed in now by an empty police car. The policeman puts on his hat and walks down the passenger side of the Capri. Stops dead. The policeman opens the passenger door. The Mechanic reaches for the passenger seat –

The policeman is first to the shotgun. He puts it to the Mechanic's stomach –

Fuck –

The Mechanic looks up into the policeman's eyes –

Just. Like –

Neil pulls the trigger.

Neil Fontaine stands outside the door to the Jew's suite on the fourth floor of Claridge's. He listens to the silence and the shadows inside. He thinks about coincidence of circumstance, meeting of motive and convergence of cause. Neil Fontaine opens the door to the Jew's suite on the fourth floor of Claridge's. He thinks about the end of a war and the start of an era. The timing of a meeting and the opening of an envelope –

The closing of a pit and the calling of a strike –

The writing on a wall. The knocking on a door –

Neil Fontaine steps inside the Jew's suite. He closes the door behind him.

There are bottles on the floor. There are bodies on the bed –

Drunken scabs and their wanton wives, satiated and salacious.

The Jew benumbed and naked upon the bones and the sheets –

Hair matted and moustache stained, his carcass bloated and cock limp.

Neil stands at the foot of the bed, a candle and a knife in his hands –

A white bandage around the blade, six inches of Sheffield steel naked at the point.

He kneels down and rests the candle and the knife on the carpet before him –

He sits cross-legged. His head shaved. A white towel across his knees.

He undoes the buttons of his blazer. He unfastens the collar of his shirt –

He loosens the belt and buttons of his trousers.

He pushes the white towel down between his underwear and skin.

He begins to massage his abdomen with his left hand.

He folds back his left trouser flap to reveal the top of his thigh.

He draws the blade lightly across the skin. Blood runs. The blade is sharp enough.

He looks up at the Jew –

He moves the knife around to his front. He raises himself slightly on his hips –

He leans the upper half of his body over the point of the blade.

He cries out as the knife pierces the left side of his stomach.

He loses consciousness.

The six inches of naked steel have vanished –

The white bandage in his hand pressed against the flesh of his stomach –

He regains consciousness. The blade inside him. His heart pounding –

The enemy within.

The pain is coming –

His fist moist around the bandaged blade. He looks down –

His hand and the bandage are drenched in blood –

The white towel monogrammed a deep and violent red.

Neil looks up at the Jew again –

The pain is here.

He begins to cut sideways across his stomach using only his right hand.

He cannot.

His intestines push out the blade.

He has to use both hands to keep the point of the blade deep in his stomach.

He pulls across. It does not cut easily.

He forces himself to pull again with all his strength.

The blade cuts four inches. He has cut past his navel.

There is blood in the folds of his trousers now. There is blood on the carpet –

Writing on the walls. Darkening the doors. Painting the shadows –

A single spot on the corner of one of the Jew's white hotel sheets.

But the blade will not cut deeper. It slips out in the blood and grease.

Neil starts to vomit. The pain worse. His intestines spill out into his crotch.

He looks up at the Jew –

His head droops. His shoulders heave. His eyes close. He retches repeatedly.

He sits in his own blood. The tip of the blade exposed. It lies in his hand.

He throws his head back –

The tide of his blood laps at the feet of the bed –

He raises the knife in his right hand. He thrusts the point at his throat –

He misses.

The blade falls. He raises the knife again. He thrusts the point at his throat –

He misses.

The knife falls. He raises the blade. He thrusts the point at his throat again –

The point of the blade touches his throat –

His head falls forward. The blade emerges at the nape of his neck.

He thinks and he thinks and he thinks and he thinks –

The Earth tilts. The Earth turns. The Earth hungry. The Earth hunts –

He thinks and he thinks and he thinks –
This is the way the world works. This is the way –
He thinks and he thinks –
There are the things I know. The things I don't –
Neil thinks. Neil knows –
For both, there is a price.

Their muted pipes – That whisper. That echo – Their funeral marches. Their funeral music – That moans. That screams – Again and again. For ever more – As if they are marching their way up out of their graves. Here to mourn the new dead – The country deaf to their laments. Its belly swollen with black corpses and vengeful carrion – Rotting in its furrows. It waits for harvests that never come – The day their weeping will burst open the earth itself and drown us all. In their tears – In their sweat. In their blood – In our guilt and in our shame. Until that Day of Judgement – There will be no spring. There can be no morning – There will be only winter. There can be only night – Lord, please open the eyes and ears of the people of England. But the people of England are blind and deaf – The Armies of the Night. The Armies of the Right – We are here because of you, they say. Here because of you – And they strip us of our language and our lands. Our families and our faith. Our gods and our ways – We are but the matchstick men, with our matchstick hats and clogs – And they shave our heads. Send us to the showers – Put us on their trains. Stick us in their pits – The cage door closes. The cage descends – To cover us with dirt. To leave us underground – In place of strife. In place of fear – Here where she stands at the gates at the head of her tribe and waits – Triumphant on the mountains of our skulls. Up to her hems in the rivers of our blood – A wreath in one hand. The other between her legs – Her two little princes dancing by their necks from her apron strings, and she looks down at the long march of labour halted here before her and says, Awake! Awake! This is England, Your England – and the Year is Zero.

Sources & Acknowledgements

This novel is a fiction, based on a fact. That fact was found in the following sources:

A Century of Struggle: Britain's Miners in Pictures by the National Union of Mineworkers (1989)

A Word to the Wise Guy by The Mighty Wah (Beggars Banquet, 1984)

Blood Sweat & Tears by Roger Huddle, Angela Phillips, Mike Simons and John Sturrock (Artworker Books, 1985)

Coal, Crisis and Conflict by Jonathan and Ruth Winterton (Manchester University Press, 1989)

Counting the Cost by Jackie Keating (Wharncliffe, 1991)

Digging Deeper edited by Huw Beynon (Verso, 1985)

Enemies of the State by Gary Murray (Simon & Schuster, 1993)

Free Agent: The Unseen War 1941–1991 by Brian Crozier (HarperCollins, 1993)

Germinal by Emile Zola (1885)

Lobster: The Journal of Parapolitics, issues 1–40, edited by Robin Ramsay (CD-ROM available from www.lobster-magazine.co.uk)

Microphonies by Cabaret Voltaire (Virgin, 1984)

Miners on Strike by Andrew J. Richards (Berg, 1996)

Neither Washington nor Moscow by the Redskins (London, 1986)

One of Us by Hugo Young (Pan, 1993)

Open Secret by Stella Rimington (Hutchinson, 2001)

Policing the Miners' Strike by Bob Fine and Robert Millar (Lawrence & Wishart, 1985)

Scargill: The Unauthorized Biography by Paul Routledge (HarperCollins, 1993)

Small Town England by New Model Army (Abstract, 1983–4)

Smear: Wilson and the Secret State by Stephen Dorril and Robin Ramsay (Grafton, 1992)

State of Siege by Jim Coulter, Susan Miller and Martin Walker (Canary Press, 1984)

Strike: A Sunday Times Insight Book by Peter Wilsher, Donald
  Macintyre and Michael Jones (André Deutsch, 1985)
The Enemies Within by Ian MacGregor with Rodney Tyler (Collins,
  1986)
The Enemy Within by Seamus Milne (Verso, 1994)
The English Civil War Part II by Jeremy Deller (Artangel, 2002)
The Miners' Strike: Loss without Limit by Martin Adney and John
  Lloyd (Routledge & Kegan Paul, 1986)
The Miners' Strike Day by Day by Arthur Wakefield (Wharncliffe,
  2002)
The Miners' Strike in Pictures by News Line Photographers (New
  Park, 1985)
The National Front by Martin Walker (Fontana, 1977)
The Political Police in Britain by Tony Bunyan (Quartet, 1977)
Thurcoft: A Village and the Miners' Strike by the People of Thurcoft,
  Peter Gibbon and David Steyne (Spokesman, 1986)
Understanding the Miners' Strike by John Lloyd (Fabian Society, 1985)
Welcome to the Pleasuredome by Frankie Goes to Hollywood (ZZT,
  1984)

I would like to thank Charlie, Darren, Jim and Mick for sharing their
information, their memories and their time. I would also like to thank
Jon Riley for his faith and Lee Brackstone for his devotion.

ff

Faber and Faber – a home for writers

Faber and Faber is one of the great independent publishing houses in London. We were established in 1929 by Geoffrey Faber and our first editor was T. S. Eliot. We are proud to publish prize-winning fiction and non-fiction, as well as an unrivalled list of modern poets and playwrights. Among our list of writers we have five Booker Prize winners and eleven Nobel Laureates, and we continue to seek out the most exciting and innovative writers at work today.

www.faber.co.uk – a home for readers

The Faber website is a place where you will find all the latest news on our writers and events. You can listen to podcasts, preview new books, read specially commissioned articles and access reading guides, as well as entering competitions and enjoying a whole range of offers and exclusives. You can also browse the list of Faber Finds, an exciting new project where reader recommendations are helping to bring a wealth of lost classics back into print using the latest on-demand technology.